TENKILL

TENKILL

Shannon Kirk

Copyright © 2023 by Shannon Kirk
Cover and jacket design by 2Faced Design

ISBN 978-1-951709-91-4
eISBN: 978-1-957957-13-5
Library of Congress Control Number: available upon request

First hardcover publication April 2023
by Polis Books, LLC
62 Ottowa Road S
Marlboro, NJ 07746
www.PolisBooks.com

POLIS BOOKS

DEDICATIONS

For asylum seekers. For the ACLU. For all lawyers representing asylum seekers.

And, for our beloved Marty Foley, who died of the Coronavirus on December 11, 2020. Marty was a fantastical storyteller and amazing sculptor and painter. He left this galaxy far too soon. I trust he is continuing his role as *Marty Marty The One Man Party* up in the cosmos with his fellow angels and spinning yarns so wild, even the aliens who visit all dimensions are enthralled. No doubt he's conversing with the ghost of Michelangelo on some improvements he might make in his choices of chisels and marble.

A FEW NOTES TO READERS

TIMING: Most of this story takes place in 2020 and after. I have chosen to imagine a world as one that never suffered the Coronavirus pandemic. I do this not to be insensitive, but simply because this story requires current technology, while also requiring people to work in office buildings and travel across state lines without restriction. Please forgive the suspension of disbelief I ask in this regard.

LOCATIONS: The locations mentioned in this novel are a hodge-podge of real and fake places. For example, if you know Milk Street in Boston, you might scratch your head about a certain numbered building and a sky bridge from it to another—because that bit is super fake.

REPRODUCTIVE RIGHTS: A lot has happened since I wrote this book. The catastrophe of the Dobbs decision, which is a humanitarian tragedy and will kill people, is one. As a writer, it is critical to me that I use whatever platform I have, however small, to be vocal on this issue. As such, the reader should assume the main character had an abortion at some point in her life. It doesn't matter when or why, because it is nobody's business and it doesn't change who or what she is or does in this story. Or maybe it does matter. This whole book is about political corruption that allows few to profit, and isn't that the very root cause of Dobbs?

DISCLAIMER: This is a work of fiction, meant for entertainment, and thus not, in any way shape or form, any authority on corruption. For serious reporting on corruption, please refer to far better non-fiction resources, some of which I note in the acknowledgements. This is a *fictional* legal thriller. The reader should realize I've taken liberty with actual legal procedure, rules, and case law. Nothing in here reflects my legal advice or opinions on legal matters.

ANIMAL LOVERS: Amongst a medley of characters in this novel are a dog and a cat. Fear not, no physical harm ever befalls them. As for the humans, I can't promise as much.

WARNING - GUN USE: Please be advised that this book includes gun violence.

"Our systems of legal education, bar licensing, court review, and peer relationships simply have not been good enough to guard against this weaponization of lawyers. We need to do better. No one thing will fix it. But I'd start with the need to specifically train law students and lawyers **to take stands** when they or others are asked to do things that erode ethics or democracy (emphasis added)."

-Matthew Segal, ACLU MA Legal Director, Twitter @segalmr, December 29, 2020. Segal is featured as ACLU lead in the documentary, How to Fix a Drug Scandal

PART I

MOTION TO EXPLAIN
WHY I'M ON THE RUN

CHAPTER ONE

I look out from the covered porch onto the wide wedges of Queen Anne's lace, a sea of white blooms and orange monarchs fluttering above. It is August in Massachusetts. Standing here in workout gear, I sip chocolatey coffee, hot and sugary with frothed milk. A warm wind, a country setting, I should be at peace. I'm not. This gorgeous—somewhat otherworldly—scenery is dissonant with my inner turmoil, waiting here, hiding here, knowing I must run again.

I'm a lawyer of eleven years, a partner in my third firm, Coarse & Cotton, a Big Law international powerhouse. CoCo is what gossip law blog *Above the Law* calls it, as do all the Ivy League law students performing death matches in the coliseum of connections and pedigree and grades to clinch limited summer associate spots. It's all so insane. These Summers are spoiled with box seats at baseball games and dinners at oceanfront mansions, cocktails on Hinkley yachts, only to maybe get a job upon graduating law school, toiling 80-100 hour weeks, reviewing documents for me, the firm's Global Head of E-Discovery and Deputy General Counsel.

I don't blame them, the temptation of money is irresistible, and I'm jaded, looking backwards on the process. But the truth remains, in exchange for *all* of your time, the pay is obscene, and the environment is all halls of chrome and glass and fine art—you feel as supernatural, as untouchable, as a rich man on an advanced planet. This, this hard imagery, these inside lines of privilege and metal and cut glass, enameled white walls and sterility, this is the inner conflict I feel now, hiding here with stolen data, in a serene field of plump color and fluttering life. A purple-bodied dragonfly lands on the natural wicker chair at my side. I watch him; he watches me. His wings are translucent green with veins of pink. He is the opposite of the white walls in the straight halls of Coarse & Cotton.

Three days ago, I programmed my firm email Out of Office auto-responder. My message says the typical vacation words and how I'm not checking email "on a regular basis" and I'm not checking voicemail. I am positive that numerous partners and associates have received this auto-message and pursued me regardless, sending a counter-response that always starts with, "Greta, I'm sorry to trouble you. I know you're on vacation, but…" I wouldn't know for sure, because I left my firm iPhone in my Boston penthouse, since the firm's MDM software (mobile device management) tracks GPS to air-striker precision. I should know. I'm the one who instituted CoCo's enhanced information security governance program on mobile devices. I meant it for defensive security. I didn't know they'd use it for offensive spying.

They'll be suspicious by now, for sure. I always, as do all CoCo lawyers, respond to emails while on "vacation" within the hour, no matter what your OOO says. I haven't read or responded to one in three days. And I won't use my personal iPhone, tied to an anonymous shell company I set up a month ago, to log in to my firm's webmail, because they track those IP address logins too. I didn't tell anyone where I was going on "vacation." I certainly didn't say that I copied another partner's emails and am on the run from my own firm.

How did this all start? I consider this question as I consider the insane volume of orange and black butterflies before me. It's all so surreal. The circumstances leading me here, to this vivid and wild concoction of nature in rural Massachusetts, are jagged and mismatched. I must admit, I am whiplashed. I need time to regain my focus, pause here to regroup in the middle of the storm—although, I must accept that in reality, despite that I've taken some serious action, the storm's just beginning. There is no room for error going forward.

But *a lot* has happened up to now.

It was one of those Summers, one of those poor spoiled souls, who struck the flint on the tinder of suspicion of firm corruption I'd been worrying over since last year. A month-and-a-half ago, on a bright June morning, strawberry-blond Summer Brad came to my chrome and glass office in the Sector 8, Sentry Floor of Boston's Prudential Building or "Pru" (CoCo rejects pedestrian floor numbers). I watched Summer Brad's twenty-five-year-old eyes move across my nameplate: GRETA VINET SEVILLE. After confirming I was, indeed, the partner he'd been emailing with on the case he was assigned to, Summer Brad stepped into my office. I watched him make quick study of my floor-to-ceiling windows and how they overlook Fenway and the crew-filled, winding black ribbon of the Charles. I adjusted a photo of me and Henry, a "colleague" of mine at my former firm. I adjusted the other framed photo of me, my brother Toby, and our Aunt Violet before she disappeared. These are the only framed pictures I have ever had on any desks, anywhere.

"Hi, I'm Brad," Summer Brad said, with cracked voice and shifting eyes, too shy to look me straight on. He took a seat in one of my black-and-chrome guest chairs.

"I know. We've been emailing," I said, as a light tease and with a smile in an attempt to break the ice, make his twitching stop. It didn't. "Nice to meet you in person, Brad. I hope you're enjoying your summer so far at CoCo. Entering your third year of law school in the fall, that's exciting. Third year's the easiest," I said, trying to be nice, hoping he'd relax.

"Uh, yes. Yes," he said quickly, nervously. "So, uh, I sent you the PDF binder...and..."

"Yes, I've got it open on my computer. Let's go through it, then."

Summer Brad waited for my feedback while I clicked through his PDF binder of "key" documents. "Key" meaning they were, simply put, *very* relevant, to the case we were defending for a trade association. Brad and other associates had discovered these "key" documents amongst an ocean of three million documents we'd collected from that client. The team had been working their way through document batches using the firm's modernized document review software platforms, futuristically called CaseSpaceAI and CaseCore, which are really just marking hype words to mean really great software that helps to more efficiently organize client documents.

The lead partner who owned the client relationship had tapped me as e-discovery lead. My job, as always, is to usher the associates through "continuous active learning, technology-assisted" document review. It sounds intimidating, but the concept is rather simple. If you know how Pandora or Spotify work, how those music apps "learn" from the listener's thumb's up and down on each song, and then how the app feeds similar songs to what the listener "likes," then you understand this technology. Basically, as the junior associates click "responsive" (relevant to the given case), i.e. "like" (if it were Pandora), on a document, the technology will find more documents like that one, and so on. This is obviously an efficient way of getting through three million documents, as Brad and his cohorts did this summer with this particular trade association's documents. Far more efficient than reviewing three million documents one by one, in no particular order. Of course, it's more complicated than that, and that's why I have a job, but that's the gist.

Out of the whole summer and junior associate team doing

the document review, Summer Brad volunteered to go through the key documents with me. I wondered if he thought we'd go over things in a virtual setting, because now that he was in my physical office, he fidgeted in the guest chair, mumbling about each document in a barely audible running narration, as I clicked and read. I kept saying *mm hmm* with tight lips, wishing he'd take the hint and chill, let me read in peace. I stood, tilting to my toes in my three-inch heels, and dropped the shade on my floor-to-ceiling window, because at noon on a cloudless day, the ricochet glare on my cat-eye progressives kills my eyes and launches migraines. Brad winced over the loss of his view of Fenway, which I noted he'd been salivating over. I assumed he was longing to leave my cold office to get to the warmth of the firm's scheduled summer associate outing.

And then, click, key document #10. The font was miniscule, so I took off my progressives and put on my dedicated readers.

"Oh, oh, wait," he said, leaning over my paperless desk, watching as I speed-read a three-page email. I was on page two and not understanding why this one email had been marked key. It seemed like a totally non-relevant screed by a trade association employee on annual budgets that had nothing to do with the case at hand, the case we'd been hired to defend against. How Brad could even read what I was reading from his guest chair is explained by the fact that twenty-five-year-old budding lawyers still have functional eyeballs.

Even in my readers, I squinted to read the small font of key document #10 and enlarged the view.

"That's, uh, a mistake, uh. I remember that one. I thought I had marked that 'not relevant,' uh," Brad said, in a deeper voice. "Sorry. Sorry about that. I'm sorry."

I kept reading though, because I somehow caught, on the third page, a buried line in a dense cut/paste of a spreadsheet. The font was at the smallest, seemed smaller than four point, and the

cut/paste into the email made the spreadsheet selection grainy
and the cells wonky and merged, so I strained, but read it, and
confirmed what I'd caught scrolling. The top row indicated the
data was from 2014, seven years old. Perhaps that's what stopped
me to begin with. Why would there be seven-year-old data pasted
into a recent email about current budgets? I shrunk the enlargement, pretended like what I read in that one tiny half-line, buried
in smooshed and blurred spreadsheet entries, was no big deal.
But it was a big deal, for it said, *T. Honeywell, est. mthly $80k*. And
that, to me, based on other things I knew and was suspicious of,
was like a pink neon billboard in a black desert.

T. Honeywell, est. mthly $80k.

This did not appear to my eyes as the mashed and fuzzy four
point font of reality. It appeared as bold and twenty-six point font
to me, for reasons I hope to make clear.

"So this was a mistake, Brad? You didn't mean to mark this
key?"

His posture slumped, his white face red. "Yeah, uh. Sorry," he
said.

I studied his nervousness over being wrong, his flushed
face, the bead of sweat on his strawberry-blond brow, slumped
posture, those filler "uhs," and figured he was clueless as to the
document's value. Brad was right, it was not relevant to the case
at hand. But the reference to any payment, any reference at all,
to a "T. Honeywell," in this particular trade association's documents—a trade association brought to the firm by the partner
I was most concerned about—confirmed suspicions I had and
warnings I'd been given. Simply put, the client was a group of
private law enforcement corporations: private-for-profit prisons, hired guards, private security, private investigations. I was
concerned that the partner in charge of that client, Raymond
Honeywell, was part of an illegal campaign finance scheme relat-

ed to private prisons all over, but especially on the Texas border. The ones that caged asylum-seeking children in freezer cells after the US government instituted a zero-tolerance policy to rip said children from their parents. Based on things I'd learned earlier in the year, I had a theory that our new CoCo partner had secretly used the name Theodore Honeywell in the past, in order to hide involvement in a prison-donation-kickback scheme.

If I'm being honest, the only reason I'd agreed to be e-discovery lead on this case was I had an urge to prove my theory. I knew there was more. Had good reason to suspect more. But how to prove it with evidence that Honeywell and others couldn't deny is the hard part. And lord knows what other corruption would seep out from there.

"It's fine, Brad. No worries," I said, using all my litigation prowess to be unemotional. Give nothing away. I hoped he couldn't see beneath my desk how tight I'd coiled my legs to stem my heels from tapping.

"Cool. Cool. So, uh. Can I, uh, sort of head out, maybe? They have that Red Sox game, uh, for the Summers in an hour and, uh, I was, uh, going to get a beer with my officemate."

Brad would not be getting an offer to join Coarse & Cotton at the end of the summer. Poor thing was honest and all, book smart by landing on Law Review at Harvard, the typical, typical Summer. If he did get an offer, I could maybe have hidden him from the other less-forgiving partners and summon the patience to mold him and teach him to never ask to leave a partner's office in the middle of a case meeting to drink beer and go to a baseball game. To never slump and exude anything other than total confidence if you wished to join CoCo's high-stakes litigation group. But Brad did not have the requisite sense of theater for CoCo's litigation group, nor the innate instinct to flawlessly act your unflappable part at all times. He didn't have enough common sense to lie about wanting to get a beer, and that meant he couldn't survive the culture of CoCo. As for making a mistake on the key document, that happens constantly. But the thing was, Brad didn't realize he was *right*. It was and is key. Key enough to push me to do what I ended up doing.

My God, what have I done?

CHAPTER TWO

When lawyers write motions—also called pleadings—they are basically asking the judge to give them something. There are motions to compel, in which you ask the court to require the opposing party to give you documents or other evidence. There are motions for summary judgment, in which you ask the court to rule that you've won the case because the facts and the law are so much in your favor, you don't have to go to trial in front of a jury. Those are just two examples. Between a motion to compel and a motion for summary judgment, there's a whole bunch of what's called discovery, which is when the parties to the litigation ask for and exchange documents, data…any kind of information they think will support their claims or defenses. And this is my focus, the discovery of electronic data, or e-discovery. How to collect documents, how to review millions of documents to find the stuff that the other party requests, that's my job, amongst other client needs, like computer forensics, or defending clients against a data breach by a hacker.

In these motions, there is almost always a "Facts" section in the beginning. This part tells the judge the facts that support why you're asking the court to make the other side do something or stop something or rule in your favor in some way. So this is how my brain is thinking of the facts leading up to and after Summer Brad dropped his stink bomb of Key Document #10 into my computer a month and a half ago.

The facts, as they might appear in a motion, as they might appear in whatever future pleading is filed in a criminal complaint about all that I find myself in, would appear as follows:

MOTION TO EXPLAIN WHY I'M ON THE RUN
<u>FACTS</u>

May it please the Court, the facts presented are as follows:

1. On or about May 3, 2011, Greta Vinet Seville lateralled to her second law firm, Stokes & Crane, as a second-year associate. She practiced there for eight years, until May 14, 2019, when she lateralled as a partner to the law firm of Coarse & Cotton.

2. On or until June 1, 2020, when he resigned, Raymond Honeywell was the United States Attorney General under then President Hubert M. Davis, II.

3. On or around June 3, 2020, Raymond Honeywell joined the law firm of Coarse & Cotton, LLP, as a partner in the Boston office.

4. Given the well-publicized controversies of the Davis administration and Honeywell's role in aiding widely criticized actions taken by the Davis administration, movant, Greta Vinet Seville, voiced her objection to a Coarse & Cotton managing partner in an email, as follows:

> To: Tim Cotton
> From: Greta Vinet Seville
> Date: June 5, 2020
> Re: Raymond Honeywell

Tim, this is unacceptable. I realize I've only been
at the firm for a year, but let me be clear: I will not
agree to work on any cases with Honeywell. A lot
of associates are upset by this, too. The firm should
reconsider this decision, one made, I would like to
point out, without the majority consent of the partnership, and, therefore, a breach of that contract. I do
not consent. Had I known CoCo was going to take
in Honeywell after he resigned as attorney general, I
would never have left Stokes & Crane. Tim, how do
you justify this when we have taken on several pro
bono asylum cases? How will you answer the hypoc-
risy? –Greta

5. Managing Partner Tim Cotton wrote back:

To: Greta Vinet Seville

From: Tim Cotton

Date: June 5, 2020

Re: Re: Raymond Honeywell

Greta, you should be careful about maligning
another lawyer. Honeywell is a respected attorney,
with great client connections, and twenty-nine years
of practice under his belt. The allegations concerning
the Davis administration are just that, allegations.
Honeywell has a right to defend himself. I see no
conflict between Honeywell and our pro bono asylum cases.

1. Ms. Seville then responded as follows:

> To: Tim Cotton
> From: Greta Vinet Seville
> Date: June 5, 2020
> Re: Raymond Honeywell
>
> Tim, they caged *kids*. Period. Actually, that's the best of it. They did worse. Let's not pretend otherwise. I agree Raymond Honeywell has a right to defend himself. That is, if anyone in the current administration were to actually take the necessary steps to investigate, charge, and prosecute him. But as we have seen time and again, it is rare that men of power are brought to justice. Instead, they are forgiven by getting lucrative positions in the private sector, like Honeywell here. You know all of the parade of horribles he and Davis stand rightfully accused of, so I will not reiterate all of them here. I note you have obviously made your decision, and I do not wish to discuss this further with you, at this time. My position is clear.

2. Amongst the many *known* controversies of the Davis administration, the salient ones for this motion are as follows:

> a.   On May 1, 2019, Attorney General Honeywell ordered a private militia, hired by the White House, to tear gas journalists who had assembled to shout questions to President Davis. Honeywell later claimed he

thought someone in the scrum had shouted "attack," but no proof, out of 152 videos of the event, support that claim.

b.   On March 14, 2020, the New York Times reported that AG Honeywell had earlier drafted a directive that families crossing the Texas border from Mexico be immediately separated and separately prosecuted, no matter how young the children were. Even if, the directive stated, the child was "breastfeeding." The children were to be confined, per Honeywell's directive, at one of the private prisons the administration had contracted.

Let me reiterate that last fact: *The children were to be confined, per Honeywell's directive, at one of the private prisons the administration had contracted. The same private prison that is a member of the client's trade association, from whose documents, Summer Brad found Key Document #10 showing monthly payments to a "T. Honeywell," going back at least seven years.* The rest of the facts would take a considerable amount of work to strip them of emotion, of the colors and sounds, inner thoughts, seemingly irrelevant observations, and scenery that courts aren't interested in reading.

As I start to think about these additional facts, the noise of the only other person at this monarch butterfly sanctuary where I hide is interrupting by humming the song she always hums: Eminem's "Say Goodbye to Hollywood". Her voice carries on the wind from two acres away.

CHAPTER THREE

I close my eyes behind my prescription aviators—these ones not progressives, but dedicated to the distance side of my complex optometry prescription. I try to focus on the wind around the cabin, how it plays the aluminum tubes and seashells of the windchime hanging off the porch roof. I don't want to think on them, the culprits, the colluders, their crime—probably crimes, plural—while I try to enjoy this hot coffee in peace. A pause in the action in my head.

Who am I anymore, anyway?

Will I end up like Aunt Violet, gone? Disappeared? Or my beloved brother Toby, living alone in the woods of Vermont?

The only other person in miles shuts the door on an outbuilding across the field of flowers and butterflies. She'll walk back to the cottage soon.

Who throws away their career on an impossible mission to take down a former attorney general and their own firm?

At thirty-seven, I should be sitting at a paperless desk in any of CoCo's thirteen offices, could be Tokyo, New York, Hong Kong, London, DC, Columbia, South Carolina, or the new mothership, Boston, where I'm technically based, even though I'm rarely there. I travel most of the year. Always first class or business. I should be e-signing pleadings drafted by juniors. I should be reading a PDF binder to prep for a discovery hearing in whatever Federal District Court the firm's corporate clients wish to drop-ship me to kill a burdensome demand for too many gigabytes of client data. Or, I should be hosting an all-women business development luncheon in SoHo, at a cost of a hundred dollars a head—for what amounts to a fistful of limp leaves and an inch of salmon. But I'm in the opposite of worlds. I'm hiding out with stolen emails that could—if I'm right about their content, and if I can pull this off—nuke Raymond Honeywell, probably nuke Coarse & Cotton, and who knows who else. The firm has politicians, global corporations, CEOs, influential trade associations, even whole states, as clients.

I open my eyes, wait for her to make her way to me on the cottage porch. I hear her humming as she goes about little tasks of tidying up around the outbuilding she just exited. She doesn't deserve this risk. I have great guilt for being here, because I know deep down I bring danger wherever I go. I've crossed so many lines.

A cardinal adds garlands of red to the fluttering orange and white and green of the acres beyond this porch; he feints and swoops as I watch him, thinking, thinking on my recent past, and on my next steps. The hot mug of coffee warms my hands; the chocolatey taste lingering on my tongue. Lavender bushes that flank the porch provide their harsh perfume. I am surely awake in all these colors and scents and tastes and fear. The sound of warm wind feathers the forest leaves on the edges of the property. And because of the adrenaline zapping around my system, I'm attuned to the flip of each leaf, the sound like waves turning pebbles at the tapered ends of oceans. The offered serenity is a trick. My body knows the truth. My heart quickens to think of everything up to now and everything to come. I sip the chocolatey coffee to burn the anxiety down, drown the hard clockwork in my chest.

A monarch lands on the rim of my mug. I am startled to think of myself here, now, under these circumstances. He flies back to the acres of white flowers. This place. I remind myself I am really in this place, and I will have to leave soon. But I am here now.

How did I get here?

Eleven years ago, the partners at the first of my three firms assigned me a basic breach of contract case to cut my teeth on. It doesn't really matter what the case was about or that I won my artist client judgment on the pleadings—meaning, we didn't have to go through the expense or uncertainty of a jury trial. We won early because the facts and law were on our side, my motion game was strong even back then, and the judge didn't want the stink of opposing counsel's bullshit in her courtroom another minute. I could tell from her not-subtle grimaces—a specific type of legal face that comes with the power of the black robe. But, again, the case does not matter. What matters is that my client required our meetings take place at her remote Western Massachusetts property, which she had bought with her inheritance after becoming an orphan on her twentieth birthday.

In a field in the center of her fifty acres, surrounded by forest at the backside of a ski mountain, is where she chose to dwell. She hired local carpenters to build her a cozy cottage—one she painted from an image she'd dreamed of while passed-out drunk on funeral wine. And, given the blazingly vivid strangeness of her grief dream, she also made real the landscaping around the cottage, because she just could not get it out of her mind. Indeed, around the cottage, she cut a circle with a diameter of four acres. Within the circle, she rototilled eight wedges, fanning from the cottage in center. She then blazed walking paths between each wedge. Next, she planted the food of the only gods on this earth: Queen Anne's lace for monarch butterflies. A four-acre circle of white flowers, betwixt which a human could walk to three separate outbuildings on the edge of the circle.

I look at those outbuildings now: the first one positioned at noon, the second one at 3:00—the one she fiddles and hums around—and, turning my head, to the third outbuilding behind the cottage at 8:00. That particular outbuilding has an outdoor summer kitchen, the pergola-tunnel walls of which, covered in crawling trumpet vines and lined with wide-frond potted plants, extend to a stream at the base of the mountain. It is here, on my first client's property, on her front porch, where I watch the multitude of monarch gods feast upon her lace flowers. It is here where I hide, for she is the only soul who I trust, and who nobody else knows. I have told nobody about her. Ever. And there's a reason for that. There's always a reason for the things I do in my life, all of it stemming from my Defining Life Event: the disappearance of Aunt Violet. It defined my brother Toby's life, too.

But Violet is a different story, my backstory, my underbelly.

I must quarantine these thoughts. I need to focus on the plan to get out and prove this corruption.

Lena Atiri is my first client's name, and here she comes down one of the wedge paths.

"Greta, the horse trader says the storm comes Tuesday, so that's when you make a break for it," Lena says, walking toward me from the 3:00 outbuilding she calls The Office. She hasn't let me step beyond the covered porch, for she fears satellites and spies who might be looking to track me from the sky. Maybe she's paranoid, maybe she's right.

She's mid wedge, it's high August, and the abundant blooms are white and fat. The monarchs flutter about her, landing for a second or two on her olive arms, her black hair; they form a moving sea of orange around her, feeding, feeding, hatching, feeding. Lena's in her lime sundress with turpentine stains, for today is a restoration day, in which she'll work in the building positioned at noon, restoring a client's old baroque painting. Tomorrow is for writing, and she'll work in the building at the position of 8:00, or at the picnic table at the end of the attached outdoor kitchen, writing her latest monograph about some *very specific* sub-sub-topic within the Italian Baroque era. The day after that, Tuesday, is the forecasted hurricane, on which she'll return to the noon building to check the drying on the re-lining of her client's painting, while I escape the way she and I have plotted.

Our drawn map is rolled in her right hand, and she bounces it in her left palm. Her crooked, silver bangles made out of vintage bicycle spokes, which I bought her at an artisans' shop in Minneapolis a few years ago, clink to pierce the competing wind, adding to the windchime's symphony. She is a goddess and this is her realm. This is her orchestra. This is her world. I am a dangerous imposition. I need to leave now, long before the storm. I can't risk her.

"Also, Greta, I made an alteration on the map. We need to go over it. Make another pot of coffee," she says.

"But the plan we mapped was solid. What's wrong?"

"What's wrong, Uncle, is it's not perfect."

She calls me Uncle. I take whatever names she throws my way, especially now, since she's affording me this respite, this pause, in her sanctuary. I'm thirty-seven, she's thirty-six. We're not best friends. We're not acquaintances. We're not lovers—I've got a whole other drama in the love department going on, or wish I did, with that old "colleague" Henry, the one framed on my desk. As for Lena, I'm not sure what we are. I'd never say such an irrational thing out loud, but I think we're akin to cosmic sisters, separated in space before consummation to different bloodlines. I very much love Lena.

She pauses by the hose on the side of the cottage, turns the spigot, and begins to water the lavender bushes around the porch with one hand, keeping our rolled map clear of water spray with the other. I watch in awe how graceful she completes all actions. So smooth, so fearless. Her hair is so shiny black it has a shimmer of blue.

"Uncle, do not tell me we're out of Ring of Fire."

"We're not."

"Then why are you still on my porch?" She recoils the hose and turns off the water. "Go on, get. Make the coffee. You're not going to believe the alteration I came up with. This is far superior. And safer. Did you check the batteries in that flashlight?"

"Yes, Lena."

She's on the porch, and I'm walking into the cottage, as she rifles planning questions at me. I answer every one with a, "Yes, Lena." When I grab the mini coffee grinder and the bag of whole bean Ring of Fire, she slinks up to the poured concrete kitchen counter, unrolls the map while standing on tip-toes, and pins the corners with smooth yellow pebbles she plucked from the stream at the base of the mountain. She does all this in one fluid series of floating motions, as if a celestial ballerina pantomiming the daily actions of mere mortals. A full-size fairy, a flesh-and-bone angel, albeit one prone to doling tough love and colorful vulgarities. Indeed, Lena was a prodigy ballerina, until, at the age of sixteen, she told her manager to shove the bulimia he advised would land her better gigs up his "rot-filled, backstage ass."

Lena's kitchen is immediate upon entering the high-ceilinged, one-floor cottage. Beyond the counter where she smooths the map in elegant arcs is a living room with a green velvet couch, a puckered gray rug on a wood floor, Lena's old hound dog, Sleuth, snoring on a gigantic dog bed, and, patrolling the topside of an exposed beam as Lord of the Manor, is Marshmallow Face, a fat white kitten with no bones, just fur.

"MF, get down from there, you delusional puffball. You're not a panther," Lena coos, turning to Marshmallow Face after following my sightline. "Greta, did you make sure all of your damn spare different glasses are in the Go Bag?"

"Yes, Lena."

"I don't know why you don't get Lasix, or get used to the progressives full time."

"Can't get Lasix because of my Christmas tree cataracts in

both eyes, and the oddball astigmatism in my left eye, and progressives are a pain in my ass. They hurt. I'm only wearing them when I have to." My cataracts are congenital and rare; basically, when my optometrist— who I'm in a war with because she insists I stick with the progressives full time—examines my eyes, she can see what looks like Christmas lights blooming in my irises. They don't hurt, and, in my case, they're benign, so says the doc. But I can't get Lasix.

"Contacts?"

"Progressive contacts? Yeah, nope. I'm not going to even attempt that pain."

"Big city lawyer, but really just a wuss," she teases. She turns back to MF still up on the beam. "Get down from there, Marshmallow!" He bug-eyes her with his sweet little face, all innocent, all powerful up there so high.

"What an idiot," she says of MF, turning back to face me as I fill the pot with water and pour into her Mr. Coffee. I think of my six-grand, restaurant-grade Jura espresso machine back at my penthouse in Boston, and how, regardless of its alien-craft sleekness and perfect roast every time, I prefer Lena's cranky, knocking Mr. Coffee. When I moved over to Coarse & Cotton two years ago, I quickly learned that everyone employed there is gifted a Jura for their home. Coarse & Cotton is the kind of AmLaw 100 firm that pays partners high seven figures, and *every* lawyer a flat one-hundred-grand bonus, not once but *twice* a year. It is the only Big Law to do what the industry calls the Double Dunk, so. That's why I thought I'd won the lottery when I lateraled there from Stokes & Crane.

I miss Stokes & Crane. I made a huge mistake. And I'm going to miss Lena's Mr. Coffee, and most especially, the blessing of hiding away with her.

"I'm going to miss this place, Lena."

"Yeah? I make a good hideout?"

"The best."

She smiles, and I smile back.

At first I think it is just the gurgle-knocking of her old Mr. Coffee. But now Sleuth is up and barking, jolting toward the still opened front door. The floorboards are shaking. MF leaps from the beam to a hutch, to the floor, and bounds across the gray puckered rug to the kitchen counter and into Lena's arms. What I thought was an uptick in the whooshing wind is now too constant, too loud, to be wind. Too even to be mother nature. A second whir, more minor, but more immediate, than the one overhead higher in the sky, drops into the doorway. Sleuth is wild, barking mad at the drone hovering in the doorway. Its eye is trained straight on my face. It jerks mid-air to stall on Lena's. Over the house is the louder, booming whir, the whomp, whomp of a helicopter. So, what's going on is this: A helicopter tracked me here and someone on board sent a drone down for closer inspection. I've been found. I've been seen with her, here. I've placed my Lena in danger. Ruined her sanctuary. I could die of shame.

I lock eyes with her.

"Those fucking drools. No fucking way," she says.

"The room. Get down to the room," I whisper, my back to the drone so whoever is filming can't read my lips.

She nods in agreement, calming MF by holding him tight to her chest. She races to slam the door shut. I yank the curtains above the sink to block the drone's view.

It's maneuvered to the side of the house, buzzing beyond the pane. Knowing where it's going next, I jump up on the counter, hip-slide to the other side, dragging the map with me. Thankfully, my high-shine Sweaty Betty workout pants grease my progress with no friction. And also thankfully, I'm still in my Ultraboosts from my morning indoor cardio, because I am in the thick of it now. Actually, *we* are in the thick of it now. Son of a bitch, how could I do this to Lena?! I pop to my feet and run to a remote on an end table beside the green couch. I press "shut." The electric tracks above the large living room windows grind to life, feeding automated cords to shut the drapes.

Once free of the drone's eye, I race back to the kitchen rug, which is glued in place, and jam my heel on a hidden lever, concealed to look like a piece of the wood floor. The rug-covered hatch opens to reveal stairs down. I stand to the side, motioning for Lena to move on down the stairs, but, while I took the ten seconds to shut the curtains and return to heel kick the hatch lever, she magically slid past me in some mad ad hoc choreography and collected the map off the floor.

"Screw the map, get down there," I say.

"We can't leave this behind," she says. "They'll know where we're going."

We're? We? She's ten steps ahead in whatever the new scenario is, and I'm not accepting this yet.

She pushes past me to the sink, grabs a book of matches from the windowsill above, lights our precious and detailed map, and leaves it burning in the sink. It's gut-wrenching to watch our hard work burn, because not only was the map rather colorful, beyond the art of it, the legend contained necessary passcodes for two different car lots with plenty of cars with temp plates, all seemingly disconnected to me, but available to Lena, due to a convoluted and webbed network of her own connections. It also contained analog directions to a rental house, reserved by my forgettably-named LLC—the shell company I set up a month ago. Knowing Lena, she's planning for the worst, she's planning for whoever is here to take us and take our plans and codes.

Is it paranoia to think they'd go to such lengths? Nope. Is it paranoia to think that this drone is CoCo's and not just some punk teen spying on neighbors? Nope. Not paranoia. We are smack dab in the middle of a deadly battle, and I have the facts to prove it.

CHAPTER FOUR

Pleadings must be double-spaced, fit within non-negotiable margins, and boiled down to comply with page limits. Judges want you to get to the point without raw feeling, flowery exposition, or color. Adjectives must be used sparingly. But I deviate now from the initial cold recitation of facts as I think on how I might draft the unvarnished reality of the remaining reasons as to why I'm on the run, and why the risk is death. If this were an actual motion, by filing time, this recitation would be strongly edited, redlined in a blizzard of track changes, and reviewed by several colleagues, each with their own edits. The sanitized result would be six sterile paragraphs, each setting forth a crucial chronological event.

MOTION TO EXPLAIN WHY I'M ON THE RUN, *continued....*

Raw Narrative of Event #1: Late June 2020, two weeks after AG Honeywell resigned as US Attorney General under President Davis and joined Coarse & Cotton, the current Cotton of Coarse & Cotton, Tim Cotton, summoned me to CoCo's most elaborately modern conference room, Conference Room K, on the Tower 8, King Floor. He didn't say what it was about. I rode the eleven floors from my office up in one of the Pru's clunky elevators, slow in progress, bouncing on cables that felt like they'd snap any minute. These antique elevators are original to when pilgrims landed in Massachusetts and do not match the sleek interiors of their modern tenants, such as CoCo. At each floor, when someone exited, the wind in the fifty-two-story shaft would howl around the car, sounding like a January Nor-Easter. Someone complimented the "fashion" of my black cat-eye progressives, which I wore because I didn't know if I would need distance or reading or both. The *constant* shifting and decision-points with my eyes, honestly, that used to be my biggest stressor, and I miss those comparatively uncomplicated days—sure, long hours, hard cases, filing deadlines, demanding clients, the drama with Henry, eye strain, eye strain, all that. But compared to now, it had been a cake walk.

I exited on the King Floor, my heels clicking on the marble of the elevator bank up to the sealed, glass doors of CoCo's restricted lobby. I waved to the receptionists to buzz me in, for this was CoCo's "select" floor, meant for only those summoned, or permitted, by Coarse or Cotton. One floor up a roped-off marble stairwell, were Maurice Coarse's and Tim Cotton's suite of offices.

The receptionists buzzed me in, and I entered the spacious, white, high-ceilinged marble and enameled select lobby. Bach filled the empty air with a gentle feel, a cover to make one think these halls were calm.

In crossing the lobby, I looked up the velvet-rope-blocked inner stairwell beside the receptionists' desk, because I always did this when I was summoned to the select floor. I was always mystified by an enormous 12' x 15' quilt that hung a half inch off the wall; the top rod bolted to the enamel paneling near the high ceiling of the open stairwell. The quilt was odd, never made any sense to me. All the other art hanging on the glossy white walls of CoCo was dark oil paintings of English fields or stills of books with eyeglasses. CoCo's antiquarian art collection is, indeed, meant to clash with the minimalist design of shiny white surfaces and modern furniture and tech-heavy offices and conference rooms. Maurice Coarse has said he wants clients to feel they're in the hands of old money masters who themselves invented technology. Not fitting with this aesthetic intention, however, is the stairwell quilt.

The quilt is made of hundreds of patches of light blues, yellows, and pinks, creating a pastel medieval scene of princesses and knights around a castle. Nothing about this quilt makes sense in CoCo, and the size is something I've never seen before in a quilt. When I passed it this time on my way to Conference Room K, a corner was folded over, and I thought I saw the edge of a door in the wall behind. The closest receptionist caught my pause, my skeptical glance, looked at the folded corner, and back at me.

"People need to stop touching that quilt when they go up and down the stairs," she said. She rose from her chair, slipped the velvet rope off an anchor, passed through, made sure to anchor it back, as if blocking me from following her, which I wouldn't have, shuttled up the steps, and fixed the corner straight.

I smiled at the receptionist as if her precautions with the rope and quilt were not strange, and proceeded to the exterior hall beyond the lobby. This hall is all windows on one side, looking down upon the Charles. It's named Ventfort Hall. Ventfort Hall holds the most restricted of all the firm's conference rooms. Ventfort is where politicians, CEOs, people who need security details come for meetings with Maurice Coarse or Tim Cotton. My heels slipped on the recent wax of the marble floor beyond the lobby rug, so I settled my feet and continued on to the T at the end, where Conference Room K took up a glass-walled corner.

On seeing the two men inside, a certain kind of instant rage erupted, and I had to fight back the urge to flip them off and turn around. But I proceeded, thinking I'd confront them head on for springing such a surprise meeting on me.

I pulled the silver handle on the glass door, stepped in. I

thanked myself for having worn my most murderous black career dress, a Jason Wu, paired with my black murder heels. I fixed my posture pole-straight, adjusted my frames, and stood at the opposite head of the table. At the other end sat former Attorney General Raymond Honeywell. Standing at the window with his back to me was Tim Cotton. Tim, a lanky man of forty-nine, turned to greet me. His full head of brown hair annoyed me, for the cut was a split middle bowl cut with flat bangs, cut straight across the brow line. The undersides of his head were buzzed, and thus, his whole 'do was aggressively unfashionable, *at best.* Tim's father was the original Cotton of Coarse & Cotton, the original office of which, in Washington, DC, is still the official headquarters, even though Coarse and Cotton are in Boston "a few years" to ensure CoCo is injected straight into the veins of New England.

"Greta," Tim said.

"Tim." I nodded, no smile.

"I'd like you to meet Raymond. Perhaps we could set aside some concerns you have in person. He is here now, and he'll have an office on your floor."

I stared at Raymond Honeywell, sitting there like a king, the new guy a king, at the end of the enamel white table. He looked like a sack to me, for his arms stuck to his sitting sides, and he slumped in his arrogance. An oval of human with a mostly-bald head and wire eyeglasses. As he had appeared in all television interviews I'd seen, he had a slovenly gray stubble in patches on his jowls and cheeks. Thus, his face seemed always in need of a shave, which was at odds with his three-piece suit. He stared back. I let the silence hang two beats in the air.

I have this thing, and it conflicts with my litigation career. I do think I've honed my skills at the acting and theater parts; and I do think I'm good at curbing my emotions in stressful situations. But I am incapable of lying, and it feels like an assault to my soul to be a phony. Whenever I'm presented with a situation in which I'm expected to be false, I hear my beloved Aunt Violet, so long ago, whisper in my ten-year-old ear, "I hate phonies." So in that moment, staring Honeywell down, I couldn't smile at him. I wanted him to know what I thought of him. But I also had a snap idea, perhaps the natural tic of being a litigator: while I could not smile and pretend for Honeywell, I *could* buy myself time to consider a better strategy. So I chose to simply nod at him. I chose not to engage in recriminations or accusations, at least not yet.

"Raymond," I said. "I'm Greta Vinet Seville, the firm's e-discovery counsel. I'm sure Tim has filled you in on my role."

"She," Tim said, an arm across his belly, the other flipping a limp-swat as he talked. "Greta here, is the person who handles computer stuff so we don't need to bother with it." At this, I did provide a lie of a smile, the way Tim felt compelled to power up on me by downplaying my value. It didn't bother me, because by displaying such an outward insecurity (downplaying me to up-play himself), he handed me an opportunity. I would seize the next move and extract something I wanted from him. He knew I would, he caught his own gaffe and stifled a wince, for true power never feels compelled to express one's higher position in an open room. True power cuts you out silently, behind a mask, and behind closed doors. Tim was the current Cotton of CoCo because recently-dead Daddy Cotton forced little Timmy on the original Coarse, Maurice Coarse, ninety, still practicing, one floor up in the special suite. Tim, entitled Tim, nepotismed into the firm, had zero litigation experience. He'd spent his career in the CoCo D.C. office up to now doing lawyer-lobbying for for-profit special interest groups.

I looked at Tim and saw weakness. I looked at Honeywell and saw arrogant power. I saw them together as the biggest risk ever.

"It's nice to meet you, Greta," Honeywell said. "I hope we can overcome whatever concerns you have, so that we can work together on client matters."

I took a deep breath. Bit my tongue. Bit every rage boiling inside. These men, these men and their machinations. The fact Honeywell was given a chance at CoCo to reinvent himself, like so many before him had been given so many chances before. I bit that all back. Oh God it was infuriating. Nobody had given Aunt Violet a shot at redemption after she did what she did. Her motive maybe had been criminal, sure, but was at least altruistic. But, no, there was nothing altruistic with Honeywell. The question blooming in my mind in those seconds was *why?* Why him? Why is he given this rebirth at CoCo? What is his connection here? I didn't know then how to answer those questions, but I needed to figure out a way to find out. Instead, I focused on what I could get out of Tim Cotton for getting me into this.

"Certainly, Raymond. I'm sure we can work out something that fits for both of us. Tim," I said, snapping him to attention.

He brought a thumb to his teeth. Kept his arms crossed. "Yes?"

"So, Cal has been coming to me for help with all the subpoenas the firm gets, third party document requests for client files, legal hold orders the firm needs to do…that sort of thing. It's all somehow related to that *computer stuff* I do." I made sure to slow roll the pronunciation of *computer stuff* to signal that yes, I was cashing in on his gaffe. "All that and as a member of the firm's Information Security Committee, since we're here, where are we on formalizing that assistant general counsel role? That's settled, of course?"

He smirked. He knew under the circumstances, he couldn't say no. "Of course, Greta. I thought that had been settled. I already talked to Cal about it. So, consider it formal."

He hadn't talked to Cal about anything. He just didn't want to convey he knew jack shit about all I'd done for the firm's own legal issues or information security. He needed to resurrect the illusion between us that he was all powerful, all knowledgeable.

32

He needed to convey to me that he still held his king and his power. But, you move your pawn in a pathetic way, I'm going to take your queen. Problem is, he does still have his King, and if you're going for the king, you best nuke him off the planet. I didn't quite know what the rest of the moves would be in this chess match, but I knew that getting closer to the firm's general counsel position would matter, somehow. Indeed, my slow pronunciation of *computer stuff* was not just to chide Tim Cotton; it was to make him think my only role as assistant to Cal was helping him do typical discovery-related work. Tim forgot that the General Counsel's Office also has a duty to enforce the firm's ethical obligations and compliance with laws. Tim, the unqualified managing partner of a massive firm, doesn't really think about *compliance* with laws. He thinks about *avoidance* of laws. Two very different things.

Raw Narrative of Event #2: About a month later, still in the timeline before Summer Brad, Maurice Coarse asked me to accommodate an interview with an AP law technology reporter in a tiny, interior conference room off of Ventfort Hall. She interviewed me on the rise of A.I. and its impact on discovery and the practice of law. Once we were done, we passed a telescope in the middle of Ventfort. It was set up for close-up views of rowers on the Charles or on pedestrians shopping on Newbury Street. If I were to chance a view through the eyepiece, I could see my own rooftop garden, capping my fourth-floor penthouse on Newbury.

"Quite a view," she'd said. Her name was Samera Banerjee. I've kept her card. When she said *quite a view*, her fierce brown eyes surveyed not the exterior world, but rather, scanned, almost like a laser, the outside world, to the white surfaces of Ventfort Hall, and then my reaction. Her intelligence was piercing, and I felt that she was probing me for more. Probing me for something other than my opinion on the literal view or answers about the impact of A.I. on the practice of law.

"Right," I said, not sure if she was laying bait for me to take. "Well, the telescope sure makes it easy to determine when there's a line out the door at Apple," I said, referring to the near-constant throng of people lining up for iPhones on Boylston.

"Ha, sure," she said. She nodded and clasped her hands behind her back. The gesture of an all-knowing professor who patiently suffers your pathetic jokes.

In passing the roped-off stairwell up to Coarse and Cotton's suites, and again catching glimpse of that weird, huge, pastel, princess quilt, she slowed her steps, scrunched her brow, as if considering something about the quilt, about the stairwell. But she moved on quickly enough to the elevator lobby, and I followed. The thick glass security doors to the select lobby sealed behind, and the loud whir and howling of the eight elevator shafts surrounded us, giving the feel that we were entombed at the confluence of multiple wind tunnels. And this obscuring noise is perhaps what Samera felt she needed in order to whisper what she did.

She strategically turned her back on the receptionists. In a nonchalant manner, while seeming to stare forward and consider an oil painting of eyeglasses that capped the end wall, she leaned towards me sideways, pointing at the painting as if this was her topic, and said, on low, "Pretend we are discussing this painting."

"Excuse me?"

"The painting, Greta. We are discussing the painting." She stepped closer to it, although we were still well sealed in the elevator lobby.

I'd never been in a situation like that before, but she was an investigative reporter for the AP, and I've read many investigative reporter books, so my interest was piqued.

"Yes, this is a great painting," I said and stepped to her, twisted so my back, like hers, was kept to the select-floor receptionists.

"I have a source," she said, in a whisper. "He's presented

somewhat of a riddle for me, but it's not really my focus of reporting. You know, I'm a technology reporter. But, anyhow," she
paused. She seemed unsure on whether to ask. She kept gesturing
at the painting. "I know you've only been at CoCo a year. Your
former firm, Stokes & Crane, just a couple floors down. Right?
And you were there eight years?"

"Yes, that's right."

"I've looked into your background. By all accounts, you play
by the rules. You're tough, pretty damn zealous for your clients,
but you're honest. And Stokes, Stokes is known for its ethics.
Yeah?"

"Yes," I said, and at this, my brow furrowed. Where was this
going?

"Well, I'm curious by this source's riddle. Again, I know
you've only been here a short time, comparatively speaking. But,
have you ever heard of a Theodore Honeywell?"

At that point in time, I had not. "No. Related to Raymond
Honeywell? He's a partner here now, you know? Since he quit as
AG."

"Oh yes, I know about Raymond Honeywell."

"So who is Theodore Honeywell?"

"Ah, probably nobody."

A burst of howling wind blew our hair, announcing her
elevator car had arrived. She quickly popped in before I could
ask more. From within her otherwise empty elevator, she waved
goodbye and said, "Be careful, Greta. People have died looking
into Theodore Honeywell. You have my card." The doors shut.

I hurried back to my office, grabbed my purse, and raced
down and over a block to Newbury Street, to my place. In my
personal elevator, I passed the first-floor restaurant, the second-floor apartments, the third-floor recording studio, and landed on my floor, the fourth. I grabbed my personal laptop from the
granite kitchen counter, and raced up the inner steps, weaving

around piles of books to my rooftop garden.

There, on my outdoor table, amongst potted trees, I dove headfirst into the riddle of *Who is Theodore Honeywell?* Reporter Samera Banerjee made strikingly clear the need for strict confidentiality, the way she leaned in to whisper her questions, her severe looks, her advice to be careful, and express warning of death. I had to hide my web searches, which CoCo absolutely monitors and audits on their network. So I needed to use my non-CoCo computer and WiFi.

I Googled Theodore Honeywell. No pictures, no images of anyone named Theodore Honeywell connected to Raymond Honeywell or anyone else at Coarse & Cotton. The only slim and miniscule bit I found, after several nights and early mornings of searching and researching, was on the Wayback Machine, a website that stores snapshots of websites, so that items later scrubbed from the live web can be found there. People always say that nothing is truly gone in the digital world. And that is mostly true, but not *always* true.

It was in the Wayback where, after I performed numerous searches and followed hundreds of false-lead rabbit holes, I found a buried list of members of an obscure political action committee (PAC) set up in 2010 to represent the interests of private prisons. At this point in time, when I discovered this PAC on the Wayback, I was not yet working on the private law enforcement trade association case. I did not yet have Summer Brad's Key Doc #10.

In this list of people related to the PAC, I found a "Theodore Honeywell," his name appearing amongst a number of other people I knew had long ties and professional relationships with Raymond Honeywell, the former AG, now CoCo partner. So this is when I hatched my theory that Raymond was Theodore, Theodore was a pseudonym for Raymond. Raymond has no family members named Theodore. On the live web, this list of PAC members does not exist—it's been purged. And in this PAC's later filings and publicly available documents, there is no mention of any T. Honeywell or Theodore Honeywell, and certainly not Raymond Honeywell. Simply put, if my theory was correct, before he became the United States Attorney General, Raymond Honeywell *then* had the mens rea (conscious intent) to hide his association with a private prisons PAC. He didn't use his real name, and the fake name he used, Theodore Honeywell, has been purged from live PAC documents. All of which posed the blazing question of *Why?* And was there any other documentary proof to support my theory?

Raw Narrative of Event #3: Still in the timeline before Summer Brad found Key Doc #10, I was working late in my CoCo office sometime around Christmas 2020. My terrible firm laptop kept blue-screening and locking up every hour or so, so I asked for an emergency I.T. assist. It was Reboot Pete who answered the call and appeared in my doorway. Reboot Pete is a scrawny guy with thin filaments of hair, and I didn't like interacting with him—which wasn't fair, because my distaste had to do with him always telling me to reboot my computer. No matter the problem, he'd say to reboot. Reboot Pete had worked with me some months before on testing out how to conduct forensics on the hard drive of a commercially-available drone.

"Pete," I said, moving away from my chair and computer, switching from readers to my progressives as I went. I then launched into a charade I go through with Reboot Pete about once a month, and he always laughs along. "So, Pete, you know what I'm going to say."

He smiled back. "Go on. Let me have it, Counselor," he said.

"This has to improve. How many times are we going to have this same exact conversation? We're working on bet-the-company cases, and we need actual, functional computers. Are these toys, made by Fischer Price, maybe? Why do these crash so much? And please, I already rebooted three times. Please don't tell me to reboot."

"Greta, you've really got the rant down solid. Brava!" He said, slow clapping.

"Why thank you. But I'm going to murder that damn computer, and you, friend, if you tell me to reboot."

"Honeywell threatened me too about the computers," he said. "Yeah, big man thinks firm laptops are trash and he insists on using his own computer. So maybe the two of you can team up and raise it with whoever does the budgets around here." He moved over to my computer, took a seat in my chair. "Honeywell, though. He's using a computer that I think he used while AG. Although," and here he paused and leaned over my desk toward me. I was standing by my guest chair. "I think he wasn't supposed to use a personal computer for government business, you know. Like Hillary Clinton off-server stuff. Right? That's illegal?"

"Hmm," I said, pretending to be consumed with the drop of mail in my in-box. Catalogs and vendor invoices, a legal newsletter. Nothing that would warrant the attention I gave it in ignoring Pete's rather interesting news about Honeywell using a personal computer for government and firm work. I was also ignoring Pete's question about what's legal for government employees vis-a-vis electronic data.

"Why do you think he used it for government work?" I asked.

"Oh, I might have seen a few things when I was connecting him to the network. Didn't mean to. Looked like a bunch of financial crap too. Accounting stuff. A bunch of archived emails. Maybe I saw a bank statement from something in the Cayman Islands? Maybe it was for a relative and that's why he's prickly about who has access to his computer? I think a folder holding some of this stuff was labeled "Theodore" or something?"

He said it as a series of questions, keeping his face away from me, as he turned to my dead computer. But it was a solid statement, and he knew I knew it, and this was Pete being Pete—a rather savvy guy, alerting me to a firm risk in his sly way.

So as to diffuse the appearance that I agreed with any concern Pete might have, and which rumor he'd spread if I didn't expressly state disagreement, I said, "I'm sure Honeywell didn't use a personal computer for government work, Pete."

"Well, all I know is, that's the only computer he'll use, and he didn't like that we have to have admin access to it in case something happens. But we promised him that nobody looks at you lawyers' junk. He's got a lot of archived stuff on there, is all I know."

Reboot Pete started rebooting my computer, which always takes a billion years (and is why I hate it so much) because of all the security protocols, so I excused myself. I didn't want any confusion to arise on whether I agreed with his rather obvious warning about Honeywell.

"I'll be back. I need a bio-break," I said. And then, as if passing it off as a non-issue, I paused in my doorway and asked, "Honeywell signed the BYOD policy, right, before you connected the laptop to the network?"

"Of course. None of my team will hook up anything without that signed. You've made that clear enough, Madam Assistant General Counsel. We ain't losing our jobs."

"Thanks, Pete. And thanks for fixing my computer, even though you're rebooting it, *for the fourth time tonight*. Good grief."

"You should bring this shtick of yours to Comedy Central, Counselor," he called after me. I was already halfway down the hall.

I walked to the bathroom and considered how maybe the reason I played my move by seeking to be named assistant general counsel was coming into focus. The point with our BYOD policy, Bring Your Own Device, which I'd recently updated because of all the *computer stuff* I do, says, in relevant part:

> *By signing this policy, you agree that a du-*
> *ly-authorized person may access your device to*
> *employ security features and for compliance with*
> *laws.*

Would I be considered "duly-authorized" or a straight-up criminal if I accessed Honeywell's laptop? Would I have the guts to do that? And how could I do it without being caught? If I got caught, then what?

Raw Narrative of Event #4: A month ago, after Summer Brad showed me Key Document #10 and its reference to the trade association's $80k monthly payments to a "T. Honeywell," and marrying that with all I had been suspicious of up until then, and, admittedly, suffering a four-year rage over the atrocities of the Davis administration—the examples above being but a few—I determined *things had changed.* In reality, things hadn't changed, they'd always been this misbalanced and oppressive for many others beyond me, a person in a place of privilege. So the *things had changed* dynamic really meant people like me, well meaning but blind, subconsciously or purposefully, couldn't ignore it anymore. I felt I had an *obligation* to act. And that I had to play my part to at least do *something.* I suddenly understood some things my Aunt Violet had said when I was a girl, and perhaps why she did some drastic and illegal things. But that was her rage, and this is my rage.

It was a double rage that the new administration had not yet begun investigations of Davis and his cohorts. And given what we'd seen over the Davis years, I didn't know whether to have faith in the FBI. Seething, fog-like, helpless rage is what I felt.

I didn't quite know what I should do, but I had enough to consider prying the lid on Honeywell's emails—the ones Re-boot Pete, in his sly way, told me were on Honeywell's laptop. The implication being, by using the word "archived"—twice, no less—these were stores of old emails. So I did consider whether I had the nerve to access them and see if my theory and reporter Samera's riddle had merit. What I was contemplating might be a pure-grade violation of the Computer Fraud and Abuse Act, maybe a violation of all sorts of codes and laws and lawyer ethics, but, again, *things had changed*. And I was the firm's assistant general counsel. Part of that job requires I ensure the firm and the firm's lawyers, *even if they are named partners and a former attorney general*, are in compliance with laws. Nobody ever *said* or *wrote* the words that I was "duly authorized" to access Honeywell's laptop, but, who was authorized to give me that authority? There was a zero percent chance Coarse or Cotton, or General Counsel, Cal, would sanction an investigation into their *knowledge and aid* of whatever was up with Honeywell. Because, again, why, *why did Honeywell land at CoCo?* There was no point in tipping my hand by asking permission.

Davis's administration had been a landslide of corruption and people had suffered. In my view, the old, collegial, white-shoe politics of law firms no longer applied in the face of high crimes and human atrocities. Admittedly, I did cringe over my choice to leave my second firm, Stokes & Crane, which had strong ethics and a progressive culture. Had I not left, I wouldn't have to risk my career and be involved. To be perfectly honest, I'd prefer to continue the practice of law and remain uninvolved. The lifestyle, the trials, the intellectual rigor, the hard work and career satisfaction, even the drama with former colleague Henry, is what I want. But I'm involved. That is the hard pill I chose to swallow. It's a pill I should have swallowed long ago.

So here we are.

Not knowing what my full plan would be, I laid the groundwork for allowing myself some anonymity. I called a trusted partner over at Stokes & Crane, and under an airtight retainer, which obliged him to strict attorney-client confidence, had him set up an anonymous offshore shell company, with my name deeply buried through a series of instruments, so that I could use that company's name to get a credit card and make reservations for travel, acquire a phone, and rent places to stay. If need be. I then didn't know I'd ever use any of it.

I put myself in a position to wait for the right moment. As Aunt Violet used to say before she fled, "A wise woman is always laying the tracks of her railway line, a tie at a time, even if she doesn't know her ultimate destination. Be ready, save cash, cold hard dollars in fireproof sacks. And keep your head on a swivel at all times, girl."

Raw Narrative of Event #5: Two weeks ago, Cal Parcel, the firm's general counsel, was preparing for his annual August in Italy. In a weekly meeting he and I had to go over the status of subpoenas served on the firm (which is totally routine and happens all the time to all big firms), I took the opportunity to ask, "Cal, while you're on vacation, I should be named Deputy GC, right? In case something comes up."

"That makes sense to me," he said, not looking up from squinting at an iPad Pro. At seventy, Cal's eyes were chock-full of the visible cataracts I feared I was heading for. "Can you show me again that app on this thing that helps me edit my vacation photos?"

Cal and I were, in effect, CoCo's in-house attorneys to represent the firm's own legal needs and compliance issues. Law firms, like corporations, also retain outside firms to represent them. Firms are, when it comes down to it, really companies set up to make money—and with that comes lawsuits and risk.

I was concerned Cal wasn't really naming me Deputy GC, as he was obviously focused on the iPad. But then he said, after twisting it to face me, so I could once again bring up Photoshop, "But anything beyond the typical computer stuff you do, send it off to our outside counsel."

"Of course," I said. "I've got enough client work anyway!"
And then I did, I admit, offer a phony laugh. *Ha.*

Later that afternoon, I was sure to send Cal an email:

To: Cal Parcel
From: Greta Vinet Seville
Date: July 31, 2021
RE: Italy!

> Cal, have a fantastic time! Can't wait to hear
> about all your Tuscan wine tours. I'll keep the
> roof over the house. Thanks for trusting me as
> your Deputy General Counsel while you're away.
> Remember, don't over-edit the photos. Do just
> enough color saturation or it won't be real to
> your memories. –Greta

Raw Narrative of Event #6: Three days ago, a month-and-a-half after Summer Brad showed me Key Document #10, I waited until nightfall. A few things had converged to make that day the one I finally took action. I should have thought things through better, for the execution proved dangerous, and is why I'm on the run. My actions changed everything for the plan. I essentially catapulted myself into chaos.

Nevertheless, first, I was on the firm's Café Floor (fortieth-floor), in the gourmet café, at lunch time. I was at the guacamole station, waiting on the chef to mix my custom order, when Honeywell strolled through. The milling lawyers holding trays parted a path as if he was Moses at the Red Sea. He sidled up to the stir fry station, which was next to mine. He easy-breezily stood there in his Seville Row suit, ordering his custom stir fry, and laughing, *ha ha ha,* along to a bow-tied partner's not-funny repertoire about tax law. Here Honeywell was, having done what he did in the Davis administration, phony-laughing over tax jokes, free and money-fat in his fine suit, while my asylum client still couldn't find the baby who'd been ripped from her at the border under Honeywell's policy to rip breastfeeding babies from mothers. Just that morning, I'd taken a call with her in which all she did was sob. Hard, hurtful, rolling sobbing, the kind one does in a futile hope of drowning your own brain of the pain. She had fled El Salvador with her baby girl because a police officer executed her husband for not letting him rape her in their home; she ran immediately, the officer in pursuit, sending grapevine messages how he'd rape her and her baby girl if they returned because, "They're cunts who serve one purpose, to whore." She had no choice but to seek asylum, and Honeywell's reign called her and her baby girl criminals for doing so. They'd ripped her baby out of her arms at the border, lost track of where they'd placed her, and now we can't locate the child.

Watching Honeywell, the cruel architect of my client's pain, laugh over tax jokes and have served to him on a literal china plate a custom stir-fry, I basically lost my shit. I vowed to do *something* that night.

The second thing that propelled me to act that day, three days ago, was when the bow-tied tax law comedian said to Honeywell, "You'll be joining us at the Summers' event at Fenway tonight, right, Raymond? The kids are looking forward to your attending."

Pretty much the whole summer for CoCo is spent in CoCo's Fenway box.

"Sure, sure, the time, again?" Honeywell said.

"Game starts at 7:00. We have the box, of course."

Immediately a critical fact formed a solid hypothesis in my mind: Fenway doesn't allow bags, which means, Honeywell will have to leave his laptop unguarded in his office.

I took my bowl of guac, a family-size bag of lime tortilla chips, and returned to my office. I had promised in a call with

Toby that I'd try to do his Keto plan, but I'm a failure in this regard. I'm not as stoic as my brother. I try, I fail, I try again. I ate the whole bag of chips.

Around 8:00 that night, with most partners and associates and all of the Summers at the Red Sox game, I considered it safe enough to scoot over to Honeywell's office. The halls of the Sentry Floor were buzzing with the sound of cleaning lady vacuums. I looked right, I looked left, and proceeded down an inner corridor to the opposite hall. I didn't pass anyone. The walls everywhere shined in their cosmic white enamel. I thought about my favorite colleague at Stokes & Crane and her obsession with Star Wars, and how the interior of CoCo is like a futuristic starship.

Raymond Honeywell's corner office was dark and empty. A cleaning lady buzzed at the opposite end of the hall, her Bose headphones on, oblivious of me. Several offices down from Honeywell's, I noted the lights of a senior associate's office on, but also heard his loud music and the click of his keyboard. So I figured I was safe.

I slipped into Honeywell's office. I walked up to his charging laptop, plugged in my thumb-drive, and, because I know the admin passcode for firm-connected devices, logged in. Working off Reboot Pete's statement that Honeywell's laptop contained archived emails, I ran a search for all files with a file extension of .pst. A .pst is essentially an archive of a collection of emails stored, in Honeywell's case, on the local hard drive, and not on the firm's live servers. And wham, right away, my search yielded results. Indeed, several sets of .psts with large sizes were in one folder. In right clicking on the folder's properties, I noted the total size of all .psts together was a whopping 300 gigabytes, which meant, after they were uncompressed from being archived, I was likely looking at 600 gigabytes of raw content. Which is roughly the equivalent of 600 trucks of paper.

I began the process of copying all of it to my thumb-drive,

which thankfully has a storage capacity of one terabyte. The process was taking a long time, and my heart was near in a full attack. The vacuum sounds were getting closer, and I was sure I heard footsteps. And still, the damn copy process whirred and whirred along.

*Seven minutes remaining…..*turned to *nine minutes remaining….*turned to *three minutes remaining* as the vacuum sounds gained and then bumped up to….*fourteen minutes remaining,* at which point I crouched below Honeywell's desk and bit my thumbnail, only to creep back up to the laptop to see….*one minute remaining….*and then….*COMPLETE.*

I yanked the thumb-drive out, stuffed it in a dress pocket, and shut laptop chassis. I turned to leave, and this is when I made a fatal mistake.

In that moment, I remembered how the firm had just instituted yet another security policy: whenever an external hard drive—such as my thumb-drive—was attached to a laptop, the next time the user logged in, a window would pop up to alert the user that an external drive had been attached. The user would then be required to confirm that said connection was legit by clicking "YES" to the question, "Did you authorize this connection?" I could, of course, override the pop-up, if I logged back in and confirmed "Yes" the connection was legit, which would disable future pop-ups whenever Honeywell next logged in.

So I turned and re-opened Honeywell's laptop. I typed in the admin password. I heard a cough in the hall. I heard footsteps. I figured it had to be the cleaning lady or the associate with the loud typing moving his way to the printer down the hall. I figured I'd finish fast and crouch beneath Honeywell's desk until the coast was clear.

I heard breathing move closer, about ten feet from the doorway and moving my way. I didn't have time to wait for the laptop to load the homepage or the pop-up to bloom, so I shut the lid slowly so there wouldn't be an audible click. I turned and didn't see anyone in the doorway—yet. But here came that breathing, breathing, closer. I grabbed a pen and post-it pad off Honeywell's desk and started writing.

"What the hell are you doing in here?!"

I looked up. It was so much worse than I thought. Not the cleaning lady. Not the loud-typing associate. It was Honeywell himself.

"Oh, oh," I grabbed my chest. "You scared me."

"What in God's grace are you doing in my office?!"

"I was just writing you a note," I said. I held up the post-it and his pen. I had thought I would play this ruse for the cleaning lady or the associate, not Honeywell himself. And because I was not expecting *the king himself*, all I'd really done was draw circles and lines, no words. I didn't think the others would inspect the note.

"What's so important that you need to leave me a note, in my office, with the lights out? You could email! You could leave me a voicemail!" His voice thundered, he shook with anger. Psychologically, I knew this was a defensive outburst from him. An indicator of guilt.

I stood straight, put on my acting face, and pushed my progressives up the bridge of my nose. All the while, my heart blared and burst and my head filled with bees. I crumpled the scribbled post-it and shoved it in my dress pocket, down deep with the thumb-drive. "Forget it, Raymond. We can talk tomorrow. You know, people around here leave each other notes all the time. Your office is not Fort Knox."

This was not true. People at CoCo were expected to be paperless and respect the sanctity of office spaces. It was at Stokes & Crane where office walls were more fluid and collaborative and desks filled with papers and books. Like real lawyers.

I pushed past Honeywell in the doorway as if in a huff, and

when out of his sight, I ran to my office, grabbed my framed pictures of me and Henry and me, my brother Toby, and Aunt Violet, and any other personal item I could grab within a limit of ten seconds. I was out of CoCo so fast, you'd think the joint was on fire. I'm not sure how long it was after I fled that Honeywell noticed the pop-up. Maybe he unplugged his laptop and went on his way and wouldn't see anything until he got home, or to the office the next day. I don't know.

I wasn't ready to be on the run yet, but I knew I had to leave that night. I'd fucked up.

I crashed into my penthouse, grabbed my go bag (another Aunt Violet lesson), which was already packed with a change of clothes, toiletries, a pair of Ultraboost, my anonymous shell company iPhone and charger, and all my extra eyeglasses. Under my bed, I pulled out a tiny safe, extracted a fireproof bag with twenty grand in all denominations, and shoved that in the bag. As I ran to the kitchen, I pulled out my firm iPhone, threw that on the counter, and was about to grab my personal laptop, when two shocking things happened.

First, I noticed a box on the counter with my other mail, which included a yellow pouch, similar to the kind used to mail books. I didn't flip the pouch over to see the sender, because I was focused on the box. All of this mail the cleaning lady would have brought in and left, as typical on her Thursday cleans. The box, an 8" by 8" square, held an address label, the sender: HENRY PALANQUERO. *My* Henry. This stalled me, I gasped, and then the second thing happened. As I was about to grab Henry's box and run, my house phone rang, a shrill, piercing sound—and the absolute strangeness of it, and not my firm iPhone, ringing at all, especially *then*—hurled exploding grenades into my heart. I backed away from my house phone as if receding from a man with a knife, backward steps, eyes on the killer, in shock, waiting for the flight instinct to kick in. By the third ring, that instinct pushed me into my elevator, into my car, and speeding out of town.

I didn't grab my personal laptop.

I didn't flip the yellow pouch. I still assume it's a book.

I didn't grab Henry's box.

I didn't think of anything but getting out, getting away, escaping.

The phone rang and rang and rang as I left, and I swear I heard it ringing even when I got into my car in the private spot in the building's basement.

Never hesitate to escape the very second you think you should, girl, Aunt Violet's words screamed in my brain. *If you're wrong, big deal. You can come back. But if you're right, you will live another day for the next fight. Always, always, trust your instincts.*

I parked my car at a train lot outside of town, hailed a taxi from a waiting line, had him drop me at a bus station in some random town an hour closer to Lena's, paid cash. Called Lena from a payphone. Lena picked me up, and here we are.

So I did a dangerous thing, and then came here to Lena's to regroup. She doesn't have the computing power to be able to burn through six hundred trucks of emails; she works off a crap laptop and an iPad. And I don't want to load e-data on her devices and expose her to whatever data crimes I might be committing. And this also means I haven't had a chance to make a cloud backup of the contents on this thumb-drive. I have just this lone, local copy.

This is risky. This is awful.

Nobody was supposed to know about Lena. I've kept her a secret. And yet, a drone has found us and we're hiding.

Over the past three days, I've tried to tell myself: *Nobody knows about Lena. Relax. She is safe. You've kept her secret.* Why I've kept Lena secret for the past eleven years is another story, or perhaps, part of the story, because it has to do with my childhood, has to do with Aunt Violet and what she did and how she fled, and thus who I am today. But here now, in Lena's shuttered cottage, in the middle of her colorful field, I am desperate to get to Point A in the course Lena and I mapped out.

How wide does this corruption go, what can I prove, and how? I need to get to a place where I can examine the contents of this thumb-drive with six hundred truckloads worth of Honeywell's emails—without anyone from CoCo knowing where I am and where I'm going.

CHAPTER FIVE

Our map, which Lena has now burned, also contained reservation numbers for trains under a pseudonym. All the car lot passcodes, all the specific street addresses, gone.

She whistle-commands Sleuth down the stairs of the hatch in the kitchen floor. As she begins to descend behind him, she stops on the first tread, looks up at me, and says, "I'm the map now." She taps her temple. Ah, right. That's right. Lena has a memory. A steel-trap, weapon of a memory. She burned our map so I couldn't block her from coming with me.

As we run down, she says, "Once we get out of here, I know you didn't want to involve them. But this is too big. You cannot do this alone. You know you're going to have to pull that team together to help you."

She always forces me to see the unavoidable truth. So maybe it's true I needed a respite with her after all that went down three days ago and to realign, make a better plan. But maybe I also needed the solid rock of her convictions, and her to say the truth of the situation. She's right, I need a team, but now, in this second, I'm resisting that. I don't answer her.

CHAPTER SIX

I am the Goldilocks of lawyers. Three firms of various sizes and styles over the course of my career, and only one was the right fit. I summered and was a first year at a small three-partner firm, Lopez & Associates. The partner, Bo Lopez, is considered the best civil trial attorney in New England. I have stayed in touch with Bo.

After Lopez & Associates, I lateraled to Big Law as a second year to Boston's oldest firm, Stokes & Crane, seizing an opportunity to specialize in a budding litigation niche: e-discovery. I stayed at Stokes until my eighth year when Mega Big Law, Coarse & Cotton, swooped into the Boston market and made a play to dominate the region by poaching me and several Stokes partners. Beyond the increased salary, they promised to make me partner early, right then and there upon acceptance, even though that normally comes by flying through the eye a needle in your tenth year. They wanted us Stokes lawyers because we each own different client relationships in New England. So they made offers we couldn't refuse.

Because that is what the devil does, makes offers you can't refuse, and I fell for it. Regret comes fast when a serious decision is based on cash alone, or misdirected emotion. And I soon learned that Stokes had been, all along, the "just right" bowl of porridge for me.

It is not possible for me to contextualize all that led to me finding myself right now in Lena's hidden storage/safe room or to think on my own trusted network of colleagues. This safe room is a safety feature that Lena, a single woman living in the wilderness alone, wisely added to her construction plans. After shutting and bolting the hatch and descending the wood stairs into this ten-by-ten underground space, I tell Lena I need a minute to breathe. To think.

Her directive that I must go through with pulling together the team I've had in mind lingers unanswered. Also not yet addressed, because it's only been a couple minutes, is how the hell we're getting out of here without that damn drone or copter tracking us.

I pace in front of a metal shelf filled with books and canned goods and candles and packaged batteries. I weave between jugs of water. She, in her lime dress, sits on a distressed red bench beside the steel door that opens to an underground tunnel. The tunnel leads to her outbuilding studio at the clock position of 8:00. Typically, she uses the tunnel as her winter commute when the temps are sub-zero. She's fiddling with knobs on a tiny closed-circuit TV, set beside the red bench on a folding table. The TV has a feed to several Nest cameras around the property.

"Can you make out the drone's FAA ID? Should be on the front arm." I ask.

"Hold on." She takes her iPhone out of a dress pocket, clicks the screen, and expands the photo with her fingers. "Okay. FA88927889," she says.

"Yep. That's definitely CoCo's drone, and there's only one person who knows how to fly it. Last year I had a case that required forensic examination of a client's drone. I'm the one who expensed that same damn test drone. It was Reboot Pete of I.T. who did the tests with me."

"Reboot Pete?"

"Never mind. Son of a bitch. They know I'd know this.

They're taunting me. We're going to have to wait here until that drone goes back to the copter and they leave."

"But what if they're sending ground people now? Now that they saw you?"

I can't believe this is really happening. Everything I feared about the lengths they'd go is coming true. Somehow I had deluded myself they wouldn't be this aggressive, this fast. I believe—I hope—the rest of my plan is more thoughtful, more strategic and solid, from here on out, but I have to question my judgment in allowing myself this pause at Lena's. I know better. Son of a bitch, Aunt Violet's first rule is: *never trust your opponent for a second or a half second or a micro-second.*

"They wouldn't have anyone nearly this close. If anything, they'll need at least two hours to get here from Boston, unless they plan to repel down from that copter—and I doubt that. I bet it's the firm pilot, Stella, and she will not leave that copter. She's probably out here scouting possibilities on where I am, taking directions from some fuckhead private security asshole back at the firm with Tim Cotton and Honeywell and who knows. And the other one on board has got to be Reboot Pete driving the drone. Trust me, he has no clue why he's really here. Lord knows what crap they told him. We need to pause, Lena. Pause and think before we run off half-cocked into the forest. They're hoping we panic, so that damn drone, and that damn copter, can track us from the sky and trap us."

"We're trapped now, Greta," she says, not in a caustic retort, more as a soft statement of fact. A way to bring me back to cold reality.

"Let me figure this out."

She doesn't respond and resumes watching the Nest feeds. I can see on the screen the drone fly from one square to another. The roof camera confirms a black-bellied copter too low to the ground. The torque of whipping blades must be ruining the

Queen Anne's lace, dispelling all the monarchs. And now I'm furious.

A loudspeaker takes over the whole sound of everything. "Greta, it's Stella and Pete from the firm. Everyone's concerned about you. Nobody's heard from you in days. Are you okay? We're here as part of the firm's emergency employee assistance program."

"Bullshit," I say.

"Could that be true?" Lena asks.

"Absolutely not. Think about the lengths they'd need to go to track me down. I didn't tell anyone where I was going." It is true, given the highly confidential nature of our work, that there is an emergency employee assistance program, because lawyers who work on what we do have been known to be kidnapped for ransom. But that risk and the need for this program are for international trips to unstable countries. I'm not aware of the firm ever going to this length before for a domestic issue. At most, if working under the employee assistance plan, they'd check hospitals and morgues and send someone to my penthouse after me not responding for four days. It's been only three, part of that over the weekend, and I have my Out Of Office on. Plus, there's the whole Honeywell catching me in his office thing.

While I have doubts I'll be able to find evidence to truly support my theory within the .psts of emails I took from Honeywell's laptop, and I have a vein of doubt inside me about my perceptions sometimes, something I've had since childhood given what I went through with Aunt Violet, I have zero doubts as to why Stella and Pete are here, and it's no good. And it's dangerous. And a private security detail is behind it all, calling the shots.

I sit opposite Lena on a case of her favorite Montepulciano. Sleuth sits erect beside her, but doesn't bark, because this exceptional hound is trained to the nines, and Lena keeps giving him the silence command. MF is positively losing it, clawing into

Lena's dress so deep, his white fur weaves into the lime fabric. I palm the air at her, telling her to give me time, hang my head between my legs, close my eyes, and try to center my thoughts. I need to get us out of here.

Like a tic, my mind sticks on snapshots of my last day at Stokes & Crane two years ago. Because that is the mental trick of regret, it's an earwig, a constant infestation that insists on being heard at all inopportune moments. I can't really make sense, ever, of why I'm where I am without thinking on that last day, that monumental moment, the cold finality. For what? For the money. But that wasn't the only reason. A stark fact that rang so deep and clear on my last day, I still feel the black hole of heartbreak. I recall so much, so much in the details, in the people I'd grown to admire and who I was leaving behind. But this is irrelevant in this moment, and I push it all away to focus on the task at hand.

I must compartmentalize.

"Lena, how? How could they have found me here, so fast?"

She abandons the TV, looks to the floor, doesn't answer. Scrunches her shoulders and winces. "Uh, Greta…" She says, seemingly anguished by what she's going to say.

"Lena?"

"So, I was going to tell you. I didn't want you to worry. But, well. Okay, so, two years ago, right after you left Stokes and you came for a visit, I posted a picture of us on Teardrop, that artist social media site. And then when you showed up two days ago, when you told me what you'd done and what was going on, I deleted it. I did." She grimaces, pained to tell me this, and rushes to add, "I used your full name."

I press my thumbs into the bone of my brow line, pressing as if suffering a raging migraine. "The Wayback Machine then. Obviously. They combed through hits on my name, and there wouldn't be many, I'm not on social media, and they found the picture you tagged. And that led to you, of course. Then they triangulated to your name and number, out of thousands, in my phone records at Coarse & Cotton."

"I was afraid of this. I was going to tell you."

I'm shaking my head. "Lena, it's so obvious. Hell, it's a basic fundamental I teach the government enforcement associates when we're doing investigations. The phone record forensics is basic too. They would have seen you'd called me a few times."

"But you never call me."

"No, I never call you. But I never asked you to keep me secret. That's just my...."

She's nodding. We've talked about this. She knows the building blocks of what I believe makes up the *why* of me keeping her a secret. But she's never pushed me to say the all of it, the everything of my Defining Life Event. I have never told anyone about my and Lena's strange sistership, because it's hard to even think about the reason why, scary, maybe, embarrassing, yes, to be so plagued still by something from my childhood. Something that I better understand now, as an adult, and am able to contextualize and rationalize. Anyone at my first firm would have given Lena absolutely no thought at all after I won the case and she paid the bill. She's a matter number in the archives to them. But with Lena, our relationship has always seemed so natural, so pure and true, it could only be mine. So I've kept her a latent secret, not really putting intention behind the secrecy, but nevertheless keeping it so. The circumstances surrounding Aunt Violet, the one who hated phonies and gave me life lessons about fleeing and safety, well, those changed me. And how my brain connects what Violet did with Lena, who should be an entity disconnected, could form a whole new field of psychotherapy. But I haven't got time for psychological truths right now.

I must compartmentalize.

I always compartmentalize.

A box in my brain for this. A box in my brain for that.

I'm a litigator and also suffer the human condition, so I must compartmentalize.

"I'm sorry, Greta. I'm really sorry," Lena says.

"No, no, no. Dammit. I'm an idiot. I never should have dragged you into this. I never asked you to keep me secret, because I never thought I'd be on the fucking run." I draw a fist to my mouth and look away. I can't let them hurt Lena, ruin Lena. I should walk out of here and let Stella suck me up into that copter.

"You're not walking out of here. I'm going to run with you. You're going to see this through," Lena says. This is another thing she does, reads me, anticipates me. "Dammit, Greta, do not make me live with the guilt of you not bringing those fuckers down. You are not giving up. I am not friends with a quitter." And there's her customary tough love.

"Where are they now?" I ask, looking to the screen.

"Still there. The drone is hovering over The Office." That's at the 3:00 marker, and is in a direct line across, through the cottage, to the 8:00 outbuilding, where the tunnel out of this safe room leads. It is the outbuilding with the outdoor galley kitchen closest to the stream in the hemline of field and forest.

"Lena, if I don't walk out right now and claim you know nothing, *convince* them you know nothing, then this is it for you. You won't be able to come back here until I shut them down, if I can shut them down. They'll say all kinds of lies about you. They might even blow this whole joint up and call it a meth lab accident. You're a liability to them now. You know too much. You know that right? They will do everything they can to discredit you. I have totally fucked up your life."

She's shaking her head in disdain. "You are the dumbest smart person I know, Uncle. And you're too cocky for your own good. Sure, you might be able to convince some federal judge in your little discovery things, but you're not convincing these assholes of jack shit. They'll malign me, blow me up as a meth head, no matter what. So I'm coming with. And you're not quitting." She adds in a truthful, and yet lovingly calm way, "You are such a dumb bitch sometimes."

I stand. I pace. I face the wall. I want to say a million *I'm sorries* as penance.

And it's during this self-loathing when I look to a row of books on a shelf above the canned beets that it hits me. I twist to lend a one-sided smile at Lena.

"What?"

"Take the tent out of the go bag, put MF in. I'll leash Sleuth," I say.

"Okay? You gonna tell me the plan?"

"We're overthinking this. What do we always say to the morons in all those thrillers who find themselves trapped in the age of the cell phone?"

"Call. The. Cops," she says, a deep bounce of her head on each word. "But you said you can't go to the cops yet. You said you still have to review whatever's on that hard drive, and find more connections between Honeywell and CoCo and the private prison system, put it all together into an incontrovertible record?"

"Oh, we're not going to the cops yet. But we *are* calling the police station."

"Righty then. Whatever you say, boss." She's looking at me like I make no sense, but she doesn't care, because she's all in. "I'm sure you'll explain it, Uncle." She stands, sets MF on the concrete floor. He burrows into Sleuth's front, and Sleuth doesn't budge, ever the protector. "We don't need to remove the tent. I have a cat pack for Marshmallow. He hikes with me and Sleuth." She proceeds to yank off a hook behind the canned goods a sea-green backpack with a plastic bubble dome and air holes. She sets it on the concrete floor, unzips, and MF jumps in in a white flash. Of course she has a cat pack for hiking with MF. As she shoulders into the straps of the cat pack, I follow by doing the same with the go bag. She wraps and ties a leash, which she collects from that same hook, around her waist. "Sleuth doesn't need a leash. He's a good boy." Sleuth lifts his head high, his jowls jostle. For real, he's agreeing with his human that he's a good boy.

I take out my anonymous iPhone and click on a police scanner app to tune in to the Lenox, Massachusetts police department.

"Make the call," I say. "Stella will be listening to this scanner too, because, now that we didn't panic and run, whoever is calling the shots back at CoCo is expecting us to make the call. She's trying to flush me out, because whoever is giving her directions is telling her to force me into a place they can control. They don't know we have a way out. The second we hear dispatch, she'll hear dispatch too, and she'll buzz off. Then the hired creeps will go to the station where they'll expect me to go to file a report. Lena, dial 911."

"How do you know this is what they're thinking, what they're planning?"

"I don't, Lena. Truly, I'm guessing. But after working with lawyers of this caliber my whole career, and knowing their resources, I'm basically thinking what I'd do if I were a total scumbag criminal."

"So we call 911, and then what?"

"We run. We do the plan we mapped. And, you're totally right. We need a team. This is too big to handle alone."

CHAPTER SEVEN

On my last day at Stokes & Crane two years ago, Victoria Viglioni handed me a mug. Victoria is a savant who looks *exactly* like the actress Zooey Deschanel. But don't say that to her face or suffer the wrath. Hers was an interior office, and she decorated it in wild and colorful finger paint pictures by her twin nieces. I'd worked nearly every difficult case with Victoria for eight years, because she only worked the difficult data breaches and forensic-intense cases. Although on the young-end of Gen Y, she held the senior position as litigation technology lead. I trusted Victoria with my career, with my life. She's a literal master of CaseSpaceAI and CaseCore, using algorithms to find relevant data amongst millions and millions of documents.

"Here," Victoria said, not smiling as she handed me the mug. She stayed seated behind her desk, so I bent to take it from her.

I looked at the mug, which was brand new. She'd left the company's card in the cup.

"I didn't wrap it," she said, pursing her lips like Grumpy Cat.

I read the front, an Effin' Birds satire: the marrying of a nice drawing of a bird with snarky commentary. This one said, *I bet this problem will go away if we have more fucking meetings*, beside a drawing of a standing duck.

"I love it," I said, smiling, trying to warm her up. She tapped the porcelain sign on her desk that greeted all guests: NOPE.

"You're an asshole for leaving me with these assholes," she said.

"Victoria, I told you. Coarse & Cotton will still take you. I need you on my team."

She didn't so much as laugh at the notion, but grunted. "Uh, yeah, so nope. No way. When I did that stupid little informational interviewy thing you made me do, all those CoCo jackasses kept calling me Vicki. I'm not working for the Dark Side. And you shouldn't either."

I'd had this fight with her so many times at that point, I just inhaled, nodded. "I'm going to miss you, Vicki." I said Vicki to chide her, and she flipped me off. "We can have lunch though. CoCo is in this same building."

"Duh, yeah. I know that. Those assholes are making it really fucking clear that they want to eradicate Stokes from planet Boston. It's like the Pru is now a galaxy, and CoCo the Death Star, and Stokes a sitting duck Alderaan."

As I had done many times before, I took stock of her Star Wars pez dispensers, lined up on a shelf in lieu of binders of legal papers. Victoria is not a lawyer; she's considered support staff. But no litigator worth their salt attempts a data-heavy case without her expertise. And I consider any who do not kiss her royal ass trash lawyers.

"I don't get it. For a whole year those assholes were up there banging around with their construction crap making whatever their Death Star CoCo hellscape is up there, and you bitched about the noise the whole time. And now you're all of a sudden—poof—within the span of two weeks, going?" Her tone shifted to serious, her eyebrows furrowed, so I looked on at her with no smile, just listening. "Greta, I think the only reason you're doing this is because…"

And then she threw up her hands as a way to stop her own words. I was shocked she started to go down such a personal-professional road and call me out like that, shocked too because it wasn't until that moment that I connected the heartbreaking reason *why* I took CoCo's offer—beyond the money and title bump.

"Never mind. Never mind," she said. "You're a big girl. Your life. None of my business."

I breathed in deep, closed my eyes a beat, and switched to a smile. I wasn't ready for a conversation about *why* I took CoCo's offer, not with Victoria, not with anyone. I needed to have that conversation with myself first. So for that moment in parting, we both bucked ourselves back to the mocking collegial vibe we always held.

"I'm sorry, Victoria. I am. But look. I love the mug. Thank you. And I will be in touch. Often. But I've got to go. I'm heading up to the Death Star now, actually. I start today."

"Yeah, yeah. I'll miss you too. And please, I mean this from the bottom of my cold, dead heart, let the door hit you in the ass."

"Sure, Zooey Deschanel, I'll do that."

"You are a horrible wretched evil bitch," were her goodbye words for me.

Of course we've talked since. I've dragged her to lunch, but there's a notch of coldness from her, and a seeping regret from me, and two years in the litigation world is like a nanosecond of time. Case work has kept us both wholly consumed. Although, I did have a lunch with her last month, and I did say, without details, I might need her help in something off the books and big and I might lob an urgent request to her at some point in the near future. She clocked my serious gaze, which she matched a beat or two as her way of saying, *I note you can't tell me details now, fine, and I grant you permission to ask if I will help when the time comes.* When the moment was over, she said, "Whatever, Boss." We continued talking about her twin nieces and her trouble in finding anyone to date who, as she put it, "Won't glom on like a parasite and can deal with my work schedule."

I'm single and childless and my brother, Toby, a philosophy professor, lives alone in a Vermont cabin, rarely going beyond his land or classroom. Our parents live on the Isle of Palms, South Carolina, far away. Aunt Violet is long gone. So long gone.

My own love life, well, that, too, played into my final day at Stokes & Crane.

I turned, stepped out, and waved goodbye through the glass by her door. She returned with another Grumpy Cat grimace and a *whatever* flick of her hand. I think it was in this moment, as I walked away from Victoria, my most trusted colleague, that the fog of the last two weeks—in which CoCo approached me, interviewed me, made the irresistible offer, and I accepted—lifted. Prickles erupted all over my body, my heart thrummed. As I continued along the familiar brown-rugged Stokes halls, passing incredibly colorful art by diverse artists in all manner of style— mixed media, landscape paintings, sculptures, abstracts—as I swept through the considerately-stocked kitchenette of the thirty-third floor with its passable coffee machine and secretarial offerings of baked goods and boxes of leftover lawyer pizza, it dawned on me the undoable thing I'd done.

But it wasn't until I passed through the cozy, homey kitchenette and took a left to the exterior offices to say my farewell to Henry, I realized the delusion I was under in making what was a really poor and stressful decision. A decision, I then accepted, that had been based on emotion and not the steel career gut I should have let guide me. Because as I stepped to Henry's doorway and found it blackened and empty, all his plants gone, and the beautiful mess of his journals and papers absent, I remembered Henry had left two months before. And in that bright, spot-lit moment, regret made her merciless self known, and whispered in my mind the truth: *You've made the catastrophic switch to CoCo in order to run from the heartbreak of Henry's blackened office.*

I still see him in case meetings, those indelible hours in a Stokes' conference room, his dark hair, his big, brown eyes, his incredible calm in the face of daunting facts and difficult case law and demanding partners. How he controlled the room, no matter who was in the room, could be Stokes herself (a descendant of the original Stokes). There was an intangible quality to his assured mannerisms, his confident tone, his blinding intelligence that held all in his thrall. I see me across from him, catching his eye, him catching mine. And I still watch, over and over, the memory of that one day we were alone in a windowless case room, and he moved over to a chair beside me, and I noted the large freckle on his wrist, and I touched it, and he didn't flinch. I remember down to fractions of seconds, how he didn't flinch, how long he remained still and warm under my touch. I remember the electric pulse in my body, and I remember pressing my finger to that freckle on his wrist in a requited searing I meant to meld us as one being. This moment was the first overt *physical* act in our long series of longing glances, and even one direct conversation the week prior, and alleged platonic lunches that somehow always lasted an hour longer than we'd planned. Was he the first to act by moving to the chair beside me when he knew we were safely alone? Was I the first to act by pressing into his actual flesh? Who was first seemed irrelevant.

But I also remember that in the next moment he said, while keeping his wrist in place and not disturbing my finger on that freckle, "I'm getting back with Marie. We're going to give it one last chance." Marie being the wife who'd filed for divorce the year before. The divorce was not yet final.

I pulled my finger away.

"Didn't she move in with that guy she met in the cheese class?"

"She's moving back to Boston."

"More like cheese man left her and she's running back to you as a consolation. She doesn't deserve you." It was nasty of me to say, so I immediately said, "Sorry, sorry." I had no right saying anything like that to him. We were not lovers. Me touching his freckle was the first *undeniable* physical act between us. But we had been close work friends for years, and had recently been flirting and lunching like wild. Hence my audaciousness in touching a freckle on his wrist in a Stokes' conference room.

"I honestly don't know that this is the right decision for me, with Marie, but I promised I'd try," he said, staring into my eyes several beats. He even shifted toward my lips, and he came close, so very close, to kissing me. But he jerked back, and my heart dropped, and I'll never forget those seconds of eternity.

Something clicked for me in that room, and when I decide on something, I go in headlong. I pressed back into the freckle on his wrist. "You're not sure about this decision because you're in love with me. And I'm in love with you. So there, it's said."

I really honestly don't even know what happened thereafter. Some blurred, awful, long, tortuous conversation about the *complexities* and *commitments* and his *obligation to try and forgive* and *a trial last try* and needing *space to think*, and all of it. All the typical words that come after breaking the seal on what's been obviously brewing. The bit I focus on is how he never denied my proclamation. Not once.

Oh how I love Henry. I always feel the same pain, the gut-punch of being cut loose and unmoored, that awful blackened drift, whenever the clouds are the same as the day he left. I cannot forget those clouds. How they hung low and gray outside my Stokes & Crane office, killing the glare and shadowing his face as he sat in my orange guest chair. I stared beyond him to my framed movie poster of Gabriel Garcia Marquez' *Innocente Erendira*. All I wanted to do was scream obscenities at him about leaving, force him to slow down, hold on, think about this. And I also wanted to not break down and cry, for the interior side of my office was glass, and a secretarial station beyond was in earshot.

"Shut the door," I said, hoping to muffle whatever had to be said in my damn office.

"Greta, I'm sorry. You know I have to leave. I start at Tenkill next Tuesday. Marie's already out there. My flight is tomorrow."

Tenkill Hospital is an immense hospital system in New York City. A tragic name for a hospital meant to cure, not kill. But, alas, its biggest corporate "philanthropic" donor, Tenkill Energy, can get anything it wants, and it wants its name on as many buildings as it can get. Henry took a promotion from being a Stokes & Crane Senior Associate to being head of compliance for all of Tenkill. Similar to a general counsel position, his job is to ensure the Tenkill doctors and staff under his domain are in compliance with laws. His role, very similar to mine with respect to Honeywell, requires him to investigate possible inside corruption. It's much like internal affairs in a police department.

Whatever.

I will never give Tenkill any credit whatsoever because it took Henry. As for Marie, I give Henry credit. He *is* trying to make it work with her. But almost as long as I've known him, she's been nothing but stress. She left him for a cheesemaker, then crawled back to Boston, only to immediately start complaining about unhappiness and how a move to New York might improve things.

Do I hold a candle for Henry? Do I wait for him? Is he the most irrational thing in my otherwise structured and rational existence? Is this an impossible waste of the best romance years of my life? Do I respect the sanctity of marriage and how he should, in the least, give this one last try? Yes, yes, yes, yes, yes. Lena says I hold a candle for Henry *because* he's impossible to attain and that I'm really covering for the fact I'm a workaholic. But Lena is wrong. I love Henry in an unmitigated and irrational way, because I'm flat-out, uncontrollably, mad-crazy in love with every single thing about him. I'd do anything for him. Like I would for

Lena.

Speaking of which, Lena's just hung up with Lenox 911, and now dispatch is sending a car here, as picked up on the scanner app. We watch the Nest feeds on the TV, our two heads joined over the screen. Our backpacks jut out over Sleuth, who's waiting by the now opened steel door to the tunnel.

One, two, three, four seconds. And sure enough, there goes the drone back into the copter, and there goes Stella driving that copter away.

"Go, Lena," I say. "It's go time."

I secure my distance-prescription aviators on my face, and we're off.

PART II

MOTION TO CHANGE VENUE AND GET OUT OF HERE

CHAPTER EIGHT

The thing about these corrupt politicians, these corrupt lawyers, corrupt white collar criminals, is that they've for so long gotten away with reinventing themselves by way of philanthropy and their incestuous networks. By way of their oppressive insistence on congeniality, and how we must pay professional deference to *established* men and women.

But the Davis administration shone a spotlight on what happens when you do not prosecute and hold convictions and sentences on those who commit white collar crimes. Whitewater, Enron, so on. For fucks sake, the *New York Times* exposed how President Davis had paid near no taxes for ten years. What atrocities might we have avoided if he, like the rest of us schlubs would be, had been properly tried for tax fraud? So many examples.

The people who have watched and suffered and been disgusted by it all, well, they have their own networks, and maybe they're going to use them. Because if a network can be used to perpetrate decades of rolling crime, rolling, rolling, snowballing into the likes of a Davis administration, then a network can be used to perpetrate justice.

I have a network of legal people. Lena has a network of non-legal people. Maybe together we have a shot to play our teensy-tiny-miniscule part and bring at least one culprit down. We need to try.

Sleuth, who was commanded, "Fast forward, boy" is in the lead. Lena is running behind him with MF poking his face into the cat pack plastic bubble; his big, round eyes don't blink. I'm in the rear, the go bag on my back. Sleuth waits at the side to the underground door into the basement of the 8:00 outbuilding. Lena punches in the passcode and once again commands, "Fast forward, boy." Sleuth noses through a hanging tapestry, meant to obscure the 8:00 building's basement door, and waits again at another door, which leads up stairs into the 8:00 outbuilding, Lena's writing room. Lena punches in another code; Sleuth again noses through another obscuring tapestry, and us humans and one cat follow suit. Once topside, I take note of the papery mess on top of her antique bread table-turned-desk. All her handwritten notes on her theories about missing and unknown Italian paintings that originate from, her theory, 1575-1650. She's convinced that there's no way there aren't unknown private commissions by masters hidden in attics, on old walls, in private country homes, rectories. Several art history books and a mountain of monographs are stacked to look like guards on the sides of the door that leads to the outdoor kitchen.

Lena opens that door and takes a ginger step, not allowing Sleuth to go first. Although the outdoor kitchen is really a vine-and-plant-covered tunnel, she looks up through a break in the overhead vegetation, and then calls back to me, "It's clear. No copter." Then to Sleuth, who's beside me in the doorway, she says, "Fast forward, boy. Water."

Sleuth launches toward the stream, Lena and MF in the middle, me in the rear. I look up the whole time and catch patches of blue sky between the thick overhead vines and leaves, which weave around and through the metal fencing and twine trainings Lena installed to make this magical tunnel. After passing the grill, I note our emptied bottle of Montepulciano from two nights ago in the outdoor sink, along with our giant goblets, which remain unwashed.

Set on a two-top table is her movable Sonos speaker, and I see flashes of the many dinners we've had out here over the years, when after the main course is done, and we're good and drunk, Lena announces it's "time for the entertainment portion of the evening." She holds a firm conviction that all dinners of two or more people must have an entertainment portion in which each attendee partake. One time, after doing this entertainment portion dance in her fields to her constant *Say Goodbye to Hollywood*, I said, "Shouldn't the troupe dance in this field to Elton John's 'Tiny Dancer'?"

"Oh my God," she said, panting to catch her breath from her Eminem field dance. "You're like a Caravaggio painting. So realist, so literal. You can't dance in my summer field to a literal song about a dancer. Your turn!"

In current day, I watch Lena rub Sleuth's sides, calm him for the journey ahead—we're all on the run now, dog, cat, humans. She's whispering soothing dog talk in his big floppy ears. I will miss this green picnic table, and I long for the sanctuary of those drunken dancing-singing nights.

It hurts to leave this place, I fear I'll never return. It's awful to have this stress. To be looking at losing my law license, to losing *everything*. To put Lena at such huge risk.

"You ready?" Lena says to me now. She's standing beside Sleuth, who's calmly waiting for his next command.

"Let's go."

Across the stream, which one can get to by crossing a one-person walking bridge upriver, is a green-aluminum roof on poles, under which are a four-wheeler and a snowmobile.

"Back," Lena says to Sleuth. He pops in the canoe and takes his upright seated position in the rear. "You, middle," she says to me. I enter next and sit in the middle position of the canoe. The paddles are clasped to each side, which I double-triple-check, as Lena pushes us backwards into the current and herself pops into the front seat.

She reaches back for the paddle I hand her. I unclasp and take mine. We stroke opposite sides until the slow current catches and we ease back on the paddles to rest. Take a breath. Every now and then, depending on the shift the canoe takes, she strokes left, or I stroke right, to keep us center down the stream. To our left, we've gone past Lena's sanctuary; to the right, is the backside of Mount Luzane, a family-owned ski mountain.

Thankfully, it is August, and both sides of the stream are full of mature trees, their canopies merging overhead, such that we remain in a leafy tunnel. The sun pokes through in parts with its golden spears, spiking through the water to pepper the black surface with gold-amber holes, revealing pebbles and minnows in the shallow depth.

Here, the mountain to our right is a vertical forest of pines and oaks and maples and brush and rust leaves. Nothing, no homes, on that side. Beyond Lena's sanctuary on the left are miles of farmland, horse fields, and empty green. Any homes on this stretch are closer to the road, and so, we have some time here alone. We hope.

There is a buzzing in the sky in the distance, but every time we catch a glimpse of the sky through a hole in the merged canopy, there's nothing there.

"How long to the horse trader's?" I ask.

"About fifteen minutes of floating downriver. We just need to keep the canoe straight. And there's the difficult bend, I'm sure you remember."

"How long until that?"

"We have a good five minutes."

"I'm going to check my voicemail. There's no point in continuing to play the game that I'm not checking voicemails and haven't heard their concerns. They know I'm in Western Mass now with you, so if they're checking when I check my firm voicemail, so be it. Can you keep us straight for a couple minutes?"

"How's MF?"

"He's bug-eyed, popping his head in the bubble. But he's not yowling."

"He loves that bubble."

I turn to check on Sleuth, and he's his regular majesty, sitting chest high and still. His hound eyes droop in their calm way, but I know he's busy inspecting everything around. He could leap in a second to defend us against an intruder. "Sleuth is good too," I say.

"Of course he is. Sleuth, you're a good boy," Lena calls behind her, as she straightens us from drifting right. Sleuth half barks in answer.

I take my phone from a back pocket and dial my firm voicemail, which is direct to a hub and doesn't track geo-location, nor will it track my anonymous number, which is blocked.

Message One, Friday (morning after I took Honeywell's emails): "Greta, this is Tim Cotton. You need to call me *now*."

Numerous other messages: More of Tim Cotton, and two from Maurice Coarse, stating, in increasingly angry tones, that I need to call them ASAP.

Numerous other messages in between: Colleagues asking me to look at my email about this or that case. And one from Summer Brad. I resolve to replay that one.

Last Message, today, Sunday, an hour ago:
"Hey, Greta, it's Henry. I know it's Sunday morning and you really shouldn't be in the office, and
I thought maybe you were. I've left you a ton of
messages on your house line and I've texted a few
times. Now I'm worried. Look, if you're mad at
me, don't want to talk to me, fine. I understand.
But at least shoot me a text to say you're fine. I
assume you got the box I sent you by now. Maybe it's been so long it's unwelcome. But, if you do
want to talk, I have some things to say. I hope
you'll still listen."

"Wow," I say, under my breath. I'm staring at the screen of my
phone.

"What?" Lena asks.

"Henry. I mean, yeah, also, the firm is flipping out and there's
all kinds of scary demanding voicemails, as expected. So, it's definitely on. But, Henry called an hour ago. He wants to talk."

"You monogomites, you put your heart into just one person
and live this constant angst. Love is all around to fill you up. But
I'm not judging, you know that. You do you, Uncle."

Lena is polyamorous. I am simply single-minded on Henry
in that department.

"Hold on," I say. "Can you keep us straight another minute. I
need to replay one of the firm voicemails."

"Yep."

I backtrack through the voicemails and find the one from
Summer Brad. The same Summer Brad who I have not talked
to or even seen in the halls since he showed me Key Doc #10.
Frankly, I thought his summer associateship was over and hadn't
given him another thought as anything other than the flint strike
to all this action. The thing about the voicemail is his assured

tone, his confidence in a *directive to me*, and how carefully he measures his words. He sounds older, and not himself. But it is surely Brad. For his part, he didn't get an offer to join CoCo, so his specific voicemail to me is odd, to say the least.

Message from Summer Brad, Friday afternoon: Hello Greta, this is Brad Perdunk. I know you are out of the office on vacation, I got your out of office response. Today is my last day at the firm. I begin my third year at Harvard in two weeks. It would be advisable for us to meet for lunch, as you suggested, on Monday, to discuss Boston opportunities. Please contact me at my home number for arrangements. I'm in the Cambridge directory. Thank you.

I have never offered to lunch with a Summer beyond their summership, and I certainly didn't suggest such a thing to Brad. I have never ever called any associate at their home number; and I've certainly not been told, by anyone at all, that it's "advisable" for us to meet after I look up their number in a listing.

"Lena, this is very wrong. I think they put a Summer Associate up to drawing me out to a lunch. The Brad kid, the one who found the hot document I told you about. And, weird. He..."

"Yeah, well," Lena interrupts. "We'll have to discuss later. I need you to paddle again," she says. "We're coming up on the bend and this is the rough spot."

We paddle hard on the left. A grove of weeping willows complicates the turn, for the drapey branches snag the canoe. Lena's in the front using her paddle to push branches to the side, and I'm struggling to keep us turning and not banging into the edges. This bend is also a rougher section of water, more proper for a river, and it is now, of course, when the helicopter returns overhead, buzzing fast. At the noise and the torque and tip of the canoe, MF is bouncing in his bubble, and Sleuth is now flat on the floor. And there's that helicopter, off in the distance, I can tell from brief peeks in breaks in the overhead canopy. It stalls there in the beyond, hovering. I don't think whoever's flying saw us. But why hover there? Why?

We are tipping too much to the right with Sleuth's dead, flat weight, and I realize I'm sitting too much on the right, too, so we're about to capsize. That would destroy this thumb drive in my shirt pocket—the only copy I have of Honeywell's emails. It would destroy my anonymous shell company iPhone and Lena's phone. The current is fast here, so it will be hard to contain the animals. And, shockingly, Lena can't swim. A foot-wide break in the canopy reveals the helicopter is still hovering over a farm-house about a mile away. It would not be possible to see us, I don't think, as the walls of this bend are thick. And it's dawning on me that there's a call I should have already made. The timing on that call is critical.

I slide over to the left and correct us just in time before we dump ourselves in the water. My heart crawls into my throat as we break free of the bend and are thrust into the wide open stream, no canopy overhead. If that helicopter circles back, we will be trapped.

"How long 'til we're undercover of trees again?"

"A half mile. This is the riskiest part," Lena says.

"Shit."

"This is exactly why I wanted you to leave during the hurri-cane. Nobody can be in the sky, no drones, no satellites can see through the gray muck of a hurricane. You said I was being crazy over-protective, but look, now, my craziest fear is true."

We're watching the copter, and it jolts, but goes forward. It does not circle back.

"Fuck that was close," Lena says. "Sleuth, slow, back. Sit in back," she calls, by half-twisting and making sure to make eye contact with him. We rock a bit as Sleuth eases to sitting, nice and center, in the back.

"I need to make a call," I say.

The timing on this call is critical, and I should have done it already. Importantly, I note that I was able to still access my CoCo voicemail, so nobody has blocked me out of the network yet. And not one of Tim or Maurice's voicemails, angry as they were, said anything about terminating my partnership or title. I'm also noting that Stella had been there under the guise of the "employee assistance program"—meaning, it's fair for me to assume I am still a partner at CoCo. This is important, and why timing-wise, I need to make this call *now*, right this second. I'm wondering why it is they haven't left a message of termination, and I'm suspecting that maybe CoCo wants to keep this issue on the down-low. Perhaps they don't want it known in the world that Honeywell's cache of archived emails is floating down a river, free for anyone to read. Maybe that's why. But this détente won't last forever, so I need to make this call.

"Make your call. Fast," Lena says.

I dial a number I never in a million years thought I'd have to. Bo Lopez, the partner at my first firm, the best *civil* trial attorney in New England, gave me the number in the event I ever needed it. I told him three weeks ago I might have some legal trouble coming up, but I didn't say what. Letticia Renee Rice—she goes by L.R.—is the top *criminal* trial lawyer in New England. She's also the President of the Women of Color Bar Association of Boston. She charges $1,999.99 an hour, and I think she does that to match her 99.99% win rate. Which is pretty brass breasts of her to do, so I'm a fan.

The phone rings.

"L.R. Rice," she answers on the third ring. "This better be real bad, like some serial killer slaughterfest kind of bad, to call my exceedingly private cellphone number, in the middle of Sunday brunch. Who exactly is this? And who do I need to *thank* for giving you my number?"

"Ms. Rice, I am Greta Seville, a friend of Bo Lopez. He gave me your number."

"You've got one minute. Go."

"I'm a partner, Global Head of E-Discovery, and Deputy General Counsel of Coarse & Cotton, and I'd like to hire you to defend me against allegations that the internal investigation of firm lawyers that I am conducting *right now* is not duly authorized."

"Did they say it's not authorized?"

"Not yet."

"You have begun this investigation? And nobody knows?"

"I have begun it. It is important that you note that I have begun it, and I have not been terminated, yet. People may know that I did take a partner's emails from a BYOD device, but they do not know I am conducting an official internal investigation."

"Are we talking white collar crime?"

"We're talking that, and possibly high crimes." I actually have no idea what crimes I may be able to prove with just former AG Raymond Honeywell's emails.

"Mm, hmm. I'm listening."

I hear her typing on a keyboard. Lena's looking back at me, and I hold up a *one-minute* finger. "We have about five minutes," she whispers. I nod. The river whirls around us in foot-wide, minor maelstroms, here and there.

"Go on, keep talking. Your minute is almost up," L.R. says. Still typing on her end.

"Will you take me on? And I consider this call under the attorney-client privilege."

"Of course this is privileged," she says in a snap, because of course this is a privileged conversation and she can't tell anyone about it. I'm seeking counsel, and although she is not yet retained,

I own the privilege. "If I take your case, this is going to cost you about as much as your sweet Newbury penthouse. I pulled you up on Zillow. You get that, right?"

"I do."

"Are you safe?"

"I'm floating down a river. I'm on the run, in hiding. They have private…"

"Security. I know. I know all about CoCo's private security force and the intimidations they've been doing around town to set up shop. How long can you stay hidden?"

"I don't know. I'm working that out now. Heading to a safe house near Boston."

"Please tell me you have a burner phone."

"I have an iPhone with an account to a shell company. I should be anonymous."

"For now," she says. "They don't own the phone companies. But you know they have connections. Look," she pauses, and lowers her voice. "Get a few burners. Call me back at this number tomorrow at 7:00 a.m., and not a minute before or after. I'm going to think about this overnight. I don't know what this investigation is about, but I sure as hell know who the partners at CoCo are. So I can only imagine. We can't talk now though, regardless. You know you're on a near impossible mission, right? Your position is weak, and it will be difficult to get you out of this jam, without losing your law license, at the very least."

"I understand. I know this is impossible."

"*Near* impossible. Near is what I said. I don't lose."

"So you'll take me?"

"Tomorrow I decide, by 7:00 am. If I'm a yes, I'll advise where to wire a $50,000 retainer, which, my dear, is chump change to what your total bill will be. And let me be very clear about something. You will do every damn every, I mean, ev-er-y little thing I say. Got it?"

"Yes. Of course."

"If I *advise* you to do *anything*, it is *only* because I think it will be good for the case. If I say walk to Vermont and get me a pint of Ben & Jerry's blonde brownie vanilla, you will put on your walking shoes, you will find some damn dry ice and a cooler, and you will walk."

"Understood."

"Now get yourself out of a river, which, yes, I heard you say, and we're not talking about whatever the hell that means right now. Next time we talk, call me L.R. Ms. Rice is what I make opposing counsel call me. You'll get my answer tomorrow."

I'm met with a dead dial tone.

Lena guides us to the shore and the Horse Trader.

CHAPTER NINE

We pull up to the backside of a big building. It's an aluminum dome, the kind you'd find at a country fair to house the horse shows. After we've disembarked, human, cat, human, dog, and tied Lena's canoe to a tree, we walk up to the building and rest our backs against the wall. Our view is the line of trees along the stream and the vertical mountain behind. It's mid-day, bright blue sky, and we've got no cover overhead, except the slanted shadow cast off the roof of the building. Sleuth stands sideways in front of me and Lena, as if a dog moat and we the castle.

Lena had tapped out a text when we first landed, and now we wait. It doesn't take long. The sound of boots crunching the top layer of white stones that surround the building approaches. I hear a cough and then a man's voice, "Lena, step out. It's clear." Sleuth's tail wags. And before we can actually step out from under this slanted shadow, a large-built man of some Mediterranean genes, I'm unsure, steps around to us. His eyes are brown orbs with slivers of green in the irises. He is immediately intoxicating, and immediately dominating, given his size. We look up to meet his gaze.

Sleuth walks to him, and the man yanks a treat from a pocket. "Good boy," he says.

"Greta, this is Parkol, the Horse Trader. But people call him Park."

He laughs. "Lena, you crack me up with the horse trader business. Nice to meet you," he says to me. I shake his hand. "Seems the schedule got fast-tracked, yeah?" Park says. "This have anything to do with that copter disturbing the peace this morning?"

"Sure does," Lena says.

"Thought it was just one person I'm accommodating. Now you, too?" He says to Lena.

"Things have changed," Lena says.

"Alrighty then. I thought you," he looks at me, "would use my building code to sneak on in and take a car on Tuesday, in the middle of the storm. But since you're here, and since it's Sunday and I'm here, and since Lena and the boys are here," he points at the cat pack and Sleuth to indicate *the boys*, "I'll get you set up myself. Come on now."

"Park, you absolutely cannot tell a soul about any of this. You get that, right?" Lena says.

His brown eyes, with those incomprehensible slashes of green, sparkle when he looks at Lena. I clock his age at no higher than forty, and I note he's not wearing a wedding ring. His cheek bones are ski-slopes, and it's just now, through the haze of arriving here in a rush and fury, that the clouds of reality are lifting, and I'm realizing Park is drop-dead gorgeous.

Lena's demand that Park hold all of what's going down right now on his property in confidence is lingering in the air, and he's still twinkling those green slivers around Lena's face. The crown of her black-haired head is about a foot, at least, below his chiseled chin.

"Now, Lena," he says in a slow drawl. "You know I would never cross you. My heart wouldn't allow it. You're still the fiercest raven I ever met. I would keep my window open for you to fly through if you'd have me."

I'm side-eyeing Lena, who, and I've never witnessed this

before, smiles at the line. Typically, such a line would earn a man her classic retort: *Keep it in your pants, man.* Instead, she says, "Buddy, you got to work on your lines if you're ever going to find yourself another wife. We'll practice some other time."

"See there," he says to me with a wide smile. "That there is my friend Lena looking out for her poor, old, bachelor man friend. I'll get it right someday, I know. Lena's the best coach in the department of romance."

I appreciate Park's boldness, which is even and sincere, and not creepy or threatening. This is a difficult balance for men to strike—the razor-thin high wire that can tip welcome boldness to threatening creepiness—and Park's figured it out. He extends a giant meat-paw of a hand to me, and I take it. His palm is warm and encapsulating, and honestly, makes me feel safe. "Come on now, let's pick out a car."

We go around the corner of the building and enter a side door. Within this gigantic structure are about one hundred cars, parked diagonal in four rows. A drivable lane cuts the center, leaving two rows on each side.

"He's the Horse Trader," Lena says. "Because he sells horse power."

"I own a few car lots through Massachusetts," Park says to me. "And Lena thinks it's a little too on the nose that people call me Park, get it? So she calls me Horse Trader." He rolls his eyes. We're walking down the drivable middle aisle; the concrete floor is a thick-painted shiny gray. All of the cars are shiny too, brand new, and the lights in here bright, providing glistening sparkles off the blacks and reds and greens and whites of the cars. Feels as if you could perform surgery on the hoods. Hoses with fat nozzles line the walls, and drains pepper the floor between cars. Most are Audis, some SUVs, a few Volvos, Mercedes, all makes and models. Park is still laughing to himself about being called the Horse Trader.

"He's the horse trader. I'm right," Lena says. "Park. Ugh, park cars. Too literal."

"Lena hates literal things, realism. And yet her whole career is restoring and studying baroque art," I say.

"Miss Lena is a contradiction. And that's why we love her," Park says to me, winking when he turns his head. I could see myself having a crush on him. And although, knowing Lena well, Lena is not *into* Park that way, she, like me, has hot blood pumping through her veins, so she sure appreciates his God-like form. I catch her scanning his high ass. Sometimes Lena can be a hornball. Or maybe I'm the hornball, because I'm picturing his long, solid legs, which *glide* up ahead down this center aisle like he's the longest, tallest drink of water on the planet, wrapped about my hips. Lena coughs, and we exchange knowing glances.

"Stop checking out my ass, you two," Park says, halting at the hood of a black XC-90 Volvo station wagon. "Now here, I think you should take this one. You got the boys with you, and they can be in the way back. You know I'd keep 'em with me, but you know I can't. That rescue German Shepherd of mine is too broken from those assholes who broke him, and his Prozac is on short supply. He can't handle other animals."

I'm looking over the Volvo as Lena follows Park to the hatch. They're busy shuttling the boys in the back, giving them water, and petting and soothing them. Settled back in his pack, Lena's cooing to MF through the holes in his plastic bubble, telling him he's a good boy and she loves him and he's the softness most beautiful boy she ever did meet. Sleuth is getting fistfuls of treats from Park and ear scratches.

"Are the plates good?" I ask.

"They're temps, and they're good, and if anyone traces them, they'll trace to my headquarters in Saugus. Not to here. You get pulled over, say you're on a test drive."

Park hands Lena a fob. "This one is the latest model, so you just need this fob in the vicinity and you're good."

"Got it," she says, as she slips into the driver's seat. To me she says, "Get in, Greta. Stop staring into space."

I realize I am, trying to center myself on this wild ride we're on, and the steps to come. Park takes the go bag from my back and sets it on the floor in the back. I take my seat up front with Lena.

"Oh, oh, hold on," he says. We watch him walk to a corner of the building, grab a box, and return. Setting it on the seat above my go bag, he says to Lena, "I was going to text you to tell your friend to grab this box when she came Tuesday," he looks at me, the friend, and back to Lena. "I pulled together all of Deanne's old wigs and such. You may need disguises."

Lena turns to me, "Deanne was Park's wife. She died." She looks to Park, "Sorry, Bud." Then to me, "She died five years ago. She was the head of the community theater."

"Ah," I say. "Sorry for your loss."

He winks at me. "Well, you know, young love, lost love. The only way to the soul is through the scars on your heart. And I don't regret an inch of the scars etched on this ticker. Now," he says, bending and leaning in to Lena's open driver's window. "Now, listen." He's serious. A tone shift from his sexy, confident glide until now. "I don't know all you got yourself into. But I know that copter is no joke. If you get in a real jam, remember the other horse trader I told you about in Saugus. Tell him Park sent you. He would kill for me and any raven I send his way. And, of course, you're already hooked up with my boat man, yeah?"

"Yes, Horse Trader, yes we are," Lena says, smile-winking at Park.

And with that, he stands and knocks the window frame. Lena starts the engine, and we pull out. We drive down the aisle toward the end, which Park saunters to, presses a big red button, and doors slide open for us to exit. I wave, and he salutes back.

"Next stop, Salem," I say. "No, wait. Boston. Before we go to the rental, we need to scout out the faces of the private security I know must be waiting outside my penthouse. I want to be able to ID them."

"And how exactly do you expect us to do that with a cat and a dog?" Lena asks.

"Okay, the Salem rental first."

"Yeah, thought so."

We're driving the speed limit along the country road beyond Park's. We're listening for that helicopter, listening for cops, listening for anything that would stop us. But we're seeing only quiet clouds and empty roads, the summer trees and green fields around country homes. As we're about to get on the highway to head east toward Boston and then north to Salem, I look over at Lena. "How in the solid hell have you not slept with Park yet?"

She smiles, sends me her eyes, keeping her face toward the road. "Oh, Greta, yes, ma'am, he's delicious to look at. But we're friends. We get together and play Monopoly Deal cards all the time. He's just not, you know. Not what I have in mind. I'll know when I meet someone who I'll let blow up my world. In due time," she says, in all the confidence in the world.

CHAPTER TEN

I have had this confidence with Henry.

I suppose there was a separate overt act between us, before I pressed my finger into his freckle and told him he was in love with me, and I with him. This first overt act was, as I think on it, just a week before that freckle-declaration session. We were in Henry's Stokes & Crane office. We'd been there for fifteen hours, pulling together our idea for a 3-D model of a timeline for a hearing we had coming up. The issue that was central to that hearing, although for an entirely different case and client, is the same issue I'm concerned about with respect to data at Coarse & Cotton, stuff I haven't had a chance to acquire yet. So while it's true I always, feels like at all times, call to mind any miniscule memory about Henry, I'm probably now thinking on this particular memory because I know it's going to be relevant to this crusade I'm on against CoCo.

Our hearing had to do with how the opposing party, a competing company to our client, had committed a series of bad acts to eliminate or hide evidence. When all of those acts were wrapped together in one package, in a convincing demonstrative (a 3-D digital model in our minds) for the court, we figured it would demonstrate the opposing party's spoliation. Spoliation is the intentional destruction, or bad faith loss, of documents and data that the party has a duty to preserve and produce in discovery. For example, if you're being sued for stealing a company's secret sauce recipe, and you delete emails in your personal Gmail showing that company's recipe, that's spoliation.

In our case, we'd imagined arguing, by walking the judge through our 3-D model, something along the lines of, "Your Honor, they changed the email servers on the day our complaint was filed; then their CIO claims he lost all the email back-up tapes from March-October, which happens to be the exact time-frame when all the relevant actions to our case took place; then there's three emails from the CEO to all his VP's, constantly re-minding them to 'clean up old records,' ...and then list a bunch of other records retention misdeeds. In isolation and out of context to the relevant case facts, each of these spoliation facts might not prove intentional spoliation of evidence, but together in a digi-tal 3-D demonstrative, they would show an entire *ecosystem* of spoliation. This is what Henry and I were trying to map out in his office, so we could then, the next day, show the award-winning Stokes & Crane graphics team our barbaric prototype, and they could take it from there to digitize a proper demonstrative for use on the court's A-V system.

Henry and I pulled digitally highlighted passages from doc-uments marked "key" in the document review platform (as Sum-mer Brad and his cohorts did in the trade association case this summer). We wrote those passages on Post-it Notes, hung some from strings of varying length from his ceiling, some we taped to his wall—after removing a painting Henry had done of his father reading Stephen King's *Misery*. Colors stood for the source of the information, red for key documents, yellow for financial infor-mation from invoices the competitor had produced in discovery, green for deposition quotes the junior associates had highlighted in the deposition software, and so on. Henry's office, after fifteen hours of this work, looked like a deconstructed rainbow of float-ing squares.

Spoliation is bad. It means a party to a litigation torched

discoverable information, when it should have preserved and produced it in discovery. And if you bring a motion to the court and ask the judge to sanction a spoliating party (a motion for sanctions), sometimes those sanctions can mean you automatically win the case. This proves the maxim that *sometimes the best evidence is the lack of evidence.* And this maxim may be true in my fight against Honeywell and CoCo, because I am near certain they are busy torching their digital footprints of crimes. I'll just need to find a way to prove said torching in the context of actual evidence I do find, so as to demonstrate an ecosystem of spoliation. Or, maybe, they torch nothing, I get nothing, and this is all a wild goose chase that lands me disbarred, fined, or jailed for hacking.

These are the stakes. We are living in extremes now.

Henry and I were sitting on his brown-carpeted office floor, atop a red-and-blue oriental rug he'd lain under his desk and which reached to within a foot of the wall with Post-its. His painting of his father was leaning against the wall of windows in front of us. The word *Misery* on the spine of the painted book was a clash with what I felt. Sitting side-by-side with Henry, I felt the exact opposite of misery. It was black night outside, 10:30 p.m. We sat under the floating Post-its. It felt like high romance to me. His long, long legs formed a wider pretzel than my shorter ones; his blue-collared shirt was rolled to his elbows, his tie long gone, strewn on civil procedure books on his cluttered desk. His left knee was one inch from my right knee. I turned to look at his black hair, the beauty marks on his jaw line, a tempting one on his neck, the freckle on his wrist I didn't know I would press into a week later. I inhaled his—by then failing—scent of Irish Spring soap, mixed with end-of-day sweat, and a layer of coffee. To me, the combo wafting off of him was a powerful aphrodisiac.

"I think that's it then," Henry said, capping and dropping a black Sharpie.

"Fifteen hours," I said, looking at the wall of black night

outside. His office faced the back block of the Prudential, where several buildings were in the progress of being built, but not yet fit with electrical. Looking up to the floating, colorful squares of our mock-up model. I took off my progressives to rub my eyes. Put them back on. "Not bad, actually. It was a good thing we had the juniors highlight the hot stuff in the review platforms and in the depositions. Made it much faster. That was Victoria's idea."

"Yep. She's always right. Hey," he said, tilting his face to me. His razor-straight nose was six inches from mine. His massive brown eyes sparkled. I squeezed the remaining yellow Post-its in my hands above my criss-crossed legs.

"Hey, what?" I asked. His eyes searched my eyes, and I immediately knew he'd switched topics from the professional to the personal. My heart beat so hard, it cleared my ribs and fell into my hands.

"But what if we….what would happen?" He asked, smiling, his voice a gravely low hum, a register I'd never heard from him before. His eyes were dream-like, throwing white glare off the brown, sleepy and wet. A calm ocean, an invitation for a warm swim.

"Are you asking what I think you're asking?"

"Yes, I'm asking."

"Okay then," I said, closing my eyes and giving one hard exhale. "Okay."

He shifted his shoulder to hit mine. "So what would happen?" He said, leaning closer.

"Well, we'd have mad passionate sex all the time, of course," I said.

He let out a deep laugh, and just as I was about to change my joking answer to a, *No, but seriously, beyond that, we'd*….serious answer, a voice interrupted from the doorway.

"Oh…" Victoria said. "What are you doing?"

"Uh…" I said, jumping. She stood above us, we remained on

the floor, our sitting bodies twisting to face her.

"What the hell is this weird-ass Post-it art project?" Victoria said, setting a Red Bull on Henry's guest table, adding to our garbage pile of empty coffee cups and take-out Wagamama containers. "Don't tell me you guys worked all night trying to mock that 3-D timeline you were yammering on about last week."

"Yes? We did?" I said, questioning her questioning of what was typically a normal lawyer thing to do late into the night, in prep for a pivotal hearing.

"Oh," her face dropped.

"What?" Henry said, his forehead creased.

"Never mind," she said. And suddenly she seemed uncharacteristically shy.

"Victoria, *what*?" I said.

"Fine," she said, in a way that indicated she'd made up her mind to explain. She moved over to Henry's computer. "Can you log me into this thing?"

Henry got off the floor, walked around his desk, and logged in. He towered over Victoria, and I ached for the leanness of his long body to be folded beside me on the floor again. One side of me, the greedy, lovestruck side, thought that whatever Victoria was trying to show us could wait, dammit. But the other side of me was anxious to see, because I can't recall a single time when Victoria didn't blow me away with some technological solution she'd cooked up, in secret. And I knew in the way she approached us and approached Henry's computer, she'd cooked up another Victoria Special.

"So," she said. "I was working on this before, but then, last week, you kept yapping about how you wanted this 3-D timeline. So this is why I told you to have the juniors highlight all the hot stuff in all the different platforms, the review platform for the key docs, the forensic accountant's separate review of invoices, the deposition platform, also the associates' highlighted interview

memos stored on the Q drive—all of it." She was clicking and
navigating to a shared drive on the firm's network. Henry had
moved back to me, so together we leaned over the guest side of
his desk, as Victoria worked away on his computer.

"So anyway," she continued. "Like I said, I was already trying
to sort this out a while ago. But then I fast-tracked things last
week. I knew you had the hearing. But I want it to be perfect."

"You always want things to be perfect," I said.

"Yeah. And I was going to show you this tomorrow, I think. I
don't know if it's perfect yet." She stopped, scratched her forehead,
seeming to stall before clicking whatever was next.

"Victoria, I'm sure whatever you did is *perfect*. What is it?"

She clicked, and up popped a digital 3-D timeline of exactly
what Henry and I had worked on all day and night.

"So," she said. "Basically, I built a multi-platform code that instructs all the various platforms and drives that the associates and
accountants are using to feed all of their highlighted portions of
Key documents, invoices, depositions, and memos into the firm's
3-D graphics software, and…"

"Woah," Henry interrupted. "Are you saying you automated
the creation of a 3-D demonstrative from multiple platforms and
drives so as to create a timeline in a click of a button? Is that what
you did? Ho. Lee. Shit. Victoria."

"Holy shit is right," I said. "Holy shit."

"Yup," she said and popped her lips. She got up from Henry's
chair and walked to the door, grabbing her Red Bull on the way.
"I mean, I'm sure you need to edit the text content and move
things around, but you can do that within the digital version
now." She waved dismissively at the deconstructed rainbow.

Henry and I were huddled up to his screen, *ooh* and *awing* at
the genius and efficiency of it all. "Oh my God, this is amazing," I
said, looking up at her in awe.

"Yeah, well, call me next time before you two go play school with your crayons and your scissors and your tape. This is Stokes & Crane, not my nieces' Montessori."

Victoria has always revered the high-level technological and legal competence of Stokes & Crane, and it's why she'd never leave to join CoCo. The regret I have for leaving Stokes and her is fierce.

I take out my iPhone while Lena passes cars on the highway. Sleuth provides a gentlemanly *harrumph* in the back as we pass another hound in a red pickup.

As I dial Victoria, I'm assaulted by the next memory of that night, after Victoria left with her Red Bull. Henry's desk phone rang; he picked up. His face changed, a total reversal of the dream-sexy look he'd given me on the floor only moments before. It was Marie, the wife who'd fled for a cheese man, calling him for the first time in eight months. As they talked, I gathered my things, took off my progressives for my night distance glasses, and walked home. I'm sure I left my favorite hooded, black alpaca sweater in Henry's office, but he claims it wasn't there when he checked.

Now, in my ear, a ring, another ring, and by the third ring, Sleuth has quieted, for Lena has maneuvered us past the other hound in the red pickup. The traffic is light, we're moving quickly towards Salem, the location of our secret rental.

Victoria picks up. "Who is this with a blocked number calling me?"

"Greta."

"Well, well, well, to what do I owe the pleasure of Greta on a Sunday?"

"Victoria, hi. Look, I'll jump to it. I'm going to need you to meet me at the Salem train station after all, tonight, 8 pm. Like I said at lunch last month, I'm into something, and I do need your help. And like last month, I can't explain what it's all about until we're secure. Nobody can follow you. You can't tell anyone. Are you in?"

"Is this illegal?"

"Maybe. But I might have a lawyer lined up."

"Is this against CoCo?"

"What do you think?"

She pauses. "Hmph," she says.

"Well?"

"So you're asking me to suddenly take, what, like a week's vacation?"

"Yes."

"You are such a bold bitch."

"Victoria, you know I wouldn't ask if this wasn't critical. This involves what Honeywell did at the border to the children. I can say that much."

"You're saying we might have a shot at taking him down for that?"

"We might. A long shot. But we might. Nobody needs to know you're involved."

Silence on her end.

"Well?" I ask.

"The good thing for you is I've got someone trained up to handle my active cases. The other good thing is I harbor vengeance for people who hurt kids. But the bad thing for you is that I don't know if I'm a yes. You'll see if I'm in if I'm in Salem at 8:00."

"If you come, bring a couple of dummy laptops with mega storage and access to CaseSpaceAI and CaseCore."

"Duh."

"And…"

"And, I know what you're going to say. We're going to need Carolin for forensics, too."

I grimace, because Carolin is difficult. At thirty-two, she's already a former FBI cyber forensics expert, a former Navigant computer forensics expert, a former Stroz computer forensic expert, and a former SEC computer forensic expert. A multi-time *former* because of the searing scowl she lends to just about everyone, not hiding her opinion that everyone but her sucks. She's not a team player. And when she eats, she chews so loud, you're forced to stop eating yourself, because it's nauseating. But. But, the truth is, she's the absolute best in the business, and she now runs the Northeast Regional office of a boutique forensics company I like out of Indiana. On top of all that, Victoria is best friends with her. And I happen to know, given something Victoria let slip once (although Victoria denies it and claims she was "joking"), Carolin has done some white hat hacking a few times, "for fun" to "poke around" and to "mess with some bad guys."

We do need Carolin, because Carolin has a forensics lab, in which, if it comes to it and we can get them from CoCo, she can copy hard drives and analyze those hard drives to see if there are signs of spoliation. Carolin has been certified as a forensic expert in two dozen federal cases. So, in addition to us needing her expertise and her lab, we may need her to testify as an expert.

"Yes, unfortunately, I have to admit, we may need Carolin. But let's not bring her into the bubble yet."

"Right, Boss, whatever you say," Victoria says, her way of agreeing with eyerolls, because she knows I know we're going to have to engage Carolin.

CHAPTER ELEVEN

I wait in the Volvo outside the Salem property I rented through my anonymous shell company. I'm on look-out, watching for anyone looking for us. This tree-lined, brick-paved street of colonials and Victorians is fairly empty for a summer Sunday, just a lady with a grocery bag, and a mom with a stroller. I'm assuming most everyone is out and about in town or down at the public beach paddleboarding or sailing. Seagulls squawk and swoop overhead, for this property is oceanfront on a private inlet on the outskirts of the busy downtown area. Lena punches in the access code on the front door. She's got with her the thumb-drive, which I've asked her to hide by taping it on the bottom of Sleuth's dog bowl. I don't want to risk taking it to Boston for our next mission.

She returns to the car and begins shuttling Sleuth and MF and all their gear inside.

This property is an entire home on the water, and I made sure it came with a dock. Tomorrow, we'll pick up a rental boat, which we secured through Park's friend, under a completely made up name. I had figured it would be best to rent an entirely self-contained place to hide and work, a place with one side on the water, so as to more easily secure ourselves and to flee, if needed. Salem is perfect in that it has multiple potential exits: the boat we'll rent, the roads with several directional exits, and a commuter train. There's also confusing malls embedded within crooked streets, all of which are haphazard, forming a jagged map that grew organically over centuries of New England fires and re-roading and reconstruction and deconstruction. It is full of ancient homes and new homes and historical homes and tourists, constant tourists, all seasons, all year. If you're unfamiliar with Salem, like a private militia guy who doesn't live here, you'd have a tough time keeping track of your prey.

Salem is twenty minutes out of Boston, so close enough for my team to come here, if, indeed, I have a team and they agree to come. And it's close enough to L.R. Rice in Boston. Also, I'm pretty sure the CoCo folks who are looking for me wouldn't think I'd hide so close to them, and in an old Salem home on the historical register, of all places.

I'm reading a plaque on the door, waiting for Lena to finish settling the boys:

1687, HOME OF JUDGE RUDOLPH HANPAR
WITCHCRAFT ADJUDICATOR

This is a six-over-six white colonial with black shutters, two chimneys, and a finished attic full of dormers. I believe the attic remodel must have been done before Salem's Historical Society swooped in and declared this joint a treasure, because nowadays, that construction would never happen. Salem's entire economy is built around witch trial tourism, which is sort of gross, to think about it. Commercializing what was, in large part, gendercide. Sure, men were killed too, and religious hysteria was fueled by men motivated by politics and property ownership *because evil is always stoked by profiteers*—but the victims were mainly female, and the message was to punish those who didn't conform.

All of the evils, whatever those evils are, and the victims resulting, in what we are trying to uncover right now, for sure there are profiteers manipulating sectors of society who hate, fueling them to rage, boiling them up, because at the end of the day, behind secret screens and plausible deniability, behind why some keep quiet and let it all happen and do nothing, somebody, somewhere, is making a profit. I am sure of it.

Malevolent action and willful ignorance of malevolence is always fueled by the money. And I'm positive my investigation will evolve to focus almost solely on following the money.

Lena's back, and I'm in the driver's seat. She's brought with her some wigs and clothes from Deanne's box, which she dropped inside the rental.

"It good inside?" I ask, as she sits in the passenger's.

"It's huge. The WiFi is good. The thumb-drive is safe. You don't want to go in and see?"

"I saw the pictures on line. I just want to get to Boston and scope out my penthouse. See the faces I'm sure are lingering outside, looking for us. Are the boys okay?"

"Sleuth inspected and smelled the entire house, and is now curled up on a blanket in the living room. MF is nuzzled into his belly. I think they're good. MF smelled his new litter box, so I think we're fine there. Sleuth will need a walk in about three hours. We're good, right?"

"We can do this in three hours. Lena, you seem nervous."

"No, I'm not nervous. I'm just. Shit, I've never been on the run before, and I certainly have never gone on a stakeout to see who might be stalking me."

CHAPTER TWELVE

Across from my penthouse on boutique-lined, tourist-filled Newbury street is Trident Bookstore, an indie bookstore staple of Boston. Outside hosts café tables and chairs, and inside, it's half old-school diner, the rest books, books, books. It's basically heaven, and truly, part of the reason I bought my penthouse where I did across the street. Aunt Violet wouldn't be happy, because she always taught me to choose living accommodations based on multiple points of exit, and one exit is to always be on the water with access to a boat. I figured out by my twenties that I didn't have to live like Violet said I should; and yet, turns out I do. So her Armageddon-prep lessons were not all for naught.

Lena enters Trident wearing a mousy-brown wig and a forgettable beige cardigan over a thread-bare, off-white Fleetwood Mac tee and a billowy, brown corduroy skirt with deep pockets. She's kept on her Keds and added round-framed eyeglasses to her face to make for, all in, her decoy character of an invisible woman of muted hues and bland fashion.

I'm a block behind, scanning the summer Sunday crowd. It's late afternoon, blue skies, and hot. Bright light and sunny. People are everywhere, kids with cones, ladies with Ted Baker shopping bags, crowded restaurant patio tables filled with cocktails and cold beers. So, too, the Trident outdoor café tables are filled with people reading and drinking coffee.

Across the street from Trident, I clock two men in black

101

and muscle-man sunglasses, sticking out like beetles in rice, as they're anchored on the sidewalk, flanking the entrance to my penthouse. They do not budge or speak or even seem to notice invisible Lena. Once Lena enters Trident, I follow. I'm in a brown wig of flouncy, floppy curls and a zip-up, polyester dress of brown and dingy beige flowers. There is no lining in this hideous scratchy *thing,* so it is with great effort I do not stop and scratch my torso until it's raw. This is the exact opposite of something I would ever choose to wear. My costume shoes are blocky white sneakers, only a half-size too small. I had no choice but to wear my distance aviators, or I wouldn't see a damn thing, so I hope the moppy curls hide what makes for my regular face.

The Volvo is a block behind, parked in an underground labyrinth below the Pru, with its multiple entrances and exits into malls and streets and hotels and offices and catwalks, which, as such, counter-intuitively to our current situation because CoCo is in the Pru, makes for the best parking option for us. We exited through the Mandarin Oriental in the mall portion of the Pru, avoiding the Tower 8 elevator lobby to CoCo, which is in an entirely different wing. Nobody should be in on a Sunday anyway, and we're in these costumes, so I figured it was a risk we could take. The fob is hidden somewhere by the car in the event one us gets lost, or one or both of us lose the contents of our pockets. *When stepping into a situation that might require fleeing or physical confrontation, never carry the keys on your body if you can avoid it,* another Aunt Violet lesson.

As I pass by the café tables outside Trident, I note another muscle-faced man, alone, paying too much attention to the crowd and the identically-dressed men across the street. All three of them, the one in the café and the two flanking my penthouse door across the street, don't try to hide the wires that lead from their shirts to at least one ear. Unless you were looking for it, you wouldn't see it. But I see it, it's what all regular security personnel in CoCo wear. These guys are some other team, I've never seen them before, but they are certainly private security. And given their location and their proximity to my door, they're most definitely here for me.

We obviously can't mill around in the outdoor café portion or waltz across the street. While we are in costume, true, I don't want to chance being too close for too long. I have a different plan to get the pictures of their faces.

I walk through Trident, pass the cashier, the diner on the left, circumnavigate a table of bestsellers and round the table of New Non-Fiction, turn right, and, looking around, note Lena in the way back, by Mysteries & Thrillers. She nods subtly. I turn to face scuffed white stairs, which are blocked by a green rope and a sign that says "STAFF ONLY." I unhook one side of the rope, which is reminiscent of the one strung on the stairwell of CoCo's select floor lobby. I move quick up the staff stairs, remembering more advice from Aunt Violet: *Girl, when you're in a place that maybe you shouldn't be, but you need to be, act like you belong. No hesitations. Same is true if you're ever trying to get a job. You walk in like you already have the job. Got it?* I responded as I always did: *Yes, Aunt Violet.* And here now, I say in my mind, *Yes, Aunt Violet. I got it. I belong. I am staff at Trident.* I erase from my thoughts the next part of her lesson: *Because sometimes you have to take jobs in terrible companies so you can infiltrate them from the inside, and burn them to the ground.*

At the top, I turn right and wait for Lena in a nook with an old-school payphone. I don't wait long; she walks right up and passes me with a convincing staff-like ease, because she's truly *got it* and belongs everywhere. I step out of the nook and follow her. I already told her where to head, which is a separate and skinny stairwell by the staff bathrooms. This one leads to an empty floor two more floors up. I know this because I've watched the construction crew demolishing it from my fourth-floor penthouse across the street. And I know it's empty, because it's Sunday, and also because the city shut construction down due to violation of a noise ordinance. So, the fourth floor is empty, stalled in renovation.

We reach the empty level miraculously, as it seems nobody saw or heard us. I shoulder the door open, Lena tiptoes on the raw pine floors to the street-side windows. It's a stuffy loft, wood rafters and beams, naked load-bearing walls with no sheetrock. No interior walls, so no rooms, no closets or cracks, which is problematic if we suddenly need to hide. One wall is exposed brick, and the only thing on it is a black, iron ladder, embedded in the mortar.

We slide easy onto our bellies, taking care to avoid twig-sized, old-pine splinters, settling in to watch the two men across the street through grime-layered window panes. We cannot see Café Man, who should be right below us. Lena wipes a small circle out of the grime with her cardigan sleeve and starts taking pictures of the men by my penthouse. We'll expand them on the laptops I'm hoping Victoria brings tonight at 8:00. Then we'll know the faces to look for when we inevitably have to step out. Also, if I'm able to pull this off, these pictures will be evidence in criminal trials for charges against colluders.

As Lena is taking pictures, I settle in and clear my own circle in the glass. I set my anonymous iPhone on video and prop it in place on the sill. I'm watching for one of them to talk, so I can zoom in and maybe try to lip read, anything. Maybe I'm grasping at straws. I'm watching, recording, studying everything, and Lena's taking pictures and watching too. Maybe an hour goes by, and nothing of any importance happens other than two men standing by the entrance to my penthouse. My arms are aching now, and Lena's drawn away from the window to shake her shoulders of cramps.

But a person appears, and my adrenaline rockets.

"Lena, look," I say.

I'm squinting because I can't believe what I'm seeing. I see Summer Brad turn the corner onto Newbury from Mass Ave. He's walking toward my penthouse with a straighter posture and more confident stride than I witnessed in him in June. His strawberry-blond hair, his young face, his white collar shirt, his khaki's are the same, but nothing else about him is the same.

"Holy shit," I say.

"What?"

"Wait. Hold on. Take pictures of the redhead in the white shirt." I can't even summon the words to explain what I'm seeing, because I do not understand. I keep watch. Brad is about ten feet from the guys by my door, when he stops short, stares at their unsuspecting profiles two beats, dips his head, turns, and fast-walks back to Mass Ave, where he turns right and disappears.

"Who the fuck was that?" Lena asks.

"Summer Brad."

"The Summer Brad, with that hot document #10? The flint strike?"

"Yes, *the* Summer Brad."

"Didn't you say he left you a weird message? You said that in the canoe."

I don't have a chance to engage in any speculative conversation with Lena about this bizarre scenario with Summer Brad, because right now, voices carry to us louder, more distinct than the typical under-mumble of bookstore customers below.

"Thank you for showing me up," a man's voice says in the skinny stairwell. "I've got it from here. The city wants me to confirm there's no work," he says. There's some indistinct murmuring from someone who seems to retreat away from this man, who starts up the steps—I think he's alone—toward us.

Lena stands, shoves her phone in a deep skirt pocket, and points to the iron ladder embedded in the bricks to our right.

Looking up, it appears to lead to a push-hatch, leading either to an attic or the rooftop. She tip-toes to it, and I stand and freeze, hoping whoever is coming can't hear us up here. We've got no place to hide. No closets. No offset rooms. This is one rectangle of wood and brick. We have to scurry up that ladder.

He's stopped on the stairs, but he's only maybe five steps from bursting through the door. His voice is clear here, and he's talking to someone. "I've gotten past the staff. Heard customers talking about this empty fourth floor. I'll watch the street from the windows."

Shit. This is Café Man, who's, of course, figured out this is the most excellent perch.

Lena drops all pretense of being quiet and hurries up the ladder; I follow. I'm mid-wall, my fingertips tight on the rung, my knuckles brushing against the brick behind. She's at the top, struggling with unlocking and pushing up the hatch. Café Man bursts in. He immediately spots me, his muscle-man sunglasses on top of his head. My wig slips forward as I hustle up to Lena's feet. He's moving fast toward us and could reach me with no effort, so if Lena doesn't smash that hatch open and suck herself up to the top in the next two seconds, we're toast.

"Lena!"

"Come on!" She yells down. I look up, and she's slithering through the now-open hatch. Café Man reaches the ladder as I'm strong-arming up. The only thing I can think to do to slow him is throw this awful wig down on his face. Lena throws hers too, and it's the two seconds of him yanking them away that gives us a shot at this impossible escape.

He's yelling into whatever microphone he has, "Roof, roof! I'm in pursuit." And I can only assume he's calling to Penthouse Men across the street.

I thrust my torso through the hole and draw my legs up as Café Man grabs the toe of my right foot. I kick, free my foot, and

Lena smashes the hatch closed on Café Man's skull. We're running onto the white-painted roof, and I'm sure, I hope, I believe, I hear Café Man's body fall from the ladder and land on the splintery pine floor.

The roofs on this side of Newbury all connect, so we're basically running down Newbury four floors above ground. This direction leads into the heart of Newbury's high-end shopping: the flagship Nike, the concept Adidas, Max Mara, Valentino, several spas, Shake Shack, and galleries that sell six-figure masterpieces. Thus, we are running away from my penthouse, and away from Mass Ave, where I saw Summer Brad disappear. With a quick glance across the street, I confirm the Penthouse Men have vanished, so we must assume they're in pursuit. We get to the third white-painted roof away from Trident, when a voice yells for us to stop. We turn to see Café Man emerging from the roof hatch.

Lena points to the alley-side roof edge of the next building, behind a giant heating and cooling unit. "Fire escape," she yells. This scratchy house-dress has no give, so I've hiked it high up my thighs. It's hot up here on this late afternoon in August, the blue sky bright, and the rooftop is searing. Lena is pulling off her cardigan as she disappears behind the heating/cooling unit on the next roof. I jump over her discarded sweater, swoop around the unit, and see her jumping, no hesitations, to a fire ladder landing one floor down.

Behind me, two roofs away, is Café Man, so I, too, must woman up.

"Greta, jump," Lena is yelling, as she scuttles down the ladder to the next landing.

I jump, land wrong, my ankle toggles and bends in these shit shoes, and I'm sure I've sprained it.

With no time to rub the instant throbbing, I move to the ladder down, and soon realize we have a problem: the ladders aren't extended to the alley floor. And, just now, the Penthouse Men have burst through Trident's alley door and are jogging down the alley toward us. Above, we have Café Man, below, Penthouse Men. We're trapped.

Café Man looks over the edge as I'm looking up, and the motherfucker grins. His eyes are light green, and those damn combat sunglasses on top of his head are mirrored, causing ricochets of rainbows with the sun.

"Greta Vinet Seville, you're going to give us that hard drive, and all the passwords to any cloud copies of it, and you're going to do that today."

"Got you, asshole," Lena says beside me. She's taken a close-up picture of him.

"Whatever, lady, you're trapped," he says. He's maneuvering over the edge and about to jump to the platform above, when loud honking interrupts, coming from a black SUV that is positively roaring into the alley, going far too fast. An arm reaches out of the driver's window and sticks a cop light on top; the spinning blue light bounces around the red-rust brick walls. The Penthouse Men turn and run to the Mass Ave end, and up top, Café Man has disappeared. The SUV slams on its brakes directly below the landing where we're trapped, a story and a half up. Lena is struggling with releasing the next ladder.

The driver's door opens, a strawberry-blond head emerges, Summer Brad. He throws the cop light into the front seat.

"We don't have time. Get down, even if you have to jump," he says.

As he says this, Lena releases the next ladder, but it jams halfway down, so if we climb down and hang, we'll have to drop about a half floor onto the roof of the SUV. My ankle is screaming in pain, this scratchy housedress is up to my ass, and Lena has already maneuvered her ballerina body to the bottom stuck rung.

She dangles above the SUV roof, while Brad is coaxing and yelling for her to, "Jump now, jump now, hurry." So she does. She sticks it. He helps her to the ground.

My turn. I shimmy down the ladder and try not thinking about a broken neck, two broken legs, death. And once I'm dangling straight and not swinging on the last rung, I let go. I try to land all my weight on the un-sprained ankle, and this is a mistake, because it means I land in a lean, and my momentum topples me head first over the edge. I'm thinking of a broken neck and instant death, but the fall is short, stunted as I crash into Brad, who is braced to catch me. He and Lena stand me straight. We take a collective breath.

"In," he demands, as he opens the back door. In goes Lena, who pauses, for I don't know what reason, but then climbs back to the seats in the third row. I'm next, and now I see why Lena paused. In the other back bucket seat of the second row, sits AP reporter Samera Banerjee. Her brown eyes are wide, and her lids are blinking in anxiety. I sit, as Brad guns it to the end of the alley and we squeal onto Mass Ave.

Samera holds her hand up. She moves her head in quick shakes, *not now, don't speak,* is the message. I'm looking back to Lena, and we're exchanging confused, confounded, frightened looks. My ankle is on fire, rubbing it does nothing, so I can't imagine what the real damage is under the adrenaline.

It is not until we are over the bridge and into Cambridge that Brad slows, makes several turns, and we blend into the hustle and bustle of MIT that Samera's shoulders loosen, and Brad looks in the rear-view to us.

I turn to Samera.

"So, Brad's undercover law enforcement?"

"Nope," she says. "That cop light is bogus. And he's not FBI, CIA, nope."

"He's your source? He's the one who told you about Theodore Honeywell? He was a plant? A spy?"

"Close," she says. "But not exact."

"Did you get the hard drive I mailed you?" Brad yells, as we slow our speed for a light.

"What hard drive?" I yell. "Holy shit, what hard drive, Brad?!"

"It was in a yellow envelope. That's why I was going to your apartment. When I didn't hear back from you after my message from Friday, which I figured you'd clue in on in pairing it with my mailing, I went to talk to you direct. Samera was going to join us once I confirmed you were home. And now all this!"

"What's on the hard drive, Brad? Who the fuck are you anyway?"

"Not now," Brad says in a slicing stern tone. It is a killer robot tone, the kind that ends conversations. I'm perplexed. I sit back in my bucket seat, winded by him.

"You need to head to Saugus," Lena yells from the third row. "Greta, the other horse trader," she says lower to me. To Brad, louder, "We need to ditch this SUV. They saw your plates. Son of a bitch, you did this without a plan, didn't you?"

"Saugus?" Brad says, seizing on a plan and admitting by his tone that yes, he did this, he went to my apartment and intervened in saving us, without an escape.

So we're heading to Saugus, and Brad is refusing to explain more until we're settled. I'm rubbing my throbbing ankle, and Samera is chewing her thumbnail, staring out the window. Lena rubs my shoulder from behind a few times, and I hold the top of her hand.

"Fuck!" I yell. "Son of a fucking bitch!"

CHAPTER THIRTEEN

"You think this is about some run-of-the-mill kickback scheme to benefit Raymond Honeywell for ushering through the government's contract with the private prisons? Sure, it's that, too. But the prison kickback is like a bite of a free bun at a restaurant. It's not even an appetizer in this smorgasbord of crime. Almost nothing compared to what's really going on. It's so much worse than a simple kickback," Brad says.

This is what Brad finally says, after refusing to talk the entire time we were in the SUV and even after we switched cars. We had ditched the SUV in Saugus, at Horse Trader II's lot. Horse Trader II gave us a non-descript Ford, out of a row of non-descript Fords, and a box of plates to change out if needed. Apparently, the plates are all registered to "randos" (Horse Trader II's word) who give their identities in exchange for cash loans from Park.

About these loans, Horse Trader II said, "So, works for us. 'Cuz, see, the randos are good people, single moms busting ass and just need some money, you know. And we need clean identities to hold in a Getaway Bank, what Park calls it. Park always says to me, 'You never know when you're going to need to hide, or hide a loved one. You should always be ready. Getaway transport with clean registration and cash is all you need.'"

I nodded in agreement and smiled. "That's what my Aunt Violet used to say," I said. "Constantly."

"Yeah, well," he said. "It's true. Especially for ladies. So, here," he plunked keys in Lena's hands. "Head out back, take the third one in. Change plates when you think you've been made. I'll hide your SUV in a shit lot we got in Gloucester and take a cod boat back up the coast."

After we were all in the Ford, Brad still refused to speak details until we were safely in place. And I only agreed because I needed time to think and to catalog both Brad and Samera's body language. Also, whenever it was that they both told their stories, I wanted to be sitting firm, in control of the questioning, and looking them face-on so I could evaluate how they talked and how they said it and all the body language clues so important to tracking credibility.

I trusted them enough to take them to the safe house, given the actions they'd taken thus far. And in intangibles I so far caught off of them, my instincts were not blaring major alarms. But if I was wrong, I was prepared to abandon the safe house and flee with Lena, Sleuth, and MF.

So on the ride to Salem, while Lena drove the Ford with the falsely-registered plates, with Brad and Samera in the backseat, I dialed my penthouse's landline to access the voicemail. Several screaming messages from Tim and Maurice of the same varietal as on my work line. And three new ones from Henry within the last hour.

>*Message 1*: "Greta, what the hell is going on?
>Your firm keeps calling me, asking where you
>are. Apparently, they've checked your phone
>records at the firm and saw I called you today."

>*Message 2*: "Greta, for fucks sakes, call me. I'm
>worried. Dammit." And then under his breath,
>not so much to me, before hanging up, he said to
>himself, "I should never have left Boston."

Message 3: "Greta, if you don't call me back, I'm
flying out there tomorrow night after this thing
I can't miss at Tenkill tomorrow. Look, I don't
know what you have going on. I miss you terri-
bly, and I'm scared. I sent you something. You
should have it, a box, by now." His voice cracked
and dropped on this last part. A sadness or a
feeling of lost hope, tied to whatever is in that
box he sent and remains on my kitchen counter.

I replayed that last message a dozen times.

I can't call Henry back until I get things settled with this ad
hoc legal team for this unsanctioned internal investigation I've
got going on right now.

So here we are, we've arrived in Salem. We've parked in a
long-term parking garage attached to the Salem Cinema and several blocks away from the safe house. I give Brad and Samera the
address, and we agree to leave the Ford at different times and take
different streets to the rental.

With me limping along on my bad ankle, Lena and I reach
the rental first and are greeted by a tail-wagging Sleuth and
meowing Marshmallow. Lena puts MF in the cat pack, leashes
Sleuth, and heads out to take them on a good long walk and get
some burners. She's now in a shapeless beige housedress and
floppy beach hat from the costume box.

Brad and Samera arrive, and the three of us agree to quickly
tour the house, pick bedrooms, and meet in the dining room for
my inquisition of them.

The first floor has spacious rooms with high ceilings. Off the
foyer and flanking a center stairway are a formal living room on
the right and a formal dining room on the left, both decorated in
antique furniture. The floors are pine, covered in old and expen-

sive rugs. The formal dining room is anchored with a twelve-person oval dining table of the federalist era. The art is oil paintings of New England sailboats and whales. This will be our war room.

Walking through the war room, we find an open kitchen with a commercial-grade gas stove with lots of heavy knobs. The center island is an antique butcher's counter, that must have been ripped out of an old general store somewhere in New England. I grab an orange from a bowl. There are no kitchen cabinets, as there is a walk-in dry goods pantry on one side of the stove, and a walk-in refrigerator on the other. Opposite the kitchen, and still within this grand open space, is an informal TV room, and I smile to see the blanket bed Lena had placed there for Sleuth and MF. Beyond this and with view of the water and the home's dock, is a four-season sunroom. A couple of loungers and tables out there look inviting for breakfast and coffee and boat watching.

"Let's hurry upstairs, figure out bedrooms, and then let's talk," I say. It has been unsaid that they are not leaving and this is the team now. I had intended to call up a trusted Stokes & Crane associate who I happen to know feels how I do about the asylum atrocities. But now that Summer Brad is deeper into this, I'll stick with him as the team's associate. Samera is a bonus. While normally I'd reject having press on a legal team, as that would ruin privilege, she's my insurance policy.

While I am beyond anxious to hear the rundown of what Brad knows and the explanation of their odd pairing, I need to check on the security of the thumb-drive first. Sure enough, under Sleuth's bowl, there is my thumb drive. Phew. I follow Brad and Samera up the stairwell off the kitchen.Brad and Samera are walking down the upstairs hall. "I'll take this one," Samera says of a bedroom with an ocean view.

"I'll take this one," Brad says of a street-side view.

I poke my head in to Samera's room and see her set her bag on a king with a white coverlet. This room is sparse with wood floors and a blank blue rug. It could be in a monastery. Across the hall is what I think must be a kids' room, for there's a bunk with the skinniest beds—seem smaller than twins. I'll tell Victoria, if she shows up at the train tonight, that this is her room to tease her, but there's four other rooms like Samera's with nice king beds.

Although I'd like to end the agony of walking on this damn ankle, I drag leg up to the attic with the finished dormers, as I know from the online pictures, the entire floor is a bedroom suite with bathroom. There is a four-poster bed, a clawfoot tub in a gorgeous bathroom of white with dark cherry floors, a fainting couch, and two walk-in closets. Each of the dormers is cushioned for window reading. Lena knew I'd want this space, so she left my go bag on the bed. I would have given it to her, but she said she prefers to be as close to the boys sleeping in the TV room as possible. I had promised the landlord (in the online rental form) that pets would not go beyond the first floor, which was easy, because when I secured this place through my anonymous LLC, I didn't think I'd have Lena and pets with me.

I achingly change out of this awful scratchy dress and into my clean, spare, shiny Sweaty Betty workout pants, my grip socks, and black T-shirt. I put on my progressives and stash a pair of readers in the T's chest pocket.

I'm going to depose Brad and Samera now.

CHAPTER FOURTEEN

(IN WHICH I DEPOSE BRAD AND SAMERA)

Depositions are formal events in which one party questions the other party's witnesses or employees. The deponent must give an oath to "tell the truth, the whole truth, and nothing but," which oath a stenographer administers. If a lie is told, that's perjury.

A witness interview is not as formal as a deposition, as there is typically no oath and the interrogation and answers are not transcribed verbatim—frankly, in most cases, lawyers conducting witness interviews shouldn't transcribe witness interviews verbatim, because, as I advise my corporate clients, it's easier to protect whatever is documented out of the interview as the *thoughts and impressions* of counsel in hearing whatever the witness says.

Here, in my questioning of Brad and Samera, I will be expecting them to answer as if under oath in a formal deposition, but obviously there's no oath giving or a stenographer, so call it an interview. Call it whatever gets me answers. I'll be reading body language. I'll be watching for credibility tics in facial expressions, the tone of their voices, the evasiveness or directness of their answers. I want cold, hard specific facts. Names, dates, times, and specifics, and I will generate in my mind my thoughts and impressions on how they provide me that information. Although the claim would be thin, I consider Samera's presence under an expectation of confidentiality—and thus, protected by the work product doctrine (therefore to remain confidential and not subject to disclosure to anyone). She's press, so, we'll have to wink-wink, nod-nod, that she's taken off her press hat for this present mission in my *duly authorized* (by me) internal investigation.

I take a seat at the head of the twelve-person formal dining table, after finding a blue tarp in the basement to use as a sturdy tablecloth. In addition to this dual deposition-interview-whatever gives me answers interrogation, we're prepping to set up this war room. And I definitely don't want to scratch the neoclassical high-shine gloss of the antique varnish. Would cost a few grand in damages.

Brad enters with a pot of coffee and three red mugs.

Samera has the cream and sugar.

"Please sit," I say, grabbing my mug, and pouring a cup. I add three huge heaps of sugar and a ton of cream, because fuck the Keto I was trying to do. *Sorry, Toby. I miss you, Brother, I do. I'll come for a visit in Vermont when this is over, I hope I can. And I'll try your Keto plan once again, when this shitshow is over.*

"So, do you want to know about the hard drive I mailed to you?" Brad asks.

"Yes, I want to know about the hard drive. And thank you for saving our lives on Newbury. But, for cripe's sake, I still don't know either of your angles—your roles here—and I need to know who the hell you are. How do I know this isn't part of some elaborate plot to get what I have? CoCo has lots of resources to do something like that." I look at each of them in turn. Of course I want to know about this hard drive Brad mailed, but I need to control the tempo and order of the questions and answers. I'm still evaluating whether I trust them. They need to follow my question outline, the damn one I've drafted in my brain and am following, in the order I want. Son of a bitch, I need order. Control.

"I want all the details. First off, Brad, please confirm, you acting like a bumbling knob in my office in June, that was a ruse? That was you testing me?"

"Yes." His affect is flat, straight. No tics, no hesitations.

"Right. So we'll circle back on that. Who exactly are you two?"

Samera points to Brad.

"Well, I would have thought you'd want to know about the hard drive first. But fine. First off, I was not born Brad Perdunk," he says.

He's staring at me, no blinking. No indicators of lying on his forehead. His hands are flat and calm on his lap.

"Who are you then, Brad?"

"I'm Brad Vandonbeer."

He pauses, letting that bombshell sink in. Samera flips her iPad in my direction, having called up a screen.

"You're a *Vandonbeer*?" I say, incredulous. The Vandonbeers are the oldest and richest family, by tenfold, in New England. Richer and more prominent than the Kennedys could ever hope to be. And they're exceptionally private and not known for embroiling themselves in politics or on corporate boards. They are the truest of old money, probably in the entire country, except the Fearz of Fearz Oil of Maine, but that family is the opposite of the Vandonbeers. Had Brad said he was Brad Fearz, I would have kicked him out on the spot and changed safe houses.

"I am from a branch of the Vandonbeers. Not the main branch from Rye. But my side has enough to live on, yes. Yes, I have a trust fund. Yes, I don't need to work. I could be a playboy on a yacht. And, by the way, the rest of the Vadonbeers know nothing about any of what I'm doing. I am very much on my own. Except for Samera."

I'm looking at the screen Samera has shown me. It's an old newspaper picture of a much younger Brad, around ten years old, I'm guessing. He's standing with his parents in front of *The Truth*, a Vandonbeer-owned regional newspaper. The caption names the people pictured as Pentington "Pent" Vandonbeer, the newspaper's owner, his wife Marjorie, and their son, Brad. Although he was only a boy when the picture was taken, there is no mistaking him.

"That's the only picture we ever allowed printed of us as a family," Brad says. "My father was just as private as all the other Vandonbeers. Also, he didn't like people to remember that *The Truth* is a Vandonbeer press. Conspiracy theorists claim that the articles are old money publishing propaganda. But my father used to publish the truth."

"Used to? I thought *The Truth* was still in circulation?"

"It's run by different Vandonbeers now. Ever since these assholes we're after killed my parents fifteen years ago." His chin quivers. He closes his eyes. Shakes his head, trying to shake away the pain. His reaction is more on the rage end of grief than sadness. Nobody could fake this. I believe Brad. His pain is raw, and I can tell that expressing his recollection of it is jarring, likely because he never gets a chance to talk about this loss out loud. I know this feeling because this is my reaction in rare moments when I mention Aunt Violet out loud, and not just remember her in my head, and the loss of her, after she disappeared for good.

"Oh, Brad, I'm so sorry," I say. I look to Samera, who shares her own empathy for Brad.

Brad waves us off, collects himself, and continues with his story. His story is horrifying, and I know now why he did what he's done and why he legally changed his name. If I were to write a legal memorandum of my *thoughts and impressions* of Brad's factual story and the way he tells it, and my own internalized observations, it would look like this:

MEMORANDUM
PRIVILEGED AND CONFIDENTIAL
ATTORNEY-CLIENT PRIVILEGE
ATTORNEY WORK PRODUCT

TO: **FILE**

FROM: **GRETA VINET SEVILLE**

RE: **WITNESS INTERVIEW BRAD VANDON-BEER (PERDUNK)**

DATE: **August 22, 2021**

Herein are my thoughts and impressions of the interview of Brad Perdunk, formerly Brad Vandonbeer. Myself interrogating, and Samera Banerjee attending, as assistance to counsel. Ms. Banerjee assisted with confirmations of Mr. Vandoneer's facts, by way of various internet pages and documents she, herself, has accumulated during her separate investigation.

Biographical Information: Mr. Vandonbeer states he prefers his given last name, and that Perdunk was a legal name change before he turned eighteen, done with the aid of Vandonbeer attorneys. Mr. Vandonbeer asserts he had long ago planned on infiltrating law or politics under a pseudonym so as to seek justice for his parents from the inside. In 2019, he was admitted to Harvard Law School, made law review in his second year, and clinched a summer associate spot at Coarse & Cotton for the summer of 2021, which he'd aimed to do, specifically because he'd learned former AG Raymond Honeywell had become a partner in 2020.[1]

---

1   Mr. Vandonbeer speculated that when CoCo conducted a background search on him, the researcher would have seen sealed family court records pertaining to an undefined "probate issue," and thus,

Brad Vandonbeer, 25, was born at St. Jerome's Hospital, Boston, on February 16, 1996, to Pentington ("Pent") and Majorie Vandonbeer. He grew up in the family's Victorian mansion on Bakers Island, which sits off the shore in sight of Manchester-by-the-Sea and between Salem and Marblehead, Massachusetts. Bakers Island is an exclusive and restricted community and does not permit non-residents, unless invited guests. Also on Bakers is the office of the regional newspaper, *The Truth*, a Vandonbeer-run press, formerly owned and run by Pent Vandonbeer.

Defining Life Event: On or around early 2006, when Brad was ten years old, he was awakened around midnight by loud banging and yelling in his family home's living room. When Brad relayed this, it was obvious that this singular moment has left a deep scar. As he told the story, he took several breaks in another room. Ms. Banerjee collected tissues in the kitchen and a glass of water, but it wasn't tears I observed from Brad, but rather, a seeping rage. His fists clenched, his eyes reddened. And while they did cloud with tears, his words were of anger at the memory. The way he described the screams of his mother in their Victorian living room and the frightening sounds outside, for it was a night of screaming wind and high waves, made the horror of the moment all too real.

---

would not know, because he was a minor at the time, that he'd undergone a formal name change. The researcher might have been tipped off if they'd asked a single question, given that the probate attorney was a known Vandonbeer attorney. But alas, Mr. Vandonbeer/Perdunk has no criminal record and his Harvard pedigree, law review status, and immaculate grades put him at the top of the heap for hiring. Anecdotally, from my own experience, having served on the hiring committee at Stokes & Crane, I note that hiring attorneys never look at the background reports unless a flag is raised, there being a near complete disconnect between the hiring committee and the background researchers.

Brad heard a man's voice—that was not his father's—yelling. Brad heard his father beg, "Don't hurt her, don't hurt her, she's not involved in this." After leaving his bed and walking softly down the stairs, Brad hid in the hall outside the living room. It was hard to hear everything said over the thunder cracking and the crash of waves just beyond the cliff of their island home, in addition to the screaming wind, which braided with his mother's screams. And yet, Brad heard exactly what the raucous was about.

The man's voice, which Brad did not recognize, said, "Pentington Vandonbeer, what a fucking name. Fucking prick. You're still asking too many questions about Theodore Honeywell, and we warned you to stop."

"Please no, please," begged Pent. "I was only investigating the PAC." It was difficult for Brad to relay this part of his Defining Life Event, as it was obvious he was full of rage and grief, his hands white from clenching, and his eyes red from wiping away and holding back tears. I looked to Ms. Banerjee, who suggested Brad take a break, expressing that he hadn't told her these details before. He'd only informed her of the event, which she verified by way of buried police records of the unsolved double homicide. There was not, she said, any press coverage because, "As you know, the Vandonbeers use the purchasing power of God to keep their names out of the papers."

Brad insisted on continuing with his story. He stepped into the doorway of his childhood living room, and in that moment, lightening cracked the sky outside a large bay window, illuminating in electric green his mother's tear-stained face and his father on his knees, begging a man with a gun to please stop. The man then shot Pent Vandonbeer in the forehead, then Marjorie Vandonbeer in the forehead. Brad screamed over the screaming of the wind and waves. The gunman turned and shot Brad in the head as well; Brad fell to the floor, thinking he was dead, but instead lay there in the doorway, seeing his parents shot and falling to the floor, over and over. Blood pooled under Brad's head and shoulders while he listened to the gunman open every drawer in the house, push over cabinets, slam doors. The gunman was looking for something and yelling to himself throughout the house, "Where the fuck is it, asshole?" The asshole being Brad's father, who was dead on the floor, ten feet away. Brad is unsure how long it took for the gunman to finish ransacking his home. Brad had assumed he was immobile because he was dying.

A long while—and Brad was unsure how long—after the gunman left, Brad opened his eyes, and realized he might not be dead. He stood, looked down upon his parents and stared for "a very long time" at the way both of the tops of their head were split open, and the misshapen pools of blood around their bodies. He believes he saw brains. I have omitted here the exceptional level of gruesome details Brad delivered about this double homicide scene, but I note Brad laid them all out in minute detail in a somewhat disconnected, hazy manner.

Brad was unclear what happened next or how the authorities came. He was unsure how he recovered or how long it took. He was told a bullet grazed his scalp, and that he was very lucky and very smart to play dead.

"But I wasn't playing dead," Brad said to me and Ms. Banerjee, as a statement of simple fact. "I did die, in fact. In very real ways, who I was before died. Nevertheless, I obviously have had top mental health care as a Vandonbeer. And I've obviously recovered, physically. But my life's work has always been to root them all out. I didn't know what a PAC was back then. I didn't know who Theodore Honeywell was, but I researched. And I got myself admitted to Harvard and, now, as you can see, because I'm sitting here, I'm making headway in my plan for revenge and justice."

       The next part of Brad's story is chilling and central to the next stage of this investigation. Brad has taken a short bathroom break, and I'm rehearing what he just said—the bombshell he just dropped—that he knows I will be exploring in detail as soon as he returns. Samera is looking at me with serious eyes, saddened eyes. "It's awful, right? Terrifying. We have to see this through, Greta," she says.

       Brad returns. The poor kid's eyes are so bloodshot, his face flush, I just want him to rest. But his voice is no longer cracking in grief, crackling in rage. And he seems determined to keep going. I completely misread, underestimated, Summer Brad. I chastise myself for having done this, as it is a lesson I've tried to train myself on time and again. I recall seeing a photo of a woman on a Central Park bench, another woman laying on the bench, her head in the woman's lap. This was chronicled by the photojournalist who runs *Humans of New York*. I assumed these women were well-to-do, middle-age New York women of means who were probably on some frilly shopping trip. But then I read the caption of their interview. The sitting one said the one whose head was in her lap had been her best friend since they were little girls, and they were taking a break to enjoy the sunshine and avoid their deep grief, as the one in her lap was dying of inoperable cancer. I am so saddened whenever I think of that picture, because I then immediately saw them as me and Lena, and I was disappointed in myself for so quickly judging them as shallow.

       I thought I'd never forget that lesson, but I did, and I misjudged Brad.

But then again, to be fair, he had put on quite an act in my office back in June.

"Brad, before your bathroom break, did you say that you found your father's journal under a floorboard and you believe these are the notes the killer was looking for?"

"Indeed I did," he looks to Samera, who nods.

"I'm pretty sure we can trust her now, Brad. Go ahead, show her."

"Woah, woah, trust *me*?"

They both look up at me with a *well, yeah* face.

"Right. Sure."

So I guess we were testing each other all along, and now, *now*, we're a team.

Brad turns in his chair and opens his backpack, which I hadn't realized he'd kept with him. He pulls out a broken-in Moleskine, and turns to a page he'd flagged with a Post-it note.

"These are my father's reporter's notes."

In Pent's own handwriting, it says:

Theodore Honeywell? PAC funds? = priv. prisons?
Racial concerns.

> Dormant/underground supremacy groups…possible connection to St. Louis or all over country? Something about a Wisc. fish or snake or wildlife or something?? Source has seen "shocking" documentation. Bottom line: Source says there's $ in the *idea* of population control, on "tough on crime," dogma, exploit extremism, in works decades. Lots have invested. Some suggest a "ghost market on money falling in from polarization."

I read the "bottom line" several times. And after the weight of it sinks in, I look up. Both Brad and Samera are staring at me, unblinking, resolute.

"Who is the source?" I ask.

"No idea," Brad says.

"I don't know either," Samera says.

"What documentation?"

"No idea," Brad says.

"No idea," Samera says.

"Money in the *idea* of all this? A ghost market? What? Like a secret trading or investment market?"

"We don't know. That's what we're investigating. I believe part of the answer is in the emails you took from Honeywell—and by the way, I only know about that because I heard you talking to Lena before she left. And, I believe part of the answer is on Tim Cotton's old hard drive I stole from CoCo. One from when he did lobbying work out of CoCo D.C. The one I mailed to you."

"The thing you mailed me was an old Tim Cotton hard drive? And how exactly did you pull off stealing that? From where?"

"So my summer associate office was in the dregs of the firm, by the I.T. department. At some point this summer, I overheard Pete from I.T."

"Reboot Pete?"

"He does tell you to reboot a lot. Anyway, at some point I heard him talking with other I.T. people late at night. They said they had strict orders to preserve a bunch of firm hard drives, including one Tim Cotton brought with him from his government lobbying days. Something about a firm hold order for some litigation. Pete said they were to be locked in a fireproof safe in the I.T. department. Nobody was to touch them without permission from the general counsel's office."

"I see. So you broke into the preservation safe and took the one labeled for Tim."

"I did. And you as deputy general counsel gave me that permission, right?"

"I suppose I did—*do*—Brad."

The three of us sit in silence. Boats in the harbor ding, as do the distant calls of summer boaters and seagulls. I note the time as 6:30 pm, an hour-and-a-half until I need to meet Victoria, hope to meet Victoria, at the train station. Lena should be back from walking the boys by now, and I'm vaguely nervous that I'm not hearing the front door open. But she said she was stopping to get burners, so I'll give her another ten minutes before a full-out panic.

I turn to Samera, who is refreshing her red coffee cup from the pot that's still hot on the blue-tarped table. This is one of those Techni Vorm Moccamaster coffee pots that keeps coffee hot for hours. It's what I use when I'm working on my rooftop and don't want to keep going back down to the kitchen for a refreshed cappuccino from my six-grand Jura. #firstworldproblems

"So, Samera, what's your story? I still don't know how you two connect."

"Brad called me. I'm mentioned in Pent's journal." Brad turns the page. It says:

> *Samera Banerjee is working own angle; I trust*
> *her. Will call, compare notes. Dual byline? Story*
> *too big for one.*

"Brad called me when he was sixteen. That's almost ten years ago now. I was thirty then and just hitting my stride in journalism. I was very young when I started working this story with his father, just starting out really, and we hadn't made much headway, and frankly, I gave up pursuing it after he was killed. I had no leads. Then Brad called six years later, but the most we ever got is Pent's journal here, and we also found on the Wayback—as I'm sure you did—the reference to Theodore Honeywell in that old PAC document. Then Brad got himself assigned to Honeywell's trade association case and found what you call Key Doc #10. Also, I have a new source, and they've been telling me they'll help for the last year. But we need to uncover more on our own first."

"Who? Who is your source?"

"I don't disclose sources until they wish to be disclosed. You'll have to trust me."

"Seriously, Samera? After everything, and our lives on line here? Brad's parents murdered in cold blood? Who is your source?"

"Greta, no. I have a code, and frankly, just no. Not yet. I'm not giving up my source."

"Code? Code? Look what I've done? I'll probably lose my whole career. My license."

I'm standing now, and yes, I'm yelling. I shouldn't be. She remains seated, her nostrils flared. She's mad. I get it. I do. It is critical that the press protect sources. But all bets are off now. I jumped off a roof today.

In a severe, measured tone, with her jaw clenched, she says, "Greta, please trust me. I cannot disclose who it is, because frankly, you're too close to this, it's too personal for you, and this person's life is in real jeopardy. I can't risk you letting this out, even in a subtle way. So trust me, if it comes down to us having to pull that card, I will. We will."

I sit back down hard. I'm about to press Samera, when the front door opens, and Sleuth scrambles in and through the dining room to the TV room. I hear Lena release MF from his cat pack, and he meows his way through the dining room to join Sleuth on their blanket bed in the TV room. Lena enters the dining room with two stuffed bags: a black garbage bag and a doubled-up paper shopping bag. Both seem heavy.

"Hey, O," she sing-songs, as she sets the bags down and removes her floppy hat. The shapeless beige housedress from Deanne's costume box is so roomy on her, I don't even know where her tiny body is within it.

"So," she says, holding up the garbage bag. "Found a consignment store that stayed open late for me. I stuffed this mofo with all kinds of clothes in our sizes, stuff they'd never expect us to wear. The rest of Deanne's costume box is costume accessories, no more clothes. And this," she says, holding up the shopping bag. "I found a second-hand electronics store. Got us several burners and even an iPad. You can Facetime Henry on it, Greta, if you want. Maybe call him back. Also I got spaghetti and hamburger and Pecorino Romano. I saw a jar of sauce and breadcrumbs the landlord left in the pantry."

We're staring at her, nobody saying anything, as we're frozen in the emotions of my interrogation and the revelations and refusals still bouncing around the dining room like de-pinned emotional grenades. From my perspective, I'm relieved Lena's back, but I'm furious with Samera for refusing to disclose her source, and I'm still stirring in the horror and sadness of Brad's story. For sure I know Samera is right and she's playing by the rules, but I just simply do not have a rational mind when Lena's safety is on the line. It would be the same if Henry's safety were on the line. So yeah, I'm mad, I'm irrationally mad at Samera for following the fucking rules. Brad's eyes are low; I think he's working himself back to steel. Hard to tell, he's quiet—near devoid of emotions, unlike in the telling of his tale. And Samera's jaw is clenched.

"Guess I stepped into some kind of thing. Geez. I'll go put together spaghetti and meatballs for dinner," Lena says.

"I'll help," Brad says, seemingly eager to leave the tension in the room. His chair nearly falls over he stands so fast.

As she passes by, dragging both bags, she stops at me, sets down the bags, takes a smaller plastic bag out of the brown one and tosses it on the table. "And I got you an ACE bandage, one of those crack'em ice packs, and ibuprofen for your ankle."

CHAPTER FIFTEEN

As Lena and Brad work in the kitchen, and Samera returns to her room to type and research, I go to my room to wrap my ankle and take a breather. It's almost time for me to head down to the train station to hopefully get Victoria, because this thumb-drive is burning a hole in my soul and we need to get into it asap. Having left my apartment without my own laptop was such a colossal mistake. But, I don't have predictive coding or analytics software on that computer, so any review I did would have been inefficient and a long process we don't have time for, but it would have been at least something. God willing, Victoria is at the train with the CPUs and software we need. Or we'll be starting from scratch tomorrow. Somehow. I don't know how.

I stop in Samera's doorway. She's standing by her bed, putting stuff away.

Turning to me, she says, "Oh, Greta. Heading down for dinner? Lena just called up."

"Actually heading out to pick up Victoria, hopefully. The person I mentioned who will have the computing we need. We're stalled, screwed, without her."

"Right."

I pause, hands in the pockets of the beige housedress that Lena threw up to my room for my venturing out. I'm also wearing her big floppy hat from Deanne's box. The consignment store clothes are in the basement washing machine.

"Samera, I'm sorry I yelled, but I have to protect Lena. I should never have dragged her into this. Me, I don't care about me. I've got enough in savings to muddle by, and, if I lose my license or go to jail, well, so be it, I have to do something. My family, my Aunt Violet, to be specific, has a history of, well, rebellion, I guess."

"I did read about your Aunt Violet in researching you."

"Yeah, well. It's…"

She stands straight, hands clasped, listening.

"It's just. When I run a case, I need to be in charge. *Someone* has to be in charge, or it's chaos and falls apart. Managing a case team is not a democracy, it can't be. Can't have too many chefs in the kitchen because then you get the baby in the pool situation."

Her eyebrows furrow, confused.

"You know. Everyone thinks someone is watching the baby in the pool, but nobody is, and the baby drowns."

"Good grief, Greta. That's a horrible analogy."

"Yeah, people don't like it when I give that analogy. I need to come up with a better one. But, that's not my point. We need some sort of order here. We've been all about chaos up to now. So I'm not exactly liking that a team member has information, a source, that I don't know about." She starts to interrupt me, and I hold up a hand to pause her.

"But. Look. This isn't exactly a case, right? This is some crazy mission. And you've been working it a hell of a lot longer than I have. So, I'm sorry for yelling. I trust your judgment on keeping your source. I won't give you any more grief about it. But, you will use that card and call that source on the carpet though, if needed, right?"

"I absolutely will."

"Great. Thank you. Still, there is one thing, and I hope you don't think me rude in rushing you on this, because I simply have to go. But I know next to nothing about you. Tell me, what do I need to know?"

Samera smiles. She seems to appreciate the efficiency of the ask and the trust implicit in it in how I trust her to encapsulate her own salient biographical details. Could be I'm reading too much into her smile, layering onto her my own wish that people would trust me to encapsulate my own details and how I define myself, rather than them making assumptions or peppering me with presumptive questions with their preconceived notions.

"I do think we'll make a great pair, Greta. I was born in Bombay. My parents moved us to New York when I was one. I am forty-eight. Married. No children, by choice. My husband is a medical physicist at Mass General. I love working as an investigative journalist. I love satire, like VEEP, and true-crime shows. My biggest vice is cream cheese with Ruffles potato chips."

I am smiling so wide, I nearly forget the stress we're under. "Oh that's just wonderful. So you're not Keto, like me!"

"Keto? Hell no! I'm a carb addict."

"Good thing, because Lena gets prickly if pasta meals go cold and uneaten. I suggest you get down there."

Samera smiles. "Lena's quite a gem. I see why you care about her so much."

~~~

After scoping out the tracks from the roof of the parking garage, I don't see anyone lurking around watching. And nobody ought to tail Victoria, she's just a former colleague amongst hundreds. I never once called Victoria from my CoCo landline. She never called my office number. I never emailed her from a CoCo email. I always used my home landline to set up a lunch, or my personal Gmail account. Looking back on those subconscious decisions, those lines I drew between CoCo and the people I care about, who I respect and want to protect, I wonder if I all along took the job at CoCo because I, on some buried mental level, did want to uncover fraud and that I always knew, somehow, that I'd need a team. Maybe that's insane. Or, I wonder if I kept Victoria quarantined for the same reason I've kept Lena a secret, because that is the natural tic Aunt Violet wove into me, and probably Toby, too, after she did what she did.

The train from Boston rolls into the station. It's 8:00 on a Sunday night, so the platform has a fair amount of tourists. Not a lot, but enough to make one not too scared to be alone, just cautious. Also, the sky is not fully dark; it's a sheer navy. A summer dusk in the streetlamps. Looking through all the people, I'm not seeing Victoria. The crowd disperses. No Victoria.

The platform is empty.

It is darker. Shadows move.

"Hey, ya, dingus," a woman's voice calls from behind, on the top floor of the parking garage. I turn to see Victoria next to a beat-up maroon Toyota Corolla.

"Did you think I was going to take the actual *train* here? For crying out loud, I've got the whole kit with me in the trunk. And don't worry, nobody followed me. Plus, this is my dumb neighbor Derek's car. He flipped the fuck out that he gets my Audi all week in our trade."

We extract from her trunk two ginormous rolling cases. Not those little ones you can shove in the overhead on a plane. No. These are basically steamer trunks on wheels. We've used similar kits to set up war rooms in hotels when our trial was in a state not near one of Stokes & Crane's offices.

"Give me the juice on what's going on," Victoria says, as we're wheeling down the uneven brick sidewalks of Salem. We pass a granite church and ice-cream shoppes. People mill around and take selfies at the Samantha from Bewitched statue at a little park in front of a pizza joint and a witchcraft store. We're hunched over, whispering to each other, each in shades and hats, trying to remain unseen. We slip into the most crowded and chaotic convenience store we pass so we can gather whatever snacks we can as if part of the crowd and within a two-minute limit we afford ourselves. All the while, I tell Victoria the entire story, and describe each of the people on the team at the safe house.

After all that talking, all that explaining, the one question she has is: "So we have a doggo and marshmallow cat on the team this time?" Which makes me laugh, and gives me comfort, because she's so calm and clinical about it all. And inside, I'm now agreeing with Samera that I am too close and personal to this "case." I need to try to get back to objective, to compartmentalizing, if we're going to get any order and headway.

Back at the house, we find the crew eating spaghetti and meatballs at the dining room table, on top of the blue tarp. I introduce Victoria. "Team, this is Victoria. Victoria," and here I point to each person, "Meet Brad, Lena, and Samera. Sitting on Lena's lap is Mashmallow Face, and by her side is Sleuth."

Sleuth barks a hello.

Victoria waves, smiles bright, which I know from experience is the last big, bright smile she'll lend the team before she becomes their drill sergeant. This is her trick, her little first impressions trick, that she allows sink into brains for a good three seconds.

And now those seconds have passed.

"Right, so. A few rules," she says.

Here we go. I take the handle of the heavy case she rolled and set it next to the one I rolled. I stand offset behind Victoria, giving her the floor.

"Rule number one, never call me Vicki. Rule number two, no more food in the war room, ever. Rule number three, I control the software and the computers. Nobody tries to re-program or code anything at all without me knowing. Rule number four, do not unplug anything. I have many, many extension cords and plug ports in these kits, so there's no need to mess around with plugs. Rule number five, I do backups three times a day. This is necessary and non-negotiable. I do *not* want to hear grief that you're in the middle of something." She looks around the room. Nobody is disagreeing. Nobody is moving. Brad's posture is straight. He seems keen on having a set of rules; he seems almost more pleased than I am to have order.

"Good. Glad we're all on the same page. I'm going to need you all to clear out, because I obviously have to do everything," she turns to give me a grimace on the word *everything*, "to set up this war room. Brad," she says. He's staring at her, a meatball frozen midair on his fork.

"Yes?"

"I'm going to need you to go out to the garage or down to the basement and find me any scrap of wood with a paintable surface. Something you can cover with the chalkboard paint I brought. There's always a piece of scrap wood in old joints like this."

Brad looks to me with a blank stare, which I assume means he is confused on the directive.

"Victoria's the boss of the war room, Brad." I shrug.

Victoria turns to me. "Where can I pull down a copy of that thumb-drive you mentioned? Dropbox? House Store? Where did you put the backup?"

"There is no backup, Victoria. This is it," I plunk the thumb-drive in her hand.

She closes her eyes, exhales her disappointment. "You are a disaster," she says. "Go. Get out of here. I have work to do," she says, waving me away. She turns back to Brad. "Brad, really need that board, please."

As Brad gets up to do Victoria's bidding, I drop the convenience store bag with Ruffles and cream cheese in front of Samera. I slink out to head up to my room to call Henry. Order is here now, and we will begin work tonight. But I finally have a good amount of dead time to attend to my struggling, if present at all, love life.

~~~

Henry's beautiful face with his dark birth marks, his brown eyes, his black hair, blooms into focus on Zoom on the dummy iPad Lena got me at the second-hand electronics store. He's still in his office at Tenkill at 9:30 p.m. on a Sunday. He's as much a workaholic as I am.

"Greta, oh my God, Greta. Are you okay?"

"I'm fine. I'm fine. There's a lot going on."

"People from CoCo keep calling me. They think I know where you are. Apparently, the few times I've called your office, and especially because I called your office *today*, they think you're hiding away with me? What?"

As I did with Victoria, I bring Henry up to speed.

"Holy shit, Greta. So you're safe now, in a safe house?"

"Yes. I think so. We've tried to be careful. And I find out tomorrow morning if L.R. Rice will take me as a client. Obviously I need some cover."

He's quiet, leaning back in his chair. Getting through the whole story and all his questions took a good forty-five minutes of breathless back and forth. Now he's pausing, shifting. I feel it in his demeanor. His leaning body language telegraphs calm and confidence. The entire aphrodisiac of *him*, tangible in the air, even as a flat image on a screen and across the distance of states in-between.

As I have always done in Henry's presence, his very specific alchemy, my brain downshifts to admire the vision of his chest, as his collar is open. The beauty marks on his face. His brown eyes, staring into mine. His black hair, messed at this time of night. He notices me noticing him; he notes my downshift, the drooping of my eyes in the intoxication of his quiet calm, his red lips.

"So," he says. He's still leaning back, holding his hands together below his chin.

"Yeah," I say, smiling ruefully. Because I can't help it.

"Did you get the box I sent you?"

"I saw it. But it's still at my place. Didn't have time to open. What's in it?"

He winks. Leans forward, closer to the screen. "Maybe another time."

I give him a side-eye.

"I, um." He pauses, switches to serious on a deep inhale. "Marie and I split for good a year-and-a-half ago. The divorce has long been final." He holds up a palm to stop me, because that is *huge* news I would have expected him to tell me before. "And, hold on. Yes, I could have told you this in any of our banal text messages up to now in the last two years. But I needed time, Greta. I didn't want to hop from one big thing to another. I took a three-month sabbatical, actually. Just got back. Visited my parents in Bogotá. They're back living there again. I hiked Peru. Argentina. A grand solo trip to think. Solidify my decision on where I was hoping to go next with my life. Yeah. So, I didn't tell you any of that. I did text you, sometime in July. We were joking about something on the news. I didn't tell you where I was or why I had to hike by myself, which was to have uninterrupted time and space to think of *you*. And I thought of only you. Which was stupid of me, because I've wasted time. Maybe you've met someone else."

"I have not met someone else, Henry," my voice cracks.

I could cry to hear him say this. It's as if all the time, the years I've been waiting for him, never happened. He is here now. He is present. As if he were mine all along.

He leans back in his chair again, and I could rip my clothes off, crawl through the screen, and straddle his lap to maul him. The moon is bright outside his window, revealing his office is opposite the famous church on the Tenkill campus, across a green quad full of flower beds.

"What are you up on the fourth floor there, opposite the church?"

"You're so good at details, Greta. Yes, fourth floor, office 17-A."

"Ahh," I say, and lick my lips.

"What are you thinking right now?"

"I'm thinking about that time in your office with all the post-it notes, that rainbow we made for a 3-D timeline, before Victoria came in. The night I left my black sweater in your office, and you claim I didn't."

He's laughing. "You and that black sweater." He shifts his eyes to the corner of his desk to something I can't see, like he's remembering my black sweater on his Stokes' desk.

"That was the night when…" I start to say and stall.

"When you told me we'd have mad, passionate sex all the time." He tilts forward, his beautiful face to the screen. His lips are a digital inch from mine.

"So you remember?"

"I think about it all the time. Is that still your answer?"

"Henry, if I could crawl through this screen right now, I'd straddle you in that chair and show you how much that is still my answer."

"Well if you did that, we'd have to lock my office door, because I would throw you on this desk, rip off whatever you're wearing, and lick every square inch, especially the quarter inch that really matters."

His tongue ever-so-subtly wets the surface of his lips, which are a fraction open.

I'm going to have to take a shower after this call.

~~~

After my lava-hot Zoom call—and shower—I'm in a pair of

PJs that Lena kindly washed from the consignment store garbage bag and left on my bed. It's time to work. It's midnight. I enter the converted dining room to see eight powerful laptops; extension cords snake over the table and on the floor, but are securely duct-taped in place. MiFi's are plugged in, in the event we lose house WiFi. Speakers at each terminal. There's a bucket full of gel pens, the good glider kind, no shitty ballpoints. Three piles of notepads, and several sets of Post-its. In a basket, we have colored chalk, rolls of tape, highlighters, and index cards. A large plywood board, painted in chalkboard paint, leans against the far wall. The oil paintings that were there now lean against the opposite wall. This is a proper war room now.

Victoria looks up from a laptop at the end of the table. "The chalkboard needs to dry until morning. And I need another few hours to build the CaseSpaceAI concept clusters with all these .psts. That laptop," she points to where Samera sat during the interrogation. "That one has all the blow-ups of the pictures you guys took." I walk to it and click through our photos and videos of the three men who chased us today. "Everyone has studied those photos. No worries," Victoria says.

"What's the volume of data on the thumb-drive?" I ask.

"Uncompressed, we're looking at four million emails and attachments. It's a shit-ton, Greta. These aren't just Honeywell's emails. And Honeywell himself had multiple archived accounts. I know that much, so far."

"So there's nothing for me to do right now? How much longer?"

"Not ready until at least three a.m."

This is the reality that TV lawyer shows never really capture. The downtime, waiting for data to load, to process. Dead time in which you can't really do anything.

Brad walks in with a fresh thermos of coffee. "In the meantime," he says. "Victoria is training me on how to review clusters in CaseSpaceAI on publicly-available Enron data. So I'll be ready to jump right in when it's ready at three. And we've got to figure out how to get that Tim Cotton hard drive from your penthouse."

"Tomorrow, Brad. I need to talk to L.R. first."

He sits without reaction. He gave me information. I gave him information. Outside of discussing his parents, I'm starting to wonder about Brad being a transactional man. A *just-the- facts- ma'am* kind of man.

I take in the room, Brad sitting next to Victoria for a tutorial—something I've witnessed her do a thousand million times with junior associates.

"Okay, then. Seems you two have it under control."

CHAPTER SIXTEEN

I wake up to absolute bedlam. This house is very much *not* in control. I'm waking up to panic and chaos, again. There's yelling, and Lena is shaking me awake. I look at the clock. It's 6:00 a.m.

"You need to get up. This is bad."

I pull on a guest robe left by the landlord and follow Lena down the stairs to the second floor, having to hobble and lean on the rail, as this ankle is definitely inflamed. Now we're down the narrow stairs, through the kitchen, and into the TV room. Brad, Samera, and Victoria are on the couch watching breaking news. Sleuth jams into Lena's side, and MF has hopped on the back of the couch and into Lena's arms.

"Shh," Brad says.

My firm profile picture takes up the screen. The chyron says, "Coarse & Cotton Partner, Greta Vinet Seville, Missing, Possible Drug Ring Connection."

Victoria turns the volume up to max. Lena puts a free hand on my back.

The anchor speaks over my face, which takes up the whole screen, "Ms. Vinet Seville was last seen in seemingly good mental health on Thursday night. Coarse & Cotton partner Tim Cotton released a statement that the firm is concerned for her well-being after she disappeared during a wellness check yesterday morning at the western Massachusetts residence of a previously-unknown acquaintance, Lena Atiri. Ms. Atiri is a baroque art restorer, but

Mr. Cotton states that locals revealed their concerns that Ms. Atiri may run a methamphetamine lab in one of her outbuildings." The screen now switches to an aerial feed of Lena's sanctuary.

"Oh my God, Lena," I say, hugging her.

With the live video still hovering over the wedges of Queen Anne's lace, much of it bent, broken, trampled, I assume from the helicopter and God knows, the anchor continues. "The name Vinet may sound familiar to locals. It was Ms. Vinet Seville's aunt, Ms. Violet Vinet, believed to have perished in the 1994…."

I don't hear the rest because Victoria smashes the off button. A black screen.

They're all looking at me.

"Holy shit. You said they'd do exactly this when we fled my house. How did you know that was the misinformation they'd spew about me?" Lena asks.

"Because Tim Cotton joked about that once to me and Cal, the General Counsel. He was spun up about a malpractice lawsuit served on the firm. He wanted to discredit the client, that was his idea. Cal shot him daggers, and I did, too. Tim told us to chill, that he was kidding. But I knew he wasn't. He's stupid. He's evil. Holy fucking shit. Victoria, put on WHDH. They won't report meth lab rumors without verification or allude to a person's mental state. Those fuckers are on a disinformation and discredit campaign. I thought we had more time. Son of a bitch."

Victoria puts on WHDH, and there's my face. This anchor is saying, "This is, to say the least, a strange press release from such a powerful law firm. I don't know that we've ever encountered anything like it. We note Raymond Honeywell, former US Attorney General, is a partner in the new Boston office of Coarse & Cotton. We also have reports from neighboring farms and properties to Lena Atiri's in western Massachusetts of a helicopter buzzing in the region yesterday, which fits with Coarse & Cotton's press release about using their Emergency Employee Assistance

Program. While many neighbors we spoke with did not interact with Ms. Atiri, and knew only that she restores Baroque paintings, one area gentleman, Parkol Calestri, of the Park Motors car dynasty, wishes to speak to the media to clear up what he says are misunderstandings about Ms. Atiri. We're going live to Mr. Calestri in three minutes after the commercial break. Please stand by."

I'm pacing around the kitchen.

"Oh my God, Park," Lena is muttering.

I crouch behind the butcher's block island, hold my head in my arms.

Oh my God, they went nuclear so early.

"Greta, Greta," Samera is saying.

I don't respond.

When the news is back, I stand and watch from behind the counter.

The anchor is not saying anything. She's listening to someone talking in her earpiece. Holding her earpiece, she says, "What? Seriously? Say this live, they're cutting to you now." The video switches to the front side of Park's big building where we took his Volvo. The man standing next to the local live reporter is not Park. It is green-eyed Café Man who chased us out of Trident and along the Newbury roofs.

"Holy shit," Lena says.

"That's Green Eyes from the roof," Victoria says, having studied our photos.

The reporter, taking the handoff in the field, says, "Thank you, Lisa. I'm standing here on the property of Parkol Calestri, owner of the Park Motors dynasty. This is not Mr. Calestri, but rather, a business partner who came for a visit late last night. Although Mr. Calestri called our station early this morning to set up this interview, to "clear the air," as he put it, Mr. Calestri's business partner here, a Mr. Matt Drexel, says Mr. Calestri is not here. He has disappeared. Is that true, Mr. Drexel?"

"That is true. We are very worried for Parkol. If anyone has seen him, please contact the Lenox police."

Lena is dialing Park's number, it rings and rings.

"Greta, he's not picking up. What the fuck are they up to? Have they hurt Park?"

"This is a scare tactic. They want to show they have control— of the narrative, and of us and our friends, physically. I need to call L.R."

I hobble-run up to my room and dial L.R. from one of the burners Lena got us. It's before 7:00 a.m., but this is obviously urgent. She picks up on the first ring.

"You watching the news?" She says.

"Yes."

"Okay, here's what we're going to do," she says, not missing a beat, and apparently several steps ahead of me. I can tell in her confident tone, not hurried or frantic, just sharp and direct and sure, why she earns every penny of her $1,999.99 an hour. "Listen up. We have to turn a low tide to a high tide this very morning. First off, this is a predictable pattern, in that they are trying to spin this in their favor. But this is deadly serious now, Greta. Obviously Parkol has been quieted, somehow, but I don't think they'd risk hurting him with this many news teams out there, and now local cops involved. This salacious discredit campaign they've started, they're painting you as some wackadoo druggie with a druggie friend. This will dominate the news unless we turn this around. Now. This morning. You with me?"

"Big time."

"Okay. So. We are not going to mess around. There's a hog's ass chance that we can prove CoCo silenced Parkol—in the immediate future. First off, obviously, I'm taking your case, and obviously you're going to send me that retainer. Correct?"

"Oh yes. And…"

She cuts me off. "Good. I assume you're out of the river and you're somewhere closer to my office, yes?"

"Yes. I'm…"

"No, nope. Nope, nope. Do not tell me where you are. Do not tell *anyone* where you are. Got it?"

"Yes."

"In the fastest way possible tell me what this is all about."

I give the fastest version possible of what I know about Honeywell and my suspicions and questions about complicity within CoCo, and how Brad's journals suggest a criminal ghost market, like a secret investment market, of sorts, which we have not yet defined or understand. I don't get to the part about Brad Vandonbeer and his parents' murders, nor that there's a whole other hard drive at my penthouse, before L.R. interrupts.

"Okay, then. Good, good. I get it. We're talking major corruption, and you need more evidence, and you think you might have it, but you need time to review documents. Got it. Nobody knows I'm your lawyer yet, but that's going to change at 9:00 a.m. sharp. Gives us a little over two hours to do what we gotta do. Everyone's going to be looking for you now that your face is on every channel everywhere. Boston is not a city, it's a teeny tiny, ass pimple of a town, so people will see you if you trot into my office free and clear faced. But you do need to get to my office by 8:45. Listen up. Do all of the following: disguise yourself, big honking sunglasses, whatever kind of hat you can find, everything you can do to make yourself not look like you. Too bad it's not one of our miserable winters, that'd be easy. You can do that?"

"Absolutely."

"Next, get in a taxi, pay cash, have the driver drop you in my underground parking, because if God forbid someone is following you, they won't be able to drive in. I'll give security clearance for you. You need to get here, so we can take back the narrative."

"Are you sure?"

"One hundred percent. Look, when someone punches you in the gut, you do *not* bend and wheeze. You *immediately* knee them in the groin and punch them in the throat. You must, absolutely must, *always* control the narrative."

She pauses. Exhales heavy.

"And Greta, you do get that we need to do this right away, not only to control the narrative. But also, this is their cover, that you're unwell somehow, to get the police to break into your place for a wellness check. You know damn well that they have a dirty cop or two in their pockets, who will take shit and probably plant shit. So, look, I know your penthouse, I know the builder sold it as highly secure, it's locked up tight, security on the lift, can't crack those windows of yours, but, tell me, do you have anything in there that you don't want them to have? Because their real motive is to toss your joint."

"Someone mailed a hard drive to my place, and it's there. So yes."

"Thought you might have something they want. I've sent over one of my own private guys to stand guard on the street, stall any cops who try to gain access, give us time to do what we need to do. Can you drop a team member there to get the hard drive, while we do what we need to do this morning? I'll send a larger security crew over there."

"Yes, Victoria. I'll drop her. Will your security keep her safe?"

"Nobody touches my crew, anywhere, ever. And if they do, they're toast."

CHAPTER SEVENTEEN

After dropping a very-cloaked and head-covered Victoria with L.R.'s now four-member security crew at my penthouse to get the Tim Cotton hard drive Brad mailed and the package Henry mailed, I ride up the elevator to L.R.'s twenty-third floor on Milk Street. This mid-scraper is buried within the serpentine streets of Boston's Financial District. Looking in the elevator's mirror, I consider my costume. Lena's garbage bag of consignment store clothes included a gray bucket hat, gray sweatshirt and matching capri sweatpants, along with an armload of other horrible outfits I'd never wear and are not in season. I figured it would be best to wear the non-descript gray sweatsuit to L.R.'s today. Also in the bag were green Hunter rain boots, so those are my shoes, and that's fine, because rain boots, any boots, are ubiquitous in Boston. I look like a misplaced fisherwoman air-dropped from a country stream into the city, a *music-montage-before-the-makeover* woman who doesn't know how to dress for the ball, but I blend into Boston's eclectic, come-as-you-are fashion like I was crafted out of the very steam billowing out of T's sidewalk vents. I just waft through the crowd like invisible fog. If anyone were to look too closely though, I am certainly absurd, given the ridiculousness of both pairs of eyewear stacked on my face: my spare thin-rimmed progressives under a pair of huge, drug-store sunglasses. I figured anyone looking for me would never expect me to wear these sunglasses, since I'm always in my prescription aviators when outdoors. They were the only things big enough to fit over my necessary eyewear, which are rather distinctive and could call me out if someone were looking.

The elevator comes to a smooth stop, unlike the rocking jolt of the Prudential's. I step into L.R.'s green-and-black marbled lobby. The supermodel receptionist, sitting behind a half-circle reception desk made of polished mahogany, smiles brightly at me. She sits beneath a modern painting of a highly-detailed, category-five tornado, which is hung on a wood-paneled wall. Above the tornado painting is a gold sign that says, "L.R. RICE & ASSOCIATES, LLP." The message to opposing counsel being, *I will chew you up, and spit you out.* For clients, the message being, *Fear not, I own the wind.*

"Ms. Seville?" The receptionist says.

"Yes."

"L.R. will be right out." She presses some buttons. "Please, take a seat." Her arm washes in the air to indicate a set of green velvet bucket seats to the side.

I don't have time to sit though, because within five seconds, L.R. steps out from a side hall, dressed in a classic, fitted, gorgeous, peachy-beige with black piping suit. And I happen to know this suit is Chanel and sells for over two grand in the pre-owned market. I'm certain L.R. purchased this number retail though, so lord knows the price tag. Her heels—I crave her heels—are nude Christian Diors, the most perfect work shoe on the planet.

Her black, sparkly eyes look me up and down. "What are we wearing here, Greta?"

"You told me to disguise myself."

"I didn't say to dress as Richard Simmons gon' fishin'. And what are these sunglasses?" With one arm across her mid-section, she twirls the air with a finger to indicate all of me, and says, "We need to do something about this. Follow me."

I follow after L.R. as she crosses the lobby and into the opposite hall she came down.

"This is the associates' hall," she says.

I've removed the sunglasses and shoved them in the fanny pack (also from the costume box) buckled around my waist, and under this bulky sweatshirt. In the fanny pack, I have all possible eyewear that might be needed, cash, an anonymous shell company credit card, and, my actual driver's license, which I had to show to get permission for the taxi to enter the underground parking, and then again to a guard manning a private elevator from parking straight to L.R.'s.

The left side of "Associates' Hall" is full of offices with exterior windows and people working—I can tell from the chatter and the keyboards and lights on. The right is full of interior offices, most of which are empty of people and unlit, as it is 8:45 a.m., so I suspect those are staff offices and will soon be filled. The first office on the right holds a name placard by the door for a JOSEPH P. CARMICHAEL. Inside is a young white man with brown hair. From behind his desk, he looks up to see the named partner of this joint, and his eyes bug in a fright at the sight of her. He swallows through his awkward surprise, and says, "L.R., good morning."

"Good morning," she nods.

I hear the ding, dinging of IM messages exploding down the length of the hall.

L.R. leans in and whispers, "I rarely come down this hall. They think I don't know Joe IM'd them all a warning that I'm on patrol. Watch, the rest of them will be busy, busy at work, and will give me a cheery good morning."

Sure enough, at the next office for a Melanie Bump, we're greeted with a busy-looking young woman who says, "Good morning, L.R.," without surprise.

As we pass, L.R. leans to me and says, "She's too short for

you."

We breeze past several more doors of associates sitting, look-ing busy, and saying good morning to L.R. with bright smiles. Af-ter each one, L.R. says under her breath, either, "No; not camera ready; too casual; you'd swim in his suit; too many colors; I don't like that pattern; too tall for you. Pink paisley should be a federal crime."

Coming up on the next, L.R. slows her pace and stops in the doorway of a Sophia Maria Calabria. This associate is the only one standing with her back to the doorway and not at her desk. She's got blue Beats over her ears, and she seems to be timing whatever she's listening to with the bounce of her fingers.

"This one's the strongest of the bunch, and my favorite, but don't tell her," L.R. says to me. "Also, she's just right for you."

Sophia is wearing a classic black skirt-suit from Ann Taylor. I assume she's wearing a completely appropriate white blouse underneath, but her back is to us. Her basic black, matte pumps are just so, just exactly the two inches that never stand out in a crowd, but do the job—like standard-issue Timberland work boots on a jobsite. Her brown hair is in a low and tight ponytail. Her entire look screams efficiency and professionalism. No frills.

L.R. knocks on her open door. But Sophia doesn't hear over whatever she's listening to. L.R. takes a step toward her, leans, and taps her shoulder. Sophia turns, startled, nearly dropping her iPhone, and quickly works to remove her headphones.

"L.R.," she says. "I'm sorry. I didn't hear you coming." Her face is flush, hazel eyes startled. Her prominent cheekbones and name tell me she's full of Italian blood.

"Good music?" L.R. asks.

"Oh, no," Sophia smiles. "I had the library convert all of the tapes of your openings and closings into digital .wav files. Did you know that you," but she stops herself. "Never mind, of course you know. Never mind."

"I what?"

"Well. The thing is, sometimes you rhyme. You bleed in rhymes, like mini poems, in your openings and closings. It's subtle. That's intentional, isn't it?"

L.R.'s eyes widen with a grin, and she swivels a bemused look to me, then back to Sophia. "Got me," she says. "A cadence, a poetic prose, it's all part of the storytelling. Hooks into brains. Litigation is theater. What is the most famous rhyme you can think of as used in a trial, Sophia?"

"If the glove don't fit, you must acquit," she says. "The O.J. Simpson trial."

"Exactly."

"Still…" Sophia says, making a quick cringe of her face, but nevertheless owning what she's about to say. "I'm sorry, I'm not shoveling compliments on you because you're, well, L.R. Rice. But that OJ line is not as clever as your lines, not as subtle. And while *glove don't fit* was obviously effective, your lines are infectious, on a subconscious level, not a hit-them-over-the-head level. And I like your style more. It's why I'm studying the tapes."

L.R. takes the compliment with a kind smile. Sophia's compliment was not dripping of brown-nosing. It was a sincere fact-opinion. I can tell why L.R. likes Sophia.

Sophia smiles wide, finally gaining her footing at this surprise visit, and taking me in. She looks back to L.R., and I can tell she adores her mentor. I can tell she's so proud to be working with L.R. Rice. She seems beyond her age of what must be about twenty-seven, more like a person to have weathered a thousand board meetings, because she soon morphs into a straight-backed executive host in her little associate office. "I'm sorry to have not greeted you properly," she looks to L.R. and then me. "I assume you are our new client, Greta Vinet Seville?"

I affirm I am Greta Vinet Seville, and that she should call me Greta. By now, I've removed the absurd bucket hat and clutch it to my legs. I'm now in my skinny progressives and the gray sweatsuit.

"Sophia," L.R. says. "I would like you to switch outfits with Greta for the press conference."

I take a step back out of Sophia's doorway and into the hall, shocked we're having a press conference. I had no idea this is what she had planned; I figured we'd be working on a typed press release, at most, and that L.R. would handle any inquiries by phone. L.R. notes my reaction and turns to me. "We're doing a press conference very soon. So get that in your head." She turns back to Sophia. "And for that favor, obviously, I give you my great personal appreciation, and I'd like you as lead associate on Ms. Seville's case with me. What do you say?"

"Yes, absolutely," Sophia says in a serious affirmation full of confidence, and not the groveling excitement that I'm sure she's hiding inside. I can see the glorious victory she feels, however, in her brightened eyes. I see myself at her age and remember the excitement I felt when I got a huge opportunity with a big partner at Stokes & Crane.

"But," Sophia continues. "No need to switch outfits. I've got a spare suit hanging on the back of the door. Same as this one. All of mine are the same."

"Of course they are," L.R. says. "Of course. Wonderful."

"Greta, please follow me to the ladies' room," Sophia says. "Oh, and," she says, scanning my green boots while pulling open a desk drawer. Holding up a duplicate pair of basic black pumps, she asks, "Size six-and-a-half?"

"Yes," I say.

"I told you she's just right for you," L.R. says, already walking away, leaving me no chance for questions or to air my panic about Park—about everything.

~~~

Sophia and I, now dressed as twins, enter a conference room, in which the conference table is lengthwise along an accent wall painted fern green, covered in interlocking gold frames. Each frame holds a copy of a jury verdict, every single one says: NOT GUILTY, NOT GUILTY, NOT GUILTY, all charges: NOT GUILTY. The wall is a bold declaration to anyone who enters that the law firm of L.R. Rice & Associates does not lose.

The remainder of the conference room is being set up with chairs, and other personnel are setting up mics and a phone on the grand mahogany table, behind which L.R. sits in a blood-red, armless chair. She sees me eyeing the victory wall.

"Sit here, next to me. We need to make a call."

I take my seat next to L.R. in a matching red chair. Sophia stands to the side.

"Alright," she says. "We're calling Tim Cotton. I do all the speaking. You say nothing."

"L.R., wait, wait. I have no idea what you've cooked up, and we haven't talked at all. You've thrown me into new clothes, and I don't know the plan here, but fine, I will trust you, okay. So I'll do what you say. But I'm scared out of my fucking mind. This whole morning is a whirlwind. They've ruined me. They've ruined my name. They've ruined my friend's reputation. And they're strong-arming, probably holding captive—maybe even killed—an innocent man. L.R., I happen to know they've killed before. We need to talk about that. And, look, they're going to destroy all of the rest of the evidence. I'm screwed. I wish we could go over to CoCo and seize all the servers and hard drives right now."

L.R. looks away from me, nods at Sophia. Sophia nods back as some unstated affirmation, and then turns and leaves. Before I can ask what that was all about, L.R. is dialing. The phone rings once, twice, three times, and on the fourth, Tim Cotton picks up.

"This is Tim Cotton," he says. His voice is guarded, clipped.

"Mr. Cotton, this is L.R. Rice," L.R. says slowly, changing the tempo, taking control. "I know you were expecting my call. I've left several messages this morning. Talked to your assistant. So I'll get down to it. I've got a press conference starting at my firm, 212 Milk Street, 23rd floor, in one half hour. My client, Greta Vinet Seville, is with me. Now, this press conference can either be with you or without you. If it's with you, how chummy it could be, you expressing your relief that your star partner is safe and fine and this was all a misunderstanding. How she is working a very confidential case for a shared client, with me, and through some, oh, I don't know, missed calls and secretarial confusions, y'all over at CoCo feared she'd come to some harm. All of which is true, if you think about it, Mr. Cotton.

"Or, this press conference can be without you, and we will talk about Ms. Seville's internal investigation of yourself, Mr. Coarse, and oh, former AG Honeywell. I'm sure the international press, already salivating for dirt on Honeywell and the Davis administration, will lose ink over that salacious tidbit. Oh my Lord, won't all reporters of all the lands descend upon Boston then, bang, bang, banging on CoCo's doors." She says *bang, bang, banging,* slow, ever so slow, and knocks the table each time. She takes a pause to inhale, and continues, "And you know, Mr. Cotton, Boston is a small town. The corporate clients of New England, they don't like much fuss, is at least my observation of things, having practiced here twenty-seven years. They walk away from firms that make headlines for anything other than victories. You're new in town, aren't you, Mr. Cotton?"

Anyone moving into and practicing in Boston for less than fifteen years is *new in town.*

Tim clears his throat. He starts to say something, but is hushed by an older voice. "Ms. Rice, this is Maurice Coarse. Why don't you cancel that press conference and let's talk, eh? Lawyer to lawyer. Come on over to the Pru. We'll see you right away."

L.R. presses the mute button. She sucks in her cheeks, as if steeling herself to go back into the ring for Round 2. She un-mutes them.

"Mr. Coarse, I appreciate you being reasonable about this. And I'm sure you know, I can't cancel this press conference. I trust from your willingness to talk with us about the situation, one of you will be at my firm in time to take questions. WHDH can be a bit aggressive in the questioning, so be prepared. Now I do have to go, they'll be here in twenty-five minutes. Thank you for your time. I do hope you'll join us this morning."

She hangs up. Turning to me, she says, "I don't bluff. And I always follow through. Opposing counsel learns best that way. And, like I said, we have to take back the narrative. We are still on the defensive. And I much prefer being on the offensive. Michael…" She's turned her attention to a man standing in a corner. "Make sure that if anyone from CoCo comes over here, *only* Tim Cotton or Maurice Coarse are allowed in, and none of their private security."

"Yes, L.R."

Through a walkie-talkie, Michael is now giving directions to other security personnel, who I imagine are stationed on the ground floor lobby where all guests have to check in to get to the public elevators.

I'm staring at L.R. in wonder. I'm thinking how jealous I am of Sophia that I never had a mentor quite like L.R. I've had some great mentors, sure, but none compare to her. Whether L.R. is right or wrong in this morning ploy to take back the narrative, I almost don't care. I feel inspired. I'm in good hands. I feel less afraid, even though the road ahead is so daunting. I hope if I'm ever able to practice law again, I can take what I'm learning from L.R. and make my own clients feel as protected.

"We'll talk about the murders when this is done," L.R. says, after taking a folder of papers someone hands her and reading through the contents, her one eyebrow raised the entire while.

"Hmm, interesting," she says at one point on whatever she's reading.

Soon enough, the receptionist and administrative staff are ushering in people with press credentials. Boston is not a heavy breaking news kind of city, so for something unprecedented like this….well, the big names in media are going to show up

L.R. instructs me in whispers to "sit still" and "look normal" and "not crazy." "Pretend you're in federal court in a bet-the-company case for a client," she advises. And so, I do. I compartmentalize that all of this is personal to me, that they've silenced Lena's friend, that Lena's in danger and her reputation tarnished. I pack it all away, close and lock the brain rooms that hold those thoughts. I put on my courtroom face and make cleared-eyed contact with everyone. Even the jag-off from the far-right affiliate.

L.R. checks her watch. The room is full. Admins have been advising press not to approach the conference table, as L.R. wishes to start it all together, at once.

Neither Tim Cotton nor Maurice Coarse have arrived.

I note the time on a round wall clock behind the press. As soon as the minute hand clinks into the 9:30 spot, L.R. begins. She doesn't give any grace period to CoCo. "Well," she says. "Thank you all for coming at the last moment. Let me introduce you to my client, Greta Vinet…" A commotion in the hall interrupts her. Loud voices approach. The entire room turns to the noise. The closed conference room door opens, and in steps Tim Cotton. Upon sight of the full room and snapping cameras, he smooths his split-middle bowl cut. I can't stand to look at him.

L.R. stands. "Tim Cotton, glad you could make it after all," she says. "Please, do, join us here at the table." She motions for him to sit at a third red seat next to her. I'm on the other side. He lends her a lightening-quick scowl. He hates every minute of having to be here, that he's forced to go along with her ploy.

"Of course. Apologies everyone for being late," he says to the audience. "Hurried over in the helicopter. Greta, you know Stella, she flew me over as fast as possible. This is exciting, good news."

I play my phony part and smile at Tim.

The press conference goes exactly as L.R. scripted. And when a couple of members try to ask about my felon Aunt Violet, as she was included in CoCo's press statements about me, L.R. shuts them down, scolding the press on how none of my childhood history is relevant and how I am a distinguished Boston law partner, not some New York City celebrity, subject to the low-brow fodder of the *Sun Times'* gossip pages. Something like that. Basically, somehow, she's turned this press conference and the topic of Aunt Violet into the age-old war of *Boston vs. New York, Red Sox vs. Yankees,* her tactic to throw them off the scent, and it's working. The Boston press is playing it highbrow, abandoning questions about Violet, and sniggering how they're better than low-brow New York media and even how the Yankees suck. I will never understand how this rivalry is so easily woven into every conversation in Boston.

But here we are.

Five minutes of L.R.'s short statement about me, Tim agreeing with everything she says, some laughs about it all, until L.R. reminds everyone of the concerning disappearance of Parkol Calestri, that she hopes is just another misunderstanding and disconnected entirely—upon which L.R. flashes Tim the quickest of glares, as a warning, like she's telegraphing to him to stay in line, because, yes, we are accusing him of serious crimes.

There's a couple of benign questions lightly probing for specifics on this "confidential case" we're working on (which neither L.R. nor Tim answer), and that's it.

It is now 9:40 a.m.

Once L.R. feels the room is on our side and buying all this, she directs me to say something, and I know what I must do: appear totally competent and not a meth head. So I laugh about how this is a humorous misunderstanding. And I comment on how my friend, Lena Atiri, has been unfortunately maligned, as she is a talented Italian art restorer and published scholar. I weave in a vague threat of possibly filing a slander complaint against whoever suggested she was a meth dealer. Tim plays it off as an unfortunate rumor someone somewhere heard and then the press ran with it without fact-checking. *Bad press, bad bad press*, was his insinuation.

"Well now, we're done, thank you for coming," L.R. says, making it clear it is over. "No more questions." In a choreography that appears to be one well practiced between L.R.'s staff and the press, they usher all of the reporters out of the conference room and down to the lobby within a matter of minutes. No stragglers, no ambitious journalists approach our table for one-offs. They must know they'll be denied. Tim, L.R., and I sit quietly and wait for the room to clear.

Once everyone is long gone, Tim glares at L.R. "How dare you. She stole firm data. She's violated a million laws and ethics."

"She's conducting an investigation, Tim."

"Nobody authorized that. Nobody."

"She did," L.R. says. "*She* authorized the investigation."

Tim is about to retort, maybe terminate my partnership, which would effectively end my investigation and turn this into a he said/she said wrongful breach of the partnership agreement, whistleblower action, but Sophia enters upon a loud bang. She holds an envelope.

L.R. directs her with a wave to hand it to Tim. Sophia does.

"That, Tim, is a preservation demand. You are on notice that all firm devices, and *all*, and I mean all, of your, Mr. Coarse's, and Raymond Honeywell's personal devices, all email, everything, every single gigabyte, megabyte, every piece of paper, must be preserved. You already knew as of at least Friday that you had this duty to preserve. And trust me, if anything from then going forward is erased, we will find out. And then, then we're talking spoliation. And we will automatically win whatever case we might bring. And we will also—if crimes are uncovered in this investigation—refer you to law enforcement for obstruction of justice. All right there, in that preservation demand."

That's what the strange nodding was between L.R. and Sophia, a directive that Sophia draft this demand. I should have known. I'm the one who always crafts these same preservation demands for our cases. The letter itself won't stop Tim and Maurice and Honeywell from purging data, but the letter makes it clear that we will argue that they have a present duty to pre-serve, such that, if they don't, we will file a motion for sanctions (civil relief) and also, possibly, refer them to law enforcement for obstruction of justice (criminal relief) if they destroy anything. Corruption always covers both sides of the legal coin: civil and criminal.

"I heard you were a bitch," Tim says on a growl and as he stands.

L.R. remains seated, crosses her arms, doesn't budge. Goads him with her smile.

"If Parkol is not returned to the land of the living by this afternoon, we will be calling in a tip to the Lenox police that you had something to do with his disappearance. My client has pic-tures of the man on the news at Park's chasing her off a Newbury Street roof yesterday. Not a big mystery there for the media or police to connect the dots to you. So, you know, Parkol Calestri won't be suffering a convenient suicide or anything, Tim. Do you hear me? I'll spell it out. We will connect such a death *directly to you*."

Tim looks as if he's swallowed curdled milk. It's an odd reaction. Putting on the phoniest of smiles I've ever seen—this man would never win an Oscar—he says, "I heard Parkol Calestri went on vacation to the Bahamas. He's got a place there, is what I heard. So you can quit with your threats, L.R."

"These are not threats, Tim." She says *Tim* as if she is biting his name with megalodon teeth. "These are facts. I know somebody like you would much prefer to avoid facts, but around these parts, we follow facts and law."

"Be at my office, tomorrow morning at 9:00. We'll talk about this, you, me, her," he points at me, "and Maurice." He swallows something, air, blood in his brain, I don't know, and grimaces. Then, as if steeling himself to say it, he says, "I apologize for calling you a bitch."

L.R. doesn't answer, just shrugs.

"No apology for me, L.R.?" He smooths his hair down again.

L.R.'s lost her smile, and those black eyes of hers are no longer sparkling. They're more like death lasers. "You, Tim, *you* call me Ms. Rice," she says. "You okay with your hair there?"

Tim makes a huff from the back of his throat, like a society lady insulted by the garishness of a guest showing to her black-tie in jeans. "Well, then," he says. "Tomorrow. 9:00 a.m., or we will really go nuclear on all of this."

After Tim is good and gone, I release my shoulders.

My brain is back to panic mode. "L.R., I can't go to CoCo tomorrow. I…"

She interrupts by laughing loud. "Oh hell no, we are *not* going to CoCo tomorrow. No way. You need to get me something solid, more than what you've got now. Anything. Some kind of hard proof of whatever these crimes are and get it fast. We need that to take the offensive. I'll try to buy us until Friday." She taps the papers lengthwise on the table. "Look, we got him flustered there when he left, thinking about how he can avoid an investigation regarding Park, of himself, so he didn't say the words. He didn't say your partnership is terminated. And he sat through a whole public charade saying how happy he is that his star partner is back and safe. Which means you're still deputy general counsel, right?"

"Right."

"Yeah, so. Some things might be obvious to CoCo, like you being cut as partner. Like you being stripped of the title. Like this investigation not being duly authorized. But that isn't obvious to me. It's Monday. Like I said, I'll try to string this out as long as I can, but at some point, we, too, are going to get a letter. So you best be getting on. Is there something Sophia can research about these murders you claim they've committed?"

"Look up the unsolved double homicide of Pentington and Marjorie Vandonbeer on Bakers Island, fifteen years ago."

"Vandonbeers? *The* Vandonbeers?"

"Yes."

"Well then. Okay, okay." L.R. scratches her head and makes an explosion noise. "A big case, alright. Sophia, show Greta the way out, the way the press and CoCo's creeps don't know. And, Greta, change back into that Simmons Gon' Fishing outfit. And my God, for the sake of decency, murder those atrocious sunglasses as soon as you get back to wherever you're hiding. Get me some solid proof, ASAP."

After changing, Sophia leads me down the associates' hall, and we pass the same first associate, Carmichael. By the time we reach the second associate door, like a bee sting that is just now flaming into pain, it seems that Joseph P. Carmichael was a little too intent on watching me pass. And it might be my paranoia, but I swear I saw him pick up his phone, cup his hand, and say something. But I've got to keep moving, as Sophia is several offices beyond Melanie Bump's now.

She leads me to a door at the end of the hall, which leads into a stairwell that crisscrosses into an adjoining building. "Go through the next building and then go to the fifth floor. There's a skybridge to another building, cross that. Then, go to ground, go through the Au Bon Pain, exit, and take a taxi from the taxi line.

Fortunately, I don't think anyone saw you in this fishing outfit, and nobody should know about this way out."

But I'm still bothered by Joseph P. Carmichael. Still, I say nothing and thank her for her help. I do have a good instinct coming off of Sophia, something intangible, a quality I learned to trust from Aunt Violet's lessons. Added to that are body language indicators, such as Sophia's earnest, unblinking eyes, her confident tone, and her unflinching posture, which lend credibility. These are factors litigators are trained to observe, for we're always evaluating witnesses in investigations, in depositions, and on the stand.

And so, I thank Sophia for her help and depart. Following the course she set forth, I'm through the building, up to the fifth floor of the next, across the sky bridge, down to Au Bon Pain, and straight into a waiting taxi, as the line moves fast.

When I see a black SUV behind my taxi taking a couple of similar turns, and when I look back and see men in it with those muscle-man sunglasses, and not a regular Uber driver with a fare, I look up to my taxi driver, who himself looks like he might be a bouncer as his second job. His laminated placard says his name is Nicolas Cage. Okay. Sure. Of course it is.

"Nick?"

"Yeah?" He's looking in the rearview at me. He's young, maybe late twenties. In leaning forward, I see a Charlestown bar band on his wrist that says "STAFF." So he's a moonlighting bouncer, or a moonlighting driver. And this Charlestown bar is a notorious one for brawls; it's not where you take your visiting tourist friends for a drink. It's for townies. This guy is grade-A townie bouncer, and I trust that he's bounced many bad eggs, and that he knows the streets of Boston as well as he knows his way around a gym. Like breathing.

"Nick, so my asshole ex-boyfriend is stalking me in that black SUV behind us. Any way you can maybe lose him?"

He glances in the rearview, and then, staring straight ahead, says in a heavy Boston accent, "Your boyfriend a private militia man, Lady? Cuz that ain't no regular boyfriend." (But he pronounced it "regulah".)

"How do you know?"

"I can tell from the plates. And I hate those fuckers, for the record. These private asswipes come into Boston and infect our boys in blue with their supremacy, if you know what I mean. They make all kinds of offers for private jobs to the susceptible cops, so long as they earn their stripes on the force. Sorry for my mouth here, Lady, but I fucking hate 'em."

"Then you and I are on the same page, Nicolas Cage. Can we lose them?"

"You bet your ass, we can," he says, glaring through his mirror. "Buckle up, buttercup."

So I do, I buckle up.

Sure enough, he's a bad-ass Bostonian with that accent and build and fearless hatred of outside forces that harm our city. His muscles twitch and contract under his pink, collared shirt, as he speeds and bobs and weaves and squeals in turns, turns, turns, with no signal ever. We crank around corners throughout the financial district, speeding down alleys, sharp turns, left turns when I thought we'd be going straight, and all along I'm plastered into my seat by the speed, or slamming into the door like I'm on the tilt-a-whirl at Canobie Lake. Mostly, I keep my eyes closed for fear of death, or I fix on the grip he keeps on the steering wheel, and the alarming hugeness of his knuckles.

Since my eyes are mostly closed, the city goes by in a blur of buildings and pedestrians on sidewalks. Lena would call the ride impressionism of city life.

Many minutes—or even eternities—pass without me taking a breath.

"We lost him, honey," he calls back, after we've slowed. "I

think I lost him in Chinatown, but I kept coming to Back Bay to be sure. Maybe you should hide in the station a bit, yeah?"

I open my eyes to see we're at a light, in between the Back Bay train station, and the Neiman Marcus end of Copley Mall. This is a good spot for me to get out, as there are multiple exit points here: through the Copley to the Pru, and several parking areas under both connected malls (and also our Volvo from Park, still parked beneath the Pru); the Back Bay train station beside me; or the grand Fairmont Hotel, up ahead, with its constant taxi line. There's also, across from the Fairmont, the gargantuan Boston Public Library, with its old wings cobbled to modern wings, a courtyard in center, and numerous confusing floors and halls in-between, that if you're unfamiliar, is easy to lose your way within if you're chasing someone like me, who is familiar with the multi-dimensional landscape of the Boston Public Library.

But I don't think I need to hop dimensions in the library today, as I'm planning to scoot into the train station twenty feet away and take Nick Cage's good advice to hide in the station a bit.

I thank Nick, throw him two one-hundred dollar bills for his expert stunt driving, and open the door to exit.

Before scooting out, I look up and find he's staring at the money.

"You didn't need to pay this much, honey," he says.

"Do you have a card?"

He scribbles a number on the back of his driver's calling card.

"The number on the back is how you get me if you're in an urgent jam. And I got my own SUV, too. Got a license with Uber, Lyft, you name it."

"Thanks, Nick. And forget my face. Like if you see me on the news or anything. Nobody needs to know I know you."

"I don't remember faces of ghosts, Lady. You look like smog to me."

I smile and move out of the taxi. Nicolas Cage drives off.

Looking around, I don't see anyone following. I enter the Back Bay train station, as I think this is the best place to hide and wait, to be sure I'm not followed to the safe house, whichever way I figure best to get there. I suppose I could have had Nick take me direct, but who knows if he lost our tail for absolutely sure. It should be good to hide in the ladies' room, which is a disgusting prospect even in the best of circumstances, but certainly a less likely spot for men to search.

As Aunt Violet always said, *always trust your instincts*. And my instincts are telling me they don't like the way Associate Joseph P. Carmichael looked at me and made that cupped call and wham, there's cars taking too many similar turns behind my new friend, Nicolas Cage.

CHAPTER EIGHTEEN

I keep my head down, so all I'm seeing is the orange to brown brick floor of Boston's Back Bay station, and I'm smelling the burnt coffee and traveler sweat. It's a hot summer day, and this joint isn't exactly air conditioned and cleaned with Febreeze. I know exactly where the ladies' room is, as this is the station I use to get to South Station for Amtrak, so I shuttle and duck myself into the four-stall bathroom. I'm not really here to ride the T, at least I don't think that will be my next move. I first need an update from the team, and then I'll decide.

As soon as I'm inside, gagging on the heavy scent of musk mixed with urine, because there's no exhaust, no exchange of air, it's hot bathroom stench, I yank out a burner from the fanny pack under my sweatshirt. I dial Lena.

"Brad found something," she says when she answers. "Here he is." I don't even have time to explain I'm trying to make sure I've lost a tail so I don't lead anyone to our safe house and all our data.

"Hi, so," Brad says, as he takes the phone from Lena. They must have been standing side-by-side. "I've been working concept analytics in CaseSpaceAI on the Honeywell emails. Victoria built me a focus on the concept search of 'profitable extremism.' So this will bring up anything that conceptually fits with that phrase. Ah shit, hold on." I hear a keyboard clicking. Back to me he says, "I need to get back into the platform, it crashed. Hold on." Women are walking in and around me to stalls, and I keep having to shift so they can reach a sink or the paper towels or the trash can.

It's cute that Brad's telling me how concept analytics works, since I'm the one who speaks on national forums about this technology. But I'll let him have his moment. Basically, it works like this: Using the same example as the three million trade association emails Summer Brad reviewed with his cohorts in June, if you were to take all three million emails and put them into CaseSpaceAI's concept analytics, it would help organize those documents around clusters of concepts. For example, if a concept search were run on the concept of "Christmas," the tool wouldn't just organize emails that hit on the literal term "Christmas," it would include emails discussing Christmas items, such as Santa, presents, holiday shopping, ornaments, string lights, etc. Of course there are many other features, far too much to explain all, but this is the gist, and this is how we can run investigations into enormous data dumps in a short amount of time. Here, the concept of "profitable extremism" should yield some rather on point communications out of the four million Victoria loaded from the .psts I took from Honeywell's laptop.

"Okay," he says. "I'm back. Back online."

"Hold on. Have you heard from Victoria? Did she get the hard drive from my place?"

"Yes. Well, at least she's confirmed it's there. She's stuck at the penthouse under security until L.R.'s crew says it's safe to switch locations and strategize on how she gets back here."

"Got it. Go then, keep talking."

I'm thinking of Victoria sitting on my very white, single-woman-no-kids—*did I say white?*—couch, dunking tortilla chips in the salsa I just bought. Her defiance of me, defiance of the laws of salsa physics, defiance of being detained. I know she's safe for the time being with L.R.'s crew, so she can paint the couch with salsa for all I care. I wanted to upgrade to a Neiman Marcus Haute House, tufted velvet Vaughn in emerald green anyway. *Buying furniture at Neiman Marcus is impractical always, and definitely now. Focus.*

A woman shoots daggers at me because apparently she needs *all the space* to put on her tangerine lipstick. I wedge my body into a corner between a concrete block wall and the diaper station. Hopefully no butts need a change in the next few minutes.

"Brad, you're going to have to talk fast, and whatever emails you found that you think are hot, you need to speed read them to me, because every word matters," I say.

"Okay. We still have millions of emails to get through in what you extracted from Honeywell's laptop, and then there's the hard drive I mailed to your place and Victoria has. But, in this concept focus for 'profitable extremism' in the data we have now, if you narrow it to items that mention 'T. Honeywell' or 'Theodore,' well, a few items come straight to the top and we need to talk about them right now. Because we need to take action on them *right now.*"

"Okay, I'm listening. Read fast."

"Right. So you just have a burner, don't you? I can't share a screen or anything?"

"No. Just read. Hurry."

"I'll hit the top super-key ones then. There's more. First one is from 2009, the second from 2019. Both are between a Raymond Honeywell Gmail account, a Raymond.Zeta.Honeywell@gmail.com, one that seems dedicated to communications with this one other account, that of a WisconsinAlbatross@Gmail.com. This fits with that weird reference in my dad's journal to a 'Wisc. fish or snake or wildlife.' Put a pin on Wisconsin Albatross, because Victoria has been sleuthing on that lead and it's important.

"First one, in 2009, is from Wisconsin Albatross to Raymond Zeta Honeywell. It says:

> *Theo, now we can confirm via email, instead of letters. Herein, confirming, as with the others, the papers with the plans for private prisons and other privatizations are in same locales. Safe undergrounds. Multiple undergrounds. We within Zeta shall keep our oaths. Investors growing, donations will climb. Confirm oath and that you will delete this chain when done reading.*

"Raymond Zeta Honeywell writes back:

> *Confirmed, -T. Please confirm that all of the MDs confirm same, and that all of their papers are in the undergrounds.*

"To which, Wisconsin Albatross responds:

> *Confirmed. Most literally underground, some in cabinets, all in hosp. archives. NY, Chicago, Pittsburgh, St. Louis, LA, Seattle, DC, Miami MDs all confirm.*"

Brad pauses his breathless reading, inhales. He continues, "Okay, so I think with that, we can confirm that, for sure, Raymond Honeywell is, in fact, Theodore. And he uses that name in connection with whatever they've been cooking up for private prisons and other privatizations, and, given the mention of investors and how donations will 'climb,' maybe that's part of the ghost market mentioned in my father's journal. But there's more. So then ten years later, *while* Honeywell is AG, we get this exchange in early 2019. First, again from Wisconsin Albatross to Raymond Zeta:

> *Theodore, ten years hence and the plan is trucking. Good job on the rollout in Texas. Zeta investors are very pleased with already realized gains. Again confirming all Zeta members will keep their oath, please confirm. Noting all MDs papers still in same hosp archives in MDs board books, board notes, and folders they've been instructed to label "population de minimus." Nothing digital. Preservation intact. Confirm you will delete this chain when done reading.*

"Raymond Zeta writes back:

> *Confirmed, T. Concerned oldest papers trashed or being digitized given age. Need, as those are leverage for fallout. Can't risk acquisition. Profit potential now expanded on polarized topics to push.*

"And Wisconsin Albatross responds:

> *All is well. No worries. Archives, same. Intact. Hidden. Moldy, but good.*

"So, obviously, Mr. Raymond, Theodore, T, Zeta, Theo, Honeywell didn't delete these chains like he said he would," Brad says in a matter-of-fact tone.

"Hold on, let me think a second."

I turn and cover my free ear, while a woman by the trashcan sneezes in a series of blows that may sever her nose. But even this bodily function isn't breaking my concentration, because I can barely believe what I'm hearing. I'm laser-focused on one particular part of what Brad just rattled through. "Brad, did I hear you correctly when you said, 'Good job on the rollout in Texas?'"

"Yes. And, yes, Greta, that is exactly *one week* after AG Honeywell sent a team of private doctors to a private prison, contracted with the government to attest to the heath of detainees—which we all know did not involve legitimate medical evaluations. Wait, because there's more for you to hear on how vile this all is. Victoria has found *more.*"

"Hold on," I say, because now that the nose blaster is gone, three chatty chats bustle into the bathroom with shopping bags, yammering about sales at Saks and lunch plans. Must be nice to not be on the run.

I shimmy past them out of the bathroom, inhale a waft of less-awful air, although it's still stagnant and unfresh in the terminal. I find a clear spot by an overflowing trashcan.

"Okay, I'm back," I say.

"So, those are the emails. They're talking so free about obvious corruption. Raymond using his own name on a private account and not deleting what he was asked to delete—the ask itself reeking of corruption. Definite spoliation. Probable obstruction of justice."

"Well, Brad, but we know it's obvious corruption, because we know what we're looking for, and we are reading a bit into it all. And, you'd be surprised how blatant arrogant men, who weren't born into technology, and who came to technology kicking and screaming, can be in email. Take a look into the Enron scandal and the emails they uncovered there. And those were *company* emails. They weren't even private accounts, like these."

"Fair point." Again his tone is hyper matter-of-fact.

Fair point? It's a lesson, Brad. What is up with this kid?

"You need to hear about Wisconsin Albatross, the sender," he says.

"Wait, wait." I have to pause, because those chatty chats are clomping this way in their kitten heels, aiming to toss more Dunkin' cups in the trash. I step back, adjust my bucket hat lower over my face, because one of them looks at me a little too long, and then toddles off. Does she recognize me from the morning news? Oh God, I hope not—that's all I need, these three birds chirping on the sidewalk about the woman from the morning news, now in the train station in a disguise. I watch them walk out, and I think I'm okay, because they seem entirely engrossed in a conversation about the Fairmont's infamous charcuterie board. The one woman looks back at me on her way out, and I move over to a blocking column, pressing my back behind it fast and tight. Free again, with just train passengers milling around, I take stock of the crowd and see no tails. I'm not focusing on the scenery I'm in. Right now, everything is blurred people and orange-brown bricks. I need to focus on this call and get it over with. I'm wondering why the team feels I need to hear these details right now, before I get back.

"So what about this Wisconsin Albatross?"

"Hey, it's me, V." Victoria has been patched in and now this is a three-way call.

I hear Sleuth bark and Lena calling for MF to get down from the kitchen counter on Brad's wing of the call. Lena's voice sounds sad, deflated. Brad says on his end, "Are the train times lining up for us?" I don't know who he's saying this to, Samera or Lena.

Now I'm really suspicious why they need me to hear all of these key findings, *right now*.

"Brad, how's Lena?"

"Not great. She's worried about Park. But we need you to focus on this right now, and Lena agrees."

"Must be huge. Okay, hit me."

"Here's the deal," Victoria says. "Wisconsin Albatross, if you dig in the dark internets for this bad bitch, pops up a couple of times in a right wing dark web chat group, which they think is encrypted, but hil-air-ee-ous. Not for me. I crack on in and of course it's total poison. There's reams of chat logs going back years, no way to read it all. So I asked Carolin—and do not give me shit on that right now. Carolin is working on this under my direction in her lab. So it's under control, and I trust her. Alright?"

"Fine. I trust you, Victoria."

"Good. So, I asked Carolin to social engineer that on her end to extract all references to Wisconsin Albatross. She found all of four. They are all in reference to a 1965 newsletter by a man who signed it *Wisconsin Albatross*. Greta, this is bad. The newsletter…"

"Wait," I say. I have to cut her off, because right outside Back Bay station, I see a Man in black milling on the sidewalk. He's talking on a cell, and I can't hear what he's saying out there, but surely he's looking for me. I hope he didn't hear something from those chatty chats. I maneuver behind the column again.

"Okay, hurry. I think I'm going to have to run again."

"You were on the run *again*?"

"None of you have given me a chance to give you an update. But go, what's Wisconsin Albatross?"

"Right. So, the newsletter Carolin found in the far right chat group is all about doctors who discussed a population control plan at a small conference at St. Louis Medical Center, on March 16, 1965."

"And so, what, Honeywell's doctors who rolled out in Texas 2019 are connected, somehow?"

"That's our theory. I mean, the 2019 doctors that Honeywell

sent to Texas are part of a chain of doctors who we believe began in 1965. Like, maybe a pyramid scheme bringing more doctors under their evil umbrella, or maybe an evil chain of doctor mentorships. Something like that. We obviously need more evidence to tie it all together, and how these docs, maybe, are part of a coordinated attempt to legitimize certain messages that drove investments, somehow? Donations, maybe? Not sure. But, I think we might have discovered reference to the *source material*, G. That's our theory. We obviously need to get to these underground hospital archives. It's just our working theory, somehow tied to some profit scheme. Maybe like cold market profiteers working with—or manipulating—racists, extreme conservative positions, like population control, crime, like speculators manipulating pockets of extremism for profit, maybe? That would explain, possibly, the 'ghost market' reference in Brad's dad's journal, and the profit references in the emails he read you. How it all connects, what the whole 3-D image is of it all together, I don't know. We need more to fill out, figure it out. The picture is not exactly in focus yet—we have only a few disjointed pieces."

"Fucking monsters."

"I'm pretty sure whatever is in the source material is worse than either of us can imagine, and, or, will lead to worse than we can imagine. But, for now, so we know where to start, I found the 1965 St. Louis conference and all the names of the doctor attendees and their affiliate hospitals, by searching the online archive of the St. Louis Medical Center. Found an old agenda—and the agenda is absolute horseshit and benign, compared to the truth of what they discussed, if we're to believe the Wisconsin Albatross newsletter. All of the hospitals match the list of locations that are in the cities listed in the emails Brad read you."

"Who's the doc and hospital in New York?"

"Yeah, so we knew you'd focus on the one in New York. Samera did some digging in corporate records. Here's what she found. On the St. Louis agenda, the New York doc is a Roger Hoff of Meriview Medical of Midtown. Meriview Medical was acquired in the 1970's by Midtown Medical, and that was then acquired by none other than…"

"Tenkill."

"You got it."

"So we need to ask Henry to gain access to wherever the old Meriview archives are and what Tenkill did to them after acquisition."

"Yup. This is why Brad wanted you to know ASAP. Lena's looking at the Amtrak schedule. Can't take the Ford, because even you can't control traffic between here and New York and back. And the road construction on 93 has things down to a half-lane."

I poke my head around the column, and of course the sidewalk man enters the train station in this exact moment. He's looking all over, so I slink back. He's one of the ones who flanked my penthouse yesterday. He'll be over here in a flat second as there's not a lot of space for him to cover. If I run back to the bathroom, he'll see me. So my better bet is to dash across the station and down the stairs to the trains and hope to catch whatever comes next and hide in the crowd.

"One sec, one sec," I say to Victoria. I breathe in, my back flat against the column. I think on something Aunt Violet once said, somehow it floats out of the mist of my memories as the clearest, ringing decision on what to do. She said, *if you've been had, then think of yourself as a clever tuna with a shark friend. Let those fishermen follow you as you drag them around the deep blue sea, while your shark friend cuts the line with his teeth. Do the double dupe.*

I never understood what she meant by that. And I'm not sure if I'm remembering it now because I'm dressed as a fisherwoman. But suddenly I know what to do.

"Guys," I say. "Obviously we're going to New York and we're

getting into those old Meriview archives. I've got someone on my ass here at Back Bay, and he's going to find me any minute. Brad, tell Lena and Samera that all three of you need to meet me ASAP at South Station. We need four of us to be able to carry back old boxes if they're there, or run diversion, or whatever. And we need Samera and her press pass. We need to get this done in one night, one shot, no time to waste. Victoria, when L.R.'s crew figures out how to transition you back to the safe house, can you...."

"Yes, I will process this Tim Cotton hard drive. Yes, I will keep care of Sleuth and MF. Yes, I'll check to make sure the rental boat is tied tight to the cleats. Oh, speaking of which, did you hear about this boat? Samera and Lena picked it up from somebody they call Horse Trader Boat Guy, and um, wait until you see this sea dog of a boat"

"That bad?"

"You have no idea."

"Fine. Brad, you guys need to hurry. South Station and fast and dressed so you'll all stick out in a crowd, but with heads covered. And tell Lena to pack us a change of clothes that are normal, blending clothes."

"Yes," Brad says, succinct. Direct.

"Like ostentatious-style sticking out. Like crazytown outfits that nobody would miss."

"Understood. Will do."

Which is the best associate answer to give to all requests.

CHAPTER NINETEEN

One more call behind this column before I start the double dupe. I call L.R., make an urgent request, haggle fast through the particulars with her, ask that she make sure Victoria is able to safely transition from my penthouse back to the safe house, and lastly tell her my instincts don't trust her associate Joseph P. Carmichael and why.

"I'll look into Joe," L.R. says.

I slip the burner back into the fanny pack and adjust my hat and plaster the sunglasses back over my progressives. Ready, I stroll from out behind the column into the belly of the station. This station is for the Orange Line, which might be the most detested of all the subway lines in Boston, even worse than the despised Green Line. And they're not called subways here. It's the T. Why is the T so bad? All of the stations smell, and, seems to me, none of the rusted tin cans that comprise each of the color-coded T cars have been upgraded since the pilgrims landed and held witch trials. As for running on schedule, or riding without having to push your body sideways between bodies bearing face-smashing backpacks, well, that's like pinning your hopes on winning the lottery to get out of a terrible job. Asking Boston politicians to open the purse and modernize infrastructure, with upgraded technology, safety, good lighting, and reliability, so that regular people and women traveling alone can travel on time and safely, is like asking the city to root for the Yankees. Nobody really

knows how many sexual assaults or men stalking women occurs
in these poorly-lit, understaffed stations and T cars. I don't know
if I can count that high.

And I've got one of the men outside my penthouse yesterday
stalking me in this crumbling station of screeching iron wheels,
of a cauldron of heavy scents, a mixture of burnt coffee, hot summer air, smoke, and crowd scents. I step on a fresh wad of gum
and pry-pull my green boot in a snap of rubber.

Scanning the track signs, I head down a dark, greasy, brown-
brick stairwell built decades before my birth, to the track with the
rusted orange T that will hurl me down a rat-filled tunnel with
broken lightening to Downtown Crossing. There, I'll transfer
to the Red Line for South Station. At the bottom of the stairs, I
casually turn and confirm that the Penthouse Man saw me stroll
down these stairs. He's trying to make it look like he's not following me. For sure, I am confident, this guy is one of the two men
from yesterday.

The screeching iron wheels are so loud, I cup my ears. But
this is good, because here comes the Orange T I need. Of course
the platform is full of people. People in suits, moms chaper-
oning camp trips to the library, women with strollers, a Swiss
band dressed in Sound of Music garb. Each band member holds
a space-consuming instrument. And filling in like dark matter
everywhere are the year-round, ubiquitous college students, each
with a seam-busting backpack. Lots and lots of space competition
on the platform. The train doors open, and it's already crammed
with standing people of the same types as those on the platform.
The Swiss band pushes its way into the back doors, and thankfully I'm at the sweet spot at the front doors, so I'm able to cram my
way deep between backpacks and bodies and a couple of babies
in strollers. It is unclear in this crowd if Penthouse Man was able
to work his way in, too.

The driver jams the doors shut, and a woman screams her

backpack is caught in the doors. He opens the doors in a loud, mechanical whoosh-crack and slap.

"Get off," he yells.

She doesn't. This is a short play that runs a hundred times a day between Boston train passengers and drivers.

He closes the door again, and just as soon as he does, rockets the train forward like this is a NASA blast-off. The collective glob of us standing humans falls and bounces back.

"Hey, bud, easy on the gas," some guy yells up to the driver.

"Piss off," the driver says.

I'm holding firm on what appears to be a stainless steel pole, but I'm sure is really a solid shaft of flu germs and virus strains, Hep C and the Black Plague. It is 1,000 degrees in here, and even my ass cheeks are sweating in these sweatpants. My feet swim in boot sweat.

I still don't know if Penthouse Man got on. I fall into the lap of a lady in the seat I'm standing next to when the driver takes a hard right. I'm sure she doesn't hear my *sorry* over the screeching screams of the iron wheels—sounds like a jet plane is racing beside us. Looking up after I regain standing once again, I see the dark sides of the grime-covered tunnel pass in a black blur. We lurch into the Tufts Medical stop, more people cram on. We rocket off again, and we all fall back again. We lurch into the Chinatown stop. A couple of people get off, and more people cram on.

I still don't see Penthouse Man anywhere. Too many people, and I'm not exactly tall enough to see over many heads. My feet are drenched in sweat in these rubber boots. I might get sick.

Up ahead, the lights of Downtown Crossing dimly illuminate our approach. Plastic shopping bags flutter from the floor of the tracks. I imagine fat rats scurry fast to avoid the iron wheels. In jerky steps in this rocking car, I begin inching toward the doors, as I can't miss this stop. I don't know if I'll make it, because a clutch of college boys with backpacks is making it impossible to pass, and none of them are moving. I elbow one in the arm; he looks at my hat and scoffs. Doesn't move. I jam a green-booted heel into his foot; he calls me "Tit Eyes," and his friends laugh, which is absolutely moronic and makes no sense. Nobody budges. And now we lurch to a stop, and I fall into him; he snaps at me, "Geez, lady." Still he doesn't move. He turns, and his damn backpack, which must be stuffed with all the books his college sells, smashes my face, knocking the sunglasses to jam hard into my nose. I'm smarting from the bag-to-face punch when the doors open. I'm rubbing my sore jaw, sore nose, adjusting the sunglasses. And I'm still deep in this mass. I know from experience, the driver won't give any grace period for exiting.

A couple of people make their way out, almost victorious, like sperm breaching an ovum, gloating to the billions who fail. I look up through the arms and butts and torsos and see the driver's hand on the lever; he's about to close the door. I'm solidly wedged in the middle of these fucking backpacks. I'm about to yell to the driver, but I stop myself, because it would be good to lose Penthouse Man in the morass of the Orange Line—if indeed he's somewhere in this sea. But I also don't mind if he follows into Downtown Crossing, because I'm planning on the double dupe at the ultimate destination: South Station. Turns out, though, I don't need to yell, because here's a saving grace: a woman with a baby.

"Driver, hold on! I need ta' get off, and I got a baby!" She yells.

The driver turns, scowls, and yells, "Move it for the lady! I told you all not to cram. There are more cars coming behind me!" There are never cars coming behind, and if there are, they're just as crammed.

"Piss off," the same guy who the driver earlier told to *piss off* says. His buddies laugh. The driver flips them off.

The politicians get kickbacks, and we're all here, left to fend for ourselves.

The lady and her stroller part a path, and I follow in her wake. I've done this transfer to the Red Line at Downtown Crossing many times, as it's the fastest way to South Station, my preferred spot to wait for an Acela to New York. It's still a maddening scramble of cramming and late, lurching trains, but it's at least swifter than the gridlock of Boston's illogical streets.

I run to catch a Red T to South Station and make it just in time. In looking behind me, sure enough, in the next connected car, stands Penthouse Man. He's good at his job. I almost salute him. But I don't. I avert my eyes and keep up the charade of being oblivious to his presence.

I'm sweating my ass off and fanning my face for air. I try to tell myself to simply focus on the plan, the double dupe, to not concern myself with anything else. *I got this,* I tell myself. I hear Aunt Violet in my brain, *you got this, girl. You own this.* She used to say this to me about everything. Spelling bees, dance recitals, book reports, 4-H, everything. And she said it to her vision of future me, assuming I, like her, would someday be a fugitive. *You got this, girl. You own this. Never let them catch you.*

At each stop, more people cram on than get off. So I guess the whole damn world is going to South Station today. When we finally reach the destination, I jump out of my door, don't look behind at Penthouse Man, and find my way into the heart of the station.

Imagine an airplane hangar, that height and size. Imagine there are multiple points of entry and exit, and they are in constant flood of people coming in and out of the main entrance on the street side or at the tracks end, opposite and across a football field or more in length from the main entrance. Imagine as you enter the main entrance, you're immediately met with a Mexican restaurant on one side and a CVS on the other. Beyond that, into the heart of it all, the essential kiosks dot the space in a way that if you were any of the dozens of rafter pigeons looking down from on high, your bird self would see a wonky circle of vendors: Barbara's Bestsellers, an open-air (open to the interior of the station) bookseller, the newsstand with an indoor roof, a Dunkin' Donuts, a bar, Au Bon Pain, Annie's Pretzels, and a florist. In the middle of the kiosks is a black electrical board looming overhead and continually clicking through the arrivals and departures of regional trains and Amtrak. Beneath that are tables and chairs full of travelers. This is where I land, looking up to the black board, standing at the border of travelers at tables, and between the Dunkin' on my left and the bar at my right.

Ten long minutes pass, and I'm not seeing Penthouse Man, or any other Men, anywhere. But I know, I just know they're lurking around, because their mission, I'm sure, is to track where I go, thinking I'm going back to a safe house that holds all the data. None of this *yada yada rigamarole* between Tim Cotton and L.R. about meeting at CoCo tomorrow, lawyer to lawyer, means anything. There is no stalemate.

Checking the time on the train board, twelve minutes have passed. I spin circles to get a view on all the doors around the station. And finally, here they are. Up ahead, coming in through a track-side entrance near Barbara's Bestsellers, you can't miss them. I'm once again thanking Deanne's costume box. Lena is dressed as a nun, with full wimple and a backpack—which I trust is stuffed with our changes of clothes. Brad is dressed as Brad in his khakis and white shirt, but he's added a two-foot-high top-hat. Samera doesn't walk with them, she comes in behind, un-costumed, and hides herself in the stacks of Barbara's Bestsellers. I understand why she took the risk she took and why she's not costumed, as I don't think anyone knows she's on the team. We need her and her press pass, because even if Henry can use his position to get us access to an old acquisition's ancient archived files, we may need the resources of an AP press room to make expedient copies with powerful copiers or other document logistics beyond

Tenkill's probably standard and basic copy machines. We do not have a minute to spare in New York. It's possible, though, that I've overprepared. That by having three members join on this escapade, I've not decreased, but *increased* risk.

I wave my arms high so Brad and Lena see me. They do and come my way.

"Lovely," I say when they reach me.

We are a fisherwoman, a nun, and young man in top hat. Samera is hopefully an unknown and remains in Barbara's stacks. I, Lena, and Brad, shoulder to shoulder, stand between the Dunkin' kiosk, which has a line twenty deep, and the station's bar, which is set off by a decorative iron fence. The train sign looms in the sky in front. Looking up, I note we need to aim for the Acela to New York in a half hour. But Acela now requires advance purchase of assigned seats for First Class and sells out in Business all the time, so we need to get the tickets in the station, and not trust we can buy on the app after boarding. I call Samera's cell. "Can you get us four tickets for the next Acela to New York at the counter? We need to use names associated with my anonymous LLC."

"Lena already gave me an LLC card and some names to use. I'll use my own in case they need the buyer to verify," she says, and moves along the side wall, away from Barbara's to the interior nook of the Amtrak ticket seller windows. This is when I note definite Men standing at the self-serve ticket machines in the area in front of the doors to the full-service windows. Samera slips in behind them without being seen. I am definitely not in command of my wild emotions right now, but I'm trying. I'm fearful and anxious, but trying to be still.

The Men seem to be looking all around, given their head swivels—I can't see behind their muscle-man sunglasses to their eyeballs. Their disguises are pathetic. Obviously they've seen us. Can't miss us. While not in all-black this time, they match in center-creased khakis and crisp, navy polos, which outfit I imagine

they acquired in whatever locker room city creeps congregate—
because creeps like this must have a locker room somewhere and
it must be dank and devoid of any aesthetic value. They look like
private militia Ken Dolls. There's that same curly wire from their
shirts to their ears—the kind I know to look for. And I'm sure
Penthouse Man is somewhere behind us, alerting the Ken Dolls
to look for me.

"Don't look now. We have company at the ticket machines," I
say, looking forward and up at the train sign.

"Shit," Lena says.

"No, this may be good."

"Right," Lena says, full of sarcasm.

"We need to flush them out and divert them. I got a plan."

I'm about to tell Brad to go to the CVS at the main entrance
behind us, but a man jumps in front of us, blocking our view of
people sitting at tables under the clicking board.

The man is roly-poly and jolly and drunk. He must have
wobbled over from the bar—which I assume started serving him
as soon as they could at 11:00. It is now near noon. His cheeks
are ruddy with those drunk red circles. A pink splash colors his
rounded nose. He reeks of Sam Adams. I imagine with a white
beard and red suit, he could be Santa.

"Hey, I got a joke for ya," he says, in a booming voice, slurred
with his heavy Boston accent. He looks at me, and with two
hands, which wobble, not so much shake, he blades through the
air as if taking in my whole body and says, "A fisherman," and
then to Lena, same gesture, "A nun," and then to Brad, he pauses,
toggles his head in a way that might dislodge it, and says of Brad,
"And Bugs Bunny, walk into a bar."

I don't know what the punchline is, but Lena is giggling,
which given the circumstances, and her underlying worry for
Park, I'm sure is more nerves. Anyway, with this loud, drunk
man, whose voice carries like a bullhorn in the surround-sound

acoustics of this train station, we've certainly made a spectacle of ourselves, so mission accomplished. People sitting in chairs under the train sign, people on stools and at standing tables in the bar, and people in line at Dunkin' are all looking at us. And, check, Ken Doll Men at the ticket machines.

I look around and find Samera making her way toward the newsstand with tickets in her hands.

I elbow Lena and say through gritted teeth, "On to stage two. Brad, go into CVS, and get whoever follows you off your ass. Whatever you do, lose him and the hat. I assume you're wearing a different colored shirt under that white?"

"Yes. Got it." Brad files off. As I suspected, Ken Doll Men don't budge, as I'm sure they're tasked with trailing me and Lena. I have no idea if another muscle man is following Brad, but I assume so. I underestimated Brad earlier this summer, and I was wrong. I trust he's got this, given his expert test of me in my office, his driving maneuvers in saving us in the Newbury alley, and how he stole a whole hard drive from a locked safe. And yet, this is dangerous for us to be separated, even though a benefit of separation is separating the attention of these men.

I'm about to pull Lena to where we need to go, when the joke man pops his eyes open; he's wobbling on his feet. "A fisherman," and to Lena, "and a nun…" he blurts. A policer officer taps his shoulder from behind.

"Ralph," the cop says. "Enough, guy, come on now. Let's get you a coffee."

As the cops usher poor, drunk, funny Ralph away, Lena and I make for the ladies' room. Making a quick side-eyed glance, I note the Ken Dolls peel away from the ticket machines and follow behind. This is dangerous. I could have totally miscalculated, and they might have no qualms in barging into the bathroom. Looking across and to the entrance of the station, I see Brad enter the CVS and, sure enough, black-clothed Penthouse Man follow behind. So the Brad ploy has smoked him out of his hole. I hope this plan works. It's dangerous for the four of us to be separated in acres of train station. Dangerous for Lena and I to pin ourselves into a closed space, within a doorless hall. But we need to dupe these men. They can't know which train we take. They can't follow to New York. While I maybe could have taken a chance to avoid the Double Dupe and had us try to stay concealed in boarding the train to New York, that would mean I was not controlling the situation. There would be unknowns, and the risk of being wrong would have been high, given how Penthouse Bloke did find me in the Back Bay station, even after Nick Cage's expert evasive driving. So, we have to smoke them out.

It seems my entire life now is spent in nasty train station bathrooms. The glory of spy work, of being on the run, I guess. I'd prefer the James Bond version and me getting sex from numerous hot men in the middle of action scenes. But here we are. This is reality.

The ladies' room is packed with midday commuters, a couple of moms at the diaper station, and three older ladies with pins that mark them as part of a Freedom Trail tour group. Waiting at the end of the mirrors, punctual and efficient as my retainer is paying them to be, is Sophia and Melanie Bump from L.R.'s office. I had asked L.R. to send Sophia along with another woman associate that *both* Sophia and L.R. trust. There were no male associates they both trusted to play the role of Brad in this dupe.

Lena and I join them. None of us speak, for I already hammered out the plan on the phone with L.R. when I called at Back Bay. And I whispered on the way in to Lena, "L.R. sent women to wear our costumes as decoys." I take the backpack from Lena. Sophia enters a stall, and I the one next to it. Melanie Bump and Lena hold tight at the sinks. Under the divider, I pass Sophia my Simmons Gon' Fishin' outfit, including the sweaty green boots and big sunglasses. Poor girl was not going to avoid switching costumes with me today. We exit the stalls. I am now in a long, blonde wig, a black zip-up dress with flip flops, and a spare pair of distance eyeglasses. Sophia is now Simmons Gon' Fishin'. I can tell her soul is dying to have to wear those damn sweaty boots. Melanie Bump and Lena take our spots. Lena exits in a red wig and flowery summer dress. Melanie is a nun with backpack, which is now stuffed with her and Sophia's lawyer suits.

Looking in the mirror and brushing non-existent crumbs from her face, Sophia says to me, out of Melanie's earshot, "L.R. looked into Joe's emails. Even before you came along, he was emailing for a job at CoCo. Seems your presence today caused him to provide them intel on your exit path through Au Bon Pain and your outfit, in hopes he'd get a job. L.R. is handling it. She says to be safe and get back ASAP."

"Understood. And thank you for doing this."

"It's better than working on a motion for sanctions. I'll never forget this case."

With that, Sophia and Melanie Bump bump on out of the bathroom with their heads down, one in a bucket hat and sunglasses, the other in Nun wimple. From behind the door opening, Lena and I poke our heads out to watch Ken Doll Men follow after them toward the main entrance and opposite the train tracks where we need to go. Outside the main entrance, at the juncture of several merging serpentine streets, I see exactly what I expected: Sophia and Melanie safely enter a waiting town car and the Ken Dolls whistling for a driver to pick them up and follow. Ken Doll Men will be blocked at L.R.'s underground parking. Most of the double dupe is done, and now we need Brad to have pulled off his part.

I look over to the CVS and see in through the glass, above all the typical CVS window logos and posters. My hope dies. Penthouse Man has grabbed hold of Brad's arm, and he's pushing him out of CVS. Brad's still wearing the top hat when he, forced and constrained, exits CVS. He tries to torque away, but Penthouse Man has a death grip around his bicep. Brad is arm-dragged forward with such force, his hat topples off, end over end over end on the sloped floor to the doors. I'm not sure what to do here. I'm not sure how to save Brad. I can't have him taken, because they'd torture him to reveal the location of our safe house, and likely kill him.

"Dammit," Lena says.

Penthouse Man is pushing Brad toward the trackside, and thankfully he doesn't see us in our new wigs and outfits. But I'm not seeing a way to cut over and make a useful distraction either. They're passing the offset food court on that side, people crossing before and around them in no particular pattern. The McDonald's in the far end is packed. I'm hoping Brad has some plan, anything at all, to get away and run. Like fleas to fur, Lena and I walk his way, even though we probably should listen to the self-preservation alarms wailing in our brains and stand back. It's not like we're trained MI6 agents. Hell, I can't even throw a punch and my ankle burns in pain, especially since I can't wear the bandage, and I have to walk normally and not give in to the limp, both of which would no doubt mark me.

I'm three steps ahead of Lena when I realize she's not at my side. I spin around to find her in the grip of the *other* Penthouse Man who flanked my door yesterday. He glares at me, I feel it, through his muscle man sunglasses. "Did you honestly think we were duped by that little bathroom costume stunt, bitch? Keep walking nice and calm or your friend gets a prick of the paralytic I've got at her back."

I slide my eyes to see that, indeed, he's got one hand death-gripping Lena's arm, and the other with a tiny, but possibly deadly, certainly harmful, needle, which he quickly shows me and returns to her spine, cleverly hiding what he's doing by his closeness to her and the folds of her flowery dress.

"Walk," he says. "Nice and calm. We'll meet your friend with my friend at the pretzel stand. Tell your friend to stop flinching. I wouldn't want this needle to slip. You call for a cop, the needle slips. You don't walk the way I like, the needle slips."

"Lena, stay calm. Walk calm," I say.

We're heading toward Brad and the other Penthouse Man, and none of these busy, oblivious tourists notice a damn thing. Everyone is so self-absorbed or absorbed in phones and tablets, it's no wonder the stats are so high on human traffickers moving victims in plain sight on trains and planes and buses, in motels and name-brand hotels. Nobody is watching. Besides, our Penthouse Man looks like any other muscle man, walking with a couple of Boston broads in public.

Lena is trembling. That needle can't slip. A paralytic could be fatal.

There's no way out of this. I can't scream. I can't call for a cop. He could puncture her and flee and she'd be done. I'm sure they have a getaway car to disappear within a second flat. So I've screwed up again, thinking I could dupe trained assassins with multiple fly eyes each.

We're just about at the pretzel stand when our Penthouse Man says, "Now, listen. My friend has another paralytic on your boy there. We're all going to walk out of the station all chum-fucking-chummy and you're taking us to wherever the data is. Got it?"

I don't answer. We've caught up with Brad and the other Penthouse Man, and now we stand as a chummy, screwed-up pack of five friends in line for pretzels.

"I said, you got it?" our Penthouse Man demands.

I'm about to say yes, when suddenly, like a shock of silver in the sky, Drunk Ralph pushes into the middle of our five-person chummy friend circle. I don't know how he got away from the cops and here. But here he is with Brad's top hat. And here booms his drunk voice, the acoustics carrying his slur and accent.

"Bugs Bunny, old pal, ya' lost ya' hat!"

"Move it," Penthouse Man says to Ralph.

"Hey, I got a joke for ya! Bugs Bunny and ah," he pauses, looking Penthouse Men up and down, and adds, "a horsie horse and a Chad and…." But he again can't deliver his punch line because now Brad's Penthouse Man lets go of Brad and jabs the paralytic needle in Ralph's gut, but all of Ralph's fabric or a button blocks the needle, and the syringe, still full, clatters to the floor. Our Penthouse Man maybe has no field skills, because he says too loud, "Get the fucking needle off the ground, asshole," as he one-arm choke holds Ralph to back the fuck up, and in so doing catches the attention of cops. He's dropped Lena's arm.

Lena and I jump out of the way, while four of Boston's finest practically fly out of their black-booted feet and quadruple-team pounce the Penthouse Men, wrestling them to the ground, as four more finest hog-pile the hog-pile.

We race to Samera at the newstand.

"Track 8, now," she says.

And so we run out to Track 8.

Looking behind, the Penthouse Men are still under a pile of Boston cops, and Ralph is wobbling around the pretzel stand.

~~~

Turns out, Samera got us first-class tickets, because that's all that was left. So we're seated at a shared table in our assigned seats, but together. Thank God, we're together. Samera faces me in the aisle seats. And Lena, next to me, faces Brad in the window seats.

As Samera shows our tickets to the attendee, Lena starts reading the first-class menu.

"Tid Bits is one of the quote meals," she says, reading the

menu. "Literally they call this dish Tid Bits. You ever have Tid Bits on this train? I have. More like Shit Bits."

"This is what you're going to focus on right now, Lena? After all we just went through, you're still sweating from the run. Friggin' Brad can barely breathe. Look at him, he's wheezing. And you're critiquing the Tid Bits?"

"Shit Bits."

"I'm fine," Brad says, in that matter-of-fact voice I'm now realizing is how he talks. "I'm out of breath from running for the train is all." Another fact from him. Nothing about how a big scary dude dragged him through the station and almost stabbed him with a paralytic.

I look to Lena and shake my head. She says it to be funny to cover our obvious distress, but I know it's forced. I let it hang. I say nothing. After ten minutes of silence, and when we're good and rolling to New York, Lena falls into me, hiding her face in my shoulder, and says softly, "Is Park okay, Greta? I'm so worried." I yank an arm around her and hold her close, rub her head. I want to endlessly apologize. I will never be able to make any of this up to her. Again, I ask myself, *What have I done?*

"Babe, I'm sure he's okay. They wouldn't risk hurting him when we have pictures proving the guy at the café was the same one who claimed to be Park's business partner on the news. L.R. spelled this all out to Tim Cotton, so truly, I don't think they have much leverage over Park." I think she buys it, because she calms. And truly, I do think Park's okay, especially given L.R.'s direct warnings. But I do think they'll hold Park's well-being and whereabouts over our heads as leverage. Tim Cotton says Park is in the Bahamas. Maybe. But I don't know if that's true, and I don't want to spin Lena up on unverified claims. If I was a bad guy law partner, I'd do what CoCo has done with Park—likely lured him away to sit this one out with some kind of threat to his business, to something. Opposing parties always secure some kind of leverage against the other. But since I am not a bad guy law partner and don't hide or kill humans, my game is to get more leverage through documents. And I hope we find those documents in Tenkill's archives.

CHAPTER TWENTY

Lena reads a book Samera hands her. Brad sleeps, seemingly peacefully, or stares out the window the whole time, silent. Samera works on her iPad researching, writing. I watch everyone around us, constantly on guard. We don't talk, and it's good to get this reprieve. This time for reflection and rest.

When we cross the border into Connecticut, I call Victoria. She confirms L.R. and her security crew have finally given word that a solid transition plan is in place for Victoria to take herself and the hard drive back to the safe house.

"And the box from Henry?" I ask.

"Yes, I've got that," she answers.

Since I can't trust talking on the train too long, I ask her to call Henry and give him the deal on what's up and to expect us.

"Already did," she says. "He's expecting you. His office is at…"

"I know where his office is."

"Within the whole Tenkill complex? It's a convoluted city itself, inside Manhattan."

"Yes. I know where his office is."

"Geez, would you two get a room already?"

"Be careful heading back to Salem. You'll process that hard drive straight away?"

"*Greta.*" And then a dial tone. This, her way of reminding me not to repeatedly ask ditheringly, obvious questions to ease my own anxiety about the work plan. To shut up and trust the team.

And to never micromanage her. I exhale a relief, as I always do when I work with Victoria.

After exiting the new Amtrak Moynihan Station in New York, we load into an Uber SUV at 31st and 8th, behind a food truck. So far, we don't see anyone following, and we're heading to Tenkill. Lena and I remove our scratchy wigs.

It's late afternoon on a summer day. It's sunny, and people are out and about, filling up the sidewalks, lengthening the taxi line outside the old Penn Station. We're passing restaurants, shops, banks, buildings, specialized restaurants—like one dedicated to meatballs—all of the typical New York sights and sounds. I miss my regular business trips, and how I'd normally be heading over to my comfy, colorful hotel in SoHo, the Crosby Street. I'm thinking on my former, solo, opulent work life of fancy hotels and Alexander McQueen dresses. It's impossible not to compare my to-now norm of glam with this chaotic life on the run in ill-fitting clothes and scratchy wigs.

I look over to Lena and can see in the window's reflection her eyes move up and down the skyscraper trees of Bryant Park. I know in her mind she's mixing tubes of paint to capture the hues of their white, brown, black mottled trunks. She could restore any painting, any forest, any park. She could be Mother Nature and paint us a new earth. I take her hand, give it a squeeze, and smile at her meditating on trees.

"Lena," I say, softly, touching her arm.

"Yeah?" She's still bright-eyeing the mind-painting of the trees.

"Park is fine and we're getting him back. And, I'm going to get you back to your restorations and your riveting monographs about lost classic paintings. Promise."

"You read my monographs?"

"My favorite is the one with your theory that there's many unknown baroque works by masters, commissioned in secret by private collectors."

She turns to me, squeezes my arm. "Just a theory," she says, sending a small and short smile, and returns to sizing the world for a canvas.

My anonymous iPhone breaks me out of this singular second of peace. It's Victoria.

"V?"

"So, I'm still at your place. L.R.'s crew was about to transition me back to the safe house with Henry's box and Brad's package with the hard drive. But…."

Our Uber driver honks and jams on the brakes. We all lurch forward, our seatbelts yanking us back into place. I have no idea what Victoria just said.

"What was that?"

"L.R.'s guys stopped a guy at the door, street level. He says he's your brother Toby. He's down there still. I talked to him through the intercom. He told me to tell you this, 'Salamanders in the window by St. Peter's toes.'"

Oh my God, Toby's there.

"That's Toby. That's my brother. Tell L.R.'s guys he can come up in the elevator. Put him on the phone with me. Now. Please."

I can hear Victoria walk to my elevator intercom and buzz the directive down to L.R.'s guys and Toby on the street. And while we're waiting on Toby to come up in the lift, which is a separate shock I quarantine for the next minute, I ask, "Is L.R.'s plan on how to get you out of there and back to Salem solid, and nobody will follow?"

"Yeah, and it's weird as hell. She's obviously had to do this a bazillion times for her infamous clients, but yeah."

"I don't trust everyone in L.R.'s office."

"I got this, boss. Chill."

The whoosh and ding of my lift sounds in the background.

"Here's your brother," Victoria says, handing Toby the phone.

"Greta?"

"Toby. Oh my God, Toby. What are you doing there?"

"What the fuck is going on? Mom and Dad are freaking out. I convinced them to go into hiding, like we always planned we might have to because of Violet's shit. Oh, but no, it's not Violet, is it? It's you!"

I go to respond, but he interrupts. I've never heard Toby raise his voice, ever. He's a calm philosopher. "Oh no. Nope, Greta. I'm talking. People from your firm have shown up at both our places. They trespassed in my woods! We all saw the news this morning. I do watch TV up in Vermont, you know. I'm not a total fucking hermit. Your press conference with your lawyer was horseshit, and you know I know it. You're up to something. You're up to something, just like Violet. And I'm sticking around to make sure you don't end up like her. Where are you?"

I am floored to hear Toby so loud and so vulgar. This is a whole new range of Toby, but I need to quarantine family right now, because we're a block from Tenkill.

"I don't have time to argue. Victoria will take you to the safe house. I'm in New York. I'll be back early tomorrow. Victoria will fill you in. I trust her. And *only* her. Got it?"

He exhales loud in his annoyed, but listening, way. He's contemlating, philosophizing with the morals he battles in his head. I picture his tall and lean body, toned from his Keto life-style, from all the firewood he cuts. From all the grounds-keeping and hiking and snow-shoeing and cross-country skiing he does on his land, so as to pontificate and consider life, as he does. As he always does.

"Got it?"

"Got it," he says. And in a snap, we are colluders once again, as we were long ago, as we've been our whole lives, since our Defining Life Event with Aunt Violet. We've kept her secret between the two of us, a heavy burden to carry since we were children. Maybe this is why we've each separately decided to live mostly isolated lives—it is difficult to be true to someone else when you have a blinking, blaring secret on your mind. Maybe this is why he's single, and I have harbored what I must now recognize was, for a long time, an unattainable love. I don't know. A split-second image of Henry pops in my mind and my heart races to realize, I am on my way to see him. I've been in battle mode this whole time, but *I am on my way to see Henry, and Toby is on the phone in my penthouse.* I catch my breath because I gasp. All of my deepest loves are now dragged into this deadly game: Henry, Toby, Lena. *Lover, brother, cosmic sister.*

Toby hands the phone back to Victoria, and I hear him walk away, probably checking out my place, which he's visited all of two times in the last few years. He might be looking at the pebbles I have lined up on my windowsill. He'll be pausing at them, as he's the only one who knows what they mean. He keeps pebbles on his windowsill too. As remembrance of—or a calling card for—Aunt Violet.

Victoria whispers into the receiver, "Is he, like, single, because, do you even know what your brother looks like?" She says this over the scrape-slide of something heavy and metal.

"Victoria, just," I sigh. *How do I say this?* "Look, Toby is a whole story, and I'm pretty sure he's not for you. I'm glad he's there to go with you to Salem, though. What is that noise?"

"Did you think I wasn't going to totally steal your Jura? We're taking it to Salem, and then it's coming home with me. This is my payment for having to twirl my thumbs on your impractical couch for hours, and, well, for everything else. Hey, Toby, can you give me a hand?"

I've got Lena complaining about shit-bits, Victoria stealing my Jura, Brad snoring and clearly reaching REM, and Toby, *wham,* showing up. Samera's fine. She's doing normal stuff, like actually researching our case. I hang up.

No, Victoria is not Toby's type. His type is the near-violently independent, reclusive type, the type that would spurn an office job. The kind that might build herself a cabin in the middle of a field of flowers and restore old paintings and theorize about unknown classic paintings by classical painters and refuse monogamy, in favor of a diversified love or until someone extreme— probably otherworldly—showed up who she'd allow to blow up her world. Toby is extreme and otherworldly. Toby has the potential to blow up her world. But I'm not about to play match-maker with Lena and my backwoods, philosopher brother. No way.

CHAPTER TWENTY-ONE

It's 6:00 p.m. when we reach Tenkill, what with the New York City traffic, and the typical Amtrak delays we encountered during our train ride. Every time the train slowed, or stopped altogether, Lena would say, "Is it infrastructure week yet?" And Brad, if not sleeping, would say in his matter-of-fact style, "No. Not yet." I can't tell if he has a dry humor, or he's just full of facts and nothing else.

Samera, Lena, and Brad are waiting down in the courtyard between Henry's office and the 1890 church made of granite blocks and a slate roof with a steeple that could be from Transylvania. I can see them down below Henry's office from his fourth-floor window in a brick building of gargantuan size, built in 1905, room 17A. The radiator under his leaded window has so many coats of white paint, it's shocking any heat comes out in winter. A portable air conditioner is doing nothing to cool his old office with a tin-plated ceiling, which has water stains from lord knows how many storms. Speaking of storms, I do want to get our work done fast, as tomorrow is Tuesday, and we need to beat the predicted New England hurricane.

I haven't seen Henry yet, although I wait in his office. He left a post-it on his door:

Greta, wait here. I went to get us waters. -H

I folded and pocketed his note, because I have saved every

scrap of anything he's ever written to me, no matter what it's about. The anticipation to see him in the flesh after two years of nothing more than benign texts and a couple of quick catch-up calls that didn't dive below the surface of general work status and what shows we were binging has me practically vibrating. My veins are full of electricity.

Henry's office is as it looked on the iPad last night. Fairly small, full of books and papers, the leaded window behind him, courtyard below. Fairly standard hospital administrative office in an old, New York building made of millions of bricks. The architecture of the entire campus is such that every possible style and era is represented and cobbled together, connected by tunnels, by sky-bridges, married end-to-end in mad Frankenstein blendings, or by crooked walking paths. A whole fifteen acres of this potpourri of buildings. It's a whole world, inside the world of New York City, inside the world at large. Looking for source material to our investigation within this nesting is a great metaphor for how the corruption we seek to expose is really just one, single, buried grain of sand within a whole beach of corruption.

At this time of night, nobody else is on Henry's floor, except maybe a straggler or two on the opposite end. I'm looking down on the team in the courtyard.

"Greta," Henry says behind me, upon the slam-shut of his door. In a flash, he's here, he's back in my physical world, and nothing else exists. A web of lightning zaps every inch of my skin. I turn to see him throwing water bottles on a chair as he walks fast to me, grabbing me, embracing me. I'm burrowing my face into his chest and clutching around him for life; he's holding me so tight and saying my name over and over and I never want this *epic era to end*. Ever. Ever. He smells of his typical blend, the one I've fallen in love with five million times, his Irish Spring mixed with coffee.

"Greta, I have so much to say."

He pulls away, his hands on my shoulders. His darkest of brown eyes are wet, his irises huge. He's saying everything I've wanted to hear in how he's looking at me right now, and how he's breathing so hard, as if he ran around the circumference of the planet to find me, and now he's found me. I believe I must have died.

A knock at the door.

"Henry Palanquero," a woman's voice says. She sounds annoyed.

"That's the archivist. She's early," Henry says.

I want to take the water Henry threw on the chair and drench my electrical skin.

~~~

Henry directs the three of us out of the building to join Samera, Lena, and Brad in the courtyard, as the archivist is going to lead us to her office in the new glass and steel building behind the church. Like the senior staff who have offices there, she lobbied and won the right to have her records department take up the first floor and basement.

She's out of central casting for librarians. Hollywood's version of the quintessential woman of books and records, with a light green cardigan, over a collarless, navy and white blouse, paired with a knee-length navy skirt. Her shoes are practical Naturalizers, perfect for walking the stacks, and her hair is in two tight buns. I have no idea what her age is, she could be forty-something, she could be thirty-something. Her name is Cecilia Brown, and she doesn't like any one of us. She's made it clear she does not like surprise records requests, nor does she appreciate Henry's disregard for procedure and failure to fill out a Form 29, which, I've learned, is Tenkill's Records Request Form. She doesn't like how Henry keeps reminding her that an urgent legal compliance issue trumps procedure. She makes it *quite clear* that she is going along with our crusade and taking us to her office over her objections and with her most severe scowl. She says she's emailed the chief operations officer, a woman who oversees the operations of the whole campus, because she wants it on the record that she is complying, but in protest.

Henry says he respects her for doing that, but we are going forward with our search. All of this is said, this banter, this tension, as we walk to Cecilia Brown's first floor office in the glass and steel building. I know Henry hates to play the heavy, but he is also unrelenting and firm about it when he has to. A very big part of me wants to ditch this whole crusade and drag him to the closest bed, hide away, run away, and never return. Have one hundred of his babies on a tropical beach and read erotica novels between naked swims with him.

Thankfully, Samera is on the same page as I am, because when we get the chance to introduce ourselves to Cecilia Brown, Samera says, "I'm part of the legal team." Henry had said we're an outside legal team, helping him with this internal compliance issue.

I want to hug Samera. Because telling Cecilia that Samera is with the press would shut this show down, right now. We'd have to file a Form 29 and follow regular procedure.

We are crowded standing around Cecilia's desk, for she has no guest chairs, and I'm betting that's intentional. I think she prefers the company of plants and records. She sits behind her desk, typing on a clicky-clacky keyboard, attached to a dinosaur desktop from the Mesozoic era. Her ancient technology clashes with the building. But Cecilia Brown has made this blank space her own, for every surface, the floor, shelves, the top of her desk, her windowsill, the tops of her cabinets, are covered in a multitude of plants. We're basically in a greenhouse.

"Now," Cecilia says, while loud typing away at her old computer. She pushes up the glasses on her nose; her buns are so tight, the skin around her eyes and her forehead stretches sideways and up. She is like a cartoon of a librarian, so entirely stereo-typical, and it's impossible for me to not make assumptions of her, like I did with Brad, so I'm fighting hard against presumptions in my mind. She's still typing, typing away and saying "mm, hmm," every few seconds.

"Well?" Henry asks. He stands closest to her desk. I am attuned to any movement his body makes, so I'm fixated on how he lightly thrums his long fingers in the pockets of his pants—his way of keeping command of any nerves he may have, and which he never betrays in his work face.

I'm standing in a corner between a potted tree and a hanging spider plant. A frond tickles my cheek. Lena, Samera, and Brad are in the other corner, likewise wedged between tropical vegeta-tion in a New York office.

"So, this is odd. The doctor you're looking for, Dr. Roger Hoff, he was with Meriview Medical in the 1960s through the 1980s. Most all of those records should be in the basement here, in this building, as we're working up chronologically through the years to digitize everything."

I step out of my rainforest. "Excuse me, Ms. Brown. Two questions. First, you said digitize old records? Here?"

"Yes," she says, as if saying *yes, dummy, that's what you do with old records.* "And I know most all of the records up to 1990 should be here now, because the copy machines we've rented to do all the glass work of scanning old paper, and OCR'ing it, have to go back to the vendor next month. I'm running out of budget and time to finish up to the 1990s."

To do "glass work" means the laborious, manual process of copying paper documents on a photocopy machine, a page at a time, because old records typically don't come in uniform sizes and in a nice stack to send through an automatic feeder, as you might modern documents. Old records are often of mismatched size, style, in bound journals, random folders, and of varying

quality. To OCR means that in the glass work—scanning process—the copy machine "extracts" the text in a manner that
converts it to something searchable. So, for example, a .PDF or
a .TIFF is a picture of a paper document, a flat image. And if the
text that appears on that paper document is "read" by the copy
machine (to "OCR" it) and thus made searchable, that OCR will
"live" with the .PDF or .TIFF image, and people can then search
the text of the scanned paper document. Without OCR, you'd
have just a picture of the document.

We need Dr. Hoff's records scanned with OCR, as that would
make for a much faster and more efficient review. The fact Cecilia
Brown's mentioned they have two such machines to do so in the
basement is like winning the lottery.

"That's great," I say. "About the copy machines and OCR ca-
pability. That means we don't have to take original boxes."

"Take original boxes?!" She shouts. She's half out of her chair.

"Oh no, Ms. Brown. We won't be doing that. Counsel is just
concerned about the urgency and importance of this confidential
investigation," Henry says.

"We would never allow originals beyond this campus," Cecilia says in a snap.

"Yes, yes. Of course, Ms. Brown," Henry says.

"Apologies, Ms. Brown. I didn't mean to alarm you. So, in
your mind, all of the records up to 1990 should be in the basement?" I say.

"Well, yes, most all, yes. I'll have to put in for more rental
money to finish the remaining decades in next year's budget." She
narrows her eyes on Henry. "And I'm hoping, Mr. Palanquero,
you will join me in that request, given the need for legal to get
at old records with such short time leads and with such great
urgency."

"Of course, Ms. Brown. Of course I will join you in that budget request."

"Mm, hmm," she says. Her grimace should be bottled and sold. It's the best grimace, the most pure, I've ever witnessed. And good on her for extracting something out of this deal. She doesn't give a fuck who Henry is, his title, or that he's the hottest man on the planet. I'm beginning to love Cecilia Brown.

To me, she says, "What was your second question?"

"Ah yes, thank you," I say. I push a spider plant frond off my face, that I think has its own brain and circulatory system because it keeps finding a way to brush me. "You've said a few times, 'most all,' of Dr. Hoff's records are in the basement here. What did you mean by that qualification?"

"I meant his records are in the basement."

"But that's not what you said."

She stares at me, but not in an angry manner, more in an introspective manner. She sends that same look to her computer screen, squinting at whatever she's reading, and looking back to me, back and forth between the screen and me. The thing is, I've done this dance many times with records keepers and department managers at numerous of our corporate clients. I've learned, dozens of times over, to press in on any slight indication of less than 100% confidence in an answer on where records might be. All of the following are finds I've uncovered upon pressing into a person's slightest indication of a lack of confidence:

*A back-up hard drive with critical evidence inside an old sock, stuffed in a white sneaker, at the back of a filing cabinet;

*After laying on the floor of a janitor's closet, a critical box of 1990-era board meeting minutes, stuffed behind a rack of old coats;

*Pressed a former company president to check her garage one more time, upon which she found old invoices from her former company; they were under an oil-stained quilt, under her husband's VW Bug, which was up on wood blocks;

*Pallets of backup tapes, kept by a client's I.T. manager, in a shed on his Alabama property. Every week he a drove a batch to his shed in the trunk of his red Corvette. He did this in secret because he feared head count reduction if he pushed for allocation of more storage. The balancing of overly restrictive budgets is almost always the downfall of proper information governance.

I could write a whole book of examples, these are just four. And I know, I just *know*, Cecilia Brown, Tenkill Archivist, is suspecting there might be more Dr. Hoff records *somewhere*, which is why she baked in that qualification of "most all" in her answer. I don't think she's trying to hide anything. I just think she wants the world to be as orderly as it's supposed to be, as she prescribes it to be. And her mind demands that, by now, per her plan, *all records up to 1990,* should have been gathered and placed in *this* basement to be digitized.

"The thing is," she says, finally, after more clicking and clacking and scrutinizing whatever she's reading. "Well, no. It can't be. But," more clicking. "So when Mr. Palanquero called and said he and outside counsel needed to review Dr. Hoff's records, I went down and counted fifteen boxes in the basement, here. They're about to be scanned and shred, if I could get the temp to work overtime. But now I'm seeing an old index," she pauses and nods at whatever she's seeing on her screen. "Looks like someone recently scanned an old index of Meriview Medical's archives, and that shows a count of twenty-five boxes for Dr. Hoff. So?"

She looks up to me.

Bingo.

"Where were the old Meriview Medical archives?"

"All over this darn campus. That's one of the reasons I had them all gathered and put in the basement, here, for digitizing, like I said."

"But are you sure all of the places were double-checked? That's a big difference between the fifteen you have and the twenty-five the old index tells should be here."

She's thinking, her forehead creased. In conversing with herself, she says, "Oh, no, no, that's empty now. Must be empty now."

"What must be empty now?"

"Should be empty now," she says, half to herself, half to me.

"I think we should check whatever you're thinking about, Ms. Brown," I say, trying to sternly, but delicately, prod her consciousness back into this real tropical room.

"It's a waste of time," she says, in a defiant resolution and crossing her arms.

I have literally had this same exact conversation probably fifty times in my career with corporate and institutional client personnel. I look at her with a knowing look, and she knows I know we must check whatever this random place is in her mind that *should be* empty of all archived records. I really hope I don't have to do that annoying lawyer thing where I explain all the times I've pressed on this exact issue with people in her position, and after forcing a search, found critical information in a sock or behind old coats or under a Bug or in a shed in Alabama.

"Fine," she says.

Thank God. She, too, is experienced in the wayward ways of historical records, and their magical ability to live forever in the dark nether-regions of institutional spaces.

"Great. Thank you. Where do we look?"

"You're not going to like it. And I'm sure this is a waste of time. But, you insist, Counsel. You're going to wish you had more formidable shoes than those flip-flops you're wearing, but fine." She's standing and peering over her desk at my flimsy footwear. "And I'm not taking a whole train of you into this labyrinth." She turns to Henry, "Mr. Palanquero, since you're Head of Compliance, I guess I can trust you to head down to the basement with two out of the group and start looking at the Dr. Hoff boxes I did pull. They're on the table in the middle of the room, by the two rental copiers. I'll take Ms. Seville, and who else?"

I look to Brad. I'm bringing, as I would on a case, my junior associate. I point to him.

"Okay then, get ready. It's a trek."

She walks over to a white closet door, pulls out a flashlight, and says, "Come on. And someone better be ordering me a dinner if I have to work with you tonight."

"Whatever you want, Ms. Brown," Henry calls, as she heads out her office door, and we follow her. She walks fast with a forward-leftward-lean, and she's muttering under her breath about the inconvenience and colossal waste of time all of this is, and I love her so much for all of her raw, real theater. I love her for being who she is and unfazed and thorough and true and openly bothered by the head of compliance making her deviate from a standard records request protocol. Under normal circumstances, I prefer people who follow rules.

We're about to step outside. Her floor is entirely empty, so her voice carries through the glass and steel atrium, when she turns and yells to Henry and the others leaving her office, "I want pho from Cha Pa's in Hell's Kitchen."

"Right away, Ms. Brown," Henry yells back.

"And extra beef!"

"Hey, Henry. Same for me," I yell.

"Me too," says Brad.

Cecilia scoffs, annoyed we would copy her.

Outside, she's hurrying along the outer perimeter of the courtyard, and we slip into a yellow-brick building in a back corner, behind Henry's red-brick building. "This is the old morgue," she says. "This connects to the ear and eye research building, which connects to the cafeteria, which connects to the auditorium, and no map would show you the way we're going. The auditorium is closed up, locked up, right now, so we're going to have to access *via* the buildings. And, trust me, we need to not be seen by campus security, because even I don't want to be slowed down by their insipid questions."

"Thank you, Ms. Brown."

"Please, call me, Cecilia. I bet I'm younger than you."

"I didn't mean to offend, really. Apologies. Cecilia."

She doesn't respond. Keeps moving along in her left-forward-leaning fast walk. The morgue has the feel of underwater pressure in the deep end of the pool, along with the disorienting buzz of fluorescent lights zapping. This type of atmosphere always bothers me on an existential level, so I'm thrilled when Cecilia butt bumps a door into an exit stairwell, we descend one flight, and enter a narrow ramp that leads into another building. "Come along now," she says. "These pictures here on the walls, delivering us into the ear and eye research building, these are medical oddities found in eyes and ears."

I stop at a blow-up of a person with my rare condition.

"I have this," I say, stalling at the picture. It's an enlargement of an iris with baubles and bubbles of colors.

She stops to look. Brad is behind me.

"You have Christmas tree cataracts?" She asks, suddenly warm.

"I do. Yes."

"So do I!" She's beaming. And now without the scowl, and looking at her anew, imagining her without the tight buns, and under her rimless glasses, I do see that she is younger than me. I'm guessing early thirties. Her whole vibe, and how she used the word *formidable* in reference to shoe wear, made me think she was older. But I was clouded by my mission and my presumptions about her to see her for who she really is.

I smile wide.

"I've never met anyone else with this congenital anomaly. They say it's benign, can't do anything about it," I say.

We're moving along again, heading into the research building.

"Well, mine's not benign," she says. "Hold on, let's be quiet for this part. Just in case." She's leading us through snaky halls, up service stairs, down, down, down service stairs, and now into the cafeteria.

After passing through the empty kitchen, for apparently it only serves breakfast and lunch, we descend several flights of stairs into, what I think might be, the bottom layer of hell, given the depth we're mining. I'm hung up on Cecilia's cliffhanger about her Christmas tree cataracts not being benign. This is one of my greatest anxieties. This possibility.

We enter an underground tunnel.

"Okay, so this tunnel leads under the old auditorium. They have concerts up there. It's a theater. Great sound."

As we walk this dark, underground tunnel, she says, "My Christmas cataracts are the kind that are dangerous. They mean an unavoidable neurological degradation, over time."

It's that same *Humans of New York* truth. Never ever assume you know a person by how they first appear. And yet, it truly is important, especially for women, to heed Aunt Violet's advice to *follow your instincts*. But instincts are different from presumptions. My instincts on Cecilia are bright, trusting. I want to hug her for sharing something so personal, so scary. At least scary to me, since it's the thing I fear.

"I'm so sorry," I say.

She stops, turns to me, "I'm happy for you that they've said yours are benign."

This issue, this exact issue. I breathe in heavy, close my eyes. I think I've made my optometrist confirm that I am fine, and mine are benign, at least a hundred times. But that doesn't ease the anxiety of reading what the internet says. "Cecilia, I'm really sorry about your cataracts. I don't know what to say."

"It helps to work a lot, keep my mind focused, you know."

"I understand. Thank you so much for helping us. I know how important it is to keep records and follow procedure. In fact, part of my job is to write those procedural policies, like your Form 29. And I know how incredibly rude it is for us to spring ourselves on you, on a nice summer night, no less. I promise you, I will personally make it up to you. I hope you know we will take great care of whatever we think we need to review."

She stops at the end of the tunnel, which is arched and shadowed, the plaster walls cracking. Looking at me with an openness she didn't have when we started, she says, "Thank you." Looking to Brad, behind me, she says, "Okay, you guys ready?"

She opens a heavy wooden door that I think was ripped out of and shipped over from a medieval castle. She flicks on her flashlight. If we were to scream down here, nobody would hear, and our bodies wouldn't be found for years. Nobody comes down here, it's obvious. The dank, musty smell hits us from a whoosh of cold air that meets our faces. It is black beyond the gray cone of Cecilia's flashlight.

"No lights down here. This is the auditorium basement, and some brainiac had the bright idea to stuff old boxes in the nooks in the 1980s. They were always shuffling boxes around, building to building, basement to basement. There truly shouldn't be anything else down here anymore. But, let's be sure"

She's poking her way through cobwebs, shining her light in

cubbies and nooks and old basement rooms that are empty, but for disconnected vents and unused boilers. "See, nothing." The smell is that of heavy mildew, wet dirt, and seeping concrete.

At the end, about six feet up off the cracked concrete floor, is a wooden hatch, or a door, I can't tell. It's a square, about three by three.

"What's that?"

She shines her light. "A doorway to the crawlspace, beneath the stage, I think?"

I move past her; she hands me her flashlight.

Brad, behind me, is rummaging in a separate room, and comes up to me with a wooden crate. "This was in there, by an old boiler," he says. "You can stand on it."

He sets it down, I stand on it, and find a metal pull ring on the crawlspace door. The ring is grimy, and the grooves in the wooden square are filled with bugs, cocoons, and spiderwebs. I'm positive this door has not been opened in decades. So if there are old records stuffed in the underbelly of the auditorium stage, they were not moved to Cecilia's basement as instructed.

I pull. It doesn't budge.

I pull. A little creak.

I pull, and the damn thing flies open, forcing me backwards, toppling off the box, but Cecilia catches me in time and pushes me straight. I shine the light in the crawlspace. Two red eyes stare back—a rat. I shout, and it scurries off.

I wash the light over the space, revealing dozens and dozens of boxes. Maybe hundreds.

Cecilia is up on her toes beside me, looking in.

"Son of a bitch," she says. "Nobody does a thorough job anymore. I told them to look everywhere for all the boxes."

"Ayup," I say. "I know you did."

~~~

212

After we discovered the boxes in the crawlspace, I climbed in and dragged, one by one, each box to the edge, at which point, Brad took it, and he or Cecilia either threw it in the boiler room as irrelevant to Dr. Hoff, or, if a Dr. Hoff box, stacked along the hall. It took us a good hour to do this triage work, and all the while, I had to shout back rats. It was horrifying. When I finally emerged, I was filthy, knees dirty and muddy, hair full of spiderwebs, and even a spider, which Cecilia kindly flicked out. The three of us took a box each and made the roundtrip three times, until all of Dr. Hoff's boxes were shuttled into the basement where Cecilia had wanted them in the first place.

Cecilia sent me to a staff shower by her office and gave me a change of clothes, a spare jogger suit, that I quite like. We're friends now.

We're all working in the basement of the glass and steel building, taking shifts doing the glasswork on all twenty-five boxes of Dr. Hoff's records. It's slow work, as the papers and folders include index cards, thin rice paper, double-sided records, handwritten notes on all sizes of paper, brochures with notes, and so on. The boxes are stuffed with thousands of pages each. Upon spot-checking, we've seen numerous items that seem directly on point. But they're also somewhat coded in isolation and strewn in no particular order throughout—we haven't found yet—as was promised in the emails between Honeywell and Wisconsin Albatross—one folder labeled "Population Deminimus." We have seen that phrase though, and phrases like, "Identify and train new MD's, sheen of validation," "Return investment from campaigns—policy must push privatization," "What is ROI on population control? What incentive? What is the hedge investment?" And, most telling is a small handwritten note in the margins of a medical record, "Zeta fund for back-end ghost market speculators. R.J. Cotton to use firm for trade tips to group." *Insider trading.*

Bingo. And here's our first connection to Coarse & Cotton. R.J. Cotton is Ram Jude Cotton, *the* original Cotton, Tim Cotton's daddy. And him using firm information for "trade tips" can mean nothing other than he was supplying confidential client information for insider trading. It's seeming to me that the Zeta group ghost market was pulling from different lines of funds, campaign donations, kickbacks, and insider trading—which likely means what we're talking about is money laundering. But I need to see all the pieces together and build the story, the ecosystem. The pieces are being found, but we still need to put this all together.

So now the question is, did daddy R.J. Cotton rope in baby-boy Tim Cotton into the whole ghost market Zeta scheme? We need to get back to the War Room, piece it all together, fill in holes with full document review, and map it all out. Make it clear in order to demonstrate an understandable and convincing ecosystem of corruption.

We don't have time to read everything in depth and connect dots, because we need to scan and OCR and get out of here as soon as possible. Cecilia is "very bothered" that there were, on our count, 200 boxes under the auditorium. She is suspicious as to why they were ever put there in the first place. She notes the COO, who she had emailed earlier in the evening when she hated us, has been at Tenkill for, "as long as dirt on the Earth" and is "sketchy."

The copy process is long and exhausting, and we're all exhausted anyway from a long day, so, knowing we have hard work ahead when we get back to Salem, those of us not scanning at one of the two machines nap on the floor. Or, others of us stand guard at the basement door, listening for any sounds, anyone who might want to stop us. At some point in this long night, Henry lays on the floor next to me, and holds me. The feeling is like I finally found a home. That I am home. Despite the danger and stress and exhaustion of our current reality, I could lie like this forever—it doesn't matter how cold the floor is, my soul is warm. Still, as the hours grow into the night, I become paranoid at every little noise, so my napping rounds are really me jerking up to sitting and saying, "What was that?"

It is now five o'clock in the morning, the sun is coming up, which I can see through the slivers of windows at the basement ceiling. Our extra-beef pho is long gone and in the trash by the copiers. Several cans of Coke and Sprite and candy bar wrappers from the basement vending machine litter the table with the Dr. Hoff boxes.

"That's it. That's the last of it," Brad says, pulling a thumb-drive from one copier, and another from the other. Those thumb-drives hold the electronic versions of all our scanning. Looking around the room, I see that Brad was the last to remain awake, as Lena and Cecilia, who were to be guarding the door, are slumped beside the doorframe and asleep. Henry is next to me and snoring. And Samera is asleep under the Dr. Hoff boxes table. I feel bad for asking her to come on this trek, because she could have stayed behind to continue her research with Victoria, safe at the safe house. I do this on cases, I have been accused of over-preparing.

Cecilia is flustered as she awakes, "Excuse me," she says. "Gotta pee." She runs up the basement stairs. Samera scrambles out from under the table and runs after her, "Me too."

The rest of us, Brad, Lena, Henry, and I, spend five minutes cleaning up and gathering our items. We start to head up to join Samera and Cecilia.

I'm the first to open the basement door to head up the stairs. The last thing I recall is exactly that: opening the door. Now, I feel cold floor on my cheek, and I see nothing but black. A vague throbbing is coming into focus, growing sharper. A pool of sticky wetness under my cheek calls to me, claws at me to awake, to open my eyes, to see why there is screaming. Why Lena is screaming. But I fade back to black, into coldness on my cheek. Into sticky wetness and pain.

There's a scream again, this time a man's. I open my eyes to see the basement in shifting, uneven angles that twist into tunnels. My body is in the doorway. Two men in black have stormed into the room. I pull my body up to sitting, and remain slumped in the doorframe. One of the men cracks a metal pipe, a baton, I don't know what, hard against Lena's left arm, and she falls to the floor, cradling what looks like her arm, bendt the wrong way. Although her mouth is open wide, I can't hear her screams, because my brain blocks out all noise; I hear only the rush of blood in my brain, the surging pulse of nerves in my body.

My head is wobbling on my neck, and I can barely hold it straight. A searing pain keeps rocketing from my face into my head, squeezing muscle, pick-axing at my cheek bone. I look to the light blue jacket I'm wearing. I recall that Cecilia lent me her jogger after the shower. Blood is pouring from my face onto the light blue fabric. My mind tells me an unhinged story about how blue and red make purple, *how pretty, paint a picture,* but I somehow know that's shock talking, so I push that thought away. I train my wobbling head, my shifting eyes that perceive the room as moving angles and not static reality, to look over to the copiers, where the men in black have cornered Henry and Brad.

The worst thing I ever imagined happening is happening now, because in addition to Lena being beat with an iron pipe, now I witness, in slow motion, and at an angle, one of the men stab Henry in his stomach or his side, it's hard to tell. Henry falls to the floor, gasping. I'm screaming, I know I must be, although I can't hear me, because the stabber yells at the other one, the one with the iron pipe, to, "Shut that bitch up." I do not understand why I can hear demons speak, but I cannot hear my love screaming.

The man with the iron pipe swings hard at Brad's right calf, and Brad buckles to the ground. Brad's yelling in agony; and I'm looking at the blood flooding out of my beloved, my Henry. God no. I must still be screaming, because the stabber abandons hovering over Henry with the knife, actually no, he was aiming to plunge it in Henry's skull. This is what my brain is now telling me to accept, and why my brain kept me screaming.

The stabber stomps up to me and tells me to, "Shut the fuck up." And then he's bending and yelling in my face, "Where the fuck is it? Where is the hard drive of what you scanned?" A card falls out of his chest pocket. I don't think he sees it.

I'm oscillating my head, no no no no. I can't answer him. My heart, my brain, my every molecule is focused on Henry. I need to get to Henry. I need to get to Lena. I'm bleeding from my face, my head, I don't know. I see the copiers and the people and the boxes and the shelves in angles, multiple shifting angles and tunnels. Henry's bleeding on the floor. I see his eyes on me; he's mouthing that I need to stop. Be still. So I must be crawling toward him.

The stabber jams his boot on my back and pushes me to the floor, as if I'm a turtle under the pressure of a human hand.

"Where is the fucking hard drive?"

Brad, on the floor, holding his broken leg, is crying out, tears, snot, coming out of his face. "Please, please stop hurting her. Here, here they are, take them. One for each copier. Oh my God, please, it's all here." The stabber leaves me, snatches the thumb drives from Brad, and shouts down at him, "This is everything?"

"Yes, yes," Brad cries. He is downright wailing. His face red and contorted. "Oh my God, it's everything." He's staring into the stabber's eyes and sobbing that that is everything.

"Do it," the stabber says to the pipe holder, who whips out of his jacket a small can of fluid, which he pours over all twenty-five of Dr. Hoff's boxes. Next he takes his metal pipe and beats the ever-living shit out of both copy machines, and he knows where to aim, right at the hard drives in them, which might hold ephemeral copies of everything we scanned. He lights a match, throws it on the boxes he doused, and all those original papers go up in flames.

The stabber throws the thumb-drives on the floor and grounds them to smithereens under his heel.

All gone. All our disorganized puzzle pieces. All that proof. And I'm sure now, they are securing all of the other underground records around the country, so there's not a chance we'll get into any of those archives, even if we had a contact at those locations, which we don't.

These animals are either going to lock us down here to burn, or they're going to kill us, now that they've destroyed all copies of evidence. The stabber is walking over to Henry, who is curled in a ball into his wound. He's raising his knife high, and I can't move, I can't move because my brain believes I'm still a pinned turtle, even though I know, I see, that the man who was pressing me with his boot is now raising his knife over Henry and about to plunge.

The basement door crashes open behind me and a woman yells, "Stop right there, assholes!" And then a pop, a second pop, and I watch the stabber and then the pipe holder fall to the ground.

In my last minutes of consciousness, I look up from the floor to the doorway to see Samera holding a gun and Cecilia standing behind her. And now, suddenly, bringing Samera wasn't over-preparation, as she is the most critical amongst us.

On the floor by my nose, I see an ID which must have fallen off the man who stood on my back. I muster the strength to stuff the ID in my pocket before I pass out. My thoughts are homicidal for what they've done to Lena and Henry, my loves. *My loves, my loves, my loves, blankness, white light, nothing.*

CHAPTER TWENTY-TWO

I awake to the mad sounds of a hurricane outside my ER
bay. Whipping wind, branches from trees scraping the building
outside. So it's Tuesday.

There's a hurricane. Literally, a hurricane. A nurse walks in.
"You're awake?" She says.

"Where's Henry? Where's Lena?" I'm struggling to elbow up,
for the bed is flat.

"Okay, settle down. Please relax." She's working buttons so the
head of the bed rises to a sitting position.

She's looking at my heart monitor. And I do too. It's going
ballistic.

"Where are they?"

She breathes in and moves to stand at the base of my bed,
staring me down. She's obviously not going to talk until I lie back
and stop yelling. So I do that.

"Okay. Better. Your friends will be fine. Your friend Lena has
a pretty bad broken arm. It's being set up in ortho. Henry is in
surgery, stitching up his stab wound. Nothing vital was hit. But he
needs to be patched and needs some blood. Just got his flank. He
will be fine. It's a good thing you guys were on hospital grounds
and got into the ER so fast. That was a life saver."

"What about Brad?"

She tilts her head to the right. "Next bay to yours. He's got a broken shin. It's been set. Don't you want to know about *you*?"

"Sure, yeah. Yes."

"Seems they really wanted to do you in, because you got both the pipe and the knife. One of them beamed you on the skull as soon as you opened the door and the one with the knife sliced your left cheek, your friends said. Pretty deep. Hit bone. You've got two hundred stitches, my friend. And the doctor will talk more with you about this, but you're going to need plastic surgery."

I look away from her. Tears are free-falling now. "But Henry's okay? He's going to be okay?" I sob.

"Yes. He will be okay."

"When can I see him? Please take me to see him as soon as he's out of surgery."

"I will do that. Please, Ms. Seville, please relax. You have a bad concussion. No computer screens for you for at least a month."

I close my eyes, fight away the fear, the sadness. All of this was for nothing.

We're interrupted when my ER bay curtain opens, and in pokes Brad on crutches. His right leg in a cast up to his knee.

"Nurse, I'm sorry. But can I speak with Greta real quick?"

"She needs to rest, so make it fast," she says. "And you shouldn't be out of bed."

"Please, I promise. This was all so traumatic. I'll be quick. Promise."

After she pushes out through the curtain, Brad hobbles over to my bedside. He's wearing a typical ER gown and a Tenkill robe over that.

"I'm so sorry, Brad. I should never have brought us into such danger. Or, in the least, I should have stayed awake and on guard. I could have locked…"

"Shh," he says. His face is blank, no emotion. Serious. Just like he was after telling his story about his parents. A complete reversal to the emotion he showed in telling that horrific story, and also a complete reversal to how he sobbed on the floor of the basement. His eyes are fixed on me, and I don't see sparkle in them. They are almost dead of life. He repeats, "Shh," while walking fast to my bedside and leaning into me.

"What's going on?" I say, pressing my pained head into the pillow, an instinctual recoiling from him and his face, which is so weirdly close to and hovering over mine.

Once he's settled in a lean on his crutches, he reaches into his hospital robe pocket, extracts a fistful of items, and drops six thumb-drives on my stomach.

"Victoria taught me that you always make backups. *Multiple* backups. I had these in my pocket the whole time. And they haven't been out of my sight for even a millisecond. Even when they brought me to x-ray, I insisted that I carry them in a bag and kept an eye on that bag, the whole time."

I'm not blinking. I'm not talking. I'm staring at the thumb drives on my stomach. I'm staring back at his blank eyes.

"Oh my God, you're a psychopath, aren't you? That was all an act in the basement."

He leans back on his crutches. "A few psychologists *may* have said I'm a clinical sociopath or psychopath, yes. Hard to say how much I was born with versus what my trauma caused. But the emotions I showed when I told you about my parents were real. It's a wedge."

"A what? A *wedge*?"

My heart monitor goes crazy again, and the nurse rushes in.

"You're going to have to leave now, Mr. Perdunk. She needs rest." Right, Brad's ID says Perdunk. She's doesn't know he's a Vandonbeer and could buy Tenkill.

"Oh, yes, absolutely, nurse. I'm just concerned for my friend here," he says, in the sweetest tone. "One last second, and I promise, I'll pop back over to my bay." He smiles.

All an act. This is all an act. Brad is a sociopath or psycho-path. A real, live whatever the right label is, if there *is* a right label.

I look to the nurse and say, "It's fine, nurse. Just a minute, please."

"One. Minute," she says, stern.

Once she's gone, and Brad's blank expression is on me again, I ask, "What the hell does that mean, a wedge?"

"It means, if you consider the whole emotional range as a cir-cle, for some reason, I feel a wedge of emotion, a rage, a horrible grief, any time I think of my parents. But I feel nothing else in the rest of the circle of me, except flickers of rage if someone hurts an animal. I do see a doctor about this condition. He thinks it's how my brain chose to process my parents' murders. It's backward, right? The wedge should be the part that has no emotions, and the rest of the circle of me should be full of emotions."

I've represented a few CEOs who happened to be true psy-chopaths, and, over the course of three law firms, I've worked with a couple more, as the condition is endemic in the profession. I've done some reading on the topic. Not all psychopaths are se-rial killers. The condition, to some degree, and along a spectrum from light to severe, is prevalent and varied in the United States. So I'm not exactly jumping out of my skin right now, but I am rocked by how much I missed in my perception of Brad. Still, I do need to ensure something.

"And you don't have homicidal ideations?"

"I just have an unstoppable rage to get revenge on the peo-ple who killed my parents. I will stop at nothing. And, if you're worried about it, don't be. I would never kill an innocent person or animal. I want revenge. That's all I'm fixated on. I can act and blend into society because I study people in order to emulate and survive. That is all."

"How do I know you're not acting right now?"

"Because I'm not. And it's illogical to think I am when I've just delivered you all these thumb drives. I could have hidden them. But I didn't, because I need your help to get revenge. Remember, *I* recruited *you*, Greta."

This, the cold frankness of how he says it, the clarity in its simple truth, I believe.

But I don't know what to say to any of this. Not only did I misjudge Summer Brad as a bumbling knob, I misjudged the central core of who he is, what he is, with all of my pre-conceived notions. Yet, I did have zero instincts about him, and I wonder, maybe that's a good thing. Maybe it means my instincts detect nothing malevolent, no risk to survival. I hope that's the case. I close my eyes. It's too much. I feel him collect the thumb drives off my stomach.

"Leave two pairs with me," I say, opening one eye. "You go be Dexter all you want, Brad. You be you. I'm still the boss of this operation."

We need order, dammit!

"Nice job, by the way. Great fake out on them. Sorry about your leg."

He drops four drives on my belly and hops back over to his bay.

CHAPTER TWENTY-THREE

At some point in this long, windy, howling day, in between rounds of doctor visits and painkillers, a couple of detectives came and took our statements. None of us told them the specific "confidential compliance" issue we're working on. Brad acted his way through the whole thing, so I had no worries about him giving up the goods. And, thankfully, they let me and Lena answer questions together, so I controlled that whole show. My awesome nurse wheelchaired me in to see Henry when he woke up from surgery, at which point, I had all of one minute to whisper to him to not give any details on the investigation and that Brad has a copy of the files. He couldn't verbalize an answer, as he was groggy and had tubes in his throat, but he gurgled a yes that he understood. I kissed his hand and said, "I love you endlessly," before he slipped back into a drugged sleep.

Has he ever said the words back to me? Do I really need to hear the words out loud? I snap back at myself for fretting on such insecurities now.

Samera is down at the police station, since she was the justified shooter, and I know she sure as hell is not giving up details of the investigation she's been working for sixteen years. Turns out, she learned to shoot when she was a war correspondent. Guns were a necessity for self-defense in the regions she worked. The story is, when she and Cecilia left the first-floor bathroom, they saw our attackers enter the basement, at which point, Cecilia revealed she had a (licensed) gun in her office for late nights working alone. Samera and Cecilia ran back to Cecilia's greenhouse of an office and found Cecilia's gun, which was hidden within the well of a pot for what turned out to be a fake plant amongst all the real plants. Cecilia hesitated two seconds too long in picking up the gun, so Samera snatched it, ran down to the basement, and did the deed. Samera is the bravest of us all.

I'm now waiting to be cleared and discharged. I'm fine, other than my eventual need of plastic surgery. I snuck my iPhone out of the bag of my stuff someone left on a chair in my bay and surreptitiously texted L.R. and Sophia since I'm not allowed to use any screens with my concussion. Now I'm on the room's landline with L.R.

The hurricane is still going absolutely nuts outside, and the power has gone out twice, only to whoosh back on from the hospital's generator. And I have an equivalent hurricane on the other end of this phoneline, with L.R. in an all-out fit. She says she's "kicking this shit up a hundred notches." We're having a rather heated discussion about the next steps, when the detective who questioned me and Lena earlier pokes her head in.

"Do you mind? I'm talking to my lawyer?" I say.

"Oh, good. I'd like to speak with them."

"Detective wants to speak with you, L.R."

"Put her on."

The detective walks to my bed, and I hand her the receiver.

The cord is short, so she has to stand close. I hear L.R. tell her to leave me and my team the hell alone, we've been through enough. It's as if her voice is on a speakerphone.

"I got two dead bodies, Ms. Rice," the detective says, and not softly. I cringe at the sound, which she sees and whispers, "Sorry."

"My clients did nothing wrong. They're victims. You have their statements. Besides, you have bigger problems than two dead bodies. The Feds are going to be barking in your face and taking command after I'm done with this press conference. Which starts in two minutes, so you might want to turn on the news. Now, I need to go."

She hangs up.

The detective flicks on the television in my room. And sure enough, the New York anchors are telling everyone to stay tuned for a breaking news press conference out of Boston concerning a shooting in New York, involving warring Boston lawyers. This is a whole new angle on the New York/Boston rivalry. All of Boston's and New York's press are on this story.

The camera switches to L.R.'s green-gold victory wall, but this time she's seated in her red velvet chair with Sophia on one side, and—to my surprise and relief—Bo Lopez, the partner from my first firm, on the other side. So at this conference table, representing me, are the best criminal defense attorney in New England, the best civil trial attorney in New England, and now my favorite associate in New England, Sophia. All three of them are mad as hell.

In a far corner sits Joseph P. Carmichael, the traitor lawyer, who is still employed with L.R. This is *one* of the reasons L.R. and I were having a heated debate when the detective came in. The other reason was her insistence that we file a lawsuit on behalf of Coarse & Cotton, in my role as deputy general counsel—and myself as a Co-Plaintiff—against individual Defendants, the named partners, Maurice Coarse, Tim Cotton, and Raymond Honeywell.

In other words, the case caption would look like this:

Coarse & Cotton, LLP
and Greta Vinet Seville,

vs.

Maurice Coarse,
Tim Cotton, and Ray-
mond Honeywell.

I haven't done the case law research, but I'm fairly certain there's never been a suit like this. There's a whole quagmire of problems with it, the main one being—and they will surely argue—that I have no "standing" to file a lawsuit on behalf of CoCo. In other words, I have no authority to file such a lawsuit. In essence, this is kicking the whole controversy on whether I had authority to conduct the internal investigation to a whole new level.

L.R. doesn't care. She wants to control the narrative. She wants to be on the offensive offensive. "Attempted murder of my clients is a punch in the face. And you know what I say: When someone punches you, you knee them in the groin and punch them in the throat, immediately," were her last words to me, as I handed the phone to the detective.

And here L.R. is now on TV.

"Ladies and gentlemen of the press, what we are about to tell you is shocking. You've never attended a press conference like this before. And that is because most always, these scandals are buried under gag orders because firms and corporations want to hide internal crimes, whistleblowers, bad deeds, and they prefer to settle things quietly. Clients and shareholders don't like messy headlines. But we're not playing that game anymore, ladies and gentlemen. Because this scandal is too vast. And people are dead because of it; my client and her legal team are in the hospital because of it. I'm here with my co-counsel, Bo Lopez. In addition to criminal complaints we'll be lodging with various law enforcement agencies including the FBI, we have filed a multi-pronged lawsuit against Maurice Coarse, Tim Cotton, and Raymond Honeywell for a number of causes of action, and, importantly, an emergency motion to compel, demanding they turn over to us, lock stock and barrel, their personal devices, such as iPhones, tablets and laptops, and the firm's email server so we can conduct our own forensic examination.

"Because of the hurricane taking over Manhattan and barreling into New England, and some unfortunate issues with the court's calendar, that very urgent hearing is not set until Friday at 2:00 p.m., in the District of Massachusetts Federal Court, before Judge Whistler. I wish the hearing were sooner. I wish it were in ten minutes."

She pauses, stares into the sea of press with a laser fierceness. "I'll hand the mic over to Bo Lopez now. All of you know Bo, so I won't introduce him."

In his jury-relatable Boston brogue Bo says, "To put it plainly, folks, this all stems from a confidential, internal investigation CoCo partner Greta Vinet Seville is conducting of certain of the other partners at CoCo. Namely: Tim Cotton, Maurice Coarse, and Raymond Honeywell. As deputy general counsel she is authorized—and frankly is required—to conduct this investigation given credible concerns raised to her. But some people within CoCo want to stop her, and we have proof of that. Sophia?" Bo says.

Sophia—who has to be thrilled to have speaking role in what will no doubt be an international press conference—picks up a tiny remote off the mahogany conference table. She's in her standard black Ann Taylor suit, hair in a low pony. Efficient as ever, she clicks on a screen, which blooms to life to the side of the conference table. "This is a picture of the ID our client, Greta Vinet Seville, picked up off the floor. It fell from the pocket of one of the men who attacked her and her team in New York early this morning. They beat her with a lead pipe. They sliced her face open, down to the bone, which will require reconstructive surgery. These men then turned to the rest of Ms. Seville's legal team and beat and stabbed them. One lost so much blood, he was close to last rights." I don't know if Sophia said that last line about Henry to close the deal with the press, but I gasp. The detective turns up the volume.

"Thankfully," Sophia continues, "the assailants were shot and killed before they massacred the whole team. As you can clearly see, this ID identifies one of the men as from TELLWATER SECURITY. Tellwater just so happens to be the same private security company used for years by Tim Cotton when he did lobbying work in D.C., and it is the one Raymond Honeywell contracted with when he was the United States Attorney General. As you'll recall, Tellwater is the team that tear-gassed reporters trying to question then President Davis. And they've played controversial roles at the Texas border."

The press explodes with questions. The cameras flashing madly. So I guess this means we took back the narrative, and in grand fashion. And I guess this means we've blown open the investigation. But it absolutely doesn't mean we've won a damn thing. CoCo has powerful resources; the men at the center of this scheme have gotten away with their crimes and corruption for decades. There is apparently a whole ghost market, likely laundering illegal donations, kickbacks, and insider trading slush funds, all of which we need more details on to define and understand, along with names to connect. None of which we will be able to figure out until we can get back to Salem and conduct our document review.

L.R. saying she's aggrieved about the hearing being set for Friday was an act. Somehow, she bought us until Friday to prepare our argument on why Maurice, Tim, and Raymond need to hand over all of their devices and not block my access to the email server. I need to be able to give enough solid evidence to demonstrate to the court why such an extreme ask is needed, and ASAP. Our allegations about their role in attempted murder of us is a separate criminal issue, one that will require law enforcement to investigate culpability—and I have little faith, given their infection of all levels of law enforcement, that that goes anywhere at all.

I still don't understand why CoCo hasn't formally terminated my partnership or deputy counsel position.

L.R. doesn't understand either.

Her press conference was essentially her begging them to do so, because then our lawsuit becomes a breach of the partnership agreement, wrongful termination, *and* whistleblower action. CoCo still has me on the website. My firm voicemail is still working.

I'm not sure what they're playing at, because by keeping me in the position as deputy general counsel, it's like they're *begging me* to keep up this investigation.

Maybe we'll get the letter of termination today.

And we still haven't had a proof of life call from Park.

This could all go down the toilet fast. I have the sense we're being fattened for the slaughter. *Never*, Aunt Violet always said, *trust your enemies for a minute, a second, or a nanosecond.*

The detective shuts off the TV and glares at me as an exhausted parent of an unruly teen. She is done with bullshit.

"You going to give me this ID you picked up on the floor then?"

I point to my joggers on the chair.

"I put it back in the pocket. I forgot I had it. Sorry."

She shakes her head. "Fucking lawyers," she says.

PART III

MOTION TO EXAMINE FACTS AND PUT IT ALL TOGETHER

CHAPTER TWENTY-FOUR

"Call me the second you get back to Boston," Henry says, at two o'clock in the afternoon. They won't say when they'll discharge him, and he needs all the care of all the doctors since he holds my entire heart, and thankfully Tenkill has posted guards at his door. Tenkill is taking no chances on security. Afterall, this is a workplace attack on two employees, as far as Henry and Cecilia are concerned. He's super drugged and barely aware, so I promise I will and whisper that I left him a note in the inner pocket of his suit jacket. It is impossible to resist covering the dark splotches of birthmarks on his face with kisses, so as I pull my lips from his ear after the whisper, I plant four kisses on his cheek, slow and deep, and note a curve of his mouth in a jump of a smile, which could be the drugs spiking his endorphins.

Nobody will agree to drive us back to Boston in a hurricane, and the post-hurricane winds and heavy rain promise to stay past midnight. The buses and trains aren't running. L.R. doesn't have another crew she trusts enough to send for us. Hers is now at the Salem safe house, because we're past the point of me not telling L.R. where we are.

I used to worry for only my own safety, but now I'm desperate for so many.

I'm desperate for confirmation that Toby and Victoria are secured.

I'm desperate for Henry to recover.

I'm desperate to hear from Park.

I'm desperate for Lena, for Brad, for Samera, and Cecilia.

And I'm desperate to return to the safe house to process this data and look through everything: the scanned paper documents, the Honeywell thumb-drive, and the Tim Cotton hard drive. We have until Friday to piece together enough proof to keep the pressure on.

I call the only guy I know who might drive us.

"Nicolas Cage," he says on the second ring.

"Hey, Nick. Remember me? The ghost lady who looks like smog?"

"The same one I saw plastered all over the news during to-day's press conference?"

"Thought you didn't see my face?"

"Oh, I just saw a bunch of smog on the TV is all."

"You still doing urgent pickups and willing to forget my face? Especially seeing as it was those private ass clowns who banged me up, and I know you hate them."

"Ain't you in New York? That's what the news said."

"I am. Round trip, five grand cash as long as you come right now and don't say one word to anyone. We're at Tenkill E.R."

"I'm in."

"Excellent. Use the SUV, there's four of us, and three are pretty banged up. Oh, and, we need to make sure nobody follows us back."

"I'll be there by 7:00. Ain't nobody going to follow us. I'll take the Merrick and some sub-roads only I know. But hey…" He pauses. "You ever watch spy shows?"

"Sure? Why?"

"Well, who the fuck knows what trackers they planted on you and your friends. You should strip *all the way* down—even underwear, even shoes. If you don't have a change of clothes, grab some from the lost and found. Oh, and don't forget to ditch any cell phones, watches…anything they could track you with."

"Good suggestion. We'll do that. Thanks, Nick. Adding on another grand for that tip, which we should have thought up ourselves. We're new to this spy game, though."

"I got you, smog lady. We good."

~~~

Hopefully, none of these clothes have body lice, but we did as Nick suggested and switched everything out. We trashed all the burners and my anonymous iPhone too, and Samera got us new burners at a New York convenience store. Brad's thumb-drives from the copiers we kept, given that he trained his one-track-mind on them the whole time.

Nick dropped us in Saugus. Horse Trader II gave us another non-descript Ford. While there, Lena and I insisted he reach Park by phone.

"I'm good, Raven," Park said on speakerphone in Horse Trader II's trailer office.

"I didn't know you had a place down in the Bahamas. What did they do to you? What did they say? Are you safe?"

"Now, you don't worry about me, Raven. I got me under control, you know that. This here is my secret getaway place. Just trust that if I keep quiet and don't rebut their claim that you're a meth head, and if I agree to lay low and out of the way as if my body safety is at risk, they won't expose my whole off-the-book loans for clean car registrations. If they do that, all those single moms allowing me to use their IDs for clean getaway registrations will be at risk. Don't fret for old Park, Lena."

There's something bugging me about the timing and openness of Park's call, and I'm not sure what it is yet. I'm happy he's fine, and I do trust him. I'm happy we got direct proof of life, and

I'm happy that Lena is relieved. I'm not sure what is bugging me
so much. It's braided with the nagging concern I have with CoCo
not formally terminating my partnership or title.

Samera was the most fit of us to drive from Saugus to Salem.
And so here we are, having parked the second gray Ford next to
the first gray Ford in the Salem parking garage. We're a dispersed
band of banged up people, hobbling, staggering through the brick
and cobble-stone streets of Salem. We walk as if wayward zom-
bies. Which fits, it being Salem and all. And even though it's late
August and not October, many people are in costume. Witches
pace the sidewalks, tarot readers in wild hats and cosmic-star
robes sit at outdoor tables, and a Wookie and a vampire perform
a duel with squirt guns in front of the Witch Museum. We zom-
bies don't rate a second look.

Using a burner phone as we walk, I call Henry's hospital
room.

"I'm good," he says, groggy. "Glad you're safe. Need to sleep."

I hear the beeping of monitors and the scuff of nurse's shoes
in the background. I try to calm my untethered heart. But I won't
feel settled until he's back with me.

Arriving at the safehouse, we find L.R.'s security crew—a
team of two men and two women: one in a lawn chair out front,
acting as if he's just another summer tourist renting a house; one
in a street-side window on the second floor; two out back, one at
the boat, and one closer to the house on the lawn.

Lena rushes to Sleuth and MF, who rush to her. They're in a
jumble of human and pets on the floor, nosing each other's noses,
a cauldron of love and sniffing and meowing. I have to step over
the pile of them to meet Toby, who lunges for me, having waited
for me in the living room. He carries me up to my room on the
third floor. I don't fight him, because Victoria reports that the
hard drive she collected from my penthouse is still processing,
and she hasn't even started with the two thumb drives. Besides,

my discharge papers ban me from screen time due to this throbbing concussion—which I'm totally going to violate once all the processing is done.

My beautiful brother. He sits beside me, spooning me ice chips, an icepack on my forehead. It's like old times, after Violet did what she did, when Toby or I would sneak into the other's room and compare notes, comfort the other with a pat on the head, or by holding hands while sneaking into our strange, huge living room to watch late-night movies at the lowest volume while our parents slept.

It is here, now, as he cares for me, that I recall the Defining Life Event. Because it was Toby's too. I can only tell my side of things.

CHAPTER TWENTY-FIVE

(IN WHICH I RECALL AUNT VIOLET IN 1994)

Aunt Violet despised semi-automatic and automatic guns. She didn't mind hunting rifles or sports guns, because those made sense to her and had practical functionality. But she saw no use for anyone—police, military, or civilians—to own a weapon that spewed more than one bullet per round. When I was six, her daughter, my cousin, was murdered in a mall by a gunman who was disgruntled for being fired from Sears. He was deranged and had a long history of domestic violence, so he shouldn't have had a permit to drive, much less own a semi-automatic—which he altered to be fully automatic. It was the accessories, Violet said, the accessory gun market that was also to blame.

Anyway, after my cousin's murder, Aunt Violet quit her job, moved into our massive home—a former Catholic Church. She lived in the basement and spent every waking minute—in increasingly extreme ways—protesting the gun lobby, gun manufacturers, gun-friendly legislators, all of them. By the time I turned ten, she'd spent four years in our basement with her military cot from the Army Navy surplus store, weaving her way down there in the maze of discarded pews and lecterns and religious statues and broken urns. By then, she'd attended and organized about a million marches and protests, sometimes leading to arrest. The fights between Aunt Violet and my mother had reached the irreparable stage.

But I never had a problem with Violet sneaking into my bedroom to tell me stories long past bedtime; and I never had a problem with her giving me all her sage advice about how to protect yourself as a woman, and how to evade the law.

Looking back—and after decades of reflection—I believe I became her lost daughter. I was a replacement for my dead cousin. We were, after all, the same age, and we looked alike, too. Back then, after each fight or arrest, Violet always promised my mother she'd be better. But she always slipped back into her revolutionary ways.

In 1994, I was ten. It was six years after the release of the movie *Running on Empty,* in which war protestors blow up a napalm factory, and then spend years with their children on the run. Violet rented the film so many times, me and Toby can, to this day, recite most of the dialogue.

One night, after maybe our thirtieth viewing, she tiptoed past the historical church placard on my bedroom door; my parents, in renovating, had kept many of the original features in their eclectic design. She sat at the end of my twin bed. The moon was big and bright outside my granite arched window, so I had opened my white eyelet curtains. I liked when the New Hampshire bats swooped outside; I imagined they were witches partying in the sky, celebrating their moon master, even though I knew witches weren't real. But I did like to tell myself fantastical stories. My white coverlet was in gray tones. Shadows beyond the moon's light, and a subtle swath of blue, washed over my belly.

Aunt Violet patted my feet, squeezed my toes. Her fat single braid held her blonde hair away from her face. She, like my mother, was full Swede, and she was young. Only thirty. Her blue eyes were like two cerulean pools, glistening, calm, hypnotizing.

"Cool moon," she said.

"Yeah, lots of witches tonight," I said.

"Look," she said, scratching an eyebrow. "We need to talk."

I looked at her, my coverlet up to my chin. I knew she was serious. I scooched to sitting, leaning against an antique headboard
with a carved cross in the top. "Yeah?"

"You know I never lie to you, Greta. Right?"

"Yes, Aunt Violet."

"The thing is. This is going to be hard to hear, but I need you
to know the truth."

"Okay?"

"It's alright, Love. It's okay."

I remember feeling confused, and also frightened. She'd always been severe when she wasn't telling stories and was focused
on her escape tutorials. But she'd never seemed morose; she'd
never seemed sad, not like she did in that moment. Even with the
death of her child way back at the start of it all, I don't recall any
other emotion from her other than rage or impenetrable concentration—except, she'd laugh with me and Toby. This was a different Violet, one that seemed—in that moment in my room in the
wash of the moon, even with all the strength of swooping witches
outside my stone-strong window—to be giving up. Giving in.
And it was scary. I realized then how much I wanted Aunt Violet
to keep fighting. I sat up even more, the carved cross now at the
back of my head. "What's going on? Tell me the truth," I said.
Even back then, even at ten, I wanted to be given it straight.

Maybe I was like that *because* of the last four years with Aunt
Violet. Maybe I was so instantly rocked that she herself seemed
to stall in delivering me some truth, which she'd never hesitated
to do before. But then she said the words that brought her back to
me, but also led her away.

"Girl," she said, and she smiled. She winked. All the hesitations and sadness cleared. "I love how you love the truth. Nobody
gets anything by you."

"And?"

"Well, you know our movie?"

"Yeah."

"So I figured out what they did wrong. See, they didn't plan enough. Was actually a great idea to blow up that awful napalm plant, yeah? But they didn't make sure there were no people inside. And, they made the mistake of having their kids with them on the run."

"Okay?"

"Here's the truth. I've been planning for months. I'm leaving tonight, driving to Maine, waiting for the Markam Gun Company to clear. I got a janitor on the inside feeding me intel on when exactly it's clear, and then I'm going to blow the whole joint sky high. Boom!" She fanned her fingers. "They got their annual shipments in several bays, ready to leave, so that's going to be all gone. *Kabloom.* And all of their murder machinery on the factory floor that took decades to custom build. Well, that's all going to be gone by morning, darling."

"But...."

"Now, shh, shh. I need you to keep this our secret, okay? I need to do this, you know that. I'll have to disappear, love. But if you keep this secret between us special girls, I'll find a way to come and visit you at night sometimes."

She exhaled slowly through her nose and straightened her shoulders, which was always a harbinger of a lesson. "These shipments are semi-automatics destined for dozens of US police stations. Now ask yourself, why are they constantly militarizing the police around here? Huh? You notice them doing that? Of course you do, because I've told you. Well, it's all for profit, and I don't mean just the sales to the cops. Behind every evil idea and movement is someone making a profit. I mean, you got militarized cops, you feed all the conspiracy theorists that the state intends to control people, take property, so the second amendment people, they panic, and they too buy semis to match the cops. It's very intentional, the profiteers manipulate the emotional groups, see? It's an engineered, self-fulfilling prophecy. We've talked about this, yeah?"

"Yes, Aunt Violet."

"So, I'm going to go and staunch as much of it as I can. Because these drools in Washington, politicians and the men who work for them, they're all a part of that prophecy, and they are never going to do jack shit to stop the proliferation of murder, Girl. They get millions of bucks from them, you know. The politicians from gun companies. That's why."

I was ten and had listened to this tirade many times. So many times, my mother had banned her from saying her "conspiracy theories" when we ate at the kitchen counter, which was a reconstituted marble altar. But it wasn't a crazy rant, Aunt Violet gave me facts, and her conclusions made logical sense to me. Maybe her actions on those conclusions didn't exactly make sense, but I still wanted to listen. I loved how she trusted me, so young, with facts and truth and her opinions on those facts and truths.

"Is the gun company in Maine that you're going to blow up one of the ones who gives money to politicians?" I asked.

"You bet your sweet ass, girl. From 1980 to now, 1994, they've steadily given hundreds of thousands of dolarinos, every single year, in campaign donations to Maine's senators. Oh, they're clever and all and use PACs—I've told you about those. They hide their tracks. But, they give and give. We've talked about campaign donations, yeah?"

"Yes, Aunt Violet." In looking at her, she seemed so resolved in what she was going to do next, I knew nothing I could say would stop her. I'd been around this block with her so many times on nights she went off to some protest or other plan that often landed her in jail and my mom having to bail her out. In as serious a tone as I could gin up to convey my heart to her and my own strength, wanting to match her strength, I said, "I wish witches were real so they could take care of it and you didn't have to."

Aunt Violet smiled wide, looked out the window to the bats.

"Maybe I am a witch. And maybe you're a witch. Who can say we're not?"

She liked to tease me like this, but I've always been a cold-facts realist, and she knew that. I smiled. She laughed.

"Right. Witches are fantasy, and witch trials are gendercide. They've also been way beyond that on the global scale, men, Jews, Muslims—so racist and religious persecution. All in, means of control over populations, and by harnessing the bigotry, the few reap profit. But, either way, I'm a fighter, and you're a fighter, and those are facts. You know what the words persecution and bigotry mean, right? We've discussed?"

"Yes, Aunt Violet."

"Because with that brain of yours, Girl, I expect you to use your skills to battle all that rot. That's a duty of the wise." She tapped her temple.

"Yes, Aunt Violet."

Then she was kissing the top of my head, whispering how I needed to keep her secret so she could secretly visit me later, throwing up the heavy wood sash, and climbing out my window. I crawled over to look down at her on the ground. I'm not sure how she navigated the plump boxwoods. But there she stood in a white-blue ray of moon, looking up at me.

"Got to leave in secret too, babe. Got the car all packed. Arrivederci! Until we meet again. Love you loads!"

And then she ran off to her car. I watched her leave, bathed in layers of night blue and shadows, and stayed at my window until she'd driven off and was gone…really gone.

The next morning, I awoke to absolute pandemonium. Sirens outside our steeple-roofed home. It was like a lava flow of grief and anger had erupted out of the labyrinth hell of the basement and burst through the floor boards to the living sections

My father was comforting my mother in our living room; six-year-old Toby was sitting on the wood floor with a stuffed penguin. Stained glass shapes of red and blue and yellow washed over him. The bottom edge of the pane showed a salamander by the feet of St. Peter. That salamander has always been our secret code to authenticate messages between us.

Toby and I locked eyes. We said no words to each other, but we knew. Everything was different, and we were alone. We had to be strong in solitude. I truly can't explain those seconds of locking eyes with Toby and our shared thoughts, as one. His ultimate path to acceptance was to grow into a person who lives in Vermont, teaching philosophy and otherwise a hermit. And I work. I work all the time and remain unmarried. There is a safeness in solitude, I don't deny. The idea of losing Toby is too much to bear, so I've—it occurs to me—shut him mostly out.

But that morning it seemed a hundred officers were piling in, looking around, looking everywhere. And still, even with all those officers, the interior of our open-plan home did not seem full. My father saw me, let go of my mother, who collapsed to the floor, so looking over her shoulder he said, "Baby, baby. Please go back to your room. Take your brother. I'll be in in a minute."

"Okay, Dad." Because I already knew.

"Toby, come on, come with me," I said.

Toby and I went to my bedroom, which still held the placard outside, "Father Emmanuel Targasy." We worked on a Lego set until a woman in a navy jacket came to my door with my father and said, "Greta, hello. I'm Special Agent Claire Complex. Could we maybe talk about your Aunt Violet?" She looked young.

"Can someone get Toby and me some breakfast first? He's starving."

She laughed. "Oh, this one's a negotiator, I see. You'd make a great attorney."

I shrugged.

Special Agent Complex followed us into the kitchen. Toby and I sat on stools at the counter. My father worked behind Agent Complex, making me and Toby Pillsbury cinnamon rolls in the six-burner gas cooker. A mural on the headspace above the cooker was of Baby Jesus, along with the words: *St. Jerome's, Est. 1799*. I wondered what Agent Complex thought about us living in a former Catholic church, and how the living room, behind me and Toby on the counter stools, was a giant open space with the highest ceiling, emptied of pews for congregants, and filled with a couple of barn tables for working and reading, books on numerous shelves, potted trees and potted plants, and two six-cushion red couches. I wondered what she thought about the rainbow glitter of light that peppered Toby's mop of blond hair.

"Greta," Agent Complex said, knocking her knuckles on the marble counter, like a bartender. "Did your Aunt Violet say anything to you about where she was going last night?"

I forced myself not to blink.

And here is a sharp, so sharp it cuts, contradiction within myself. I despise lying. I need truth and facts. But in that moment, I stared straight into Agent Complex's eyes and said, "No. Why?" I had to keep Aunt Violet a secret if I ever wanted to see her again.

"Baby," my father said from the black stove. "Are you sure? It would help the officers a great deal if you remembered anything." I noticed he was trying to stop his body from shaking. I knew in that moment he was pulling every molecule of strength he had to keep it together for all of us. I turned and looked for my mother, who I found sobbing in a corner and three agents standing around her, and looking back on this scene as an adult, how isolated we all were in our own separate perceptions of grief. My mother, who thought then, and I think still does, that her sister had died. My father, too, although I suspect since that day, he's become clued in to my and Toby's different version of grief—knowing Violet's alive, but never being able to be with her—because my father doesn't live in as much denial as my mother. Still, for him, in that moment, he had to balance all of it, and his own emotions, in front of federal agents.

"Where is she now?" I asked, turning back around. "Where is Aunt Violet?"

Agent Complex looked to my father. He looked to the Tuscan-tiled floor, and after several beats looked back up at me.

"They think she died in an explosion last night. I'm so sorry."

I immediately went defensive, shoulders up to my ears; Toby jumped off his stool and ran through the congregation in the living room and down a hall to his bedroom. But I cemented myself on the stool because I needed one more fact. "Did they find her body?"

Agent Complex studied me, blinked once, and I knew she knew I knew something. She said, slowly, and staring at me, as if a test, "No." With that, before she could test her theory that I knew more, I pretended to be shocked and horrified and followed Toby's path of screaming grief. I slammed my Father Emmanuel bedroom door and continued denying any knowledge of Aunt Violet's plans to this day.

The Feds held several press conferences on the total obliteration of Markham Gun Company of Maine, and they noted how, shockingly, nobody except a perpetrator was harmed. They claimed the detonator, Violet Vinet, was a "crazed conspiracy theorist who died in the blast." And they arrested the janitor, who readily admitted he'd implanted himself, so as to pull off this destruction. During all of these early-day press conferences, I suspected the Feds lied about Aunt Violet dying, so they could contain the situation and put the public at ease. Close the case.

But I knew, I knew from Agent Complex's single blink and slow answer when I asked if they'd found Aunt Violet's body—I knew they considered Aunt Violet a fugitive.

Agent Complex, now sixty-two and retired, still visits me every two to three years, snooping around, asking if I've heard anything. She now says the Markham Blast is the "case that got away," and that now, even in retirement, she's still "curious." Active agents, who have inherited the cold case over the years, call me, acting all good cop, asking questions. Reporters and researchers and documentarians, they call too. I have never told any of them about Aunt Violet's post-blast visits that lasted until I was fifteen. And Toby keeps his tongue too, she visited him until he was eleven.

The first time she came back was on another fat moon about eight months after the blast. The witch bats were swooping that night as well, so when she knocked on my bedroom window, I'd convinced myself of a fantastical story that a bat had morphed into a full-grown witch beneath the pane. I startled and hid under my coverlet, but then the knock came again. I poked my head out and saw Aunt Violet's face. I pushed up the pane.

She was standing on a three-step ladder my father kept in an outbuilding.

"Father Emmanuel," she said. "I seek penance." This was one of our running jokes.

I smiled and stifled tears of joy to see her. Even though her long, blonde hair was now short and black, and she wore a green janitor's jumpsuit with the nametag, "Rina," she was Aunt Violet. I was confused, however, by her purple eyes.

"Your eyes?"

"Red contacts. Mixed with the blue, I look weird, right? I need to work on my eyes."

"Aunt Violet," I whispered. "You're not dead? Are you a ghost? I'm…"

"Shh," she said, and looked over her shoulder. "Listen, girl, I'm no damn ghost. You don't believe in ghosts, remember? I am as real as this dumb ladder. Don't you ever question your perceptions or instincts, I've told you that a hundred times. You remember that, right? You remember, never ever question your perceptions or instincts. Don't you ever let anyone gaslight you. You got that?"

"Yes, Aunt Violet."

"Now look, I popped over to say hi and I love you, and I'll come back. Remember, this is our secret. I need to hide, obviously. But I got more to come. Someday. I need to lie low for a while, but I'm out there. I need you to know that."

"I miss you," I said. And I steeled my belly to not allow my voice to crack. I forced my eyes not to blink, so the tears would be dammed. I wonder if these moments shaped my ability to steel emotions in courtrooms. I wonder.

"You are the fiercest and smartest girl in the whole wide world, and I am so proud. Here," she said. And she set a pebble on my windowsill. "Every time I come, I will leave proof I was here, something for you to remember how much I love you and how real this all is."

"Okay, Aunt Violet."

Then she blew me a kiss and trotted off, taking the ladder with her.

I now have fifteen pebbles on my windowsill. I carried them with me to college, to law school, to my first apartment, my second apartment, and now my penthouse. Fifteen times she visited, leaving these pebbles on my windowsill, and a set for Toby, too, as he had his own visits. I don't know why she stopped visiting. But there were no pebbles after my sixteenth birthday. I don't know where she is today, or *if* she is today. But I miss her galaxies of time. Other than Toby, I never told a soul about her visits—except Lena—because until now, Lena was special enough to be a secret, too. I'm going to have to tell Henry if we're to make a go of making us an actual us.

CHAPTER TWENTY-SIX

In the morning, Toby greets me with a cup of hot coffee.

"Victoria made you a cappuccino with the Jura she stole."

I sit up to take the hot, red mug from him and smile into an immediate sip.

"So, she's a real boss," he says. I can tell he likes Victoria, but is not *into* Victoria, as I predicted.

"Ayup," I say. "Trust her with my life."

"She's good, I can tell. She told me to tell you everything's processed, whatever that means. Everyone is already immersed in reviewing documents. I guess that's what they're doing? They're all down in what they call the war room, but is actually the dining room?"

"Thanks, Toby."

I slowly move to the edge of the bed, my legs dangling over the high mattress, as I bend over my thighs to catch my breath. I look up at him, bracing me, as if he is scaffolding, and I am a teetering building he must uphold. "You sat in my room the whole night, didn't you?" I ask. "Even though there's guards all around the property."

"Got me, sis. I was afraid about this concussion. Can't have you slipping into a coma."

I hold on to his arm. "I'm the one who should be looking after you, little bro."

"Ah, but we both know it was never going to be a big sis-little bro thing with us, right?"

"Nope," I say. "We're pretty much twins in all this." I don't have to spell out that by *all this* I mean *life* and *childhood loss of a loved one* and *burden of a shared secret that we shouldn't have been asked to carry.* "Thank you for coming. I'm so sorry you're in this now."

He nods silently, his face to the floor, a hand cupping his cleanshaven chin. He turns his back to me, shifting into his thinking gesture. I look to his morning shadow, cast long from the sun in the high window above my bed, stretching his six-foot body twenty feet long on the wood floor all the way to the door. His shadow is an extended image, a mirage of his contemplative professor interior, my brother's soul captured lengthwise beneath our feet. He turns back to me, assessing me sitting on the edge of the bed, and lands his thoughtful gaze on my face. The stitches under the bandage tingle.

"I just," he starts. "I guess I don't understand all you have gotten yourself into, but I am trying to catch up. Lena was up here—and, as a side note, I understand why you're friends with her. Anyway, Lena was up here with me last night trying to explain it all."

I note he meets my eyes each time he says *Lena,* and damn if his blue eyes don't sparkle to mention her name. *I knew this would happen if they met.*

"Okay," I say, sliding more than hopping off the high bed and moving slowly toward the bathroom. "And?"

"And, well, you know my top priority is to keep you safe. I can't lose you like we lost Violet, Greta."

I'm looking to him, sympathetically, conspiratorially. Between us is now my shadow, which stretches and washes over his bare feet, and behind him, his, which stretches to the door. A person could walk the length of this room by following the bridge of our interlocked souls. Perhaps the river beneath our bridge is Violet herself. I'm not going to fight Toby on whatever he suggests we do next, because at this point, I'm seeing me as him, and if he were me, my only concern would be to protect him. Screw all the corruption in the world. I feel like we're at a monumental coin toss, and Toby controls the call. If he calls it, we leave this impossible mission behind us, then we walk. I could have lost Lena and Henry. Things came too close. I will not risk Toby.

"Toby, look. I love you so much, and I can't lose you. I should have realized this a long time ago. We need to stop being fearful isolationists. We need to be brave enough to be with each other. So, I'm going to do whatever you say. If you say we walk, we walk. I don't want anyone else to get hurt, most of all, you."

He seems relieved for me to have given him the coin, the baton, whatever you want to call it. He seems happy that I would call us both out, serving more to the fear of loss than to the chance of life. He seems to agree with that conclusion, which took us both too many years to find. I see it all in his eyes, as he looks into mine, and he's six again, and I'm ten, and our home is full of cops, and we're alone in this trauma together.

"That's the thing, Greta," he says. "Lena and I," he pauses, and I swear he fights back a smile when he says Lena's name. *Oh my God! What the hell? So fast. I knew it. I knew they'd fall for each other.* "We hashed this out last night, and I resisted what she was saying at first. But she's right. You can't walk away from this, and neither will any of us. This is too big and things need to change. We're not going to change everything, or even make a sizable dent. But we have a shot at a nick, a teeny tiny ripple. And you know what I think about ripples."

Here, I have the urge to laugh, but I resist, because laughing sends an armload of spears through my cranium. He steps closer to try to pull me back to the bed. But I hold up a hand, still with a smile, and say, "Oh, I know how you feel about ripples." Toby's biggest-selling philosophy book (he sold fifty copies, mostly to his own students) is titled Ripples on This Conversation. In it, he theorizes on the nature of existence and how a single word in one conversation between two people, can ripple into wider and profound meaning across whole sets of generations, which thus, proves existence. It is a rather heavy and complex book on the philosophy of language. My favorite part goes like this: "Words, indeed, may change you, define you, dictate dictators to action, wend and weave the ways of the world, or fall on the deaf ears of those unwilling to take and absorb them."

"Okay, brother. It's settled. We go forward. But we are not leaving this house. And we are sure as hell doing whatever L.R.'s security crew say. You trust them, right? They're good?"

"They're good. Trust me, I assessed the hell out of them."

"Good. Then we go forward."

"We go forward. And yes, we're going to be careful. But you're not looking at a damn computer screen. I've carried one of the cushy armchairs to a corner of the war room, away from the screens. That's where you sit and coordinate with the team. Go get yourself ready, and I'll walk you down. I'll wait out here," he says, gesturing for me to go change in the bathroom.

At the doorway to the bathroom, I look back at him with a look of love and thanks, and then I switch my face to a teasing grin. "Oh, and, Toby, by the way, I saw your eyes glitter at the mention of Lena, in case you thought for one millisecond I missed that."

He pulls his lips into his closed mouth, raises his eyebrows. Doesn't deny a thing.

Shit. But also: of course.

"Henry's awake. He's talking to Victoria on an iPad down in the war room from bed, asking a million questions about you. He's talking slow and he's medicated, but he's down there, digitally, existing in pixels for you. I wish I had met him before meeting him on a screen, Greta. We are going to have to be better about being in each other's lives."

I am so very lucky to go through life with a brother like Toby and a friend like Lena. But I'm not sure how to navigate going forward if both of them agree on making whatever the hell this is a thing between them. Before all this, things were nicely quarantined: a box for work, a box for Lena, a box for Toby, a box for Henry. Now everything's swirling together. And the problem with mixing the colors of love is you could lose the satisfaction of green, the authenticity of orange, the brilliance of blue, and the passion of red. And thus, you could lose yourself. I suppose Lena would say that it is only in the beautiful blending that you might achieve a masterpiece. So I will keep her imagined advice in my head, as I head down into the blend of colors, action, work, noise, and passionate chaos of the war room.

It's time to fit the puzzle pieces together.

CHAPTER TWENTY-SEVEN

I sit in a corner of the war room in a tufted, blue armchair, conferring with the team. They read me key documents as they find them in the conceptual clusters of CaseSpaceAI and amongst the high-scored documents, according to the CaseCore predictive coding algorithm.

I have a couple of FaceTime calls with Henry, who Cecilia moved to her apartment, following a convoluted path she assures us no one tracked. She lives in a mid-rise in Tribeca with security *plus* three doormen. Her fifteenth-floor door has four deadbolts (she being a NY woman living alone), and there's no ledge or landing anywhere near her triple-paned and locked windows. Frankly, I think Cecilia's place sounds safer than Tenkill, so this is giving me mental space to focus on the work. How and why Henry convinced the hospital to discharge him so soon was the subject of a squall between us, but he insists he's on the mend and feels safer at Cecilia's. Fine.

I've been battling the need to quarantine worry about Henry, about Cecilia, all day. I've been battling quarantining concern about Park. About Lena and her own worry about Park, about her broken arm. About Brad and his leg. About Samera and the mental scar of having shot two men. About Toby, as always, about Toby.

I don't worry about Victoria. She's the rock in the room.

"Brad, here's the new focus cluster you asked for," she says, breaking my latest cycle of reliving Henry being stabbed. I listen again for the reassuring shuffle of the guard upstairs. I look out the front window to the one in a chair on the front lawn. Looking through the war room to the four-season glass room that looks upon the harbor, I can't see the guard at the boat or the one on the back lawn from this vantage point, as the terrain slopes to the water and is lower than the level we're on. But I can tell in the way Sleuth watches at a window—as he has been all day—that they're there. Also, I hear the crackle of a walkie upstairs, "All still out front." And the return message, "All still out back." They've repeated these checks all day.

We've been at this for hours. The room is aflutter with papers, pens rolling off the blue-tarped table, coffee cups, M&M and Snickers wrappers, Samera's Ruffles bag—and now empty tub of cream cheese—because the one Victoria rule that was immediately rejected and aggressively violated was the rule about no food in the war room. I don't know why she tries. Nobody ever follows that rule.

What we've uncovered is a chaos of facts, dredged and extracted out of millions of documents, from different data sources, different files, different time periods. Thankfully, we have Victoria's customized solution to auto-generate an easier-to-follow 3-D timeline as our hopefully eventual courtroom demonstrative, because we've got too many relevant dates and facts to convey; a traditional flat timeline would be so cluttered, it would be useless. Besides, to build a regular timeline would be manual and take way too much time.

The key finds hold lots of buzzwords that seem generally within the big wide world of "corruption," but are unclear, in their disconnected state, in how they connect to our specific focus. Words like: "push privatization," "polarization is a feature," "secrecy location," "Balkan bank," "ghost market," "Zeta fund," "campaign donations," "trade tips," and "SuperPac." All of these have appeared in key emails we've found, and some in the source papers from Tenkill. We've been able to tie those buzzwords to our investigation's narrow focus by way of bank statements and certain phrasing in emails. As always, you follow the money. What we're dealing with here is kickbacks, insider trading, and money laundering.

"Guys," I say, standing. "Stop, stop. Just *stop*. It's time to define the ecosystem in which this suspected corruption took place. Because that's going to define the boundaries of our 3-D model for the judge."

"Here we go," Victoria says, leaning back in her chair at the head of the table, away from her computer screen. She's heard me deliver this sermon many times.

"Well, it's a good thing you created that insta-3D modeling program to pull all these key findings together, because we don't have time for traditional graphics work to build one. I'll sketch the concept on the chalkboard, and then we build in Victoria's program."

Brad takes out a phone with a camera to capture what I'm about to draw, as the team will use that to guide the 3-D model. I love that I don't have to spell out every single step for him. He's a good associate. Samera helps adjust the chair Brad's leg is rested on so he can face the chalkboard, where I now stand.

"Ready?" I say, stepping to the chalkboard. I turn to the team, "What is the ecosystem, what is the planet, within which we find ourselves investigating?"

"Dark money?" Lena says, venturing a guess.

"Yes," I say. I start drawing shapes on the chalkboard. "We have Honeywell, the former AG. We have numerous references to pushing polarization and extremism. We have references to Tim, when he worked in lobbying in CoCo's DC office, pushing privatization and de-regulation. Something in one of these podcasts I was listening to, a TED talk by a campaign finance expert, Lawrence Lessig, struck me. Toby, can you hand me my notepad?"

Toby, who sits at the other end of the table, grabs the notepad and walks it to me. He returns to his seat, and I note Lena and Victoria eye-scraping his long legs during his entire journey. *Good grief.*

This war room smells of sweat and coffee and cheese and pheromones.

"Here it is," I say, reading from my notes with the readers I pull down from the top of my head. "Lessig, the campaign finance expert, relayed a story about how Al Gore wanted to advance legislation to deregulate the telecom industry, but another congressperson responded, 'But if we deregulate them, how will we raise money from them.' Lessig maintains that in order to continue to gin up campaign donations, polarization is not a bug, but a feature."

I add to my chalkboard drawing a header that reads: *$16 BILLION.*

"With these documents we've found, with their bold and rather direct statements in which they shockingly spell out, in no uncertain terms, their intention to push polarization, etcetera, we have a unique opportunity to publicly demonstrate to the judge a specific example of the insidiousness of dark money, which is all coiled up within this political structure, this polarization. The structure itself is estimated to be a $16 billion dollar enterprise, according to the podcasts I've been listening to."

I turn to the team. "Where is all this $16 billion, which is just the money we *know* about, flowing in from? Well, it all flows in and out and through these political and supporting groups—lawyers, consultants, lobbyists, media—four main pots of money: PACs, SuperPacs, small money donors, and straight up campaign fundraising." I draw lines to web it all together. Brad takes a picture so as to capture how the progression of this timelines and facts build should look when we auto-generate it.

"This is not illegal, strictly speaking. But what this does do is allow for what's called dark money. Dark money is simply illegal or illicit money for which we don't know the source. And it's hard to find the illegal bits, because it typically gets mixed with legitimate funds. You can see how you could hide illegal funds within a whopping legitimate $16 billion, right? How are those illegal funds hidden and cleaned? Well, by what's called laundromats, which are often money-laundering product lines at legitimate banks. Even legitimate banks get duped, often by their own remote branches.

"So, here, these red triangles I'm drawing represent various dark money schemes within the $16 billion political web. I could draw thousands of triangles if I wanted to capture all the byways and intricacies of opportunistic dark money." Brad takes a picture.

"We are focused on bad actors within CoCo, and the documents tell us that we're seeking their connections to something called Zeta fund, which seems like it must be this mysterious ghost market, or a secret fund within it, and we can fairly assume is a dark money laundromat, dependent on this structure's closed world and intentional polarization. Oa is one of these dark money triangles." Brad takes a picture of this next progression.

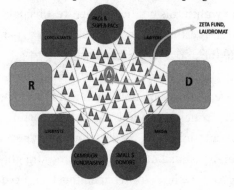

"How can we argue, with what proof, that Zeta is an illegal money laundering fund?"

Samera is clicking on her laptop. "I think it's fair to say so given these bank statements from Honeywell's data set, and from publicly available information about Zeta. Zeta Fund is a product line at the Balkan branch of the much larger parent bank, Henko Financial. All of Zeta's banking clients—dozens in fact—are bogus LLCs set up at one office building in Belize, with the same designated members. None of which have any internet presence. A classic offshore shell company factory. Honeywell's bank statements are not in his name, but, rather, the statements on his computer are for a Gray Industries, one of those benign-sounding, forgettably-named LLCs in Belize that send funds in and out of Zeta. Several statements match those $80k payments Brad discovered in the trade association documents. The funds move in and out of Zeta accounts within a matter of hours sometimes."

"Hold on, hold on," I say. "Samera, in the bank statements and other documents, do we have something to tie Raymond Honeywell to the $80k kickback payments? I mean, look, divorced from everything else, Honeywell could claim these bank statements are unrelated to him personally. He could claim he himself was investigating Zeta when he was AG, and these are his investigation files."

"I think I have the connection," Lena says. She calls up a document then leans back in her chair. Toby grumbles because I'm reading a screen, but I'm smiling as I read. It is dead-on exact and even better than Brad's Key Document #10. On Lena's screen is an email from Raymond Honeywell's CoCo email account to someone from the trade association. Raymond Honeywell writes, "Send the eighty to Gray Industries, with the subject line, *payment for electronic technics*."

Lena reads it aloud for the room.

"Lena, tell them the date of that email."

"September 16, 2020."

"Woah," Brad says. "That's on CoCo email, and smack dab when he's a CoCo partner."

"Yup," I say. "So now, for sure, a real general counsel would investigate this. Bingo."

"Let's be sure those bank statements—and certainly that Honeywell email about sending it through Gray Industries—are tagged and highlighted for our 3D model. Also, we'll need publicly-available research to explain how Zeta Fund, which is obviously illegal, can hide within a legitimate global bank," I say. We still need more.

"What about Tim Cotton?" I ask. "Let's keep reminding ourselves we are not *proving* crimes yet, we are just trying to demonstrate to the court that we have enough smoke to compel production of personal devices and the CoCo email server. That we're not on a fishing expedition."

"We have paper documents from Tenkill mentioning R.J. Cotton, right?" Toby says. "How he was using CoCo client information to give insider trading tips to Zeta members. And notes about how a special Zeta group would work with Cotton to continue to advance extreme polarizing ideas—using doctors to legitimize where medical opinions were needed. To up campaign donations, favor special interests. All of it. The notes are spread through the twenty-five Roger Hoff boxes, but when you marry them all together, that's the top-line and clear message."

"Maybe enough to pin R.J. Cotton. But he's dead, and that's not enough to pin Tim Cotton," I say. "All of it, though, could certainly be a point in our timeline to give atmosphere, if—and only if—we can tie it to some specific act or demonstrable knowledge by Tim Cotton. What do we have on Tim Cotton specifically, and what about Maurice Coarse?"

The room turns to their computers.

"We need a bigger team," Victoria says. "I've got 100 gigabytes of files that couldn't be processed into analytics and predictive coding. Like pictures and videos. Those have to be reviewed in a slog, one by one, and watching the whole thing."

"We're not getting more people, V. This is the most staff we're going to get."

I set the chalk back on the table and snatch a bag of M&Ms. I pour a handful in my palm. I'll eat all the blues first. Then the oranges.

Everyone returns to their computers, and I go back to my blue chair in the corner. Toby sets a hand on my shin in relief that I'm not looking at screens or walking around. I have to admit, I'm a little dizzy from the lecture at the board, my scar is throbbing under the gauze, and there's blooms of colors in my eyes from looking at Lena's screen. I massage my temples and remove my readers to rub my eyes.

And now, a sense of malaise washes over me. Not from the mounting migraine and eye pain and face throb, but something else. Some looming danger. I don't know what it is, this instinct, but it sure feels like an alarm about a threat to survival. Bodily harm.

I once again do a mental check on L.R.'s guards. Maybe my brain realizes it hasn't heard the crackle of their walkie-talkies in a while. I'm blocking out the noise of the war room: the clicking of the keyboards, the breathing of the team, and training all of my hearing for confirmation that our security detail is still safely in place. I note the guard in the lawn chair in the front yard. He's still there, but he's sitting upright. I wait, I hear no crackles of check-ins, and my senses, my heartbeats, are rising.

"Front status is same," the upstairs guard says after what feels like eternity.

"Back is same," one in back confirms.

I note these are different security check words from before. But I also note their voices are calm. The front guard hasn't made any sudden movements and doesn't look perturbed. The only change is that he continues to sit upright and is not pretending to read something, as before.

Brad looks over to me with his heavy-lidded eyes, that I now know would mean he's happy, if he could feel joy. And so, I know, he's found a SuperKey document.

"What is it, Brad?"

"How about an email from the backup of Tim's old firm laptop? When he was down in D.C. and using his firm email. Something he buried away in a file called *Molasses* that says, 'You're welcome on the Riser tip. Make sure it all goes to Gray, my father's typical account.'"

Gray is Gray Industries, part of the Zeta Fund.

Riser is a CoCo corporate client that went through a lucrative merger years ago.

If Tim gave an advanced tip about Riser from firm documents, that means nothing other than insider trading, just as his father did, as spelled out throughout Tenkill source documents.

"Brad, there's no way. You're teasing us."

"I'm not."

"Shut the fuck up," Victoria says.

"Nope."

"Read it again," I say.

He reads it again.

"Son of a bitch, holy shit," Samera says.

"How did you find it? Concept analytics or scored high by predictive coding?" I ask.

"Neither. Since we just learned from Samera's bank statements and Lena's email that Honeywell was directing his payouts through Zeta using the Gray Industries shell, I ran the search term *Gray*, and started reading all the hits. Obviously, there's a ton of false hits. Gray is a color, after all. But, here it is, I think this Cotton email is the missing link."

"Huh," I say. "What email is he responding to? And does anyone respond to him?"

"There are no preceding or succeeding emails to this archived message. It's divorced from the original thread. The 'to' on his email is an encrypted name, a series of numbers, and the domain of the sender is another series of numbers."

"V, how could that be?"

"A lot of reasons. One of them could be that Tim is a dumb fucking idiot criminal and thought he purged a batch of incriminating emails, but somehow allowed this singular one to stay locally on his computer."

"Well add that puppy to the timeline. And this is a perfect example of why we need access to CoCo's email server, because we only have the emails that Tim and Honeywell saved locally. Maybe the server has the emails that come before and after this Tim email telling someone to send his gains from insider trading to Gray."

"What we need is more people and more time," Victoria says under her breath.

"Well, I need water," I say, as I stand and walk to the kitchen. That malaise is growing. The truth is, I don't need water. Something is drawing me to the kitchen. Something wants me to confirm the guards in the back are there, that all is well.

CHAPTER TWENTY-EIGHT

In late August, the New England sky performs a measurable shift around six. It's something you not only see in deepening colors on the blue-purple-orange horizon, it's also a feeling on the skin. A cocooning feeling of downshift, and here close to the sea, with the constant soundtrack of waves rolling and the scent of aerosolized salt, one's breathing calms, coaxing you to end the afternoon task, or take a break.

That is, if your heart isn't racing, worrying about some unseen threat.

I watch boats docking for the night. Hear fishermen in the harbor calling about catches and the need to empty lobster traps. I hear motors on the street at the opposite end of the house. Even the seagulls have stopped swooping trashcans and tourists, resting on overpopulated perches at the apex of roofs along the water.

The guard by the boat is still by the boat. The guard up closer to the house is still by the house.

They do not appear concerned. And still. Still. Things *feel* different.

I contemplate the water, looking out over our insane rental boat, a twenty-six foot fishing vessel with twenty rod holders on the center console roof, a table for six in the bow, and the sides with highly-detailed paintings of a wide-mouthed, green gator. The boat's named—shockingly—GATOR. I'm drinking the water I said I needed, but did not need, when I excused myself from the war room. I didn't mean to invite the team to stop working, but it seems I was the one to break the seal, for now I hear feet coming closer, voices rising, laughter in the kitchen. Their lightness clashes with my rising concern.

"Time to make dinner and take a break," Samera says. "Victoria and I are going to put together a stir fry, and all of you can help."

I turn and watch Lena enter, her hurt arm cradled in her good arm. Brad hobbles in, and Toby helps him settle on the couch. Samera walks over and drops an empty paper bag on the floor beside Brad, a plastic bag full of husked corn on the cushion to his right, and the biggest colander I've ever seen on the cushion to his left.

"Can you shuck this corn? Put the cobs in the colander and the husks in the bag?"

"No problem." Again, Brad seems pleased to be given a task with rules.

Lena's pulling out a Bluetooth speaker the landlord left in a kitchen cabinet and connecting it to a dummy iPhone she bought. A sudden desire to rip the phone out of her hands and fast-ball it into a lobster boat motoring out to check traps washes over me. A flare of paranoia. There is no way anyone could hack and track her phone. No way they could know she even bought it. This is not a Ludlum spy novel. While Honeywell was once the boss of the DOJ, I do not believe the corruption we're uncovering is that deep and insidious and sophisticated.

Right?

I think what we're dealing with operates in shadows, and I don't believe its chains are fully connected and webbed throughout the US spy network. Also, pieces are wildly unsophisticated, such as Honeywell and Tim saving all these blatant emails, bank statements, and the Zeta group saving source material in hospital basements.

But we obviously do have to be careful. Why can't I enjoy Lena's happiness in scrolling for music, Samera's humming while she washes broccoli, Victoria's setting of a cutting board and her singing an ad lib showtune about *this lovely cutting board for the pep, for the pep, for the pep-pep-perrrrrs*?

I'm focused on how Sleuth and MF ignore the humans in the kitchen and stare out the back glass to the yard that slopes to the water and GATOR. Maybe that's why I came into this glassed room with my water in the first place, to see why Sleuth's back has become rigid in watching our security detail. MF's little nose is pressed to the glass.

Lena cranks the volume on her predictable dance song, *Say Goodbye to Hollywood,* and with casted arm cradled, begins to dance between the Jura on the center counter where Victoria and Samera chop vegetables and Brad on the couch. Even with a broken limb, Lena can find the rhythm with her hips and shoulders. Toby is watching with the biggest smile, and now he's raising an eyebrow as she looks at him and grinds low to the ground, legs splayed, the skirt of her dress mid-thigh. He shrugs as if to say, *fine, well done, but I'd have to see more to be truly impressed.* She turns her back to him and twerks. I'm lost in how to react to what I'm seeing between them. They are openly flirting and happy, laughing in these dance moves—as if the rest of us are not here. Victoria stalls with her mouth agape, the pepper knife in the air and not chopping.

Toby takes Lena's iPhone and scrolls through music, as Lena continues her sexy-joyful dance to Eminem. At Toby's hand, the song switches to a remix dance version of Carly Simon's *You're so Vain,* upon which Toby slinks his long legs and high hips onto the *ad hoc* dance floor, hip bumping Lena out of the spotlight upon the first line and specifically the word "yacht." He cranks out a professional-grade twerk all the way down to the floor, and oh my God, Toby can dance. This sense of humor from him is astound-

266

ing, he's alive. He's so very alive.

Victoria pours a cup of ice-chips down the front of her shirt and fans herself.

"Motherfucker," she mouths. I don't have Victoria's reaction to Toby dancing, obviously. I'm happy he's happy. He seems free, and I want Toby to be free. How he learned to dance like this, who knows. Maybe he dances with Vermont bears and moose.

The truth is, I'm not happy watching Toby and Lena. I look to Sleuth and MF, still at the windows, impervious to the party in the kitchen. This is not right. They should be in the middle of things sniffing around, yelping at the noise, making sure Lena is okay, guarding her from this tall man twerking and grinding around her. Sleuth would typically be protecting his queen. But that is not happening. Why did they let Park speak with us at Horse Trader II's? If they want him sitting this one out, wouldn't they have put a minder on him in the Bahamas? Why did they take away their leverage of maintaining the uncertainty of Park's wellbeing? Why haven't they fired me as deputy GC? How am I still a partner at CoCo? Why am I still on the firm website? Still have access to voicemail? Why haven't they ousted me?

Why are Sleuth and MF so intent on watching the back yard?

What screams for me now is this realization, one I've observed over years of litigation against the highest skilled of litigators: *The other side never gives up leverage, unless they want you to drop your guard, because they're going to take bigger leverage.*

There's a knock at the front door.

Toby shuts off the music.

We all freeze.

It's quiet now outside of the sound of the sizzle of the wok and the air-suck from the over-stove vent. The knocks continue. In a slow turn of my head to Sleuth—he hasn't budged, even with this knocking at the front door. MF is up on the sill, his tiny nose married to the glass hasn't moved either. I don't know what they're seeing or sensing. It makes no sense that they ignore the knocking at the door at the other end of the house; typically, they'd be charging the door like fearless assassins. Sleuth's back is so rigid now, you'd think his spine was a steel pole. I can't tell if he's growling or if it's the sound of my heart gonging in my ears.

Toby heads to the door, I follow.

CHAPTER TWENTY-NINE

Cecilia Brown with her tight double buns and her rimless glasses stands behind the front lawn guard, who is in the doorway. Toby's at the door before me. I can't see his face, but I imagine it's full of questions. He moves his head to the side to see past the guard and Cecilia to Henry, who is moving up the front walk in aching steps. "Is that you, Henry?" Toby says. He must recognize him from the iPad.

Henry gives a slow, pained wave.

"You verify these two?" The front lawn guard says.

"It's fine. We know them," I say to him.

Although the guard moves away to allow Cecilia and Henry to pass, he does not sit back down. He's scanning the street, the other lawns, and talking into his walkie.

This does not match the anxiety boiling in a white-hot heat inside me. I hear Sleuth bark way in the back of the house. Again, it's weird he isn't here, scanning our intruders.

"Don't worry," Cecilia says, reading my concern. I'm looking to Henry, while also inspecting the street for anyone following. The front lawn guard doesn't seem settled by my assurance that Henry and Cecilia are welcome here. "We didn't call to say we were coming because we didn't know who might be listening, or how."

Cecilia continues, "I took my mother's car from her nursing home. She never drives, and there's no way anyone would know about her let alone go all the way out to Queens to bug it."

"Henry," I call out, reaching for him, pulling him into the house past Cecilia. Cecilia shuffles in, carrying two bags. Toby nods to the front guard, steps inside, and closes the door.

"Are you *sure* nobody followed you?" Toby asks Cecilia.

"I'm sure. I've read every Le Carre. Took some other precautions and evasions..."

I leave Toby to interrogate Cecilia and lead Henry into the living room opposite the war room. I'm so worried that he's made this trip—something I did not expect, given he'd just had major surgery and almost died of blood loss. The note I'd slipped into his jacket pocket in the hospital had this address in the event I did not call him in a few days and he needed to send authorities.

I'm about to throw a million questions at him, but before I can, he stands up straight, and with the most serious face, staring into my eyes, says, "I love you, Greta," in a burst of words, as if bottled for decades under pressure. He inhales deep.

I have stopped breathing.

"I have *always* loved you, Greta. I refuse to spend another minute of my life without you. It killed me lying in that damn hospital bed, unable to speak to you with that tube in my throat, knowing I could have died never saying the words, never saying how much I love you. I'm so in love with you, Greta. I had to get here as fast as I could. Cecilia is invested in this case now. She wants in. Please forgive me for bringing her. I can't live another minute without you." He's panting, breathless. His eyes water, not from pain, but from emotion. But also, maybe pain. He's risked sepsis in his stab wound to say this, so with that, he's delivered unto me my death. He pulls me to him, kisses me. His lips burn. I am both concerned he's rocking a fever, and in a total state of bliss to feel his kiss. I pull away.

"You didn't take your meds because you wanted to be clear when you said this, right?"

"Got me," he says, and winces. Because now that he's finished his insane love mission, the pain is present and overtaking the room.

"Oh my God, Henry. Oh my God. I love you so much. Come on, you're going to bed. Cecilia," I yell over my shoulder. "Cecilia, where are his meds?"

She runs up behind me and hands me a backpack. "Here."

And so, we go up the two flights of stairs to my room, *our room*. Our progress is slow, and he's breathing hard. This is not exactly the explosive declaration of love and then aggressive sex scene I had always imagined, but he's here, and I'm here, and for a few blessed minutes of this walk to settle him in *our bed* to sleep off his wound and possible fever, I am going to enjoy this special time in history.

Henry is definitely flagging as we ascend the last set of stairs, because he slurs, half awake, "Did you open the box I sent you?"

"No, Henry, I was waiting to open it on a Zoom, while you recovered."

"Is the box here?" His voice has slipped to an inarticulate mumble.

"Shh, Henry. Shh. It's okay. It is here. Please rest."

I lead him to what I guess is now his side of our bed. Help to remove the hospital scrubs. Dole out his meds. Tuck him in. Lena tip-toes across the floorboards and sets a cold glass of water and a thermometer on the nightstand. She leaves. I take his temperature; it's a definite fever at 99.9. Not terrible, but not good, given the risk of surgical infection or a reaction to the infusion. I'll be sitting vigil and checking his temperature every half hour, even as he sleeps.

For a few minutes the world around us does not exist. All of my malaise and caution and burning instinct about danger is momentarily quarantined—but definitely present. As ever in our years of working together, I do not think rationally near Henry.

Being in love is an all-consuming insanity. It is the greatest leveler of every defense you might have taken a lifetime to build.

I am not rational. I am not sane. I am in love. This precise moment in time is the perfect moment for an aggressor to attack. The gates to the castle are open. The moat drained. This must be the bliss of an afterlife, raking his black hair to soothe him to sleep.

But my bliss dissolves, for now I hear it. Sleuth is barking and growling so loud and unending, it feels as if the walls shake. And now comes a scream and shatters upon shatters of glass. Henry is asleep. He hears nothing.

Yelling erupts one floor down, precisely where the second-floor guard was all day.

One of the burner phones buzzes in my pocket. Extracting it, I see it's L.R.

"Lost contact. Get out now!"

CHAPTER THIRTY

I walk down to the kitchen, knowing I am descending into hell. The house feels like an ice-cold ocean, its depths unending, the water black. It feels like a windstorm is cycling around outside, confusing things. As I slowly make my way down the stairs, my legs are slow, as if stuck on soggy treads. My face scar burns under the patch of gauze taped to my cheek. Reality has collided with my instincts, trapping me in horror.

I enter a melee of screaming and shattered glass.

The porch windows are blown in, debris everywhere. Looking to the backyard, I see Sleuth barking and circling around Lena, who is laying on the grass, screaming at GATOR. Several men are running from the dining room with armloads of laptops, cords dangling like open nerves, out through the opened door of the porch, crunching shattered glass as they leave in their commando boots. I do not see Brad. I do not see Toby. I do not see Samera or Victoria or Cecilia.

I look to GATOR and note three of L.R.'s crew are tied up on a bench in the stern. Men stand around the table in the bow, waiting for the others with our computers.

I don't know where L.R.'s fourth crew member—a former Marine—has gone. Given the incredible dearth in numbers of women Marines, I'm pegging all my hope on her, for she certainly has the skills if she made is as far as the Corps. But I see her nowhere.

Standing on the last tread of the service stairs into the kitchen, I sense something to my left. Inside the walk-in refrigerator beside the big-knobbed stove. Victoria is there, holding one laptop, sushing me. She presses back out of view. I look forward as if I've seen nothing, and in this moment, a man approaches me, screaming in my face, so I step into him, forcing him to step back, back, because I can't have him looking in the walk-in fridge.

Cecilia screams from the dining room, her screams coming closer. Behind the man blocking me and yelling in my face, I see another carrying Cecilia and throwing her on the couch, disturbing Brad's now-abandoned cauldron of husked corn. She lands on her right shoulder, and the corn explodes from the cauldron, shooting like mini rockets to scatter on the cushions and roll to the floor. Cecilia's top leg twists over to smash the top of the coffee table. I am quarantining everything into trauma boxes, reducing this horror to a project I must manage. A graph forms in my mind's eye of where all of my people are:

The man in front of me ducks down to my height, and now that his smarmy face is in mine, I cannot avoid hearing what he's saying. "Greta Vinet Seville, you are no longer, how shall we put it politely? You are no longer with Coarse & Cotton. We are seizing CoCo data. Do not follow, do not call anyone, or your man in the boat falls to the bottom of the Atlantic. I don't think he can swim with that leg cast. Do you understand?" He's the size of a professional wrestler, and it's possible those aren't muscles on his face, but actual embedded rats, bulging there, diseased masses of meat, squirming as his cheeks.

I don't see Toby. I don't see Samera.

I look again to the backyard. Sleuth is still circling Lena on the grass. She's sitting now, hugging into her cast. She screams at GATOR and the men hopping in with our laptops. Now that I'm looking closer, I see what Lena is screaming about. Sitting on a front cushion with two men patrolling around him is Brad. Brad keeps a stone gaze on the intruder men. He's not yelling. He's his emotionless self. He puts up no act, no effort of resistance. But I know his leg is pained to have been dragged and thrust into the boat. The three from L.R.'s security crew are tied up and gagged in the stern—there is no chance they'll be saving Brad, or any of us.

The ex-Marine, I see her now, but none of the intruder men on GATOR do. Somehow, in knowing to scan the area for her, I was able to see her belly-down on the roof of the neighbor's boathouse. She's inch-worming toward the neighbor's boat below. Maybe she intends to track Brad on GATOR. Maybe she intends to flee.

Rat Face, still crouched and leering into my face with his lingering question about whether I understand that I'm to abandon everything or Brad drowns, snaps his head toward the walk-in refrigerator. Victoria must have moved into view by mistake. I don't know. Or maybe Rat Face has rat senses and can smell her. I try to block his path. But I am a blade of grass, and he is a combine, so he shoves me to the side, and I miss cracking my skull on the island by a half-inch before landing hard on my ass.

From the floor of the kitchen, I watch two horrors. One, Rat Face drags Victoria out of the refrigerator and snatches the laptop from her. Two, from the dining room emerges the same man who threw Cecilia, now with Henry slung over his shoulder. He throws Henry on the couch, as he did Cecilia, who is now cradling her legs at the opposite end. Henry lands on his ass and crumples to the middle cushion on his side.

I go to race to him, but Rat Face smashes Victoria's laptop into the cup shelf of the Jura, stomps over to me, and—as a way to make his total dominance known—shouts, "Don't fucking move." Next, he walks over to the couch, and he and the man who carried Henry hover over him, assessing whether he's strong enough to give them a problem.

Victoria slides closer to me. As the men talk, she whispers by barely moving her lips and without turning her head, "All of our work product and my home-grown programs are on that laptop. The one on the Jura. We need to get it back."

The man who carried Henry says to Rat Face, "Found just this one mope up there. Didn't see any other electronics in any other rooms. What now?"

Because I already processed our trauma into quarantined blocks, my brain moves through a series of survival and protect commands, and I realize one thing with blinding clarity: *We are not getting Victoria's laptop back.* So the only other option is to destroy it. *Now.* Which hopefully serves the dual purpose of creating enough distraction for them to want to try to stop our destruction and thus move their horrible bodies away from Henry—while, of course, taking away from them all of our organized findings, our document coding, our highlighting, our notes. Our work product. A long shot, definitely, but we're cornered, they're looming over the love of my life, and we have to at least try *something*. What Victoria means by protecting this one laptop is that it's the central brain where all our work was maintained, and the laptops the intruders took to GATOR, were terminals without out local storage.

I hop to the part of the center island behind the Jura, which holds Victoria's powerful laptop on the cup tray. Without a second of hesitation, I unplug the beast and heave the heavy sucker over the edge onto the floor, sending the milk wand and the coffee nozzles and the bean holders and the water tank to disperse in broken parts across the floor. The laptop chassis obliterates. Keys from the keyboard roll on the floor. And in the confusion and flying shrapnel, Victoria drops to the ground, crawls and snatches the hard drive compartment, pops to her feet, jumps to the big-knob stove, throws the hard drive in the wok's remaining oil, and pours more oil in. She turns the burner on high.

"We got to go," a voice crackles through Rat Face's chest speaker.

Rat Face and his inside man are staring at me and then at the high flames, heating the wok of oil with the hard drive. Between us frozen in the kitchen and them in the living room, we're in a slow-motion triangle stand-off, one that won't last. They're still trapped in the seconds of surprise from the Big Bang of the Jura and Victoria's swift moves. Many millions of espresso and coffee beans mix as dark matter between the smashed machines. The wood floor is

Lena, cosmic sister	Yard, with Sleuth, yelling at GATOR
Henry, lover	Bed, sleeping
Victoria, litigation tech colleague, friend	Walk-in refrigerator, hiding with laptop
Cecilia, Tenkill Archivist	Couch, screaming
Brad, sociopath/psychopath associate	No idea
Toby, brother	No idea
Samera, journalist	No idea

Do we have that clear, Ms. Seville?

I nod once. I just want them to leave so I can tend to Henry, so I can find Toby, so I can find Samera, so I can figure out how to get Brad back. Make sure Lena is okay. *Leave, leave leave, leave,* I'm screaming in my mind.

"That a yes, Ms. Seville? I need to hear you say it."

"Yes," I say. "Fucking yes," I scream. "Get the fuck out of here! Leave Brad on the grass. You don't need him. We're done here. We're *done.* We won't do anything more. You have everything now. Leave and leave Brad!"

"That's pretty funny, Ms. Seville. And also, insulting. You think I don't know how computers work? Your friends wouldn't give up the passwords or tell us where there's cloud backups, so we'll be keeping Brad as insurance, until you prove that this is indeed over, and until you figure out that you're going to give us those passwords. You'll be ordered to give them up anyway soon. By the court."

"Leave!" I scream. "All these fucking huge crimes you're committing right now, as if this is going to fly? The fucking arrogance."

He chuckles, as if this is a funny, funny joke. "Come on, Rocko, let's go."

Rat Face and Rocko crunch through the glass on the back patio, soldier-jog to GATOR, hop in, and speed into the harbor and into the open sea.

Our Marine, having maneuvered herself into the neighbor's boat, and presumably found the key or hot-wired it, takes off in pursuit. How one woman, even a Laura-Croft-Wonder-Woman-level, real-life superhero, could overcome GATOR, full of many muscled intruders, is beyond me. I'm fearful for Brad, I'm panicked for Brad, for everyone, and I'm out of my mind to find Toby and Samera.

Victoria is shaking beside me at the counter. I'm breathing so hard I may puke. "Victoria, go help Lena inside. I don't think she's wearing shoes. Avoid the glass on the porch."

Victoria runs off.

Cecilia is crying so hard on the couch, I don't know if she's even in the land of the living, but she needs to answer me. "Where are Toby and Samera?" I shout to her. She stares at me, almost in a trance. "Where are they?" I keep asking, as I move to Henry, right him on the couch, check his skin—he's hot.

"I don't know. I don't know," Cecilia says. "Basement. Samera took Toby, basement."

I shove pillows around Henry so he won't fall to the floor, and race down a set of creepy basement stairs. It is an old stone basement of seeping wetness and a dirt floor. There are no rooms, just one square open space and a washer and a dryer on pallets beneath grimy skinny windows too thin to crawl through. The bulkhead is open, though, affording egress to a fenced easement between this house and the next. Nobody is slumped in a corner. Nobody is bleeding and dying on the dirt floor. No Toby. No Samera.

Footsteps overhead walk in from the front door. I run back up, through the living room, through the front foyer, and into the complete disaster of a war room to find Victoria returning with Lena and Sleuth. Cords with no computers are flung about, a decimated colony of decapitated snakes. Pens, highlighters, flashcards, papers strewn as if a cyclone hit. The chalkboard is smeared of all words, and is now white dust of nothing. MF is a coiled ball of white fur in the corner by the paintings we removed from the chalkboard wall. Around MF is a moat of blue tarp that must have been yanked from the tabletop. Sleuth crunches over the tarp and noses into MF, sniffing at him, until MF uncoils and nudges noses with Sleuth. The animals huddle together in MF's corner, beyond the blue tarp.

"Where's Toby and Samera?!" I shout to anyone who will answer.

"Samera pulled Toby into the basement as soon as she saw these guys storming in from the backyard. The rest of us didn't see them coming, but Samera was like a fucking spy. As she pulled him, she said they needed to get the Fords," Victoria says.

Lena, shaking, crying, "It's true, Greta. It's true. What the fuck is going on!"

CHAPTER THIRTY-ONE

Samera and Toby return not soon after, having waited around the corner with the Fords until the coast cleared. The plan, Samera says, was to have the vehicles close so we could get the injured in the cars and flee as fast as possible. She did not think the intruders would take anyone or hurt anyone, as they were only after the data. I suspect her source warned her they'd be executing this seizure event and want to maintain that it was simply a mission to recover firm data.

Twisted as it is, however maddening it is that she might have been forewarned, her logic makes sense. These men were not quiet in what they did. Certainly, neighbors heard and cops are likely storming the joint right now—I don't know for sure, as we fled as fast as possible so as to avoid them.

They kidnapped Brad. They took three of L.R.'s crew. They stole a boat. They committed assault. They must have high confidence they have crooked law enforcement and judges on their side—because who would commit such blatant crimes, out in the open. Or they want us to think they have everyone in their pockets so we'll back down, give up, sort of a bluff, which bluffs have worked for decades in gagging the truth. Everything is upside down.

Samera's theory, and why she grabbed Toby, was they were most likely to first detain L.R.'s security detail and then hurt the only tall, uninjured male in the house—my brother. Samera says she figured the intruders would intimidate the women and infirm, and take off with the data. Which is, in large part, exactly what they did. I'm beginning to wonder how much journalistic war training Samera has had, and I'm wondering how close her training is to actual field agent work. And I'm furious at her *again* for withholding what I suspect to be valuable intel from her source. Samera had been whispering on a call as I took Henry upstairs. I recall the image her of resting her cell to her ear as if I'm watching it now.

Had there been murders within, then homicide would get involved, and surely someone in the harbor or harbor houses saw identifiable faces. As it stands, with whatever they've filed in court to stop me and gain cover to seize CoCo data, CoCo will try to argue that this was a lawful seizure action that we resisted and thus the broken glass and screaming. It's weak, but, CoCo has connections that might allow such a weak position to fly, as long as there are no dead bodies.

I can't really probe Samera for the truth of her spy-journalism training or the forewarning she may have received, because this entire car ride she's been on the phone, talking in coded whispers with her source. She's holding up her finger at me every time I try to jam questions at her. I'm driving, I'm speeding, I'm missing collisions by fractions, but I am a certified Boston driver, skilled and trained on all the illogical one-ways and loop-d-loops and cross-dimensional, worm-hole brick alleys, just like Nicolas Cage. Of course, I shouldn't be driving with a concussion.

Samera's in the passenger's seat. Henry and Lena are in the back with Sleuth and MF. Toby is up ahead with Victoria and Cecilia.

We agreed to drive to my penthouse and park in my restricted basement. Thankfully, I paid a fortune to own two spots and my own car is still abandoned out at a stop in God knows what town on the way to Lena's. Because at this point, CoCo and their hired squad of assholes already know where we all are. With my secure building codes and me being on the fourth floor, at this point, we might as well decamp at my place.

~~~

Toby helps me settle Henry in my bed. His temperature is still at 99.9, so at least it hasn't risen. I've fed him more pain meds and antibiotics, so he's knocked out. Cecilia seems to have stopped hyperventilating. I sent her to a guest room to take a hot bath and relax. Thankfully, THC is legal in Mass now, so two edibles are working their magic into her blood stream.

Everyone, including me, needs to calm the fuck down and think.

Toby and I meet Lena, Victoria, and Samera in my kitchen. We're standing around my granite counter. Toby moved an armoire in front of my elevator, even though nobody can come up without my code or me buzzing them in. He also pushed my sub-zero in front of the stairwell that leads to the roof deck. We're locked in. Everyone is locked out. All of the windows are double-pane security glass and locked.

I hold my finger up to the group before anyone can start speaking. Up until now, we've been in battle and survival mode. Nobody talking. Nobody speculating or yelling or shouting accusations. "Hold on," I say. Lena slams pain pills in her mouth and chases them with water straight from my faucet. She cradles her broken arm tight to her chest. I just slathered topical anesthetic on my cheek and replaced the bandage.

I use my landline to call L.R.

She picks up on the half-ring.

"Greta?"

"Yes."

"Other than Brad, are you and your team alone in that penthouse? I see you're there from the caller ID."

"Yes. Brad, they took—"

"I know they took Brad. My one crew member is tracking them, but she can't get closer right now." She pauses, inhales, and launches into all of the relevant updates, "You're out at CoCo. And I've got a motion for a gag order on my desk. As you know, they took most of my crew. CoCo has threatened to file a complaint with the Bar for you violating attorney-client privilege in having a reporter on your internal investigation team, which their papers say was never authorized. Also, they demand all cloud backup passwords. So we have an entire cataclysmic shitshow on our hands. I called in a favor to a celebrity client. His bodyguards are on their way to your place. I trust my client. I trust his crew."

"They took Brad, L.R. They fucking took Brad. They're going to kill him. How did they know where to find us?"

"Greta, come on, snap out of it! Who the hell knows how they tracked you there, any hundreds of ways. I highly doubt you guys were being as careful as James Bond. You're a rag-tag legal team, at best. Let's move forward with a new plan. Focus. The hearing on Friday is now *not* what we wanted. They've shifted it to this gag order and a motion to compel passwords to whatever cloud backup they insist you must have. They say that you now have no standing to seek any devices or data, as there is now no internal investigation and you're out. As far as our complaint stands, that's somewhat technically right. The standing thing is a problem—a problem we knew we'd face. So what did you find? What can we show the judge?"

"L.R. they took everything. And we *have no* cloud backup. We worked on local computers."

"Well," Victoria says, trying to get my attention. "Greta," she's saying.

"Hold on, L.R." I look to Victoria. "What?"

"You're not going to like this, or maybe you will. Carolin has a set of the collected data, the preprocessed data. I e-transferred her a copy as a disaster recovery option— a total last resort. She's my private cloud. But it's only the raw, pre-processed stuff. We've still lost all of our work product, everything, because I was using the laptop we stir-fried as our server. We'd have to start over."

I'm trying to process this news, weigh whether it even matters at this point. We already didn't have time to finish our work into a coherent package for court. Now we have to start over? Impossible. And even if we could, we can't risk Brad's life.

"I'm so sorry, Greta, I didn't want our work product in the cloud. So I was keeping it on my laptop, and backing up only locally, and to some removable backups. But they took all of the backups, too. Will take them forever to restore though, and they'll need to know what they're doing and have all the right operating systems...and see, Carolin has..."

Victoria goes on babbling big technology words, which she does when she's nervous, while L.R. lobs questions on her end of the phone. "Who is Carolin? She has *everything*? So what is it? What did you find?"

"But L.R., if I have no standing—if I'm out as deputy general counsel and out as a partner—and they're already threatening to run me up with the Bar for breach of attorney-client privilege...how can we use any of what we learned, even if we *could* reconstruct all the details, which would be near impossible in the time we have? They'll charge me, and my whole team, with a violation of the Computer Fraud and Abuse Act and hacking for accessing and storing and copying firm data without authorization. That's what's next. But beyond all of that, listen: They attacked us and they took Brad. If we go to court on Friday on the offensive, they'll drop him in the Atlantic. And I highly doubt this is a limp leverage game like with Park. They're serious this time."

"I need to think. The new bodyguards will be authorized by me, and only me, when they show up at your door and buzz. Hold tight for that while I think on next steps. Whatever you do, make sure this Carolin is safe and does nothing with that data."

"Carolin lives in a literal fortress. I'm not worried about her."

Victoria nods a heavy agreement. I hang up.

"Greta, can I talk to you?" Samera asks. She's halfway to my guest room. "Alone?"

~~~

Beside an antique dresser of weathered white, Samera stops next to an antique dresser and turns to me. I'm standing in the doorway.

"Shut the door," she says. I do as she asks.

"I talked with my source."

"And?"

"He says to come to CoCo now. Go to the restricted floor."

"So, of course, your source is at CoCo. Obviously."

"Yes. Look. I pulled you in here because my source asked you to bring Lena. He wants to give her something—an apology for what the news said about her. I didn't want her to overhear and insist on going, unless you wanted her to."

"Who is your source?"

"You'll see soon enough."

"This is insane. We can't go there. I can't bring Lena. This is too dangerous."

"Greta, everything is dangerous now. They've taken Brad. Look what they've done to us. They've murdered before and will do so again. You know what we've uncovered. Too many people have millions at stake. They'll do anything to stop you."

"Fine, they've stopped me. I won't go."

Samera stares at me. That fury she had with me in the war room on the night she wouldn't give up her source returns. Her nostrils flare, her eyes bore into me.

"So you give up? So you let Brad hang and give them all the leverage? Just like that. You quit on all the people who've been harmed. Shackled. Caged. Murdered. Kidnapped. You give in to them? You let them walk?"

"Samera, they'll kill Brad if I keep going."

"They'll kill Brad if you don't seize back the leverage. If you don't control the narrative. Figure it out, Greta. Go to my source. I trust him. I do. But I'm not going to sugarcoat this and patronize you. Obviously, you need to be careful."

"Don't tell Lena."

"What do you mean, 'don't tell Lena?'" Lena asks from the doorway.

CHAPTER THIRTY-TWO

We're off to CoCo, Lena, Victoria, and me. Lena insisted on coming and yelled at me for making life-and-death decisions for her. Point taken. Shrouded in shawls and blending with the last dinner party to leave the first-floor restaurant, the three of us merge into the last of late-night crowds running to catch the T. We cut through a couple of alleys and dark side streets before entering one of the Pru's underground parking levels, this one dedicated to CoCo's restricted floor. It is here where CEO's and Governors take a dedicated elevator to meet with Tim Cotton or Maurice Coarse. It is ten p.m., and nobody should be at CoCo except maybe a couple of late-night juniors on the floors below forty.

Victoria's coming along because Samera had said, "And I'd bring Victoria. My source says there's data involved."

So here the three of us lady spies are, waiting at the secure elevator door in the parking basement. I can't swipe my way in, as my card was revoked. So we're waiting on some yet-identified person to greet us and take us up.

Ding, the doors open. And who greets us? None other than Reboot Pete.

"He's waiting for you," Reboot Pete says to me, ignoring Lena and Victoria. As we file in, he steps out and hands me his keycard. "I don't know what shit is going on, Greta, but just so you know, I drove that drone to your friend's place because they said you were sick. I got nothing to do with whatever crap is going on. I always liked you."

"Pete," I say. "Run. Get far away from here. That's my advice."

He closes his eyes, sighs in understanding. Pete agreeing so readily and with that somber face, sends chills through my chest. What are we walking into? But Samera trusts her source. *Samera trusts her source.*

"Meet him behind the princess quilt on the stairs," Pete says.

The doors slide shut. I don't have a chance to find out who *he* is.

"Meet him behind the princess quilt in the stairs? What the hell?" Victoria says, incredulous—I know, this is all so insane.

As we rise, ears popping from the pressure, the familiar hurricane of wind surrounds the car. We jolt to a stop and bounce on cables before the doors clatter themselves open on the restricted King Floor, which is so fucking pretentious. It's the fiftieth floor.

"Come on," I say. Clearly we're walking into the most dangerous situation. They could hide our bodies in *the space behind the quilt in the stairwell.* And we talked about this and agree, we're not backing down now.

I'm thinking all this as I touch Pete's card to the sensor, allowing us to enter the restricted floor lobby. We're greeted with the Bach that always plays. It is pitch black outside, but for the lights glittering like diamonds on the hotel that was, two years ago when Henry and I sat on his office floor, in the middle of construction.

"Stay here," I say to Lena and Victoria, stalling them at the receptionists' desk. Nobody's there, of course. It is only us up here on this dark night. I yank off the velvet rope that blocks the marble stairwell up to Maurice and Tim's suite of offices and throw the fucker on the ground. The brass hook clatters on the marble floor. I turn back to Lena and Victoria, "Stay. I mean it. Do not follow me."

"Yeah, boss, we're not moving," Victoria says, for once without her collegial sarcasm.

I pull the princess quilt to the side, finding it heavy and difficult to move, given its size and thickness. I hadn't realized it's sturdy cotton on both sides, stitched together with what must be a dense stuffing middle. I find a plain brown door with a gold knob *on the bottom,* not in the middle, like every other knob in the known world. But because the stair I'm on is lower than even this weird knob, I move up two steps to lean over and turn the knob, at which point, the door opens in and I see a folded wooden ladder at the edge of the opening. I shake my head at the disorienting feeling of being entombed within a House of Fun, within a glass-enamel-marble modern firm, within a skyscraper. I wouldn't be surprised if a demonic, two-headed clown-goat, floating on no feet, were to transcend from this opened tomb of a room, pass through the quilt, and haunt me with his eyes of glowing microchips, as a whole new genre of modern gothic horror.

"What the hell?" Victoria is murmuring behind me. I turn to see that she has moved up the stairs to gain a closer look. Of course she didn't stay at the receptionist desk.

"*What?*" Victoria says, as I glare at her for moving.

I turn away, trying to figure out how to release the ladder. Standing on my tiptoes and looking in on the floor of the room and this folded ladder in the entrance, I think I see wheels buried within and on the sides of the ladder compartment, but honestly at this angle it's hard to tell. There must be a lever or button. I can't figure how this crazy contraption works. How is it we were to meet *him,* whoever that is, in here, if he's not in here already, and helping us in? With one arm pushing the quilt, I lean from my marble stair to try to get a better handle on what's inside, but from this awkward angle, and with one arm struggling to hold back the heavy quilt, my face reaches only the bottom corner of the open doorway, making it so I can see only five feet into the room, and at that, only the ladder in its floor compartment and the carpet around it. I see no feet. I hear no voices. Nobody walks closer to help me in.

"Step back," Lena calls up to me. I let go of the quilt, and it swings back in place. Looking down, Lena has moved behind the receptionists' desk. She's hovering her a hand over a series of buttons. "I think there's a button for that ladder." She presses something, and the Bach changes to Yo-Yo Ma. "Nope, not that one." She presses another, and the lobby lights switch to a hazy blue—used for fancy cocktail parties with big clients. "Nope, that isn't it. Hold on."

"Be careful, Lena. What if the next one is an alarm?"

She looks up at me, "Then we're fucked. But aren't we already fucked?"

"Press the green one by the left side phone," an older voice says from the top of the stairs. "And hurry, before Tim returns. Hurry, *hurry*." It's Maurice Coarse. *Ninety-year-old* Maurice Coarse, at the top landing to his private suite, looking down to Lena, then to me, and limping his way down the stairs on his cane. He holds the railing tight. His steps are definite, but cautious. The tip of his cane is rubber and makes a sucking noise as he descends. I've only been in the physical presence of Maurice Coarse a handful of times. He is always, as he is right now, in a three-piece black suit and red tie. His face is smooth, almost unnaturally so at his age, and his posture is as straight as a forty-year-old. He still rocks a full shock of white hair, tight cut, waxed to the side. But for his cautious steps and cane, you might not know he's ninety. If the world had vampires, Maurice would be their king.

Lena presses the green button, and with a slight hum the wooden stairs slope out a section at a time, pressing out the quilt as they go. It is now low enough for us to climb by pushing our bodies between quilt and ladder.

Who would ever hire a company to design such a thing, in a law firm, in a marble staircase, behind a princess quilt? The ultra rich, of course. Still, *why*?

"You ladies get inside, quick. And if you would help an old man, please, climb those little steps we can talk inside. Hurry."

Victoria scrambles up fast; she helps one-armed Lena up, with me as the bottom spotter. In the time it takes me to help Maurice up and then myself to enter the room, Lena has beelined to a case at the far end of the room, like it was a giant magnet and she made of metal.

Lena is walking back and forth at the far end of the room, repeating variations of the following, over and over, "I can't believe this. I can't believe this. Caravaggios. Cara-fucking-vaggios. Oh my God, I was right all along, private commissions. Caravaggios. Holy hell, holy shit."

Maurice presses a button on the wall. The stairs do exactly what they just did, but in reverse, settling back into a folded state at the entrance. He closes the door fast. Through a monitor above the button Maurice pressed, we can see that the quilt falls straight, but is shaking from the motion, a thing that Maurice seems nervous about, for he's pleading under his breath, "Come on now, fall straight, stay still. Ladies, shh, shh, now." His concern seems fraught, since this room must be soundproofed, and indeed, as things settle, Maurice talks more confidently and louder.

"Excellent," he says, in a relief.

In the center of the room, between Lena and us, is an eight-person conference table, on top of which is a black backpack, which seems stuffed full of rectangular items—I can tell from the sharp corners bulging out. Beside the case where Lena is having a mini-breakdown is another brown door with a gold knob, this time in the middle—like a normal friggin' door. I don't know where it leads, but by orienting to what I know of Ventfort Hall, it *should* lead into what I thought was a server room, dedicated to 50th Floor conference room AV equipment.

He turns to us, and speaking in a low voice, says, "Ladies, we'll have to be quick and we'll have to speak quietly. I never trust soundproofing. I fear Tim may return from a dinner with…a certain unsavory. Please, take a seat and I'll explain."

Victoria and I move toward either side of the table, but remain standing. Maurice takes the head closest to the princess quilt. Lena is not moving from the rectangular case. She turns, tunneling her massive, glistening blue eyes on Maurice. I move closer to her so I can see what's got her so spun up.

"Are these really Caravaggios?" She asks. Literally nothing else in the world—not our recent past, not kidnapped Brad, not I or Victoria, not her broken arm—matters.

"Indeed, they are. His style is so distinctive. Knowing you are a baroque art restorer, from our sources and the news, of course, I figured you'd know these straight away. And as you can see, they're signed in that same playful style he signed his name in painted blood, 'Fra Michelangelo,' in *The Beheading of St. John the Baptist*."

"That was the only one he signed."

"He signed these too, my dear. Look closer, in the red of the tiles that are painted in each panel. See how the tiles are the same in each? These were intended to live as a set of eight for the collector who ordered them. See the signature, hidden in grooves and mortar."

"Private collector?"

"Naturally."

Lena turns and bends her face so close to the glass, I fear she'll fall through. Without turning back she asks, "Who? Who was the collector? How did you get these? Do you have provenance papers? Who was the collector who ordered them from Caravaggio? When?"

I look inside the case and see mounted atop a red velvet backing, eight 10"x10" oil paintings of the same woman. In the first, if reading the panels left to right, she is simply standing nude. In another down the line, she's sitting nude in a chair with wide-opened legs, a finger in her mouth. In another, she's on all fours, naked. The series seems a progression, for in the last one, a priest in opened cassock is fucking her on the tiled floor, and she seems quite happy about his moves. These are masterful oil paintings of the baroque style, that depth, those deep-rich colors capturing realism, but they are pure porn, not the religious scenes one would expect from Caravaggio.

"So, Lena—can I call you Lena?" Maurice asks, without answering her series of breathless questions. "I hope that's okay. I owe you an apology. I am so sorry for not stopping Tim in spreading that terrible lie about you. How rude, how low, how garish of him. And, of course, your broken arm, which I am ashamed to report I was unable to stop Tim from causing, by way of his damned security force."

I already know Maurice is not going to apologize to me for my face gash, which is tingling in his presence. And he won't apologize for Henry's stab wound. Henry and I are licensed lawyers, and Maurice is the type of lawyer who never apologizes to other lawyers. But Lena is a civilian, so she gets an apology, which is all fine with me.

"Maurice, they took Brad Perdunk. They kidnapped him. They're going to kill him. And they still have Park, Lena's friend. Parkol Calestri. I don't think we should be wasting time—even on priceless Caravaggios," I interrupt.

The mention of Park snaps Lena out of her Caravaggio hypnosis. She shudders and inhales a lungful, only to hold it. Her shoulders up around her neck.

"Oh, Greta," he says, tilting his head. "But don't you see? If Lena here walks with priceless art, it's my repayment to her, plus it will enrage Tim, and, sorry, but I do want that. I am the only owner, and Tim can't prove otherwise. We'll talk about leverage to get Brad and Park back, safe and sound, but I want more than just Brad and Park's safety secured. And if you do what I say, we'll get them back. But I also want pain. I want punishment. I want Tim and Honeywell *eradicated*. And all along the way, I want Tim to understand just how much he's losing. Even these paintings, which he assumes he'll inherit when he inherits my ownership in the firm."

"Lena walks with all of these Caravaggios? That makes no sense, Maurice. First, it's insane. Second, you keep them. You tell him he's not getting them in the will."

"Greta," and here he pauses, blinks in a way as if he's struggling with a hard truth. "I'm on borrowed time. Simple as that. Nobody knows this, but the doctors gave me six months to live, and those six months ran out two months ago. I could go at any minute, and I just want to see Tim know. I want to see that. Besides, Lena deserves them."

I don't think Lena's processed yet this whole bizarre conversation where Maurice and I are haggling over whether Lena walks with priceless Caravaggios as part of a rich men war over assets and power. I watch her struggle with the tension she clearly exhibited upon hearing Park's name and being reminded he's at risk with the confusion of the paintings in the case, for she keeps looking at them and then tensing up and looking at them. I think she wants to stem her otherwise suffocating concern for Park, because she asks, "Who was the private collector?" She says in a clipped tone.

"Ah, well. I bet you have your theories, no?"

"I do."

"I can confirm your theories. And it's interesting, because the paintings are also a good demonstration to show how the core of the corruption you're uncovering now, in 2021, has been the same for centuries. These Caravaggios were for a Vatican priest. Father Ventfort is the pseudonym he used to rent his rather private and secret Vatican apartment, where these hung for decades. Ventfort," and here, Maurice pauses to wink at me. Now I know the derivation of the hall's name. "The boys of the church had many secrets, and certainly many were not celibate. This is no surprise to you, I know. This Ventfort chap was into, as the provenance papers set forth, *elegant sexuality,* which is what he ordered from Caravaggio. The model was none other than Ventfort's favorite prostitute. The Vatican boys had to keep up the ruse of celibacy and being called by God to drive parishioner donations, to squeeze money out of manipulations and dogma. Oh, speculators always find ways to manipulate feelings, fear, faith, extremism, *polarization,* into money. Nothing changes. Right, Greta?

"But, they're yours now, Lena. The code to the case is 8833. Set the paintings, I'm sure you know how, in the carrying case. It's there, under the paintings. See? Please work fast, as I discuss the other pot of leverage with Greta."

Lena looks at me, full of questions, full of doubt. She's cradling her broken arm.

"Do it, Lena. Now. Victoria, can you help her? Her arm."

Victoria looks at me as if we're in a dream and that, of course, in this wacky case, this funhouse dream, she's going to help broken-armed Lena case up millions of dollars of Caravaggio porn, while I discuss a high-crime investigation with my boss-vampire, in a secret room behind a princess quilt, that hides a mechanized ladder in the floor. Okay.

I'm nervous, a definite skepticism boiling inside. Why would Maurice so easily give up priceless art? When things seem too good to be true, they are.

"Oh, and, dear, that little folder in the case, those are the provenance papers. Slide them down here so I can sign ownership over to you. And although it's old-school, humor me, would you? Let's get some consideration in the record for this deal. How about a dollar?"

Victoria, who has moved to Lena and helped her find the hard case, readying it for the eight square paintings, jams a hand in her pants' pocket and throws a five on the table. "Keep the change," she says. "Lena, pay me back."

Lena's not listening, she's moving the paintings into the case, with Victoria acting as a net holder below Lena's working hand. Lena won't let Victoria touch the paintings. Nobody is going to touch these paintings ever again, except Lena, if Lena has her way. I take the folder of provenance papers and set it before Maurice.

Maurice extracts a Cross pen from an inner pocket and begins signing over ownership to Lena. While he works away, he says to me, "Greta, there's not much for us to talk about, except that you need to take that backpack of hard drives and get out as soon as possible." He puts the pen down on the table. "Put these papers in the backpack." So I do, wedging the folder between several hard drives. "I think if you leave with these hard drives and taking them out, quick, before someone can overpower me, I can convince Tim, if he wants them all back—and he will—to return Brad and loosen his grip on Parkol Calestri. But that's not all. You're going to court on Friday as you planned all along. Those hard drives will help."

I'm about to list all the problems with his plan for Friday and yell about Brad, but he stops me. "Hold on, Greta. The facts from my perspective are simple, and here they are. First, I never wanted Tim Cotton to join this firm. His father foisted him on me in a Faustian bargain that has something ugly to do between Cotton Senior and myself and has nothing to do with what is going on now. Second, I never wanted Honeywell to join this firm. That was all Tim. There is, however, something relevant tying Tim with Honeywell and the whole Cotton clan and other unsavories. That is what you're uncovering. Third, I have been trying to stop Tim in this crusade against you all along. And I have been winning in some moments, and losing in others. Fourth, Pete in I.T. brought me that bag of hard drives earlier tonight. He was concerned over what Tim wanted his I.T. team to do. All I know is they're firm hard drives from laptops and a backup of the email server. So you're getting a lot, from what I can tell. But definitely not the iPhones that are part of your motion. That's what Pete said to me. Honestly, though, I have no idea what any of the other technical words Pete said mean. No idea what Tim asked for or if Pete or his team did any of it. But I know enough to know what I don't know and to hand off computer stuff to the firm's E-Discovery Counsel."

"Maurice, I am no longer E-Discovery Counsel. I am also no longer Deputy General Counsel. Tim sent clear messaging on that to my lawyer, L.R. Rice."

Maurice half smiles. "Please, just leave with that backpack and the paintings now. You'll leave through that back door to an inner stairwell, which leads to my suite up top, and to one floor below. You'll go down one floor. Don't go up to the suite. It's possible he and his unsavory dinner companion go straight up there. Go down a floor. That is the way you need to go to avoid Tim and whoever might be coming up the elevators. As for your position with the firm, and as for me playing hardball with Tim about Parkol and Brad, you let me handle things. Go."

I pause a second in considering Maurice; he slips the five in a breast pocket with another wink.

"Why would you give her all these Caravaggios? That's millions and millions. Why would you give us these hard drives? I'm betting there's data on them that will kill the firm you spent a lifetime creating. Why? I don't trust what you're doing here, Maurice."

"Oh, Greta. You know, out of all these years, *you* have been one of my favorite hires. Did you remember? I was the one who interviewed you first. We have no time to have a lengthy trust exercise or some philosophical conversation on the *whys*. I'll tell you this much." He pauses. His tone is direct, decisive, crisp. It is obvious why he is one of the nation's top trial attorneys and has been for decades. He talks from a place of confident knowledge, not condescendingly, not in a con-man way of misdirecting babble, but of holding incontrovertible truths. The man could sell a portable heater in the desert. His competence is sexy, and I'm not surprised by all the salacious stories of him with models on the Amalfi Coast and Cannes.

"What have I done with my life, Greta? I will tell you. I have built this firm. Full stop. At the age of ninety, I still pull eighty-hour weeks. It has always been so. I never married. Never had children. I have given every minute to the law. Oh, the law is a mistress, for sure. And, of course, I have had many real mistresses. But that is all, in all its naked emptiness and truth. In all its hours of loneliness and solitary scotch. So, perhaps, I find it rather serendipitous, here near the end of my long life, that I find myself owing a major apology to a baroque art restorer, the only person to have ever reacted as I did when I first saw these special paintings. Perhaps I see her as the embodiment of the law, all my women mistresses, and the wife I never had. To me, looked at from that view, it seems logical that she should inherit the

Caravaggios. And that is my final answer on that topic. As for the backpack of hard drives, you are wrong. If you do your job, they will not ruin my firm. They will save it. Now, go."

"So you authorize this investigation, Maurice?"

"I, my dear, have always authorized it. It is Tim who does not. You find yourself in the middle of major corruption, you are right about that. But you've also stumbled onto the bloody front line of this firm's power struggle. I am the senior-most member of this firm, and by God, I authorize this investigation. Unfortunately, Tim also has, technically speaking, an equal say, which is, again, the result of the awful Faustian bargain I made with his father. Now, go, and hurry. He will be here any minute. I have no idea who he'll have with him, and the private security force is under his thumb. Not mine. The big deal now, Greta—and I suspect you and I have the same goal but for different reasons—is not necessarily to prove the merit of what you're investigating, but rather, to make the facts that support your discovery request very public. You need to turn the tide of this hearing on Friday, and the number one goal now is avoid, at all costs, a gag order. Just getting the facts, the undergirding facts, that support the real suspicions here public—very public—is the real leverage we need. I don't need to tell you how powerful white-collar criminals have always avoided real punishment by hiding behind confidential settlements and cooked consent decrees. *Public*, my dear. No gag order. That is your current job."

"But the motion for a gag order was filed by CoCo, the firm. How in the world am I to overcome that and get back to my motion, *my* motion to compel, and the facts that support my quest for more data from Tim and Honeywell's phones and laptops? Tim's motion and firing me means I have no standing anymore. We could just have Samera bring all this out in the press."

"Come on, Greta. You know you can't use the press angle quite yet. You go to the press while a gag order motion is pending, and with Tim having already planted the seed of you being a loose cannon, with rumors of drug use, they'll paint you as disgruntled. They'll lodge a violation of the Computer Fraud and Abuse Act and you'll be disbarred, maybe arrested. We need the blessings of a federal court judge. And sure, maybe I could just state publicly now that you have standing, but then Tim and Honeywell immediately file some kind of motion looking into the legitimacy of that. Maybe they say you coerced me, which is laughable, of course."

"Of course," I say, and because I'm now, admittedly, a smidge under his spell, I allow a little smile.

"Anyway, I'd rather say you are authorized when you and L.R. walk into court and give them zero time to delay things, zero time to mobilize around that. Zero time to wage the age-old he-said, she-said meta news about news of corruption. Until this damn hearing, we need them to think I'm not so invested with you. They'll have no idea who I gave the Caravaggios to, and they don't know you're here."

"Still. You and I, we could just go to the press right now."

"No," he says, slamming his fist on the table. He's ninety and dying, but no doubt, Maurice is lead counsel in the room. "Greta, I said no! How many people have tried that over the decades? We'll get there. But no, not yet. We need the theatrical spectacle of a public hearing, with high-profile counsel delivering the supporting facts, such as your L.R. and Bo Lopez, for the good eggs in the DOJ and FBI to take this to the next level and avoid convenient accidents and suicides. You know that."

He says all of this, especially the last part about convenient deaths, in the most clinical and calm manner. *Good Lord, what has this man seen—what has he done—in his long life?*

The noise of men laughing interrupts us. Maurice holds a finger to his mouth, and points to the back door, telling us with the force of his finger to leave, now. *Now.* He keeps jabbing his finger in that direction. To me he mouths, "You let me worry about your standing in arguing the motion on Friday. Go. You'll have to jump down. The ladder on that side is out for repairs."

I grab the backpack.

Lena and Victoria are done filling the hard case, and we all run out through the other brown door. On the other side, we have to drop to our rears on a ledge and jump down four feet, as now I can tell from temporary boards in the floor, another ladder is usually here, like the other side. We're trapped in an inner stair-well. We freeze, not wanting the men entering the secret room to hear us on the other side of the door. Perhaps the room isn't so perfectly soundproof after all, because I can hear Tim's voice talking with one other man about oysters they just ate on Here-ford street.

"What the hell is going on, Maurice? Why are you in here?" Tim yells.

CHAPTER THIRTY-THREE

"How dare you question *me*, sitting in *my* room. How dare you!" Maurice bellows.

"Was someone in here with you? Did they leave through this door?" The gold knob rattles. We are right on the other side, down four feet.

But then the rattling stops. "Where are the Caravaggios?" Tim yells. "Maurice, *where are the Caravaggios?* My father helped you get those. They're half mine!"

"Timothy, they were never half yours. And you know that. The provenance papers make clear they are all *mine*. And I, Tim, have put them and certain hard drives—oh yes, I know about the hard drives you tried to have Pete destroy—anyway, the paintings and hard drives are long gone. You've missed them by hours and hours. Lovely of you to take a long dinner with your buddy here. The hard drives will be returned when you return Brad safely, and release Parkol. But you're never getting those paintings."

"You asshole."

"Do not speak to me like that, Tim. You are not the heir apparent of this firm. You are weak. You are nothing. Make the call, now, about Brad. And Park."

We are creeping down the flight of stairs to the next floor, as Maurice had directed.

"Now!" Maurice yells, loud enough to echo in this secret

stairwell.

"Brad is fine. He's being pampered like a clown in a mansion I rented. Relax. I'll bring him back safe and sound when you give me the paintings and hard drives."

We are about at the next landing, and moving as fast as possible to get under the upper stairs so nobody could see us from above if they burst into the secret stairwell. Sure enough, the back door opens just as we scurry to hide. I hear Tim in the open doorway, "Unless, old man, I find whoever you gave the paintings and hard drives to first. Cren, stay in here with the old man. Make sure he doesn't move."

If Tim chooses to go down a flight, we're screwed. We could bolt for the door and enter the 49th floor, but he'd hear us. I'm keeping us frozen in place in the hopes he goes up to his and Maurice's private suites. I have no idea if it would have been better for us to go up to those suites and exit that way. We likely made a huge mistake in going down a flight.

The seconds of waiting here, holding our breath, are interminable. I'm about to explode. I look to Victoria and Lena. Nobody moves a muscle. Tim is not moving, and I sense he's up there, in the stairwell beside the vacuum-sealed door, deciding whether to go up or down.

I hear him jump down four feet as we did. He takes a step. Another step. And now we hear him ascending to his and Maurice's suites. I'm timing his steps, holding a finger up to Lena and Victoria to hold, hold, hold, while I move ever so softly to the 49th floor door, set my hand on the handle, and when I hear the clicking of the suite's door above, crank, push the 49th floor door open, and usher Victoria and Lena through. I follow, and the door, now just a white-enamel panel appearing as part of the wall, vacuum-seals closed. No way to open it back up. This is a one-way door.

Here now, on the 49th floor, I mouth, "Get to the fire exit

stairwell." I point to the end of the hall, which will take us to ground, and hopefully avoid running into Tim or his unsavory Cren, should they start riding the elevators in search. But we need to make it all the way to the end of the hall, and between us and the fire exit at the end is a gauntlet of glass—a fishbowl. When CoCo re-made these floors two years ago, they cut out the middle of the 49th floor down to the 40th, making an inner atrium with false sunlight beaming down from bright lights to an inside field of grass, around which are glass-walled offices on two sides, and libraries and conference rooms on both ends, like up here on the 49th.

Victoria has already run to the end of the hall and stands between the tax law library, which has walls, and the fire-exit stairwell. In fact, she bolted. Lena and I are still frozen at the vacuum-sucked door, looking at a closed closet across from us.

I'm not sure why Lena and I have stalled a beat. I tug on her unbroken arm, which holds the case of Caravaggios. She looks to the sealed door behind us. Footsteps coming this way from the inner stairwell, and fast. We jump across the floor, open the closet door, and push our way in. Victoria is out in the open at the other end, standing in front of the tax law library. She watched us jump into this closet, so I'm hoping she's smart enough to take cover in the tax library.

Lena and I are not breathing as the stairwell door opens and vacuum sucks closed once again. Footsteps approach the closet door, and the knob begins to turn. This guy is like a bomb-sniffing dog. A loud cough from the end of the hall interrupts the progress of the knob.

"Who are you? What are you doing here?" Tim yells.

Footsteps approach. I watch Tim's shadow move, visible from the bottom crack.

"Oh my God, did I scare you? I'm so sorry," Victoria says.

"Who are you? What are you doing here?"

"I'm, I'm, Mr. Cotton, oh, I'm a new first year associate, Henna Green. They said I could start early and stay late because I have a tax research project. See? I've been working in the tax library until they finish office assignments. This book…."

"Who said you could work in the tax library?"

"Oh no, I didn't mean to start trouble, Mr. Cotton," Victoria says. Her acting as a nervous and deferential associate is so natural—likely from years of observation. I picture her out there with whatever tax law book she is trying to show Tim, which shaking is likely true to her nerves of trying to get us all out of here alive. Hopefully, he'll perceive her shaking as a young woman associate trembling at the feet of the named male partner. She's playing to his patriarchal ego. Tugging on his entitlement. I hope, because he's a sniveling-idiot-trust-fund prick, he falls for it.

"I asked: who said you could work in the tax library, Henna Green?" Tim says in a tone that is a slight step down from his fear-anger a second before. Lord knows what act Victoria is performing outside this door, likely pulling on every aspect of her innocent-looking Zooey Deschanel face, to send signals that she thinks *Mr. Cotton* is just the greatest, her hero.

"Oh, I don't know, Mr. Cotton. It was a lady in H.R. I'm so nervous. I'm such a huge fan of yours. I'm so sorry. It was Stephanie? Or Susie? Maybe? Maybe it was Sharon or S, ssss? It was an S name. Oh my goodness, I can't remember." She's breathing in short blasts, and I can tell she's trying to summon tears for her act.

"You mean Sue-Ann Miller?"

"I think so? How unprofessional of me to have forgotten. I'm so sorry, Mr. Cotton."

Sue-Ann Miller is the head of H.R. So now I know Victoria is a con-woman, cranking out, on the fly, a con-woman's game, like a Salem fortune teller who shotguns a series of options until you flinch or provide the answer she was fishing for. *Noted.*

"It's fine, it's fine. Have you seen anyone else on this floor? But wait, how do you know who I am anyway? I'm sure we haven't met."

"Oh, Mr. Cotton, I researched all the partners before I accepted my offer at the end of last summer, when I was a summer here."

Victoria took a calculated gamble with that answer. She—correctly—assumed Tim Cotton, the not-worthy named partner, who was last summer flying around the globe, trying to find new office locales (and maybe Victoria stored that fact in her brain when I mentioned it at some lunch), would never have intermingled with the summers. And she knows from working with so many egotistical partners like him for so many years, that he'll never admit to not knowing something about his firm, about the hires, about the details. Victoria's answer is either going to clue Tim in to the ruse, or seal the deal.

Silence. Tim's shadow hasn't moved.

"Right, right, of course," he says, in a tone that is rushed, somewhat accepting the story she's telling, but somewhat distracted, hurried. "Have you seen anyone on this floor?"

"No. It's just been me. I've been concentrating, but I would have heard. Look at this thing, I'm sure you've read it already, a total game-changer and riveting! Oh, I can't wait to be on cases with you, Mr. Cotton. Do you do tax law, too? You must, it's the most fascinating of topics, and this book. Wow, this book." Her quivering voice from a minute ago firms to a happiness in the course of this bullshit monologue. Now she's just having fun, and she needs to stop. This is the problem with working with extreme geniuses. They sometimes toy with people they deem inferior, and in the process, ignore warnings.

"Assembled Strategies of Tax Preparers of Toledo, Ohio, 1983-1993?" He asks. "That's riveting to you?" *Victoria, you better not have fucked this up.*

Victoria snort laughs. Tim is still right outside this door, his shadow not budging. She needs to get him out of here, and fast.

When she's done snort laughing, she says, "Oh I know, I'm such a nerd. Hey, I got a joke for you, Mr. Cotton. A litigator, a corporate attorney, and a tax lawyer walk into a bar." *I am going to murder you, Victoria.* "Oh wait!" She yelps. His shadow jumps. "Oh my God, now that you asked. You know what? I think I saw this super sketchy guy in the elevator when I went to get a snack about, like, twenty minutes ago? I think he got off at the 39th floor, maybe? I thought he was one of the late-night partners who work on that floor."

"Thank you, Henna. I'll check it out." He says *Henna* in a tone that tells me he's not 100% buying who she is, but is mostly there. Still, he's got enough skepticism remaining to want to burn her name to his brain. "You stay here, Henna Green. Don't leave."

And with that, Tim's shadow moves away, and I hear footsteps down the hall. We wait here in the closet. Lena is breathing tiny sips of air. If Tim is moving to the elevators to go down to 39, he'll need to cross the end hall with the tax library, cross half of the glass hall on the other side, and enter the elevator bank. Typically, Pru elevators take a century to come when called, so I picture innocent, fake, green associate Henna Green, watching her hero, Mr. Tim Cotton, with her adoring eyes, while clutching the most supremely boring book ever written. And although I can't see a damn thing, I'm positive Tim is texting his unsavory Cren in the secret room and telling him to come gather up Henna Green for more questioning. We have a sliver of a window to escape once Tim's in the elevator, if that. We may be cooked by Cren coming down the inner stairwell now.

A literal eternity passes.

Finally, Victoria cranks open the door. "He's gone," she whisper-yells, looking over her shoulder at the enamel-paneled wall behind. "Hurry. I heard him call Cren to come get me," she says.

We all run the gauntlet of glass, constantly looking through the false atrium to the other side and to the visible floors below, worried someone, somewhere, will see us in this fishbowl. Worried Tim will return. Worried Cren will bust onto the floor any minute. We reach the fire-escape stairs. We don't stop. We don't talk. I've got the backpack of hard drives secure on my back; Victoria takes the case of Caravaggios so Lena can use her unbroken arm to hold the railing. When we reach the 33rd floor, Victoria swipes us into Stokes & Crane, and where Cren, if he starts running down the fire escape stairs, can't follow. We race to Stoke's private service elevator, landing ourselves on the main lobby's ground floor. We rest here, Victoria holding the *close doors* button, panting for breath. For a break.

~~~

Victoria says, "I wanted to jam that boring ass tax book lengthwise into Timmy's windpipe and then the soft spot of his skull when he bent into the pain. I learned that on a self-defense YouTube channel. But it's better, right, that he doesn't know we were meeting with Maurice? Make him think Maurice has his own security team, or whatever story he's selling him? Maurice would push Tim off our trail, right?"

"Agree. Although, Tim and his creeps might look at security footage. Let's hope they can't really do that tonight, though. Pete's not there, and he won't help anyway. Great job, V," I say. "And *twice*, a walk-into-a-bar joke has been an escape mechanism. Who knew terrible comedy could be self-defense?"

"Now what?" She asks.

"Now," Lena says. "We scoot as fast as possible to the Volvo and get the hell out, asap."

"Nobody will know about the Volvo, so, yes, we need to do that. If by some miracle they do look at the security footage and they see us coming up the elevator and in Ventfort Hall, they'll know they should be looking for three women walking or running. But they don't have video beyond CoCo floors. Not of this elevator, not the ground lobby, and not the main parking garage. You two will hide in the way back, laying down, and we'll bomb on out of here. We need to get to Carolin's with these hard drives tonight."

"Ugh," I say, because Carolin is the most annoying forensic expert on the planet.

Standing straight, now breathing easy, Victoria hands the case of Caravaggios to Lena, looking her up and down in a mock disdain. "So, you get the hot guy and the priceless art, and I get an obliterated Jura? Great." Victoria's smiling, cutting the tension and fear for a two-second break before we race off to the next risk.

"Oh, I don't know, Henna Green. Seems you have major chemistry with Mr. Cotton," Lena says. We all snort-laugh a blast of momentary joy at the absurd notion of any sentient being having chemistry with *Mr. Cotton*. Victoria is laughing through saying, "That hair, that horrible hair." It's all so insanely hysterical to us in this paused anxious moment, because now we live in the wackadoo world where it is more believable that we have a case of Caravaggio porn than anybody having chemistry with bowl-cut Cotton. The moment passes, we step down our laughter, breathe deep, and return to serious intention.

I say, "Okay, to Carolin's. Let's go. Keep your heads down. We are getting Brad back. We are getting Park back. And we are winning that damn hearing on Friday."

CHAPTER THIRTY-FOUR

As soon as we were safely out of the Pru and I didn't see anyone following, Victoria climbed up to the front passenger seat. Lena, what with her broken arm, and protecting the Caravaggios as if the case were her newborn triplets, stayed in the way back. I called Toby and warned him that maybe someone might know we met with Maurice, but we're not sure, and that he needs to re-double the security at the elevator and the doorway to the rooftop garden. He said L.R.'s new verified crew of bodyguards had arrived and things are locked tight.

I can tell it's time for more topical anesthesia on my face scar because a growing throb is mounting under the gauze. I wince from a migraine that I can't tell is from tension or pain or stress, my concussion, or these damn progressives. Probably all of it. Victoria is on the phone racing through explaining to Carolin what's happened and that we're on our way with hard drives.

On the Volvo's speaker, Carolin's mean voice is amplified, "I come to you. You don't come to me."

"Carolin, gonna need you to work with me here," Victoria says. We're nearing the end of Storrow Drive and about to head to 93 North, to Carolin's allegedly uber-secure lab in a Marble-head mansion. I've never been there. According to Victoria, it has vaults and biometric locks and stainless-steel work tables and two stocked panic rooms. What's true, what's science fiction, what's over-bloated, vendor-consultant, marketing bluster, doesn't matter in this moment. We're heading to Marblehead, to Carolin's forensics lab, whatever it is.

"As I always say, I come to you, you do not come to me. You want this fortress of mine to stay a secret and protect your data—and me, your most important asset right now—then you stop. You turn around. You meet me in front of Trident in one hour."

"That's right in front of Greta's," Victoria barks back.

"No shit, Sherlock. That's where you meet me. Holy stupid, Victoria, do you know what my boss would do if she found out I let clients in this regional lab? Besides, we have security protocols for things like this."

"And you don't think meeting at Trident, across from Greta's, is the most obvious and dangerous place to meet? Especially since they might know we just met with Maurice Coarse?"

"Did they see all of your faces?"

"We don't know, Carolin!"

Carolin now takes on a contemplative, not combative, tone. She says, indicating she listened, stored, and hyper-processed all of the fast facts Victoria just hurled at her, "Let's go with they didn't see your faces. I don't think they did. No way Tim and whoever this Cren is— likely a muscle dope—could figure out security footage on their own, that fast, at night, without I.T. And I bet Maurice spun some crazy-ass tale about who he gave the paintings and hard drives to, because, surely, he'd put Tim off your trail. I don't think they'll have too many people outside Greta's. Just regular dopes on stakeout, and they're probably asleep in their dumb car. The mass of them are likely with Brad in Tim's rented mansion. And your team already killed two guys in New York. Disabling two more stakeout dopes is a good opportunity for us. Definitely worth the easy trap. You meet me at Trident. In one hour."

"Worth the easy trap?"

"It's called a honeypot. What are you dumb? I'm the pot of

honey. They're the bears. Geez, V, you need to think a little more."

She is so severe, so sure of herself, so abusive, even to Victoria.

"You cocky little bitch, listen to me," Victoria says. "A honeypot, if we're talking about the term applied to computer forensics, is a virtual trap to capture computer hackers, duh. This is the real world with actual physical human beings, and I'm telling you that, because you never interact with actual physical human beings. These guys are super dangerous. You can't be thinking you can grab these hard drives like it's picking up thumb drives at Best Buy."

"Yes, I can. One hour."

"Oh my God, fine. Fine!" Victoria exhales loud. "Wait," she says, bracing herself as if pained to say what's next, which seems an embarrassment for her. "And also, we need more computing power. They took all ours. And we destroyed my local server so they couldn't have our work product and my source codes. Carolin, don't lecture me. I know, I *know* I shouldn't have saved local. We need your help with mega storage and review software."

"No, you don't. Remember? I'm processing all your backups of the collected data, and it'll be hosted on my network with my instances of CaseSpaceAI and CaseCore. What you need are dummy laptops with Citrix. Then you Citrix into my network with my RSA fobs. Which is exactly what you should have done from the start and not risked a local server."

"Right. You're right."

"Geez, V, you're slipping. I guess I'm doing everything on this case, like always." She hangs up. My brain seizes in the total annoyance that we are once again, as in near all cases we work together, reliant on a forensic expert consultant. Especially this one.

The air in the car is stilted and cold.

"Victoria, you know she grates on my last nerve, she's going to get us killed and the hard drives taken. And also, this is how you two besties talk to each other?"

"Oh that? She was being nice, actually. For Carolin."

~~~

Carolin arrives dressed as the regular version of herself when she's not testifying in a federal court. A backwards gold-black ballcap, gold sunglasses with red-tint lenses, oversized white T-shirt with the word RAD in a pink-black spray across the chest, coral cargo shorts, and pink wedge heels with crisscrossing laces around yellow fishnet stockings. I'm not sure what this style of fashion is, other than Carolin. It's aggressive, it's ostentatious, it is all her, so I'll give her that. I admire her for owning herself—no matter how maddening her inside self is to me.

"You," she says to me as an ungracious greeting. Victoria and I are standing with the backpack of hard drives to the side of Trident, leaning on an adjacent building and in shadow. My door is across the street. Two of L.R.'s new crew guard the front. Lena returned to the fourth floor already, since we parked in my garage, and she could go straight up.

The only other people on this late-night street are a couple of bros, a half block beyond Trident, in a matte-black Audi with purple rims and a purple LED strip. The thump of their music is so loud, their car vibrates. I'm pretty sure clouds of pot are wafting from the cracks of their windows and stoning up Newbury. I see nobody else.

"Hey, *you*," Carolin repeats, pointing her finger, jabbing the air at me.

I point to myself, "Yes, Carolin?"

"Give me the hard drives. And my invoice needs payment by tomorrow."

"No problem on the invoice." I'm still clutching the loop on the top of the backpack.

"Are you going to give me the drives? Geez." She's moving to take the pack from me. I clutch it tighter to my chest.

"Are you sure you weren't followed? I mean, how in the hell would nobody see us, out in the open, across the fucking street from my place?"

"Who cares? Give me the bag. We're losing time."

"Give her the bag, Greta," Victoria says.

I glare at Victoria as I start to give the bag to Carolin. As soon as I hand it off, she turns, jogs a half-block to the matte-black Audi with the purple lights, knocks on a window, it rolls down, and throws the bag in.

The flashy Audi pulls out and drives to the end of Newbury, stopping at the intersection with Mass Ave. Carolin holds a hand up to us, telling us to stay put. She's looking up and down Newbury, listening, looking, waiting for something. The Audi is still stopped at the intersection, even though I don't see any cars on Mass Ave. that would prevent it from turning. A loud squeal forces us to look down Newbury, away from the Audi. Turning onto the street is a black SUV. It drives past us, nears Carolin, but passes. She jumps to the middle of the street with her hands in her coral cargo pockets, and once centered behind the SUV, pulls out her right hand and hurls a wad of something gray at one back tire.

Into her wristwatch she says, "Stuck 'em. Tell me when it's clear."

"10-4," a male voice says through her watch, as the Audi turns right onto Mass Ave. She's transfixed on the SUV. It turns onto Mass Ave in pursuit of the Audi, *which has our hard drives.* I note the symmetry of how only three days ago on Sunday, this is the same escape pattern Brad took. I look all over. So, it appears as though Carolin was right and that the only tail—which she lured out—was whatever regular dopes have the night shift to monitor my penthouse door.

"I'm waiting," Carolin says into the wristwatch when too many seconds of silence pass.

She's hovering her fingers over her wristwatch.

"Clear," the male voice says.

"No humans?"

"None."

Carolin jams a button on her wristwatch, and immediately, an explosion rockets the night from up on Mass Ave, and we see the SUV that was in pursuit somersaulting backwards, and landing roof-down in the middle of the intersection of Newbury and Mass Ave.

Carolin turns to us and in a fit of fast words says, "Wow, that was only supposed to blow out their back tires! My boss will be thrilled I got to field test her invention. Amazing. I'll need to consider the physics of the explosive tipping that big beast backwards. Now run, get back in that penthouse and bar yourself in, A, fucking, SAP. And take these hats, a present from my employer." She bends to grab a plastic CVS bag, which was propped against the building we're standing at. I had thought it was garbage. Victoria accepts the bag.

"Thanks?" Victoria says, as confused and breathless as I am. She's looking to the smoking SUV. Its front tires are spinning in the air, the back wheels obliterated.

Hats? A gift from her employer? This was a field test?

"Carolin," I yelp. "What about all the security cameras on this street. They'll see what you did. They'll see we were involved."

Carolin sends me a derisive scowl, as if I am the dumbest person in the world. "V, you need to train your lawyers better, geez." Still nose-curling at me and my stupidity, she says, "Obviously, I hacked all the cameras on this end of the street on my way here. They all use the same cloud-video security service nowadays. Whatever. Go, get inside. And there's a big box for you in the alley, by where you drive in to park. Go," Carolin yells to us, as she races down Newbury, in the same direction Lena and I ran on Sunday, away from the exploded, top-down SUV. When she reaches the next intersection, her now unlit matte-black Audi hauls around the corner and slows enough for Carolin to take a running leap into the backseat, and she's gone. From the point at which the SUV landed top-down to now, a total of twenty seconds have passed. If those guys aren't dead and are coming to and about to crawl out, we need to move. Surely the cops will be here any second.

We run to my door (L.R. had already cleared us with her new guards when we dropped Lena), punch in my code, hop in my elevator, and press for the fourth floor. I call Toby to move the hutch at the top. Victoria takes one of the hats out of the CVS bag. It's blue with embroidered green letters that say, *15/33, Inc.,* the name of the boutique forensics company Carolin works for, Carolin being the head of the Northeast lab.

"She's giving us vendor swag in the middle of a car chase and explosion?" I say. My tone is angry, confused, my hands are clawed. I can barely breath because my heart is beating the hell out of my lungs.

"These hats are not vendor swag. There's cameras in the lids."

"Okay, sure. And she was running a field test?"

"Ayup."

"Her employer invented an explosive and this is Carolin's honeypot?"

"Seems so."

"What the actual fuck, Victoria?"

She presses her face in a non-committal shrug, a *what can I say, that's Carolin,* face.

"And she decides to wear those shoes to execute an explosion?"

Victoria looks up from the hat with one eyebrow raised. "Dude, she just saved our asses. And maybe you're not the best authority on practical footwear, ma'am."

The lift delivers us to the fourth floor, and I get out. Victoria tosses me the hats and doesn't exit.

"Come on, V. Where you going?"

"To get the dummy laptops that Carolin left in the box in the alley."

CHAPTER THIRTY-FIVE

We have less than two days to get Brad back, get Park back,
reconstruct our findings into some semblance of a coherent
argument, hopefully find more solid connections of Tim's mal-
feasance and connection to Honeywell, figure out if anything is
worthwhile in Maurice's bag o' hard drives. But if any team could
bend time and space, it's this team. Plus, Sophia's here now, having been sent by L.R. to be in on all the prep.

I have no idea what happened to Maurice once we fled. He's
not picking up Samera's calls. From L.R.'s Marine guard—who is
an unstoppable warrior and has been camped out with night-vi-
sion goggles, alone, outside, for hours—we know Brad is, indeed,
sitting on a couch in a coastal mansion, watching movies. This
could all be futile, and Brad could die. I have no witnesses that
Maurice authorized this investigation, except the biased Lena and
Victoria.

At this point, I haven't slept. I'm in total violation of doctor's
orders for my concussion and have been reviewing documents all
day. I think it's maybe Thursday evening. I'm working at a desk in
my bedroom; Henry's in my bed. He's looking better, sitting up,
free of fever.

"Henry," I say.

"Yes?"

"Did you really sit in a car for four hours with a fever after
being stabbed to tell me you love me?"

"I'm sorry it took me being stabbed and almost dying of blood loss to tell you I love you. I love you and I'm never leaving this very comfortable bed. Why have I never been in this bed?"

"Because it apparently took you being stabbed and drained of blood, Henry Palanquero."

I'm smiling at Henry, considering whether I can ignore the integrity of his stitches and the deadline we're under and just go ahead and join him in my *very comfortable* bed. But a loud voice interrupts from the living room.

"Oh wow, hold on, everyone stop," Cecilia yells.

I run to the living room, Sleuth lifts his head off the floor and barks at the sudden break in concentrated silence.

We'd tasked Cecilia to review all those image and video files that Victoria warned about and couldn't process through analytics or predictive coding. Sitting next to her is white puffball MF.

Everyone has dropped what they're doing and come to the living room. "What?" I ask.

"You need to watch this video."

CHAPTER THIRTY-SIX

The team had two conference calls this morning, starting at 7:00 a.m. One with Carolin, in which she gave her forensic findings of Maurice's hard drives. And one with L.R. and Bo. It is now 9:00 a.m., and I'm standing at a Providence, Rhode Island dock. I just hung up on a call with Park, who returned home last night. Last night, Park's partner in Saugus gave us some valuable information on a boat slip Park owns down here in Providence, Rhode Island.

So, late last night, I called Tim Cotton. "Tim, if you're not at Adam's Wharf in Providence with Brad by 9:00 a.m., with my boat, I'm calling your bluff. I've got the video of you and Honeywell and others—who I'm sure you don't want to be seen—at The Arsenal last year. *Everything* is in that video, tied in a bow. Zeta. Gray Industries. The polarization you've been doing for years. You didn't think anyone would record that? Seriously? I don't care what you do to me anymore. I'll release it if you don't bring me Brad. And it needs to be *you*, Tim, who brings Brad. Got it? And I better get a call from Park that he's on his way home."

Yes, Tim, I am extorting you. I've got the leverage. Bring Brad. And my damn boat! Send Park home.

"Understood," he growled.

"It's very public at Adam's Wharf, end of summer and beautiful, so lots of spectators. Don't make a scene. You bring me Brad, then this can all end. There's a free slip waiting for you to dock and return the GATOR and Brad. Don't be late."

"I'll be there. But I'm not giving a damn thing over without confirmation that L.R. calls off the hearing and withdraws your complaint with prejudice. The whole thing needs to end."

And it was this, which I should have expected, that equalized our seesaw of leverage, his leverage (Brad's life) meets my leverage: Arsenal video, the Caravaggios (which I didn't even mention), Carolin's forensic findings—all the facts we've uncovered, and the threat of the public hearing. But if I don't demonstrate that we will tank the case, Brad winds up in the harbor like all bags of English tea.

But we are not at Boston Harbor. We are in Providence, Rhode Island. And that is legally important to what I hope is about to go down.

Regardless, in this Faustian bargain, I obviously choose Brad.

Down at the docks, and this prime-location slip, owned by Park, is empty. It's 9:02 a.m. I'm standing in workout clothes and my hair is shoved in one of Carolin's *15/33, Inc.* swag hats. Samera's hiding nearby in the back of Nick Cage's SUV. Sophia is back in Massachusetts at L.R.'s office, having gone there to help with a call to the Judge's clerk.

The late-summer morning sun glistens off the black water. Seagulls wait for tourists to drop their lobster rolls in cans outside the Crazy Crab. The cashmere slide of boats in the harbor slip and swish out to sea. And motoring in is a 26', twin-engine named GATOR. I didn't think it would happen.

Brad sits in the bow with his leg on the cushion. Tim sits in the middle of the bench at the stern, with his arms across the top cushions and his legs spread. His positioning matches his split-middle bowl cut in a display of gross arrogance. A random muscle-man, the size of an oak tree, drives GATOR.

I walk down to the dock after the driver ties her up. Tim

remains seated like an asshole. Doesn't budge. I wish the gull
swooping GATOR for scraps would shit on Tim's upturned face.
And, miracle of miracles, I think the bird heard my thoughts,
for it swoops low. But all it does is caw near Tim's right ear. Tim
flinches.

"Still don't have confirmation that L.R. called off the hearing
and withdrew a damn thing," Tim says, holding his phone up
high, indicating he has someone trolling the docket.

"It's 9:00 a.m., Tim. I'm sure she's just now getting through to
the clerk. Check again," I say in a frantic tone. "Please, please just
leave Brad," I add, practically in tears.

The driver glares at me and moves to Brad. He picks Brad up
in an embarrassing—for Brad, I'm sure—cradle, as if he's a baby
to be rocked to sleep. Brad has the most placid, unreadable face,
as usual. I know he's thinking about how to brutally murder these
guys. For I am too, to be honest.

The driver holds Brad over the edge of the boat. Brad can't
swim with that cast, he'd sink.

Tim is talking on his phone, "Uh huh, uh huh. You sure?"
Then he looks at me, smiles, and says, "Good." He hangs up and
washes the air with his hand toward his driver. The driver winks
at me. A second of pure terror overtakes me as I watch him lift
Brad higher, as if he wishes to really dunk him hard in the water.
I blink—not wanting to see—and when I open my eyes Brad is
falling. He lands in a horrible crumble on the dock. His broken
leg crashes.

I run to help him. In a flash, another motorboat pulls in swift
and fast. Tim jumps into it, followed by GATOR's driver. The
motor boat idles, while Tim, standing in the bow, yells to me,
"We have a deal, now, Counselor. If you ever release the Arsenal
video, I know where to reclaim Brad, or Lena, your brother, or
Henry. And I'll say you, and your tech losers, created a deep fake,
you being E-Discovery counsel and all, and so smart with all that

computer stuff." As the boat races away, I want to flip him off and launch a grenade, followed by firing a bazooka as insurance for his total obliteration, and then summon all the covens of all the lands to hover like carnivorous bats over his blown, floating body parts, swooping to eat him into total eradication. But I have to help Brad walk.

"How could you? How could you throw it all away!" Brad yells at me, ignoring whatever pain must be rocking his body from within his cast.

I look at Brad's twisted, angry face as we walk together, him using me as a crutch, toward Samera, who runs out of the Crazy Crab shadows to help. As a calm mentor, I smile, indicating I'm going to give Associate Brad a legal lesson. "Brad, did you know that the most important skill of being a litigator is *not* mastering case law or statutes?"

He stares at me in his stony way.

"It's acting," I say, and wink. I tip the 15/33 hat at him.

Tim's motorboat speeds into the open sea around Providence, Rhode Island, and is soon a distant dot on the horizon. Samera takes on some of Brad's weight. "Come on, our car is over here," she says. We settle Brad into the back of the SUV and scooch in on either side. I take out my firm-issued iPhone, because I don't have to hide my location or identity anymore, and dial Tim's cell once we're on our way to L.R.'s secure parking, an hour twenty up the highway to Boston.

"Oh, Tim," I say, when he answers. "Who fed you that intel about the court clerk?"

Silence. I hear the roar of his motor and water slapping.

"Wouldn't by any chance have been Joseph P. Carmichael, associate at L.R.'s, was it? You're playing in the big leagues, Tim. Something you were never trained on, because you were never a proper associate, ever, anywhere. Sure, Joe *thinks* he overheard L.R. calling the clerk. But the real call was taking place in another room by another lawyer, and that lawyer was asking the Judge's clerk to ensure we'd have access to high-grade tech for this afternoon's hearing. And thanks for doing a command video performance this morning. In *Rhode Island.*" I touch the lid of the hat again. Thank God for nerds and microscopic cameras.

As I hang up, my elation and adrenaline high are immediately deflated when Samera, reading her phone, says, "Maurice is hospitalized. He won't be there today. We're screwed, Greta. They'll get their gag order."

CHAPTER THIRTY-SEVEN

"All these people for a discovery hearing?" the judge's clerk asks. The courtroom is packed, and people are still milling in and talking, as we're all waiting on the judge to enter and feed the entirety of the plaintiffs' table, where I sit, through a buzzsaw and then a woodchipper. Ours is a lost cause without Maurice's confirmation that he'd authorized this investigation. At plaintiffs' table, there's me, L.R., Bo Lopez, Sophia, and a couple juniors from both firms. Sophia is in her typical, functional Ann Taylor suit. I am me—normal lawyer me—dressed in a black Carolina Herrera career dress. My Tom Ford stilettos camouflage as somewhat practical, but I know I could wear them under a ballgown if I wanted. I certainly do not compare to L.R.'s powerful aura and impeccable ensemble, which I will dwell on in detail as we sit in this hearing as a way to focus on something other than Tim Cotton's awful face and the anger I have. For now, together us women demonstrate modern-woman lawyer fashion, a spectrum of professional attire that matches each woman's personal style and strength, a far cry from any obligatory bland brown tweeds with thick pantyhose of yester-bore.

At the defense table sits the entire militia of a several nation-states, or so it seems from the intimidating faces on the glowering men over there. There's Tim Cotton, two intimidating-looking outside counsel representing Tim and Honeywell as individuals, and several severe-looking associates, who I think were hired out of central casting for twenty-something, homicidal psychopaths. I think of my own psychopath associate, who is currently being treated at Mass General for dehydration and another fracture of his leg. It's best that Brad stay contained for now, as he is, for sure, homicidal. Like, literally. I don't care about the men he'd butcher. I'm just looking out for him, hoping to keep him out of prison.

Notably, Raymond Honeywell is not here. Because the powerful find ways to not show face when redemption might come calling. They use pawns, always. And these lawyers and Tim are his pawns. Tim's too stupid to be embarrassed by the fact that he's a pathetic shield, a disposable asset, at risk for one of those *convenient deaths.*

Breaking my stare-down with opposing counsel, Carolin walks into the courtroom, with Victoria behind. Carolin proceeds toward us, dressed in the most expensive, lined suit I've seen since I saw L.R.'s this morning. Carolin's hair is professionally blown out, and you'd never believe she wore yellow fishnets just two nights ago. Victoria is in the pews, trying to find a seat.

"You ready?" I ask Carolin.

"Are you?" She rolls her eyes at me.

"Please take a seat in the row behind us. We saved a spot," I say. And she sits next to Reboot Pete. Victoria decides to sit in the pews behind Tim Cotton's side of the room, as she still works at Stokes & Crane and it would be improper for her to be publicly working this case with us in the courtroom.

I note Lena standing a pew behind. She leans over the front pew, and I walk to meet her there, bending myself. She leans her forehead on mine.

"Whatever happens, Greta, you gave it your all. Love you no matter what. You're the sister of my soul."

"Love you, Lena."

She stands, winks, and adds, "Now go fuck 'em up."

"I'll try."

I turn back to plaintiffs' table.

Tim has gotten up from the defense table and walked to where Victoria is wedging herself between a journalist with sketchpad and a brown-suited partner woman from CoCo's Mergers & Acquisitions Department. I've never worked with her. Frankly, I can't remember if she's a Mary or a Maureen or a Mathilde. As Victoria might bluster, she's an M-name. I don't know why M name is here, other than sport. She smiles at Tim, and Tim nods back.

"Henna, Henna Green," Tim says, talking past the M-named M&A partner to Victoria.

Victoria stares straight ahead, ignoring him.

"Henna Green, *Henna*," he repeats.

She looks at him with a confused expression. "Me?" She says.

"Yes, you, Henna. I know you came to watch the show and all, and good on you and your enthusiasm. But can you hurry up and run across the street to DelMarco's and reserve a table for four, so we have it as soon as this hearing is over?"

Victoria laughs in his face. Laughs and laughs and doesn't stop, until the bailiff interrupts everything and yells, "All rise!"

I rise, my heart hammering, because there's no way—not a damn chance—we're overcoming their argument that I have no standing. Maurice is in the hospital. I can't prove he authorized a damn thing. The judge and all her power change the tenor of the room to icy silence. I sit after she sits, and my nerves make me miss the preliminaries.

Tim Cotton's individual lawyer steps up to the podium and hits hard all of the points we expected. How I'm a rogue and dis-gruntled employee. I've been let go from CoCo. I am not Deputy General Counsel or a partner. How I was never authorized to conduct any investigation of anyone at CoCo. And how I have no standing to file suit on behalf of CoCo against partners of CoCo for anything at all. That I have committed unauthorized access to firm data and a personal laptop and that all of this is a violation of my attorney ethics, client confidentiality, and so on and so on, and at some point, he raises his voice about referring me to the bar and to law enforcement for my various breaches and data crimes. All of it. In the middle of his grandstanding, I hear disturbance in the audience.

I turn to see Cal Parcel, General Counsel, now apparently back home early from his Italian vacation. Tim notes the disturbance as well and holds his hand open wide as a hello to Cal. Cal nods back. *I'm fucked.*

The M-named M&A partner scootches closer to Victoria to make room for Cal. Cal sits. He again nods to Tim, and to Tim's individual counsel, who turns to see him from the podium.

"And, given all of these serious violations of law and ethics, Your Honor, we ask that you throw out Ms. Seville's complaint immediately. Or, in the very least, seal these proceedings until such time that you rule to dismiss her complaint," Tim's attorney says.

"But, counsel," the judge says. "I'm sensing a rift, a power struggle at Coarse & Cotton, and Ms. Seville's allegations are serious. She *was* a partner. She *was* Deputy General Counsel. Essentially, with what she's filed on behalf of CoCo, and then your motion to dismiss and your motion for a gag order, CoCo is suing and gagging CoCo. Which is ludicrous, of course. I'm concerned I'm not hearing the true and aligned Coarse & Cotton position."

Cal stands. "Your Honor, pardon. I am Cal Parcel, General Counsel for Coarse & Cotton, may it please the court, I can address your concern if you would permit me to approach the podium?"

"Approach," she says.

Cal proceeds to the podium, Tim's attorney sits back down. Cal taps a folder of papers on the podium. I'm so screwed. He looks so credible and trustworthy. Every bit the Boston Brahman attorney.

"Thank you, Your Honor. For Madam Court Reporter, my name is Calvin Parcel, General Counsel for Coarse & Cotton. Apologies, Your Honor, for being late. The reason for my tardiness is that I flew back from Italy on a red-eye for this hearing. And, I just left the hospital bedside of the firm's most senior member, and named partner, Maurice Coarse. As Coarse & Cotton's General Counsel, I am here to report that with my return, Ms. Seville is no longer Deputy General Counsel."

He clears his throat. Tim winks at me.

"Rather," Cal continues. "Ms. Seville is returned to her standing title of Assistant General Counsel, and she is, as she has been during my absence, fully authorized to conduct this investigation and pursue all of her individual claims, as well as Coarse & Cotton's claims. In addition, Maurice Coarse, currently a named defendant, seeks leave to join CoCo's lawsuit, as filed by Ms. Seville, as against the individual defendants. In other words, he seeks to switch parties, as it were—should the Court grant our motion for leave of court to amend the complaint, which we intend to file after today's proceedings. Given that the individual defendants, Mr. Cotton and Mr. Honeywell, do not have standing to have filed these motions on behalf of Coarse & Cotton, I, as General Counsel, withdraw the pending motions. It is Coarse & Cotton's position that the proceedings be public as against the individual defendants, as they are meant to be. Being that the firm's position is aligned with Ms. Seville's, and the firm agrees there is urgency to the discovery motion, we do not wish for today's proceedings to be stalled for purposes of Mr. Coarse's motion for leave to join as a plaintiff. Thank you, Your Honor."

"Is that all, Mr. Parcel?"

"Yes, Your Honor."

"This is a surprising turn of events, counsel. Quite dramatic, no?"

Yes, Judge. This is a surprising turn of events, indeed. I'm shocked my heart still beats.

"Apologies for the last-minute turn of events. We do not wish to surprise the court."

"Well, counsel, I do hope there will be less surprises as we proceed. This is an honorable Boston Federal Court. We are not the Southern District of New York, full of dramatics. Now, will you be arguing for Plaintiffs, or shall I be looking to Ms. Rice?"

"If the court would please look to Ms. Rice, she is lead counsel for Plaintiffs. Thank you, Your Honor," Cal says, as the old-timey, unflappable trial attorney he is.

The judge nods, indicating she has no more comments or questions for him. With this, he is released from the podium and may return to sitting. Cal slides in on the bench behind Plaintiffs' table, sitting between Reboot Pete and Carolin. Him sitting in the pews was theater to trick defense counsel he was on their side and they wouldn't pre-empt what just happened. Stunning move. I'm shocked.

The lawyers representing Tim and Honeywell pop up. One says, "Our motion for a gag order as to the individual Defendants still stands," one says, and the other repeats.

I pop up, even though it is not my place, it is L.R.'s, for she is lead counsel. But I am Assistant General Counsel of CoCo, that is affirmed, signed, sealed, delivered, and *duly authorized.* Waiting on defense counsel to finish, because interrupting would surely irk this judge, I wait for her to look at me. And when she does, I say, "Your Honor, the individual Defendants are the most complicit. They should not delay these proceedings or hinder the public's knowledge of these events. We respectfully ask the court to deny their motion and allow us to present our facts and arguments."

Defense counsel goes to make another point, and I'm still standing to counter-point whatever drivel he's about to spew, but the judge bangs her gavel to stop all of us.

"We will have order in this court," she says in a loud, commanding voice, staring everyone down. Everyone is immobile. She bangs her gavel four more times. "Now, counselor," she says to the attorney who argued on behalf of Tim as an individual. "You would have me expel the members of the press from the galley and all the public spectators, seal these proceedings, and institute a temporary gag order on all parties, until such time that I rule for good on your motions? Is that the request?"

That was not his specific request, but that's what she feeding to him to request, this half measure to what he wants as a permanent measure, as that is what she's going to do. *Shit.*

"Yes, Your Honor, thank you," defense counsel says with a smile.

The Defendants win if they get *time*. They'll drag things out. They'll tarnish our arguments, our reputations. They'll make it painful and—most of all—expensive. They'll drown out the facts with counter-facts, before we're allowed to divulge them, making anyone in law enforcement and the public unclear on what the truth is. They, in short, will control the narrative.

"Don't thank me, counselor, I haven't granted such an extreme request. In fact, I'm not going to. Your motion for a gag order is denied. Settle in, sit down. Ladies and gentlemen of the press in the audience sit down, take your notes, we have a public discovery hearing to attend to." She sits down in a thud and the audible swoosh of her black robe. "Ms. Rice, please approach the podium and present your argument."

Wow.

I'm not breathing.

L.R., the Queen, the Magnificent Trial Attorney with a

99.99% win rate, strides to the podium in a powerful ease, as if none of the preceding drama happened, as if all along she predicted this result, or commanded this result, and as if anyone shouting frantic objections or seizing in fear upon the judge's gavel are all, very truly, very much, beneath her. She is the only person on the planet, commanding the spin of the Earth. Commanding the sun and the moon. Wind. Oceans. Time. All hers.

At the podium, in her red Alexander McQueen *Grain De Poudre* suit jacket and matching pencil skirt, she says, "May it please the Court, Letticia Rene Rice for Plaintiffs. Your Honor, we coordinated with your clerk earlier today to display a three-dimensional timeline of facts, documents, images, and videos, which together form an incontrovertible and urgent need to forensically examine Defendants' personal devices. Urgent in that, and this is a fact, for they already have spoliated evidence. Your Honor, we have proof, and an expert who can—with your permission—testify to Defendants' shocking use of BCWipe, a Department of Defense wiping software, to purge data on several relevant hard drives. We also have Coarse & Cotton's I.T. Director, who will testify that Tim Cotton directed Coarse & Cotton's I.T. staff to use B.C. Wipe on these relevant hard drives on Wednesday, as this matter was pending."

L.R. turns and accepts a glass of water from Sophia. *I know it's practiced theater, but the galley doesn't, and a jury wouldn't. They'd just be enchanted by her delicious competence.*

I look to Carolin and Reboot Pete, who have the best poker faces. They're listening in a way that gives nothing away, showcasing the impression that they are unbiased technical experts. I look to Victoria, who is doing the same. So, it is, as always, the forensics expert, the litigation technology genius, and the Director of I.T. who will, once again, save our asses in court.

L.R., done with her slow-roll theatrics of pausing for water, to allow her shocking facts to sink deep, returns to the podium.

"This is just one shocking fact, as we'll demonstrate in walking along our timeline. We will also play a video of Mr. Cotton, partaking in the very corruption Ms. Seville's investigation seeks to uncover. And then, a video of Mr. Cotton *just this morning* extorting Ms. Seville at Adam's Wharf, in Providence, Rhode Island, while he and his private militia man violently returned a team member they kidnapped and also a boat they stole. Surely, beyond this civil hearing, criminal complaints will be filed. But, if I may, Your Honor, whatever criminal proceedings may unfurl, they should not curtail the procedural and routine, albeit emergency, discovery motion before this honorable court."

The facts boiled up like this are strange and surreal and mind-blowingly specific, and anything but *procedural and routine*. Anyone else delivering them would have done so with a tone of exasperation and elevated voice, so as to heavy-hand yank on the shock of the court. But doing so would upstage the undeniable shock of the facts, which speak for themselves. L.R. is the finest of pros, so she delivers her opening as a clinical vampire, using her honey-drenched sotto vocce, and at a controlling pace. She is the finest trial attorney and actress, combined.

After a one-second pause, allowing her opening to sink in, but before defense counsel can interject objections, which they seem primed to do, she says, "May we proceed with displaying our 3-D demonstrative?"

Tim's individual defense counsel pops up and hurries through objections to any videos and clamoring for a side-bar about evidence authentication and how any video of Tim at Adam's Wharf was done without consent. "Massachusetts is a two-party consent state to record his voice. He did not consent. This video is a felony," he bellows. He goes on about not having had the chance to review what we're going to show and how he's concerned about the irreparable harm of publicly disclosing confidential CoCo client data that might be wrapped in our presentation, along with a slew of other quick-scratch objections he can blurt out before the judge slams her gavel again, which she's surely going to do, for it's raised.

"Sit down," the judge snaps at defense counsel, while slamming her gavel. "Your objections are overruled. This is not a hearing on the merits of the claims. This is a civil discovery hearing in order to get evidence to address those claims. Your objections are not applicable today. Ms. Rice has represented that the video was shot in Rhode Island, which is a one-party consent state, and Ms. Seville, I gather, consented to recording it. Besides, I want to see these videos. I'm sure Ms. Rice, a highly respected and veteran trial attorney, wouldn't show this court doctored evidence or disclose client material." Looking to L.R., she says, "Is that correct, counselor?"

"Correct."

"Proceed."

And I swear, the judge purses her lips, in an ever-so-invisible manner, to hide how entirely entertained she is by all this e-discovery drama and how thoroughly she enjoys L.R.'s dominance over the flustered men at Defendants' table.

I look to Sophia, who stifles a smile, as she taps out a rhythm with her finger on a pad of paper. I suspect she's rehearing the metronome of L.R.'s opening, the intentional wording and delivery, how she emphasized and contorted certain syllables, the subtle weaving of a couple rhyming phrases, her murderous voice, which could infuse gin with addicting smoothness, her pacing, her unruffled posture at the podium, the theatrical pleating of her red jacket in back, but the professional cut of the front, the entire package that holds all of us in the surround of this Greek play under the point of her blade, begging to be slaughtered by her capable hands.

And oh, what a beautiful slaughter it is. And in a 3-D model, no less.

~~~

I'm not surprised when the judge rules in our favor, which, at this point, for us, is a formality, as we know any evidence we might have found on Tim and Honeywell's personal phones are long gone. We were able to get enough to get this ruling from the other data sources we acquired. We needed this legitimacy of an open court hearing, because we already have prepped a full-scale international media blitz with all the gory facts, right out of the gate. We are giving the Defendants zero time to re-shape the narrative on what happened in court today.

The second the judge leaves the court room, I dial Samera.

"Let it fly. All of it. And all the videos. Go."

The press was always Maurice's and my insurance policy. The press is what we needed on this case. Samera's story is already written, and written in real time, with so much more detail than L.R.'s clinical statements in court. Samera's has adjectives and color and flavor, unvarnished facts, tales of gripping, horrific murder, chase scenes, names and pictures of co-conspirators—like a thriller novel, but delivered as an AP Special Report. And it's timed to drop *right now*, so we are in *total command of the narrative*. Bombs are dropping in news feeds this minute, around the world.

Although I wasn't surprised by the judge's ruling, I *am* surprised by what's happening now as we leave the courthouse. A swarm of FBI agents descend around Tim Cotton and cuff him, as the scrum of press watch on, snapping pictures. That M-named M&A partner walks up to me and says, "Maurice tipped me off to what was going on a few days ago. So, I looked through the firm's document management system and had Pete in I.T. analyze network activity logs. It wasn't just the Riser insider trading tip; Tim was a parasite on the network, sucking information on nearly all the M&A deals. Oh yeah, he was sending non-public M&A deal information to those same people in your Arsenal video—the ones he promised, in that damn video, to send tips to. So, you have your end of the proof, and with mine, Tim's cooked. So is Honeywell." She looks me up and down. "Nice work, Greta. See you back at the office, partner."

CHAPTER THIRTY-EIGHT

It's two weeks post-trial. Our pictures of the security team helped with a number of arrests—but not enough. I paid off the landlord of the Salem rental for all the damage, through my Stokes & Crane lawyer, maintaining my LLC's anonymity. Maurice paid L.R.'s whopping (and deserved) bill, so I'm fine in the money department. CoCo also sent me a new Jura, and one to Victoria, too. (Also, CoCo paid Victoria and Carolin well for their time). CoCo reversed itself about Brad, who now has an offer to be an associate. Brad and I have been discussing with Samera what—if anything—we can do about additional lines of inquiry our investigation opened up, so that we might make the number of arrests a landslide. Setting boundaries around Brad's rage that we didn't necessarily destroy *every single last member* of Zeta is work for him, and me. I'm committed to the cause writ large.

I'm walking into my penthouse after several hours of spa appointments Henry booked for me. He said he'd make us dinner while I was out. I'm super chill after a ninety-minute massage, facial, and mani-pedi, and I'm so excited to see him back at my place.

His energy is back. He's well.

As I step out of my elevator, I step into a deconstructed rainbow. Hundreds of post-it notes are strung on strings from my ceiling, hovering over my white living room.

Henry is sitting on the living room floor under it all.

"The box I sent was filled with all these post-its. Every one says something you said at some point over the years. Or a memory. All of the reasons why I love you are on these notes," he says, looking up, his eyes dancing around the hanging squares. "Sit next to me." He pats the floor. I do as he says. I'd do *anything* he says.

Once I'm settled beside him, as we were two years ago in his office, he looks at me.

"But what if we….what would happen?" He asks, smiling.

"When you first asked me this two years ago, I said we'd have mad passionate sex all the time. And I think we've proved that since you recovered, no?"

"True. But what if we made it permanent?"

I am an instant body of electricity. I think my arms are flying and my face is fog.

"Are you asking what I think you're asking?" My voice shakes.

He pulls from a breast pocket a giant, emerald-cut aquamarine set in a wide gold band.

"Yes, I'm asking," he says, holding out the ring.

"Henry?"

"One of these post-it notes," he points up, smiles—and I want to literally crawl into his beautiful dimples. "One of them up there somewhere, has something you said a long time ago. I stored the information for years. You said you preferred colorful gems to diamonds, and everyone should know their ring size, like they know their blood type, and that your ring size is five and a half. I have no idea *why* you delivered that information then. But, I think—I hope—I hit the mark with this. We can switch it out, anything you want. It's size five and a half."

Henry doesn't realize he could have proposed with a rubber band, and I would have thought it was the most breathtaking thing ever. Ever, ever.

"I love you so much, Henry. It physically hurts how much I love you," I say, flat out sobbing, as he slips on the ring. "Can we make twelve thousand babies, starting right now?"

He wipes the tears from my face. "So that's a yes?"

"Oh, Henry, that is a yes. A very big yes."

He stands. Walks to my bedroom. I follow. He's standing in front of my desk inside the door. My bed is made behind him.

"Stay there," he says.

I stand still.

"Shut the door," he says.

~~~

Next August

Some instinct is distracting me at our wedding. Some tempting sense mixing with my rational happiness, but not in a malevolent way, in a playful way, making for the potential of irrational happiness. An anticipatory electricity, perhaps a sense that some additional depth undergirds the joy of this day into something else, some solid and real alchemy that could turn this magical day into real magic. Magic is always dangerous, as once it's released, it's wild and can become uncontainable. But magic can also turn a glittering rainbow into a solid arch of color, with touchpoints to the ground. Something unbelievable, dream-like, but tangible. These glittering, electrical currents around me, driving through me—my skin tingles in whatever this is beyond the gorgeous ceremony about to begin.

We are blessed to have awoken to the radioman saying, "Good morning to all the weddings out there! It is a perfect summer day!" And so, it is a perfect summer day. Henry and I are on the porch of Lena's cabin with Lena behind us as our officiant. My brother is my attendee, and Henry's sister is his. They stand opposite us below the porch. And this arrangement is the closest to being traditional at this wedding.

The officiant, Lena, in a gorgeous white cotton prairie dress, has locked eyes with Toby several times while we await the singer to finish singing the procession song—Ray LaMontagne's "It's Always Been You." I catch Toby biting his bottom lip and mouthing to Lena, "I will devour you," right before she says, "Welcome, ladies and gentleman." She pauses, winking at Toby, and adds, "And delicious lovers who we let blow up our world." The wedding guests catcall, and a few clap and hoot.

Because this is that kind of wedding. Non-subtle sexual innuendos baked into the sermon and many other exotic elements for the eyes to feast upon.

I snap Toby with my bouquet and tell him to behave, adding in a whisper, "You two are a rom-com porn." All of this said with a big, wide smile.

I am in bliss, true. But I also need to define and understand this other sense of distraction. Although I appreciate the exotic atmosphere and the wild colors, I see nothing out of place, yet.

It is almost unbelievable what Lena has done, but she did it. She spent the last year devoted to this wedding. She's told me a million times that this is what she wanted to do, and that this is her "big art project." She says she's loved every minute of the planning and major construction, and, she says, regardless, she needed a three-floor barn with full-length porches at each level anyway. What she had never before envisioned, and which also made the construction of this giant barn outbuilding, across from us, here on the cottage porch, so urgent, was the need for a biometrically-locked basement under the barn—which houses the Caravaggios in temperature-controlled vaults and behind bulletproof glass.

Still. Beyond the strangeness of Lena's unbelievable sanctuary, which at this point I'm used to, there is something, something about *right now,* that's prodding me to look closer.

The field is restored, eight wedges plump with Queen Anne's lace, and the orange monarchs are abundant and feeding throughout. Within the front four wedge paths are hired dancers, who are on their knees, folded over and waiting, as if buds about to bloom. The vision of them is certainly peculiar, but also perfect and exciting—but above all, planned. However unique they are, whatever visual magic they add, they are expected and not the source of this other sense. They are dressed in sparkly turquoise sheer cloths and blue tights. Orange butterflies flutter above them.

I bring my eyes back to the three-story barn, set at the 10:00 position, beyond the front four wedges. There is a porch on the raised first floor, accessible by ramp, and where ten of our guests who can't do stairs are seated. That first level affords a perfect view over the wedges of flowers and butterflies and dancers, and to the wedding party here on Lena's cottage porch. And then on the two higher porches, ten more seated guests per floor: my parents, Henry's parents, Victoria, Brad (attending solo), Samera and her husband, Park, who's here with a beautiful date, and a smattering of friends and close family. Other than its massive size and porches, plural, the barn is painted traditional red. Within it is where the reception will occur. Caterers adjust bouquets on high tops and strategic low tops, where guests will be delivered hours of small bites, big bites, drinks, and cake. There is no planned seated meal, because what's planned is hours of unstructured and constant eating and drinking and dancing and laughing and speeches and karaoke. There's a magician somewhere in there, and also a face-painter. Kids in attendance have their own buffet of donut towers and endless pizza and even a soda machine that doesn't require coins. So, we're all good. Nobody's concerned about nutrition or tooth decay or bedtimes.

What are these nerves, forcing me to look at the faces of the waitstaff? What is it about the women and men within the first level of the barn, the ones scurrying with trays past the opened door behind the first-floor porch?

We've said our vows. Lena pronounces us married. And now Lena raises her hands to silence the clapping and cheering guests in the barn's porch audience. A hush washes over the field. I know what's coming, we've rehearsed this, and I should be fixed on the turquoise dancers in the field. But a woman is distracting me. She's walking out of the barn and toward the stream at the base of the river, beyond the wedges. I return to watching the dancers, telling myself—forcing myself—to quarantine and label her as one of the waitstaff, heading for a break.

"And now the entertainment portion of the evening," Lena says.

I'm braced for the dance in the wedge aisles to be set to Lena's long-imaged choreography to "Say Goodbye to Hollywood." But that is not the song that blooms over the field. The song is Elton John's "Tiny Dancer." I look to Lena. "Surprise," she says, with the widest grin. "We're *literally* having dancers in this *literal* field."

I hug her. "Oh my God, Lena," I say, and tears form immediately.

But.

Still.

I turn away.

Because when I hugged Lena in a happy shock at the surprise song, I studied that waitress walking toward the stream. And I can't ignore that woman.

"Pardon me," I say to Henry.

All three levels of wedding guests are enthralled in watching the dancers in the field, so I am able to quietly leave the cottage porch. I feel my brother behind me. I know Toby saw, too.

Once we are free of the porch, and behind Lena's cottage, we pick up the pace through a back wedge path that should intersect with the woman as she reaches the stream. White flowers surround us on both sides, and butterflies flutter above our heads. Elton John is as loud here as out front, as Lena added several speakers on poles around the property.

At the end of the aisle we find ourselves in the green field beyond. The woman is almost to the stream now. Her hair is solid gray and braided fat down her back. She wears black pants and a white tuxedo shirt—like the rest of the waitstaff. Toby and I run to her, and it is Toby, not I, who says, when we're five feet from her, "Aunt Violet?"

"Aunt Violet?" I echo.

She pauses, turns, and her big blue eyes light up.

"I had to see you again, forgive me," she says. "I love you," to me. "I love you," to Toby. Toby is crying. Flat out crying. I fall to my knees in my ivory dress, crying. My turquoise sash blends with the green grass.

"Oh no, my dears. Please don't cry. Greta, darling, up now. Up, my love, my beautiful girl." She pulls me to stand and rubs her thumb over my face scar, which I did not have subdued by plastic surgery. "My beautiful girl," she says, and hugs me hard and fast. Pushing me away, but keeping her hands on my shoulders, she says, "I didn't mean for you to see me. I just had to see you both. I never wanted to upset you on your wonderful day. Oh, dear." She pulls in Toby, and the three of us hug. I'm trying not to sob, because I want to hear any words she's going to have to say soon, and say fast. Toby too, I can feel him stifling his emotions for the same reason. Still holding us, her face between us, she says, "Loves, you know I can't stay. I already scouted your friend's four-wheeler across the stream. She keeps the keys on the back tire."

She lets go, steps back. She scratches her head, "Tell your friend I'll leave it somewhere close. She can find it."

"But…" I start to say, because I have so many questions. "Just stay here. Hide out here."

"Oh, baby, I can't. You know that." She's looking over our shoulders to the party behind, and we look, too, but nobody is approaching to see why we came here quite yet. I'm sure they will soon though.

We turn back to Aunt Violet. She presses a pebble into my palm and one in Toby's.

"Got to jet, my loves. And," she winks. "Just trust, my efforts aren't nearly done. Have had something huge in the works for decades. Keep an eye out in the corporate media rags for my big opus. I'm so proud of you both for living so solidly in your own truths. So proud. Arrivederci!"

Aunt Violet takes off and leaves me no chance to stop her or ask any questions. I go to do so, to run after her, stop her, but Toby slow-grabs my arm. Because, of course, we have to let Aunt Violet go.

We're watching our beloved Aunt run over the walking bridge, and hop on Lena's four-wheeler. She vrooms up the mountain trails. Of course she had this scoped out and planned.

Toby and I are holding hands and listening to the sweet song of Violet buzzing away, up the mountain, through the trees. I'm realizing that my Defining Life Event never ended, it continues, here, now, and will continue into the future.

I rub my sixteenth pebble from Aunt Violet. I hope there will be a seventeenth.

ACKNOWLEDGEMENTS

I couldn't do any of this without the incredible support and guidance of my agent Kimberley Cameron, who, no matter what wild ideas, whatever genre I say I want to try, supports me. Thank you, Kimberley, I am so honored to be working with you.

Huge thanks to my editor Chantelle Aimée Osman, whose incredible close eye and read of this manuscript saved me from several pitfalls. Further, and what I'm forever grateful for, is her total commitment to me going for the throat on political issues and not shying one second. Working with Chantelle has been exactly what I needed and I'm entirely in her debt.

I could thank a multitude of colleagues and clients, having practiced law for twenty-four years. For fear of leaving anyone out, I'll just thank all my colleagues and clients, all my inspirations, motivations, the entire E-Discovery community, and, I would have to single one person out, the colleague I've grown to know I absolutely cannot live without, Litigation Technology professional extraordinaire, Danielle Davidson. She's not Victoria Viglioni, but she does have a sign that says NOPE on her desk.

To my beta readers, MOM (Kathy Capone) and Emily Carpenter, THANK YOU! As always, their reads helped to shape the story in invaluable ways.

Thanks to my husband Michael Kirk and my son Max Kirk. It is for them, for Max especially, I work so hard at making sure I am doing what little I can to be vocal, to be out there.

If readers would like to read more on corruption or on Caravaggio, some of the resources I used to research aspects of this novel, include:

*Inspiration from a number of news articles and books about collectives of investigative journalists who worked in secret and hundreds, possibly thousands of hours, to uncover the Trump tax story, Panama Papers, and Pentagon Papers.

*The documentary, *The Dissident*

*http://www.visual-arts-cork.com/old-masters/caravaggio.html

The Lost Painter, Jonathan Harr

God's Bankers, A History of Money and Power at the Vatican, Gerald Posner

Dark Money, Jane Mayer

American Prison, Shane Bauer

*Ted Talk 2013, We the People, and the Republic We Must Reclaim, Lawrence Lessig

*Podcast series, The Dark Money Files

*Freakonomics Podcast, Season 8, Episode 10, America's Hidden Duopoly

ABOUT THE AUTHOR

Shannon Kirk is the multiple award-winning, international bestselling author of *Method 15/33*, which was optioned for film, sold in over 20 languages, and garnered critical acclaim, including three starred reviews and the coveted placement on *School Library Journal*'s 2017 "Best Adult Books for Teens", as well as *Viebury Grove, Gretchen, In the Vines* and the award-winning *The Extraordinary Journey of Vivienne Marshall*, which was given the Literary Classics Seal of Approval. In addition to writing, Shannon is the Global Head of E-Discovery at one of the top AmLaw 100 Firms. *Tenkill* is her first legal thriller. She lives in the Boston area. Find her online at shannonkirkbooks.com